NEVER Left You

STEFANIE K. STECK

Book Cover by Melody Jeffries

Chapter Headers and Scene Illustrations by Melody Jeffries

Ranch Map and Family Tree Illustrations by Erika Plum

Edited by Allie Samberts

Proofread by Tessa Frank and Vee Troy

ISBN (Paperback) 979-8-9866169-5-7

1st edition 2025

For those who thought they would never smile again. You smiled,
you loved, you *lived*.

Author's Note

Never Left You is a contemporary small-town romance that handles mature themes, following a journey of grief for both main characters, and some of the content may be triggering. This book is intended for an 18+ audience. Though it is 'cracked door' with mild spice, sexual acts are implied, and strong language is used. Mild spice is found in chapters thirty two and thirty-seven. It deals with topics that have taken research, such as day to day life of a working cattle ranch, barrel racing, and rodeo travel. Even with research, creative liberties were taken. Content warnings include death of a spouse shown on page, gaslighting, emotional and verbal abuse, infertility, mention of cheating (not from main characters), grief and loss with emotional trauma. I hope I have handled these topics with care. Your mental health matters most, so please protect yourself. Thank you for choosing to read *Never Left You*, I hope you love reading it as much as I enjoyed writing it.

Hartwell Hills
RANCH
Lake
Lottie's River
Lachlan's House
Cow Pastures
Main Barn & Events
Horse Pasture
To Gardens
Bunkhouse
Stables & Indoor Arena
Garage
Rhett's Cabin
Main House
To Town

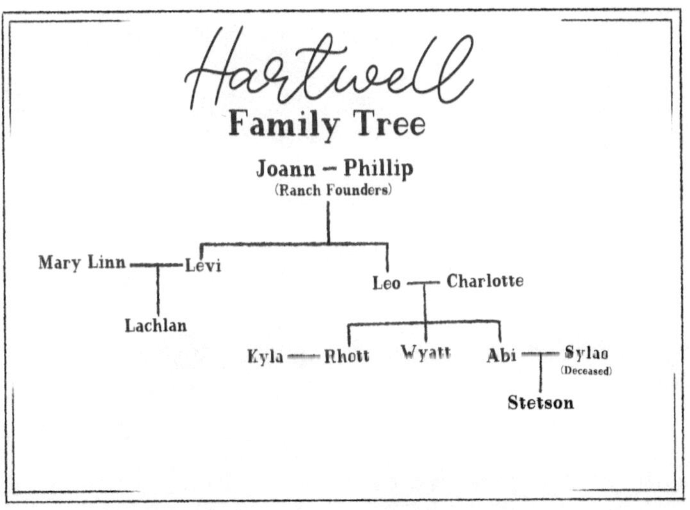

Hartwell
Family Tree
Joann — Phillip
(Ranch Founders)
Mary Linn — Levi
Lachlan
Leo — Charlotte
Kyla — Rhett
Wyatt
Abi — Sylas
(Deceased)
Stetson

ONE

Abi

F*IVE YEARS AGO*

"Daddy!" Stetson screamed from my arms, his own tiny ones reaching out as Sylas passed us.

My husband, completely ignoring me, kissed our three-year-old son's forehead before lifting him off my hip.

"You ready to ride a bull, Stet?" Sylas's Spanish accent flowed off his lips, making me want to kiss him every single time, except this time the words that he said pulled me back to reality.

"Hell no, Mr. Acosta." I snatched our son back before he could step into the arena with him.

"Oh, come on Mi Reina." He squinted his eyes, giving me a small pout as I situated Stetson back on my hip. I shook my head at the nickname. Of course, he would choose My Queen during a moment when he wanted to put our son's life at risk. I never minded it when he changed his nicknames up, but whenever the words Mi Alma floated through the air, I melted. My Soul.

I was Sylas's soul.

This man was my everything. From the moment I first saw him, I knew I loved him. Granted, it took him years to figure out he felt the same, and if I'd never made a move, I bet we'd still be circling each other. The age gap scared him at first. Not me. I was the fourteen-year-old daughter of a ranch owner, in love with the twenty-one-year-old ranch hand, and once I hit eighteen, I boldly asked him out on a date. Seven years later, we're married with the cutest little boy in the entire world, and the age gap didn't make a single difference.

His deep brown eyes widened as he held my gaze. "Abi, I'll hold him. He'll be fine." He waved his hand before holding his palms open for Stetson.

I shook my head, twisting my hips away from him before my son got taken to his death. "He's too young. Maybe when he's older, but not at three years old."

"I was six." My older brother, Rhett, called across the arena.

I looked over my husband's shoulder to shoot Rhett a 'don't you dare' glare. Catching the heat, he quickly turned his back to us.

"I get it's only practice, but no, Sy..."

"Bien, bien." Sylas shook his head. "Next time Stet." Sylas leaned over and gave me a sweet kiss. "Always the logical one, Mi Reina."

I hummed against his lips. "Someone's gotta make sure you don't kill our son."

Sylas let out a loud laugh. "We'll get him on the back of a sheep first."

"Well," I groaned, turning to my son. Stetson looked just like his father. Brown hair which I know is ruffled even though it's hidden under his small cowboy hat. His dark eyes shined as he watched his father step into the arena. His forever tan skin was a contrast to my pale complexion, and I loved the fact that every time I looked at him, I saw my husband. "A sheep is better than a bull, I guess."

I looked back at Sylas as he pulled on his gloves.

My Soul. Mi Alma.

"Make sure he's mad, Wyatt!" Sylas yelled over to my twin, who was currently getting the bull in the chute. Rhett had run across the arena, over the chutes where Sylas would mount the bull to ride for eight seconds. "You wrangling, Lach?" Sylas waved to my cousin on the other side of the arena. Lachlan stood still, his hands in his pockets as he gave Sylas a curt nod.

"Daddy." Stetson moved in my arms, his long body flailing as he attempted to move to the gate. I let him lean his feet on the metal and use me as a backrest. I was just tall enough that his little cowboy hat didn't bother me, "Mommy, the bull." He pointed.

"Yup, we're leaving soon though, remember? We're going with Daddy to the rodeo." I squeezed him closer to me, feeling his little body against mine, and I kissed his temple. "So many rodeos."

"The rodeo!!" he shouted, lifting his arms in the air.

"Yes!" I exclaimed, "but first he needs to practice."

From my cousin Lachlan leading the board last year in bareback before his unexpected retirement, to Rhett taking tie down by storm, the Hartwells lived and breathed the rodeo. Even Wyatt, who hated riding bulls almost as much as he loathed being on a bucking horse, found his place being an announcer. It was only natural that once Sylas joined the family, he joined the rodeo world too. Only he chose the most dangerous event; he was a bull rider. It was a wild sport, the one people flocked to the rodeo for. Watching Sylas for five years was what made me a fan of it, but my heart still lurched every time that chute opened.

Now, my little family of three was taking the summer to travel to rodeo after rodeo, watching the love of my life climb the boards and make it to the NFR this year. I couldn't wait to follow him everywhere and to experience it with him. Simply to see him in his element, see him truly shine.

"How many practice runs has he put in?"

The Southern drawl of my husband's best friend came up behind me, and I turned to see Cash Callahan. His tall figure appeared next to me on the gate, lifting his left leg up on the railing, leaning in to rest on his elbows before he met my gaze. He donned a white hat, standing out against his tawny skin, which was a change from the normal black hat I was used to seeing him in. The white fit him better lately anyway, as if to add some light to his world I knew was turning dark. I enjoyed Cash's company, and the fact that he still would randomly pop in gave me a sense of comfort. Even if his 'other half' didn't want him here anymore, he still came.

I gave him a smile before turning back to my husband as he lowered himself on the bull and began positioning his hands.

"This is the first one," I replied. Taking a deep breath, I looked over at Cash, whose eyes were now zeroed in on Sylas. "I didn't think you would be here today."

Cash shrugged his shoulder and shifted his gaze to me. "Carolyn—" I rolled my eyes at the mention of his wife "—is waiting out in the car. I told her I just needed to come see Sy before we left. I won't be here long."

"Ah so we're a pit stop?" I lifted my chin, turning to give him a teasing smile.

The last time they were here together ended in a huge fight, Carolyn screaming at Cash across the room until he finally broke and left the house. That was months ago, and now we were lucky just to see him for a few minutes. Cash was trying to mend something that was—in my opinion—beyond repair. But that didn't matter, he was still going to try.

Cash side eyed me, taking the tease. "Well, when you say it like that..."

"I'm only kidding," I used my shoulder to bump into him, his body swaying as he turned to give me a sideways smirk.

My attention flew back to the dirt once I heard the chute clang open, followed by a whoop from Rhett and Wyatt. My focus went straight to Sylas as his hand waved in the air and the bull bucked. These were always the longest eight seconds of my life. Even in our own arena, my heart lodged in my throat. I would count the seconds as the bull bucked and kicked, always moving slower in my head than in real time. One, two, three. I wasn't like this when any other cowboy got on a bull. Only for Sylas. Four, five, six. I bit the inside of my lip. While my husband loved this sport, there was constant fear in the back of my head every time he rode, giving me a love-hate relationship with bull riding. It was a thrill to watch Sylas in his element. I'd always support him as much as I could. Seven...eight...

I breathed.

Stetson cheered as he watched, and as soon as that buzzer went off, Sylas flew from the bull's back, making it look easier than it really was. He raised his arms in the air, and his feet began bouncing in his victory. It was then I realized my husband wasn't wearing any protective gear.

And then, time sped up.

And everything happened so fast.

Lachlan was screaming, running towards Sylas. Rhett jumped the gate from the chute and followed Wyatt as they rushed towards the bull—the now furious bull—as it began charging Sylas.

"He better get out of the way," Cash grunted.

"Sy..." I muttered, my heart thumping so loud I couldn't even hear my own words.

"Sy!" Lachlan yelled, waving his arms. "Move your ass!"

Sylas turned to look at Lachlan, eyes widening at the sight of Rhett and Wyatt—and then the bull smashed his head straight into him. He was in the air in a matter of seconds, falling flat on his back after being hit from behind by the bull's horns. I jumped, leaving Stetson there at the gate as I made my way towards the arena. I didn't even notice Cash grab Stetson's back to keep him steady; my focus was entirely on Sylas. Wyatt got to the gate first, holding me back as Rhett and Lachlan tried to gain the bull's attention. But that bull—it only had eyes for Sylas as it ran at him again.

"Sylas!!" I screamed as the bull's horns flipped him in the air again.

"Cash!" Rhett's voice rang in the back of my head, "Call 911!"

Lachlan managed to get the bull from dirt, but then everything was a blur. The silence in the arena was more deafening than the shouts coming from my brother and cousin. Wyatt's arm around my waist tightened as I tried to focus. Rhett moved faster than I'd ever seen, and I could finally hear Stetson's screams. But my eyes were solely on Sylas, lying in the dirt, completely motionless.

Wyatt's arm fell from my body.

I had never moved so fast in my entire life.

Blood seeped from his brown hair, his arm was crushed, and his shoulder was dislocated, bent in an unnatural way. I could even feel pain radiating through my bones. I moved my hand down his chest, noticing his white shirt was turning a deep shade of red as blood soaked through. I was too scared to take the shirt off—terrified of what I would see there.

"Sy..." I whimpered, running my hands through his hair, my flesh turning red and sticky from his blood that was now smearing over my fingers. I grimaced, my entire body shaking as I pulled him into my lap. Swallowing the tears I knew were coming, I tried to speak. "Why the hell didn't you wear your gear?"

He blinked. Once. Twice, before his eyes fluttered closed. "Mi Alma..."

"Ambulance is on the way." Cash called out, his yelling nothing more than a faint whisper.

"Mi Corazon." Sylas met my gaze as he spoke, "You're okay. You're okay."

Looking down at my husband, I knew he wasn't. But he wasn't saying he was ok. He was saying, 'you're okay.' He meant me. In this moment, no matter how much pain he was feeling, his mind was still focused on me. Tears began to fall on my cheeks as my hands cradled his face, his breaths slowing as he searched my eyes with his. There was too much blood. The color drained from his cheeks, the dirt that covered his cheeks sanding out even against his skin. His chest hitched as he struggled to take deep breaths as he lifted his arm to my neck, and yet...he still managed to give me a soft smile.

"You're okay," he repeated softly. "Mi Alma..."

My Soul.

Present Day

I jumped awake, my forehead covered in sweat as I pulled myself from the memory. This nightmare has haunted me at least twice a month for the past five years. Revisiting the day Sylas died over and over again. An endless cycle that, no matter how hard I try to push it down, continues to surface. I can still hear the screams from Lachlan and Rhett, still feel Wyatt's arms around me as he held me back...his sticky blood on my hands. Strong hands pulling me away from Sylas as paramedics arrived...

Letting out a loud groan, I slap my arms down on my blanket.

Pull yourself together. You got this. It was just a dream...

I've got this.

It was still dark outside, my window closed to keep the winter air out. But the sweat clinging to my brow told me I wouldn't mind the cool air. I climbed from my bed more aggressively than necessary, flinging the blankets back with a whoosh as I took the three steps to the window. As soon as it was open, I stuck my head into the night.

It was snowing.

I sighed and dropped my chin to my chest.

Of course it was snowing.

Unlike my racing mind, the world remained quiet. Not even the wind had anything to say.

According to my phone, it was barely past three in the morning. I had two options. I could climb back under my blanket for an hour and a half before my day was really supposed to start, or...I begin it early.

A quick glance at my bed gave me the answer I needed. The nightmare still sat there, Sylas's side of the bed empty as always.

"Well," I said to no one, "looks like I'm up."

I walked past Stetson's room, a calm expression across his pouty lips as he remained peacefully asleep. After another moment, I snuck away to shower quickly. Pulling my long blonde hair in a loose braid, my mind began to move with the list of things that needed to get done today and how an extra hour would be useful. I made my to-do list. Anything to keep my mind off that damn memory of a nightmare.

Hartwell Hills was slower in the winter and with it being the end of February, we still had plenty of time before things began to ramp up. Today would mainly consist of preparing meals for the ranch hands who stayed for the season, helping Lachlan fix a few doors in the arena and care for the horses. Get Stetson off to school, make lunch, double check the livestock had enough feed for the day and then, of course...the books.

I needed to look at those red numbers today.

That would take my mind off the nightmare for sure.

One nightmare to another.

Switching the kitchen light on, I took in the silence that came from the spotless kitchen. I smiled, knowing who had created the calm. Kyla. Having Rhett's new wife around has been a blessing. She had been a huge help in the kitchen, always making sure it's spotless before she drags my brother off to their cabin. She would walk across the threshold in a few hours, my brother right on her heels. Then the noise would begin. I had two, maybe even three, hours before the house woke up.

I should just really enjoy the silence while I could.

And for me—there was only one way to spend my quiet time. In one place I found peace on the ranch. The stables.

With him.

Sylas.

I brewed a pot of coffee, filling a mug to the brim, slipped on my boots and coat, then I headed out to the stables.

The mare could sense I was coming, she always did. Passing the family horses, saying a quick good morning to each one, I finally made it to her stall. Her brown head poked out of her pen, her black bangs sweeping over her eyes as they followed me. Her head bobbed the closer I got, and the minute my hand touched her nose, she stilled.

"Hey Luna," I whispered to her, brushing her bangs off to the side. "How are you, girl? You warm enough?" I peer behind her, grateful to see Lachlan remembered to put her blanket on her back. "Yeah, you are." I reached up and scratched behind her ear. "Wanna go on a quick walk with me? Watch the sun come up before it gets loud in the house?"

As if she understood what I said, she nodded her head. Chuckling, I unlocked her pen and let her step out and together—no lead needed—Sylas' mare and I headed out to the pasture.

TWO

Cash

"Up next is a rising star in barrel racing, Quinn Compton. She was well on her way to the NFR last year and this year is no different, she's going to prove to everyone..." The rodeo announcer's voice boomed through the air as the crowd died down. Everyone turned their attention towards the end of the arena to where the horse would fly through at any moment.

I could see my client, Quinn, bringing her gelding round the corner. Her face was stern, etched with concentration, leaving no doubt in my mind how ready she was for this. We had been training for months before this rodeo, gearing up for this circuit. For her, it was all or nothing. This was the first ride of the twenty-seven we had planned through the upcoming weeks, and even though I was used to that vigorous of a schedule, I wasn't sure if Quinn was. The girl was determined, I'd give her that. She insisted on this schedule, so who was I to stop her?

Seeing the drive there only brought out the spark in me I lost years ago.

But then that small twinge of electricity reminded me why I was on this side of the dirt.

Leaning against the railing, I lifted my left leg to catch my boot on the gate, my elbows keeping my torso steady as I watched Quinn gain speed. Her long brown hair flew behind her as her form on her gelding was perfect, the determination in both rider and horse unmatched. She rounded the first barrel, earning a cheer, then the second. Another loud whoop came, and Quinn smiled. I swear I could see the blush in her cheeks as she raced towards the third barrel. She had this...

Pulling on the reins, the gelding turned....

And Quinn lost balance.

My eyes widened as I froze, watching as her weight fell off to the side, her gelding's massive body following—both landing on the dirt—her horse coming down directly on her leg. The horse rose quickly, taking Quinn and her stuck boot with it. She grimaced as her hand flew up, reaching up her leg. I watched as she maneuvered, doing exactly what I taught her, removing her boot and letting the horse go. Once she was free, she flopped on the hard ground, the prideful expression she had mere seconds before now exchanged for one of pain and defeat.

The crowd gave a loud groan as she lay there, her hat near her hip, one boot missing as she spread her arms out to her side. This wasn't her first accident on this particular gelding, but it was her first in front of a crowd.

But hey—at least the barrel was still standing.

"Awe man," the announcer bellowed. "That's hard to see, especially for a rider like Compton, but there she is, up and ready to ride again. Give her a cheer because a fall doesn't stop cowboys and cowgirls. They get right back in that saddle."

Quinn slowly stood, grabbing her hat before she dusted off her Wranglers. She waved at the crowd and kept her eyes trained on the ground as she jogged back to the entrance, a slight limp in her step. I knew what that felt like. I knew the embarrassment and dread that came with a fall. I had fallen off horses before, and I did just what she did. I picked myself up and stood—limping away with a wave.

Pushing myself off the gate, I felt the pain shoot up my left leg, my hamstring reminding me of one particular fall, even years later. The one where I didn't get up. Ignoring it, I quickly made my way over to Quinn. She grabbed the reins, keeping her left foot lifted from the ground, toes pointed as she hobbled.

"We need to get that looked at," I shouted as I came up behind her.

Her back was covered in the dirt of the arena, and her cream hat was now bent. Dust flew around her as she shook her head.

"I'm fine," she grumbled.

"Your 1700-pound horse just fell on your leg; we're getting it checked out," I demanded, taking the reins from her and offering my arm to help carry her off the path. "A quick x-ray and before you know it, you'll be back on the dirt."

Her gaze met mine as a long, slow breath left her lungs. She grimaced.

"It hurts…" she whimpered, her voice low so only I could hear. She clearly recognized that not even her brave face could win against me.

Taking on barrel racing clients wasn't the first pick of training jobs for me, but since saddle bronc riding was no longer a way for me to bring in the checks, I had to start somewhere. I had saved up enough throughout my competing days that I was able to pay all my medical bills and afford life, but my nest egg could only last so long. I had known Quinn a little over a year, and she just happened to be looking for a new trainer when she joined the league. She was thrilled to get *The* Cash Callahan to train her. Last year was a win for us, Quinn gained a lot of traction and almost made it to the National Finals Rodeo. This year we were both determined to get her there, basically becoming her agent as well as her trainer. But now with a possible broken leg she just jogged on to get off the dirt, well…looks like we'd have to add recovery time to the lineup.

Quinn is a tough gal, for her to tell me it hurt…that was different.

"I know, trust me, I know," I responded, giving her side a squeeze. "Let's go get it seen about."

"I can't be out for the year." Quinn's voice rose as she took a step, a gasp leaving her lungs once we made it to the stall.

"You won't be."

"How do you know?"

"You givin' up on me already?" I raised an eyebrow.

"No," she griped. "That was going to be a good run. Hook had it." She gave her gelding a quick glance as he sauntered into his stall. I helped sit her on a barrel next to it before closing the lock.

"*You* and Hook had it." I held onto her shoulder "The horse is as only as good as the rider."

She let out a groan, closing her eyes and holding onto her knee. Shaking her head lightly, she bowed her chin. Quinn was one of the strongest girls I had met in the last few years. Basically, whatever Quinn wanted, she worked her ass off and got it. She never let anyone, or any*thing* get in her way. All of that tethered in my mind as I studied her, noticing her bottom lip quivering as she held back the failure I knew she had to be feeling.

I was in almost the same spot almost three years ago when I got bucked off and the horse landed on me, causing my left leg to shatter, along with other long-lasting conditions. The pain will still seep through the tough skin I've grown to cover it up, but it's there. If I closed my eyes I could still see everything clear as day. The reaction from the crown would still ring in my ears. If I still felt that, would she?

Watching as Quinn walked off the dirt with only a small limp until I got to her, my guess was a simple sprain or torn muscle. With training, she and Hook would be back on the dirt sooner than she thought. She would ride again. Me on the other hand...I haven't been on the rodeo dirt since my accident. I didn't see myself on the other side of the chute ever again.

Hook made a huff in his stall, pulling my attention back to him.

"I'll strip him down. You rest, and then we'll take you to the ER."

"The emergency room! Come on Callahan, I don't need the ER. A clinic is fine," she protested, a snap to her voice that would have almost worked to get her way.

Shaking my head, I heaved a sigh. She only called me Callahan when she was pissed. I raised my eyebrows and motioned towards her leg. "I'm taking you to the ER. We need to add in recovery time."

"I'll be training if I can't ride in the circuit," she bit back.

"I would expect nothing less from you, but for now, you're staying off that leg." I opened the pen. "Give me fifteen minutes and then we'll head on out."

Quinn scoffed. "How far away is the closest hospital anyway?"

My eyebrows met in the middle as I tried to recall exactly how far away the hospital was. I unhooked the gelding's reins and bridle. "An hour or so. Boise, I think."

"An hour..." she repeated softly. "What about Hook?"

"He'll be fine here."

"We can't leave him."

"Just for a few hours Quinn. You need to get looked at, and I'm not leaving him in the trailer while we're at the ER." I gave her a stern stare, glaring at her until she finally let out a long sigh and grumbled.

"Fine."

"Fine." I turned back to the gelding. "Now keep quiet, and don't move that leg."

"Well," I looked at the x-ray on the screen. "At least it's not broken."

With my hands on my hips, I turned to look at Quinn. Her leg was straight out on the bed, her back slouched as she lifted her gaze up to me. Fire brewed behind her green eyes, pure hatred for me at this point. The news that she tore a muscle and ligament wasn't exactly what she wanted to hear. She could ride, but she needed physical therapy—and a few weeks of rest before she could get back in the circuit.

"Eight to ten weeks," she lamented. "I'm down for eight to ten weeks." She emphasized the *'to ten'* bit. "That means I'm out until at least the beginning of May. Do you get how long it's going to take me to get back on top fifteen, back to the NFR?"

"If you don't make it this year—"

"I'll quit," she stated point blank, her gaze moving from me to her foot. Disappointment carved across her face as she stared at her wiggling toes.

"No. I won't allow that."

Quinn locked eyes with me. "Fine. I won't quit. I'll just sulk."

"You can train, and we can stay right here in Boise while you do your PT."

"Don't you have other clients?"

Nope...

Her eyebrows twitched. "Don't tell me you banked your entire year on me."

"You proved to me last year you were worth it. So, show me I made the right decision." I knew I had. This girl was one to watch and I was proud to call her my only client. It wasn't that I had everything *banked* on her, it was that I knew she was it. I knew she was going to go far. And I wanted to be there to watch her. "One fall isn't going to take you completely out of the running for the NFR. We'll train and go to PT and lay low. I'll work with Hook too, make it so he can go tighter, but...we may want to get Charming trained up with you too before spring just in case." I sat on the edge of the table, making eye contact with Quinn.

"Charming is calmer for sure." She inhaled. "And you think we can just stay in Idaho?"

"Think of it as a vacation." I raised my arms, giving her the cocky grin I knew could pull most people from their anger. "We don't have to, but hey"—I held up the many referral cards the doctors had already handed me—"we have a plan here already."

Quinn folded her arms, annoyance seeping from her pores at my optimism. Her bright green eyes pierced into me, almost as if she could directly send me her thoughts. Her brown hair was up in a loose braid, small whisps falling around her pale skin. She closed her eyes and her bottom lip shook. Quinn wasn't one to give up. She wasn't one to show fear. Just being here showed a different kind of strength from her—vulnerable, raw strength.

"Don't go crying on me."

She let out a laugh, "I'm not crying, I'm just…"

"Crying?"

"Yeah…" She looked up at me as the first tear fell.

"It's gonna work."

"Eight weeks," she sighed. "I can make this work for eight weeks."

"Eight to ten," I corrected.

Quinn agreed with a slight roll of her eyes. "Eight. Watch me."

With a dip of my chin, I chuckled. "Oh, I expect no less."

A few more doctors in and out, some prescriptions given for pain, and Quinn was officially discharged from the ER and comfortable in her hotel room. I checked on her horses before waltzing into my own room right next to hers. I tossed my hat onto the nearest chair, kicking my boots off while simultaneously unbuttoning my shirt. I loved this life, but days that ended in the hospital added extra stress and took the thrill away. Though I was technically employed as just her trainer, I helped put together this string of rides, and now each one had to be notified and canceled. Seeing she was fast asleep and knocked out on pain pills in the room next to me, that task was going to be left up to me.

Standing in just my boxers and t-shirt, I grabbed my phone and laptop, pulling up Quinns schedule on our shared document. I let out a deep breath when I saw the twenty plus events I had to call and remove her name from. No one was going to like this.

Especially Quinn.

The rodeo was her life.

Hell, the rodeo *was* my life, too. Or rather, used to be my life.

The last time I sat down to cancel events, they were my own.

Letting those memories fester for two seconds, I pushed them out as quickly as they came.

I never let them linger.

My phone buzzed next to me, a much-needed distraction, and the name on the caller ID pulled my lips into a soft smile.

Lachlan Hartwell.

"Lach," I answered, not even a hello between us.

"How's Quinn?" His rough voice hit my ears, and I could see him sitting on his porch back at Hartwell Hills Ranch. His feet would be on his railing, a glass of water next to him as he watched the stars. The vision was clear as day—even if it had been years since I had seen him.

"You saw that tumble huh?" I scoffed, switching him to speaker phone so I could cancel the next event Quinn had lined up.

His deep chuckle reverberated the speakers. "Rhett's wife was more concerned about her fall than the bull rider that almost got bucked."

The memory of meeting Kyla Hartwell months ago floated through my mind. She was still so new to the rodeo world, so of course she would be more concerned over a barrel racer than a 'tough' bull rider.

"Compton will be fine. She tore a ligament, up to ten weeks PT and training before she can get back on the dirt."

"Damn," Lachlan breathed.

"She'll be back before you know it. Tell Mrs. Hartwell she'll recover, but she's out for now. Currently canceling her line up."

"So, what's next? Montana for PT and rest?"

I had known Lachlan Hartwell for a long time and still thought of him as my best friend. We didn't see each often—seeing as he stayed far away from rodeos, only really attending one a year in his hometown—but the communication was always there. He was the only Hartwell that still spoke to me on a regular basis, the only one who still checked in. Rhett Hartwell, tie down's golden child as of last year, would talk to me when we ran into each at rodeos, but since he was taking the year off, Lachlan was my only tie to my previous life.

I stood, grabbing the phone as I made my way over to the bathroom. I caught my own gaze in the mirror. The dark brown eyes shown back at me, my tawny skin covered in dirt from the arena, making me look darker than I really was. Being the son of a mixed-race couple—my father Black, my mother Caucasian—my complexion was sometimes the same color of the dirt, but today it stood out like a sore thumb. Setting the phone down, I turned the sink on, cupped my hands and splashed my face, the dirt falling down the drain, almost with all the sullen memories I wish could be wiped from my brain.

"Staying in Boise," I confirmed, grabbing the towel. "We can get PT going and find a place to train here. Sure, she wants to go home, but eight weeks here won't be too bad. I just need to talk to the hotel and extend our time." I rubbed my face with my hands before grabbing the light blue towel on the rack.

"Boise? Maybe Rhett and I can take a trip to see you one day. It's been a while."

My eyebrows perked up. A night with friends? Sure. "Drinks one night? Hell, I'll even come to The Steel." I did love that dingy bar.

Lachlan gave me a curt chuckle. "Yeah, sure. I'll make sure to tell Abi and Wyatt."

Abi.

Abigail Acosta.

My heart lurched as I threw the towel, watching as it hit the small lotion bottles on the counter, even toppling over my medication bottle into the sink. Thank god the lid was on, or I'd have to stop by a pharmacy. Groaning, I grasped the little orange bottle in my hand, holding on to it tightly as I gave myself one last look as thoughts flooded my mind. Wyatt Hartwell loathed me.

Wyatt I could handle, but Abi?

I hadn't seen Abi in almost five years. Abi was, well, she was the one person I didn't know if I could see again. Given our history and the way my heart fluttered just from hearing her name—I wanted to—more than anything, but...

"Yeah, that sounds fan-fucking-tastic." I mumbled, setting my meds back on the counter, moving to rearrange the mess the towel created.

"Nah, just Rhett and I. I was just joking."

I swallowed, giving Lachlan a nod I knew he couldn't see. He knew. He didn't know the full extent of what thoughts flew through my brain whenever I heard her name—if I were being honest, neither did I, but he knew enough to let it go.

A few more exchanges helped move the topic, easing me back into my normal rhythm, and once we said goodbye, my mind went right back to work. Quinn and the rodeo.

Not on Abi, or my past.

THREE

Abi

I PLOPPED DOWN ON the wicker chair on my brother's deck, the soft pad hitting my joints and muscles in the perfect balance, the warm mug of tea sending comfort through my body. The sun had already made its way down over the mountains and the chill hit my skin. It had become a nightly ritual to watch it set from Rhett's front porch, no matter what time of year. Even though I still had dinner to make and a kitchen to clean, Kyla and I always seemed to find calm here at the end—or close to the end—of every day.

I shifted, pulling my knees close to my chest as I fumbled with the blanket, curling myself into a tight ball. Hugging my legs, I gripped the mug with both hands, not even thinking of taking a sip, just enjoying the silence. That is until the front door swung open and hard boots hit the wood.

I turned and saw Kyla, her hair up in a messy ponytail, a blanket wrapped around her shoulders.

"Need some spirits?" she asked, tilting her own mug back and forth. "We have whiskey."

"No, but my brother apparently thought you needed some?" I answered as I watched my friend sit next to me.

"He may have added a bit of whiskey to my drink." She smirked.

"I still have dinner to make, and a kid to get to bed, and I think that said kid has homework."

She hummed. "I can tackle homework if you want to tackle dinner?"

"Deal." I cheered, moving my legs just enough to lift the tea to my lips. "No plans with Rhett tonight? No *dates*?"

Kyla blushed and tilted her chin down.

My brother had married Kyla as a way to fend off her ex, but that didn't stop love from taking shape. They decided to stay married once the ex was officially out of the picture, but they decided they would 'date.' After winning the NFR in Vegas last December, my brother took the year off from his event to focus on his wife. Rhett took Kyla out at least two times a week, and the other nights they simply spent whatever time they had left in their day together. She always took an hour or so out of that to spend the time with me though, and for that I was grateful.

Kyla was a godsend, coming to Hartwell Hills kind of as a fluke, but she ended up staying and loving it just as much as anyone else in the family. She blended in perfectly. Without her, Stetson would still complain when I told him he needed to read before going to bed. Without her, the kitchen would most likely sit dirty some nights. Without her, I would most likely lose my mind.

"Movie night," she responded.

"Ah." I smiled. "So, that's why you got homework. You won't be at dinner?"

She shook her head. "We're ordering from June's."

My eyes widened at the thought of June's Pizza being brought out to the ranch. I had paper plates, I had napkins...no dishes required. "New deal. I have homework, you order June's for everyone."

Kyla laughed, "I'll pass the message onto Rhett."

"Already on it." I heard my brother holler from inside. "Six pizzas would be enough, right?"

I turned and looked at the slightly cracked window and saw my brother hunched over the kitchen island, his hat sitting on the counter as he thumbed through his phone. I turned back to Kyla and laughed, lifting my chin in the air at the simple thought of my brother now ordering pizza for the entire ranch. The blush on her cheeks deepened.

"I love him." She smiled.

"He's a good one." I admitted. "Make sure you get me—" I began to yell towards the house again.

"I got a veggie deep dish, don't worry." Rhett interrupted, joining us on the deck moments later. He bent and kissed Kyla on the crown of her head. "Forty minutes and you owe me half of the bill." He pointed at me, his eyes narrowed. "Meet you at the house?"

"No, I'm coming, I'm coming." I set my tea down on the small table next to the chair and wiggled my way out of the seat. Rhett shoved his hands in his coat pockets and watched as I hoisted the blanket up over my shoulders and bundled myself even more. Kyla snorted when I turned to get my tea, not quite sure how to accomplish that, completely bundled in the blanket.

"Here," Rhett sighed. "Allow me. You may stay a burrito."

I gave my brother a smirk. "Always the gentleman. You comin' Kyla?"

"Oh, I'll drive there."

"It's less than a mile," Rhett argued, twisting his torso, reaching a hand out to his wife. Kyla looked at it and shook her head.

"It's cold, and I'd rather eat hot pizza, so I'll drive us back when it gets here. You two walk in the snow. I'll be there soon." She gave Rhett a wink and then turned to go back into their home.

I offered Rhett a cheeky grin as we both marched off towards the main house. I had no choice but to follow my brother. He had my tea after all, so I had to keep up.

The man sitting in front of me was determined. Strong. Confident. Caring. His broad shoulders took up most of the space of the chair and his dark facial hair still refused to turn gray like the rest of his hair had. This man knew how to run a ranch. He knew how to lead the family and make sure every single need was met.

Leonard Hartwell.

My father.

And the look he was giving me and my brothers was downright terrifying.

My father wasn't a scary man. Maybe when I was fourteen and chasing after a certain somebody—but that was a different story.

Lachlan leaned against the windowsill, his ankles crossed and his arms folded over his chest. My dad looked from Lachlan to the three of us sitting in the chairs across from his desk. Rhett relaxed in his chair; Wyatt slouched and gave a yawn. I simply crossed my legs and tried to look ready for anything. These meetings with my dad weren't uncommon, but today the feeling in the room was completely different.

He broke the silence. "I'm retiring."

Right to the point, huh dad?

"We knew that," Wyatt said coolly.

Narrowing my eyes, I gave my brother a side glare.

"What?" He shrugged. "We did. He's been talking about it for years."

"I'm leaving the ranch. You're mother and I."

Oh, ok...that was a new development.

"Leaving?" Rhett parroted.

Looking over at my cousin, who currently owned half of Hartwell Hills Ranch. He gave me a slight nod.

"We're going to travel. We've spent the majority of our life here, and yes it's home and always will be, but we want to see the world." My dad leaned back in his seat.

"You have seen the world." Wyatt stated.

My father's gaze turned to his youngest son. "We've never been outside the US or Canada. It's time I focus on your mother."

Rhett took a deep breath. "I get it. I want to spend all the time I can with Kyla." He shifted in his seat. "So, what does that mean for Hartwell Hills?"

"Well"—my dad turned to Lachlan—"Lach owns half. That's what Levi's will stated. He and I owned it fifty-fifty. The other fifty needs to be split between you three."

"Equally?" I asked, knowing very well my twin brother didn't want any part of the ranch. I didn't exactly know what Wyatt wanted from life, but I did know he didn't want to be tied to a piece of land. Rhett on the other hand, this was his life. Once he was ready to retire from tie down, his plan was Hartwell Hills. I have overseen the finances and day-to-day of the ranch for five years now. Lachlan and I worked together to make sure everything ran smoothly, and it was a well-oiled machine. But, despite doing it every day, I had my father to fall back on. He was always there when I needed guidance.

He knew what was happening behind the scenes now. He knew what those books showed. The truth was, Hartwell Hills needed extra funds somehow. We weren't bleeding money, but we weren't really making a profit either. We're barely breaking even every month. We were able to make payroll and supplies, but I would like to see something come of it.

"That was a plan," my dad spoke, "but..."

"I don't need an equal share." Wyatt interrupted, moving to rest his elbows on his knees.

"And we accounted for that. So, here's my proposal." Dad stood. "Abi gets the majority."

My eyes widened. "Excuse me?"

"You're already running it." Dad leaned on his chair, placing a hand on his hip as his eyes bore into mine. "Lachlan and I talked about it."

"But...Rhett..." I looked over at Rhett, who simply blinked. My big brother was showing zero emotion here. I wanted him to protest. I had seen him get angry—granted, never at our father—but I knew it was there. He needed to claim the ranch.

"It makes sense." Rhett sighed. "I'm only here for the year, and then I'm back on the circuit. You and Lachlan already know it inside and out, more than I do so..." He met my gaze. "It makes sense for you to get the majority of my share."

I chewed on my lip to stop my jaw from dropping.

"It does." Lachlan nodded. "You know more about the finances than anyone, and you know the land just as well as I do. You have the drive for it."

The drive.

"The ranch may fail in the next couple years if something doesn't change," I blurted out. "And I don't want to be the one responsible for it."

"Wait..." Rhett sat up in his chair. "What? The ranch is failing?"

My heart pounded. "Well, not technically. But if something doesn't happen soon, we won't be breaking even every month."

"But, we do need another source of revenue." Lachlan added as I caught his gaze. I nodded.

"Yeah we do." I returned his nod before turning to look at my dad.

"Ideas?" he asked, and I froze. "You've been looking at the books for years now Abi. What do you see?"

I racked my brain, looking over at Rhett, wishing in this moment he was my twin instead of Wyatt—who had all but checked out of the conversation—hoping he could give me some telepathic answer as to how to bring in more profit.

"Well," I began, still hoping for something from Rhett. "It's winter, we're always slower but...this started about a year ago. To be honest, I was a little upset we didn't sell to David—"

Rhett's head spun my way. Bringing up the events of last year surrounding his wife wasn't an easy topic, but the man—as sleezy as he was—wanted to buy five hundred acres for 3.7 million dollars. 3.7 million dollars we could have used to update the barn and stables, get more staff, expand the garden, fix the fences, and possibly get more cattle. When dad was tip toeing around the idea of selling, I was secretly hoping he would. Lachlan and Rhett would have never allowed it, and I played their side. But, I silently wanted that to happen. I wanted the money for the ranch.

"You didn't just say that?" Rhett grumbled, leaning forward on his chair and burying his head in his palms. See—I knew he was capable of anger.

"It was a lot of money, Rhett. You never saw the total." I argued.

"It was substantial." Lachlan heaved a sigh, "But it wasn't worth it at the time."

"It really was though. There are so many things around here that need to be expanded or repaired or...hell...that was five hundred acres we didn't have to worry about anymore."

"But it was David." Rhett dropped his hands, his voice hoarse.

"I get that, but if it wasn't him and if it really was a genuine offer, not just to weasel his way back into Kyla's life, I would have loved to take the money. The issues we're facing now wouldn't be as big as they are."

Rhett shook his head, "Okay, well moving on from that..." His voice was gruff, but yet, no guilt formed in my own stomach. It was the truth, and about time he heard it. "We're not selling land, so we need to think of other ways to make money."

"We could board horses," Wyatt finally said, all of us twisting our heads at the sound of his voice. I guess he didn't fully check out. "We have what"—he looked at me—"ten empty stalls? People pay a lot of money to house their horses correctly, and we have the room. We could also rent out the arena. Rodeo training. And maybe even the barn for events once it gets fixed up."

"And you don't want anything to do with the ranch." My dad chuckled.

"Oh, hell no." Wyatt flopped back into his chair. "While you guys were remembering the asshat, I was thinking. We have room in the stables for at most ten horses. The arena isn't being used as much anymore since Rhett isn't on the circuit, and the barn sits empty a lot of the time."

"It needs repairs before we can rent it out for any kind of events," I added, thinking of the long list of to-dos that currently sat on my desk. Paint the barn. Repair the roof of the barn and stables. Fix the fences on the south pasture. A million pounds of stress began to settle in my stomach just thinking about everything that had to get down before the next winter hit.

"Easy fixes." Lachlan agreed, not a stitch of stress in his voice, which thankfully reminded me to stop stressing. "Rhett and I can get started on that. Renting out the stable—that sounds easy enough to fill—and using the arena as a training ground...I may have the perfect person who could use the space." He pushed himself off the windowsill. "I'll give him a call and let you know."

Rhett stood and followed Lachlan. "Can you look at the numbers Abi?"

Hunching my shoulders, I peered at my dad for reassurance. I nodded at him. "Yeah. I can research the amount people are charging for boarding horses."

It just may work. Wyatt was full of surprises after all.

"This is just further proof that you don't need your mother and me. We trust you three, even if one doesn't seem to care." He looked over at Wyatt, who gave our dad his award-winning smile, "Once we get the title and papers drawn up, we can talk about percentage between you two, but again"—his eyes met mine—"I think Abi needs to get the majority."

I gave him a tight smile, trying to look excited for what the future held for me.

FOUR

Cash

THE LAST TIME I drove under this gate, Carolyn was in the passenger seat. I wanted to see a friend, to give him a late birthday gift, and she was greatly annoyed that we had to make this stop. I could still see her checking her nails, making sure the bright red was still perfectly polished. I could still hear the *tsks* she would sigh loud enough to get to me. And I could still hear her shrill voice ringing in my ears...*This detour better not take long. We're going to be late. I don't understand why you can't wait to give it to him in Billings. You know I hate this place...*

Seven months later, I got into my accident.

Three months after that, she filed for a divorce.

After Sylas Acosta died, it seemed my entire world imploded on itself, and as much as I tried to move on and keep being who I was, each passing day got harder and harder. Without my best friend, without the one person who would listen to me no matter what I needed to say, I had never felt more alone.

Once I wound up in the hospital, needing surgery and PT to get through the healing process, learning I would never compete again seemed to be the breaking point. But then having my wife, who was supposed to be my rock through everything up and leave because I no longer fit into her dream world...that was the icing on top. Once the divorce was final and I could walk without massive amounts of pain, I started over. I pushed everything aside and began again.

Tugging the long trailer behind me, the three horses inside most likely hating every single turn, I pulled up to the stables. It was as if fate was working in my favor. When Lachlan called offering up the stables for boarding use and the use of their massive indoor arena to rehab Quinn—for a small renters fee—how could I refuse?

The place hadn't changed much in the years since I last saw it, but I could tell from a distance that the barn needed a paint touch up, and there were a few things on the stables that needed repairs, but that was Lachlan's to worry about. My one and only concern today was getting these horses comfortable and avoiding Abi Acosta.

It's not that I didn't want to see her. If I were being one hundred percent honest with myself, I was dying to see her, to have that connection to my friend. It was knowing she didn't want to see me that forced me to make this trip as fast as possible.

I popped my rig in park, and flung the door open the moment I saw my friend step out of the stables. Lachlan Hartwell, like the ranch, hadn't changed much since the last time I saw him either. He wore his signature black boots tucked into his Wrangler jeans, a dark flannel shirt sticking out under his winter coat, and his black hat perched on his head. He hadn't shaved in a few days, and since I was used to seeing his face bare, the scruff only added to his stoic demeanor. And yet, once he saw me, a small smile spread upon his lips. I hadn't seen that man smile in years—and I was the lucky one to get to see him lighten up just a twitch.

During the circuit it was always Lachlan, Sylas, and me behind the chutes. Lachlan rode bareback, Sylas was the bull rider, and I was saddle bronc. The roughies that were always together. Two of us were always there when the other was getting down onto their chosen animal, hyping them up as they settled, and when the nod came, we cheered just as loud. After the eight seconds buzzer went off, we each would jump off the animal and raise our arms, the adrenaline seeping from our pores. We loved the rodeo.

"Fuck, if it isn't *the* Cash Callahan," Lachlan greeted me, reaching his arm out to pull me in for a hug.

"Hey Lach." I patted his shoulder, pulling away to get a good look at him. "Still brooding I see."

He shook his head at my joke and stepped past me to my trailer. I knew what Lachlan lived through. I saw the grief that struck his eyes, but he still took my jokes.

"How many horses you got?" He changed the subject, going straight to business.

"Three. Two are Quinn's, one is mine."

"Still riding Nova?" he asked as he opened up the back of the trailer, answering his own question once he saw my blue roan mare standing between Quinn's two geldings. "She's looking good."

Leaning up against the trailer, I smiled. I loved Nova. I wouldn't trade her in for the world. "She's the one and only thing that has stuck by me. Of course it's still her. I'll be with her until the end."

Lachlan raised his eyebrow at me. "You trained her. I wouldn't think you would just get rid of her." He took a deep breath as I passed him, Nova bobbing her head as we moved. Nova hated the trailer, and being shoved in between two geldings wasn't her favorite thing in the world.

"Why is a barrel racer traveling with two horses?" Lachlan asked, pushing himself off the side of the trailer to step inside, heading straight for Hook first.

"Depending on how many runs she does, she switches horses," I answered. "Smart of her, hell for training. I feel like I have to do double the work to get both horses where we want them."

"How are you training Quinn with two horses plus other clients?"

I chuckled between my teeth, lowering my chin to look at my boots before talking. "I don't have any other clients."

"None?" Lachlan paused. "None at all?" His rough voice hit with slight concern.

"Quinn's it. She almost made it to the NFR last year, and if she sticks to the PT schedule, she can make it this year." I turned to look at him over my shoulder. "I'm proud of that girl."

"She's young, too." Lachlan stated.

"Twenty-two." I confirmed, giving him a curt nod. "Age has nothing to do with it."

A scoff left his nose, sounding more like a horse than man. "So, who's this?" he changed the subject, patting Hook's neck.

"Hook. This is the guy that fell on her."

"He didn't get hurt did he?" Lachlan looked over at me, raising an eyebrow.

His mind probably went straight to where mine went when I saw the horse fall on her. Thankfully, Hook got up with no problem. The horse that fell on me had a different fate.

I pursed my lips, not really wanting to go down that path.

He hummed, obviously sensing I didn't want to mention that night, and then jerked his head down the row of stables. "The three at the end are for you—right next to Luna."

Luna...

"Haven't heard that name in forever. How's that old gal doin'?" I approached the stall carefully, jitters running through my stomach at the thought of seeing something that was close to Sylas.

He would take Luna, Lachlan would be on Onyx, myself on Nova, and we'd roam the areas surrounding our events before we hit the bars or beds. Time with my friends was all I wanted when I needed to wind down from a ride, and I missed those quiet moments. I didn't have moments like that anymore. Life was loud and chaotic.

"She's great." Lachlan opened a stall and led Hook inside, unlatching his lead and scratching behind his ear before Hook left him to go straight for the water trough. "Abi takes her out every now and then, when she's not busy around the ranch."

I stiffened at the mention of Abi's name, glancing around the stables before leading Nova into her own stall and undoing her lead. I blinked out of my stupor. "Glad the old gal gets out."

"She's not that old. She's only twelve." Lachlan chuckled. "Onyx is fifteen."

"And still dealing with your ass half the time."

"Ha. Ha." Lachlan grumbled. "What's the other horse's name?" He locked the stall and turned his back to me, an eyebrow raised in question.

"Charming." I answered, watching Lachlan as he stopped mid step and turned to look at me.

"Charming?" he repeated, raising a brow in question. Lachlan kept to the traditional horse names, pretty sure there was an Echo in their stables.

"Quinn likes fairy tales."

He raised a single eyebrow before giving his head a shake, turning with a sigh and adjusting his hat. "First Kyla named a cow Josie, and now a horse named Charming..."

"It fits the horse," I hollered towards him.

His head down, he lifted his arm to me to wave his hand, "I'm sure it does."

I chuckled, giving Nova some love before leaving the stall. They needed to be brushed down, given hay and food and then wrapped for the night. The barn was warm compared to the winter weather outside, but I knew they still appreciated a blanket over their coat. Leaving Nova's stall, I stepped over to Luna. The brown mare gave me a slight huff as she poked her nose over the stall's door.

"Well, you haven't changed a bit." I said softly.

Memories of racing flooded my mind the moment I touched her nose. Sylas on Luna always trying to beat me as we ran the length of the ranch. Lachlan would win no matter what Sylas and I tried to do. It was always in between rides that we came here. We relaxed and practiced and trained as best we could, but we always ended up in the field with nothing but our horses, a fire, and the cattle all around us. I could still smell the smoke; I could still hear the crackling of the wood. It was a memory I wouldn't be able to erase anytime soon. It wasn't one I tried to forget. A memory like that brought a smile to my face every time.

Luna nudged her nose up and down, forcing my hand from her. Her jaw moved as she took the last step towards the gate.

"Ready to meet the last house guest?" I asked her, adjusting the hat on my head.

I turned, reaching out to pat her nose once more, then my eyes drifted towards where my rig sat, the trailer still open. Charming was waiting in the trailer—or at least I thought he was. I froze, and I swear my heart stopped beating completely.

Abi Acosta stood in the stable's doors, Charming's lead tight in her hand as she stared right at me.

FIVE

Abi

MY GRIP ON THE lead tightened when I saw the man next to Luna's stall. It couldn't be. Anyone but him. Anyone but Cash Callahan.

When I saw Lachlan stepping into the unknown trailer, excitement filled my entire body. Our first paying boarding client. Three horses for at least eight weeks. And, a person renting the arena for training space? I basically jumped for joy when I looked at the white horse in the trailer. And when Lachlan said, "His name is *Charming?*" I let out laugh and gave the gelding attention before leading him into the stable. He walked slowly next me, using his nose to nudge my cheek, being absolutely...charming. I was enamored with him, right until I saw the darker skin and black hat of the man I hadn't seen in years. The man I never thought I'd see again.

"What the hell?" I said breathlessly.

Cash's dark, rich eyes hit mine. They were different, a hint of something I couldn't quite read sitting behind them. I pinched my brow and focused on him. He was holding onto something in his eyes, but then in an instant, he changed. His eyebrows rose and a smirk spread across his lips, revealing his white teeth. His cocky smile was the same as I remembered—it was just those eyes that were different.

"Abs." He gave me a nod.

His voice. Deep and rich, that Tennessee drawl flying through the air sparked more memories than I cared to admit.

"It's been awhile," he finished.

It's been awhile!?

I bit the inside of my lips, holding back any and all words that I may vomit out. Trying to find something decent to say. Anything other than what I really, truly wanted to say to the man standing near my husband's horse.

Get away from Luna.

Get the fuck off my property.

Where the hell have you been?

Why didn't you call me back?

Why did you leave us? Leave me?

Why....why...

Why the hell didn't you come to Sylas's funeral?

I finally settled on one simple word. "No."

"No, what?" He raised a brow, stepping away from Luna's stall to come a little closer to me.

I dropped Charming's lead, noticing right away how he didn't turn his head to wander off, and took one step towards Cash.

"No." I repeated before spinning on my heel, feeling my hair whip around my back in my fit of rage. "Lachlan." I glared at my cousin. "I need to speak with you, please." I grabbed Lachlan's collar and yanked him hard, dragging him out of the stables as fast as I could. Away from Cash Callahan.

"Abi." Lachlan stumbled. "What—"

"What the *hell*"—I yelled in his face once we were out of the barn—"is he doing here?"

"*He* is paying us to board three horses while his client heals from the fall you saw the other night. *He* is paying us to use the arena to train her before she can go back to the circuit. *He* is giving the ranch what it needs right now—money." Lachlan glared at me, making sure his voice raised every time he said 'he'—as if I needed to be reminded who *he* was.

I shook my head. "No, not him."

"Abi." He groaned, shaking his head, his arms raising before they came down and hit his thighs in frustration. He chewed his bottom lip, probably so hard he was tasting blood.

"This is who you knew needed a place to board horses? This is who you called yesterday? Why didn't you tell me? Why did you think just letting him show up was a good idea?"

"Because I was hoping to avoid this." He waved his hand in between us. "You said the ranch needs money. Cash has more than enough money, and he has a need. We can fulfill that need, so guess what Abi?" His voice grew sharper, louder, and one glance behind his shoulder told me Cash could hear everything we said. "You're going to put your big girl pants on and get over the fact that he's here. You used to be friends. He was Sylas's friend. You shut him out. You made that mistake. You get over it. He has."

I clenched my teeth at his words, forcing the tears to stay back. Put my 'big girl' pants on as he called it. I crossed my arms over my chest and didn't take my eyes off Lachlan.

The way he saw it, I stopped talking to Cash. I stopped being his friend. He didn't know what had happened. He didn't know the last thing I ever heard Cash Callahan say was that Sylas had died. That the injuries were too much for his body to sustain. Then he walked out of the hospital doors. And I never saw or heard from him again.

But not because I hadn't tried.

Grinding my molars together, I looked at my cousin. I kept my teeth together, not trusting anything that could have come out of my mouth.

"Are your big girl pants on?" he sneered.

I gave him one single nod.

"Good. Now get your ass in the stable and talk to Cash like an adult." He turned his back and took a few steps but then looked over his shoulder. "No, how about you talk to him like you're old friends who haven't seen each other in four years. I have horses to settle."

He walked away from me, towards Cash, waving his arm in the air as if he was wiping what just happened between us from his mind. I watched as he grabbed Charming's lead and walk him to the stall next to Stetson's horse, Marshmallow, and then my gaze went to Cash.

He stood with his thumbs in his belt loops, his hip cocked and chin in the air. His skin was still as flawless as I remembered, maybe a hint of scruff on his chin...but he still looked the same. He still looked like the friend I had grown close to until he was gone. He raised his eyebrows and smiled, no doubt thinking it would erase the last four years of silence.

Biting the inside of my bottom lip, I held his gaze for what felt like forever...

One...two...three....four...

Come on Abi, bull riders make it eight seconds...

I blinked...and turned away from him.

I couldn't even last the eight seconds.

"Are you going to tell me about the guy in the stables with Lachlan and Rhett?" Kyla asked as I tried to focus on the food in front of me.

I ignored her. It was lunch time, and before I knew it, a few of the ranch hands would be wandering in to get their meal before heading back out to the land. I didn't want to talk about this. But maybe I did? Should I get it all off my chest? Kyla was the one to talk to about it. I need to get it off my mind and put my energy into feeding the employees. These guys deserve the best bologna sandwiches in the world. And dammit, they would get them. I spread the mayonnaise on one side, and then the mustard. Provolone. Bologna. Lettuce. Tomato. Deliciousness in square form. One down—fifteen perfect bologna sandwiches to go. And that was not making one for Cash. He could make his own damn sandwich.

I rolled my eyes at myself. So much for my big girl pants.

"He looks familiar." Kyla stood by the sliding door; her arms folded as she watched the three men leave the stables. "I swear I've met him before."

"You couldn't have," I finally responded back to her, my focus still on the sandwiches. "That's Cash Callahan, and he hasn't been here in a long time."

"Cash Callahan? He's a trainer?" Her head shot over to me. "I have met him."

I furrowed my brow and scoffed. "When?"

"At the rodeo in Utah, I'm sure. He led me over to the winner's podium. Wyatt didn't seem too thrilled about him, but he seems nice?" She shrugged a shoulder up.

I raised my gaze and gave a chuckle. "Wyatt is not fond of him."

"Why not?"

I looked out the window, catching Cash mid laugh. Whatever was said must have been funny, because it even earned a smirk and head shake from Lachlan. Lachlan never smiled.

I blinked. "It's a long story," I muttered under my breath. "He's just here to board his horses."

"That's good, right?" Kyla moved, taking a seat on the stool at the island, reaching over to gather all of the sandwich fixing. "The ranch needs the money, at least that's what Rhett's told me."

"It does, so this is a good thing. Just," I heaved a sigh and closed my eyes. "There's a history."

"Abi, there wasn't anything..." Kyla blinked as she leaned forward, lowering her voice. "...romantic between you two was there?"

"What?" I spat, almost dropping the butter knife in shock. "No. Kyla why on Earth would you ask that!?"

"You just seem—"

"No." I cut her off, fire boiling that she'd even suggest that. I hadn't known her long, but she knew I loved Sylas more than anything. She was the one I opened up to with ease when she simply asked about Sylas, and now I couldn't even bring myself to open up here. "It's just..." Dropping my shoulders, the clang of the knife hitting the marble island rang through the kitchen. "A really long story."

"What happened?" she asked quietly.

I inhaled. I wasn't ready to crack open that chest yet. I had locked it a long time ago, and only Wyatt really knew what was sitting there, but we didn't talk about it. Cash was Sylas's friend. He used to be mine. But then he was gone. I could feel the tears welling up. That stinging vibration that pushed and pushed until the tears fell. But like always...I stopped them and went back to my task.

"I'd rather not go there right now," I mumbled.

Kyla raised an eyebrow.

"Rhett will tell you everything."

Well...everything he *knew*.

Kyla's eyebrow raised higher.

"Oh, don't pretend like he won't."

"He won't. Because I won't bring it up. That's your story to tell." She hit the island and lifted herself off the chair. "You gave me time to tell you my story, just know that I'm here when you want to talk about it."

She came around the counter and wrapped her arm around my shoulder, pulling me in for a side hug. I welcomed her warmth and leaned into her slightly, the small smile forming on my lips as she squeezed me tighter.

"Do we like him?" she whispered.

Sighing, I leaned my back to look at her. "Unfortunately, he's a good guy, so don't let me not making him a sandwich sway your decision on whether or not you like him."

"You're not making him a sandwich? There's a lot of sandwiches here." Kyla pulled away and looked at the now nine sandwiches sitting on the island.

"We have a lot of ranch hands..."

The sliding back door opened, and the three men came stomping inside, tearing off their winter coats before making their way into the kitchen. Kyla's arm dropped from my shoulder as she made her way to her husband. Lachlan walked over to the counter, removing his hat and placing it top down before grabbing a sandwich, and Cash...

Cash made his way over next to Lachlan, fitting right in as if he had been here every single day. He took his hat off, his hair still flat against his scalp, a bit of cropped curl trying to escape. His hair had always changed. One minute it would be tight and short, the next, the curls I knew were there would want to break free. I had always asked to see a picture of him in his teenage years—he once claimed he had an afro. But now...now it looked the same as the last time I saw him. Sleek and trimmed to perfection. That was Cash.

Carolyn, his wife, always made him keep it perfect. She didn't care for the hat hair that Lachlan would don after a ride. To her, the shorter Cash's hair was, the better.

I cleared my throat as I watched him reach for a sandwich. I bit back *that's not for you.* Instead, I met Lachlan's gaze and tried to come up with something sensible to say.

"How long are you going to be here?" I snapped, clearing my throat again to break out my tone. Big girl pants, Abi. Big. Girl. Pants.

Cash lifted his chin, chewing that first bite of sandwich. One single eyebrow raised as his dark eyes focused on me. He swallowed, and a corner of his lips tipped up.

"Quinn's healing for about ten weeks."

"Lachlan told me we were boarding your horses for eight." I glared at my cousin, but I could still feel Cash's gaze heavy on me.

Cash's half smile turned full force. "Eight to ten weeks of PT. It could be more if she doesn't heal."

"Quinn?" Kyla's voice made Cash turn from me, and I was relieved to have the reprieve. The two minutes he was watching me felt more like an hour. I could focus back on these amazing bologna sandwiches and not on Cash. "The barrel racer who fell the other night."

Cash nodded. "That's her. She's a spitfire and really upset she's missing rides, so we train."

"I didn't know she was your client." Kyla smiled.

"That she is Mrs. Hartwell." Cash returned her smile before his gaze turned to me again. "Thanks for the sandwich, Abs. It's delicious."

Abs.

That's the second time he called me that. Not that I was counting.

"It's bologna," I grumbled.

"Big girl pants, remember Abi." Lachlan sneered.

"How's Carolyn?" I asked, ignoring my cousin completely.

The room went silent, and after a few moments, Cash finally spoke. "Wouldn't know. We're divorced. Haven't heard from her in years."

Divorced?

"Oh," I stammered. "Sorry to hear that."

"Don't be. I'm not."

His voice was so sure. No regret in his tone whatsoever. From what I knew, Carolyn was his everything. He sure acted that way when they were married, at least. I saw the way he looked at her. It was the same way Sylas looked at me, the way Rhett looked at Kyla. Carolyn and I may have had our differences, but she was what Cash wanted. For them to get a divorce was kind of a surprise, and for him to not regret it...I wasn't quite sure how to take that.

"Good riddance." Lachlan patted Cash on the shoulder. "Pretty sure we celebrated when the papers were signed right?"

Cash let out a laugh. "We sure did. In different bars, in different states, but we celebrated."

"I'm sorry I...I didn't know." I stammered.

Cash shrugged. "Didn't think you would care."

Okay, that stung.

Once again, I found myself grinding my teeth, forcing myself to keep it calm. I didn't need to let five years of pent-up anger out right here, right now. It was eight to ten weeks of this man. I would survive. But I could feel it. I could feel the anger building my bones, starting at my metatarsals all the way to my ribs, caging in my pumping heart. My body was practically vibrating.

"Oh, would you look at that," I shouted, louder than I intended. "It's time to go pick up Stetson." I dropped the knife on the counter, and pushed past everyone, leaving the kitchen as calmly as I could.

"But it's only lunch time?" Lachlan questioned, his voice growing faint as I opened the front door.

At least I lasted longer than four seconds this time.

SIX

Cash

THE MOMENT I SAW Abi was a punch to the gut. The last time I had seen her was the night of Sylas' accident. I told her he passed, and then instead of comforting her like a good friend would do, I left. I've always regretted that moment, but that night I wasn't sure how to act. There were so many things I would have done differently—but seeing as *Doctor Who* was fictional—I had to accept what it was. It had been so long, but the look on Abi's face when she first saw me and the brief interaction in the kitchen told me all I needed to know.

She was pissed.

And still just as beautiful as I remembered.

So...I smiled. Put on my cocky mask, and I tried to act as normal as possible.

And then she brought up Carolyn.

In my mind, she had to know about my divorce. She would have celebrated when Lachlan told her. Abi and Carolyn never got along. Abi put up with her because she was my wife. Carolyn put up with Abi because...well...she didn't. Carolyn detested Abi, and she made it known. One drunken night with Carolyn, she told me all about her exes, and I shared secrets about mine—including the small fact that I may have hit on Abi the first time I met her. What was supposed to be a fun, enjoyable night with my wife, revealing things about our past, turned out to be the biggest wedge in our relationship, and slowly she began to pull me away from my friends. According to Carolyn, Abi was trying to take me from her, steal me away and get her completely out of the picture. No matter what I did to show Carolyn I loved her, nothing ever changed her mind. She did everything in her power to keep me away. Once our divorce was finalized, I had one person in my mind that could help me become who I was again. But, at that time, I figured it was too late, and that I had fucked up enough that I wouldn't be able to make up for it.

Looks like my assumptions were right.

I knew it was going to be hard seeing her again. That it would open wounds I had tried so hard to stitch up and cover. A part of me was hoping it would be like any reunion. One where Abi wanted me here as much as I wanted to be here. I never thought it would be this hard.

But with a deep breath, I knew I had to let it go.

Once she left the kitchen, the silence became deafening. Lachlan took a deep breath, the rustling of his clothes becoming the only sound in the room. Once the front door closed, he let out a puff of air.

I looked over at him as he raised his eyebrows at me. "I can guarantee one of these sandwiches wasn't for you."

Pinching my brow I looked at the sandwiches that were laid out on the counter, and then the last few bites of mine that sat in my hand. I had the impulse to throw the rest away.

Kyla took a deep breath and turned to the cowboy attached to her hip. "I'm gonna go find Abi. It's only noon, and she knows I'm going to pick Stetson up today." She kissed Rhett's cheek, giving me a quick nod. "Good to see you again, Mr. Callahan."

"Please, call me Cash," I corrected her.

"Good to see you again, *Cash*. Just...please don't call me 'little miss' again.'" Kyla smiled, giving Rhett another quick kiss before she turned to leave.

I smirked, remembering the one time I used that nickname last year.

"When did you call my wife *little miss?*" Rhett asked, shoving his hands in his pockets.

"Protective much?" Lachlan grumbled, stuffing the rest of his sandwich in his mouth.

"At the Days of 47 last year," I replied.

Lachlan began to haphazardly piece the remaining lunch meat and cheese together, shoving a piece of cheese in his mouth as he worked. Rhett joined in eventually, stealing some lunch meat. I leaned on the counter and watched them, listening as Rhett defended his actions in keeping anyone from calling his wife 'little miss.'

The front door burst open, and the sound of boots hitting the hardwood followed by the loud chatter of all the ranch hands, came bursting into the house, echoing off the walls. Rhett looked at me, tilting his chin towards the front of the room before taking the few steps out of the kitchen. Lachlan spoke to a few of the ranch hands, telling them whoever could figure out which sandwiches were made by us and actually eat them would get a small bonus on their next check, before following Rhett and I to the entryway, grabbing our coats and stepping back into the chill air.

"Well." I adjusted the hat on my head, twisting my torso to look back at the main house. "I didn't recognize any of those workers. What happened to your staff?"

"Nick is still around, but mainly we get seasonal guys," Lachlan replied, reaching into his pockets to pull out his gloves.

I looked around the ranch, finally taking it all in for the first time since I arrived. I noticed the dinks and dings in the stables, but now I saw the fences that needed to be fixed, the paint chipping on the main house and barn, and the beat up water troughs. I get it was the tail end of winter, but these were things that needed to be kept up on. Lachlan knew that. His life was this ranch, so why did it look like it was falling apart? Is this why they were renting out the stables and arena? Money to fix the place back up?

"Well, there's Ryan too." Rhett's voice carried through the air. "He's been here a few years."

I shoved my hands in my coat pockets, barely listening to them talk. I could easily pick up some paint to repair the chips around the barn and mend the fences. These were things I could do while Quinn was in PT. Hell, I planned to stick around here anyway. May as well make myself useful.

Turning, I stopped when I spotted Abi.

She was moving fast. Kyla kept up next to her as she made her way to the gray Chevy, both women being followed by a small brown-and-white cow. Abi plopped her hat on her head and turned, walking backwards giving Kyla a smile. That smile, I remembered. I knew it still had to be there. I smirked just watching her, seeing her still happy underneath the anger she was sporting moments ago. Kyla raised her arms as Abi got into the truck and started the engine. She shook her head as her truck left the drive.

"I guess Kyla isn't getting Stetson today." Rhett shrugged.

"Does your wife normally pick up Abi's son?" I asked, taking my gaze from the scene back to Rhett and Lachlan.

I didn't realize I had stopped to watch the women, completely ignoring the men I was following. My attention went from the ranch hands, to the ranch, to the blonde leaving in a matter of minutes.

"Normally." Rhett added, "She's been tutoring him this year. Abi needs the help."

"With Stet or…"

"I wouldn't call him Stet." Lachlan pointed out, making his way back to the stables.

Pinching my brow, I jogged to meet up with him. I always—*always*—called him Stet. Sylas started it, the small nickname becoming what I knew the kid as. He wasn't Stetson, he was Stet.

"Why? I always called him Stet. He liked it."

Lachlan choked out a laugh. "He does, she doesn't."

"You know," I started as I opened up my truck door a few hours later, Lachlan close behind me, "I plan on being here every day. I can help with something around the ranch."

He shook his head, "Nah. I can't afford to pay you, too."

"Think of it as a thank you." I took my hat off, tossing it on the front seat. "I need this place as much as you do."

"For eight to ten weeks," he reminded me, a snarky tone fluttering through the air between us.

"So, for the time I'm around, let me help out. Your barn is looking as rusty as you." I chuckled.

Furrowing his brow, Lachlan turned to look at his stables. "I just haven't been able to keep up on the aesthetics of things. Wyatt mentioned events...I should probably fix it up a bit."

"A bit." I took one last look around. "Just a bit."

Raising a single eyebrow, Lachlan tilted his head to the side. "The roof needs patching," he began. "A couple of fences, a paint refresh, and a few things in the main house Aunt Lottie has been on about. Seeing as she and Uncle Leo want out—"

"Out?" I stopped him.

With a single node, he continued. "He's officially retiring."

"There's a lot more happening here than I thought, huh?" I couldn't imagine anyone besides Leo and Charlotte Hartwell running Hartwell Hills alongside Lachlan. "What's going to happen to the ranch?"

"I own half, that won't change, but the other half will be split between Rhett, Abi, and Wyatt."

I barked out a laugh. "Wyatt?"

"He'll get a small percentage, but the majority will probably go to Abi since she and I run the show anyway and Rhett is still on the circuit."

Last I knew, Abi wanted to travel. She wanted to see the world with Sylas and his rodeos, so what changed to make it so she was getting the majority of the ranch? I bit my cheek, keeping that question to myself. "Does she want it?" I asked, keeping the travel thoughts to myself.

"It makes sense, and she deserves it. After Sylas died, she poured herself into the ranch. She knows it like the back of her hand, just like I do. She does more than make sandwiches, you know."

I didn't doubt that at all, but it didn't fit with the Abi I knew. Then again, that was years ago.

"It was Wyatt's idea about bringing in horses to stable, but Abi took on the project. She put together the numbers and made it happen. Sure you're our first client, but we'll get more because of her. She's always been good at the financial side of things."

"Does Hartwell Hills need money?" I asked, finally letting the thought out of my brain.

He shrugged his shoulders. "We're not drowning, we're not going to go bankrupt, but it's been tight. According to Abi, we're barely making even."

"Hence the renting the arena and stabling horses. More work for Abi?"

"Nah, Rhett will take on the horses. He agreed to it, and we do have enough hands for the extra jobs. Once winter ends, things will pick up."

The crunch of gravel pulled both of us away from the conversation, as Abi's gray truck pulled up to the main house. She stopped and reached for her woven straw hat on the dashboard, a small set of hands in the front seat next to her doing the exact same motion. A slight smile grew on my lips. Stetson.

My heart jumped a little. The last time I saw Stetson, he was barely three years old. He would gladly jump in my arms and settle down on my hip or shoulders as Sylas rode the bull. He loved watching his dad just as much as he loved hanging out with me. We had tons of camp outs on the ranch. Millions of riding lessons. Thousands of laughs as the little guy was learning the ropes.

I ached to see him even knowing he wouldn't remember me one bit. It had been too long, and he was too young. The memory died the moment I remembered I walked out of their lives, ultimately his.

The door to the truck opened, and the kid jumped out. Cowboy boots, Wrangler jeans, a blue plaid shirt and a white hat on top of his head. He was taller now, probably to my torso, and his gait was that of a cowboy already. A smile tugged on my lips. He was a little Sylas.

"He looks just like his dad," I mumbled.

From the corner of my eye, I could see Lachlan turn to look at me. "He's a good kid."

"Uncle Lachlan!" Stetson cried from the truck. "Mommy told me I could ride!"

"If you muck out Marsh's stall—" Lachlan began, but Stetson's attention was elsewhere. Right on me.

"Hey." Stetson stopped right in front of us. "Who are you?" His eyes met mine as his hands hit his hips, standing as tall as he could.

"Stetson!" Abi called from the truck.

I mimicked the boy's stance and looked down at him. He was tall for a seven year old, his brown hair sticking out from beneath this cowboy hat, his dark eyes narrowing, studying me. I could practically see the wheels turning in his head.

"I know you." He finally said. "I think."

I smiled. "You do."

"Where have you been?" he asked, his voice steady as he took one more step.

"At rodeos." I answered, not sure how to give him the real answer.

I was afraid to come back, I couldn't come back.

He nodded and took my answer, and then his face changed. His tight lips opened to a wide smile and the rocket that was burning inside of him lit up. He jumped and if I wasn't ready, he would have fallen. Instead, he landed in my arms, his sweet laugh leaving his lungs. He held onto me tightly, his hat falling to the ground as he latched on for me to lift him off the ground.

"I missed you, Uncle Cash."

Uncle Cash...

Damnit.

The kid remembered me.

"I missed you too, buddy." I lowered him back to the ground. "I hear you have a stall to muck."

He scrunched his nose. "Wanna ride with me?"

I patted his shoulder, glancing up at Abi. She stood by the truck with her arms crossed, a vacant expression under the rim of her hat.

I smiled down at Stetson. "Sure bud, if it's ok with your mom?"

"Mama please?" Stetson rushed back to Abi, pulling her arms from her body as he pleaded.

Abi's vacant expression faltered when she looked from her son to me, a hesitation there. But, to my surprise she straightened her shoulders and kneeled down to look Stetson in the eyes.

"Just be back for dinner, okay. You have homework, too."

"Yes!" Stetson jumped in the air, spinning around as if he were on ice. "Let's go, Uncle Cash!" He dashed into the barn at full speed, leaving Lachlan and I behind.

"Thanks Abs." I nodded to her. With tight lips, she gave me one single nod of approval.

"Looks like I'm not leaving just yet," I said over my shoulder at Lachlan with a smile.

SEVEN

Abi

I HAD MANAGED TO avoid Cash for three days. It wasn't easy. He and his client were here constantly. I took up sanctuary in my office, away from everyone, looking at the dreaded numbers. With the income from Cash, it eased the worry a little bit, but we still needed more. I had put out an ad for boarding horses and even a few other animals. Ads were floating around on social media, which seemed to be working since my inbox had a few potential inquiries.

But with my mind fixated on a million other things, I couldn't find the focus to schedule them.

When I tried to calm my brain and clear my thoughts, all I saw was my son jumping into Cash's arms. I didn't even tell him Cash was here; I didn't think he would remember him. I hadn't talked about Cash to Stetson for five years, but he apparently had a better memory than I realized. So good in fact that he literally jumped into his arms without hesitation for the tightest reunion hug possible.

The things it did to my heart...I can't even acknowledge because it caused an ache strong enough to break me. How did he remember Cash but not his own father? For the past three days, Stetson has begged to spend time with him, and as much as I wanted to ignore it, I wanted to see him smile more. If taking a ride with Cash was what was going to give that to him, then I would gladly watch those two saddle up a horse and take a ride. Even if it tugged at my heart in more ways than one.

Taking a deep breath, I hoisted myself from my desk. I pushed any and all thoughts of Cash out of my mind. I had plenty of things to keep me busy. Clean the stables, rake the indoor arena—simple upkeep that I could start to tackle on my own. Bigger projects would need to wait until spring was fully underway, but hey...we had to start somewhere right?

Alright—here we go. Time to tackle that to-do list.

The stables housed thirty stalls, and only twenty of them were in use. The large, deep brown building opened up to the indoor arena where Rhett would practice tie-down and training sessions would take place. It was by far the largest footprint on the five thousand acres that was Hartwell Hills Ranch. The rolling hills that made up our two pastures—one smaller, one larger—were still wet with a rainstorm we had gotten, making the vibrant colors of spring want to peek out even more. Winter was ending soon, and the lush colors were about to make Hartwell Hills the most beautiful place in Alpine Ridge.

Twelve horses should be in the stables, with the others out on the land with ranchers as they worked. I knew I was capable of getting the twelve that remained out in the pasture, and then the cleaning would begin. I could spend all day in here avoiding a certain cowboy.

Luna was first. Moving her into the pasture was easy as could be since the girl didn't need a lead. Then came Buckle and Onyx. The thought only barely crossed my mind that my brother and cousins' horses were still in their stalls before I led them out to the pasture. My parents' horses, then Stetson's horse, Wyatt's chestnut horse Rusty, and then the three that had recently joined our pack.

I spent some time with Hook and Charming, getting them used to my voice before slipping the leads on them and carefully taking them out with the others. Hook had spunk, and Charming was calm and relaxed. Then I approached Nova, Cash's horse, as she grazed on the fresh hay that was there for her already. She was sweet—just as I remembered—and took to the lead with ease. Cash had let me ride her a few times before. He didn't even let Carolyn ride her, not that she would anyway. But me, he'd watched me mount her and then walked beside me as I took her around the arena with a baby Stetson in my lap. It was a good memory, and those good memories were always clouded when it came to Cash. Nova followed closely, bumping her nose with my cheek before making her way to the field. I closed the gate, counted all twelve horses and then turned back into the stables.

First task....check.

After grabbing all the tools I'd need to muck and clean each stall, I ran my hand through my hair, pulling the unruly mess into an even unrulier bun on top of my head. As soon as I made it into the first stall and gathered my first shovel full of hay, a loud bang came from over me. Then another. And another.

"What the…" I looked up, half expecting the ceiling to fall through.

Another bang.

Dropping the shovel, I made my way outside, walking out into the sunlight to see the man I had been avoiding standing on top of the roof.

"What the hell are you doing up there?" I asked, loud enough for Cash to hear me.

He stopped and turned, giving me that stupid, cocky-ass smile of his. "I'm fixing some tiles; I noticed a few leaks the other day."

"So, you just took it upon yourself to climb up there and fix the shingles?" I argued.

He smiled, "Well, I knew there was a lot going on, so I figured I'd help out."

"I had that planned for spring."

"Well, now it's getting done before spring." He leaned his palms on his knees, that damn smile only growing. "If you're boarding horses you need to have a leak-free roof. I bet your horses will like it a lot, too."

Placing my hands on my hips I scoffed. "Where's Lachlan?"

"Up here." Cash motioned behind him. "Rhett and Stet, too."

"Stetson's up there?" I asked, half worried, half not. It wasn't the first time my son was on a roof, having been up many times to shovel snow off it, but the thing that didn't settle well with my stomach was the fact that Cash called Stetson *Stet.*

That was Sylas's nickname for him.

Cash laughed. "Yeah, little dude jumped on the chance to help. He called to you when you were moving the horses. Did you hear him?"

"No I..." *was too busy thinking about riding your horse...* "I didn't."

"Oh. Well, you were with Nova."

"Abi." Lachlan appeared, raising a hand to shield his face from the late afternoon sun. "Can you move the ladder to the west side? There are more shingles to fix there. I didn't realize how bad it had gotten up here."

"Yeah well," I scoffed as I moved to the ladder.

"Thankfully Cash caught those leaks. I'm shocked the snow didn't cave it in."

"And my son is up there?" I questioned, the half worry turning to full-blown worry. He could handle himself, yes. Life skill, sure...but him falling through the roof? I did *not* need to end my day by a trip to the ER.

"He's fine. He's with Rhett." Lachlan waved me off, turning to leave, leaving me with Cash once again.

His smile faded, but didn't leave as his eyes locked on me. "He's ok. He insisted, and he's doing a great job."

"Just make sure he doesn't fall through the roof. You though—" I looked towards Cash, half tempted to point at him. He just tilted his head and gave me a grin, waiting for my cheeky reply. I rolled my eyes. "Feel free to fall through." I slammed the ladder on the gutter and turned, making my way back into the barn to finish the chore I started before I was so rudely interrupted.

I did not complete my task.

I was only able to get through half of the stables before my body had to call it quits. Half of the stables looked amazing, the other half looked like horses lived there. The ranch hands had just finished putting the horses back inside, and they all headed back to the bunk houses, leaving Stetson and me alone with Marshmallow and Luna, waiting to be brushed and settled in.

"I just wish we didn't have to clean out their poop all day," Stetson grumbled from the stall next to me.

I chuckled. "Well bud, that's what happens when you have a horse. Marsh is a poop machine."

"I didn't even ride today. Why do I need to brush him?"

"Would you want to be covered in filth all night?" His dark hair flew from side to side as he shook his head, the only part of him I could really see as he stood on the stool next to the big white horse he claimed. "Exactly, so brush him and then go bathe yourself."

He groaned.

"Did you have fun today?"

"Yes!" His body spun, and his eyes became visible over the wooden stall barrier. "Uncle Cash taught me how to replace a shingle on the roof, and then we grilled hamburgers for dinner. Even Nana Lottie ate one and loved it. Miss Kyla said she'd help me with my homework tonight, but I just really wanna watch a movie." Stetson talked at rapid speed. If I wasn't his mother and fluent in 'Stetson' I wouldn't be able to understand him.

But my mind froze on one fact. *Uncle Cash.* He didn't even call Kyla 'Aunt Kyla.' She was Miss Kyla. Why did Cash get a title that was so close to family? So close to home? "Why do you call him Uncle Cash?" I blurted out.

"Because that's what daddy called him."

"You remember that?"

"Yeah. I remember Uncle Cash. I like having him here." He turned back to the horse. "Don't you, Momma?"

"Yea, Abi, don't you?"

I heard the Southern drawl before I had any other sign that he was behind us. I turned slightly and watched him approach the stalls, leaning against the gate, letting his arms hang over the metal.

I didn't answer. My back stiffened as I tried to remember what Lachlan had said, those big girl pants I was supposed to be wearing. I took a deep breath through my nose. This was fine.

"Brushes are in the closet, I'm assuming? I know Hook and Charming haven't been brushed for a while," he asked, pointing his thumb behind his shoulder to the closet.

I nodded, keeping my focus on the horse.

Keep your big girl pants on, Abi. It's best if you don't talk to him at all.

"Do you mind if I hang around? Take care of the horses?"

"That's Rhett's job." I bit.

So much for not talking to him.

"Rhett and Kyla headed back to their place. Your mom saved you a plate of pie. You too, Stet."

Stet. He needed to stop that.

"Mom! Can I go eat the pie?! I forgot about it!" My son jumped off the stool and handed Cash the brush he was holding. "Uncle Cash, can you finish Marsh for me?"

"Sure thing. You did great work on the roof today. Ready for part two later?"

"Hell yeah!" Stetson screamed.

"Stetson!" I shouted, trying to hide the laugh that was forming after hearing my son swear. He grew up on the ranch, so he had heard far worse, but he knew not to say them...well possibly knew not to say them.

His eyes widened as Cash croaked a throaty laugh. I glared at both of them.

"Sorry, Momma." He ran, bolting out of the barn.

I shook my head.

"He takes after Sylas." Cash still had laughter in his voice.

Taking a deep breath, I didn't respond.

"Abs," Cash said softly.

No answer.

Don't. Give. In.

"Abi."

I shook my head.

"Are you going to ignore me the entire time I'm here? Are you that pissed about the roof?" He pushed himself off the gate, opening Marshmallow's stall, petting his nose before bringing the brush to his neck.

"No," I answered.

"No to what?"

"No, I'm not that pissed about the roof. It needed to be done."

"So, you're just not going to talk to me?"

"Exactly." I pushed the brush into Luna's coat, making her bob her head slightly.

The stable grew quiet, Cash working on Marshmallow while I worked on Luna. Going through the motions, forcing down any words that may want to explode out.

I wanted the answers, but I wanted to go back to how things were without him. I knew I could get through everything without him. With him here, it was harder. And I didn't like it.

"You know Abs, there's only room for one brooding cowboy on this ranch, and I'm sorry to say Lachlan has that title down." Cash's laugh filled the stall, his hand reaching up to scratch the back of his neck.

He.

Laughed.

Before I could stop myself, I tossed the brush across the stall, hitting him directly in the back of the head. His hand moved, holding the spot where the wood hit as he turned to me, his eyes meeting mine with a look of pure confusion.

"Fuck off," I grunted before leaving him alone in the stable.

EIGHT

Cash

A RARE LAUGH FILLED space as I retold the encounter with Abi from the night before. Lachlan and I leaned up against the metal gate as Quinn mounted Charming and trotted around the arena. I could see in her face she wasn't having it. This was her first time back on her horse. Her injury was still bothering her even with a few physical therapy appointments under her belt, but all I could see was my friend laughing at me. And this man didn't laugh.

"Abi really told you to fuck off?" Lachlan asked, the chuckle still deep in his throat.

"Yeah, is that so hard to believe?" I turned back to Quinn. "Move to a gallop Quinn! You're too stiff," I shouted as she passed us.

She shook her head and kept her focus on the horse under her.

"Loosen up. Remember your position."

"No," Lachlan continued as if I didn't just shout across the arena. "And it's damn funny." He laughed again.

I shook my head and gave him a slight eye roll before turning my attention back to Quinn. I had to focus. I had a job to do. The least of my worries should be why Abi was acting the way she was. I knew why she wasn't talking to me, even if I tried to joke it off. Five years of silence was too long to pretend like we were still friends. As many times as I thought about reaching out to her in those years, Carolyn would remind me that the phone worked both ways—a saying I grew to hate—and that if our friendship meant anything, Abi would reach out. I was stupid enough to believe her. Then I had my accident. My life stopped the second that horse fell on top of me. Once his entire weight centered on my leg, breaking bones and tearing muscles, I knew it was plastered all over the internet and pro rodeo channels. If you followed the rodeo at all, you knew that Cash Callahan was out for the year—possibly forever. In the back of my head, I knew Abi had to have seen that and despite everything, maybe I thought that would have been enough for her to reach out to me, if she wanted to.

But nothing.

Lachlan visited me in the hospital. So did Rhett, both coming to comfort me and make sure I was ok. Neither one of them mentioned Abi.

At that point, I assumed we were done. The friendship between Abi and me had faded the second Sylas fell off that bull. The second I didn't *truly* come to the funeral. The link broke.

Even with all of that pent up and buried deep inside that small box in my mind, I had to move forward. Forget it. And a way to do that was to train. Put my attention somewhere else. For now, that comes in the form of a brunette on the white horse whose posture was still too stiff.

"It's like she's never been on a horse before," Lachlan commented.

Glancing his way for a split second, I pushed myself off the gate, the sting of light pain hitting my left leg before I could even acknowledge the force was too strong.

"She had the weight of her horse on her. Of course she's hesitant to get back on." I opened the gate and stepped out onto the dirt. "Quinn, head over here."

"How long did it take you to get on the back of a horse?" Lachlan asked. I turned to look at him, furrowing my brow before completely ignoring the question and turning back to Quinn.

He knew the answer to that.

Too long.

"Charming's out of practice; I've been riding Hook too much." Quinn said as the horse came to a stop in front of me.

"He can feel your body. You're too stiff. What's going on?" I placed my hands on my hips, looking up at her as Charming lowered his head to lick something on his leg.

"I'm fine," she grumbled.

"No, you're not. Hop off and walk him around the arena. You two need to get back on the same page."

Quinn looked as if she was going to protest but eventually did as she was told. She led Charming over to the mounting stairs and slowly got off the saddle.

"She's nervous." Lachlan stated the obvious as soon as I approached the gate.

"Wouldn't you be?"

"I've fallen off more horses than I can count."

I glared at my friend, knowing damn well he was more solid on the back of a horse than he was on his feet. That man was more comfortable in the saddle than on the Earth.

"I don't get it." I heard a female voice from the inside of the barn. "He seems nice, why don't we like him?"

I did a quick glance over Lachlan's shoulder into the stables. Kyla came into view, a straw hat on her head and her arms folded across her chest as she followed Abi.

"He's an asshole, that's why," Abi replied, a quick snap to her tone.

"According to your story, you're the one who threw a brush at him."

"He deserved it."

"Man, you really pissed her off," Lachlan whispered before patting my shoulder. "Have fun with that."

I turned back to the arena, glancing at Quinn as she hugged Charming's nose and walked him around the arena, the slight limp still in her step.

"Walk three times around, then ride. Slow. Let's not push it," I hollered.

Quinn gave me a thumbs up before returning her attention to the horse, and I left her alone in the arena to make my way into the barn.

"Come on Abi," Kyla drew out. "Rhett talks highly of him, so does Lachlan—"

"Doesn't mean I have to tolerate him. I have two showings of the stables today and then a horse moving in this afternoon. You're still picking up Stetson, right?" Abi emerged from the tackle closet, only to stop once her gaze hit mine.

Kyla turned, a smile on her face as soon as she figured out I was behind her. "Oh hey Cash," she said.

I tipped my hat. "Mrs. Hartwell."

Kyla let out a small chuckle. "You gonna help us clean up the stables?"

"It's clean," Abi said, zero emotion in her tone. "You're busy anyway, right Cash?" She turned to me and for the first time since she asked about Carolyn, she made eye contact.

I looked at Abi raising an eyebrow, tempted to rub the back of my head where I could still feel the contact from the brush.

"Quinn's here for another hour, then I'll take her to PT." I never once broke Abi's eye contact. "I'll be back tonight though, to make sure the horses are ok."

"That's Rhett's job," Abi snapped, reminding me as much as she was reminding herself.

"Yeah, but I can help. Two showings today? For?" My attention went to Kyla, hoping she would be more talkative.

She nodded. "Boarding horses, right Abi?" She turned to Abi.

"Obviously," Abi mumbled.

She locked eyes with me, boring into me as if to silently tell me to...what were the words she said so graciously yesterday? Fuck off?

I narrowed my gaze and gave her a slight smirk before turning back to Kyla. "I'll get out of your hair." I motioned towards the arena, taking a few steps back before finally turning my entire body.

"Abigail Acosta," I heard Kyla whisper sharply. "What the hell has gotten into you?"

"PT isn't working," Quinn complained as we got to her hotel after her appointment. "Training isn't working. Nothing is working, Cash."

I shut the door to her hotel room, watching her stumble to the bed before plopping down head first onto the mattress. "Quinn, you've trained once and have had two appointments. It takes time."

"It shouldn't," she groaned into the mattress, before turning her head to look at me. "Just pull me out of the running."

"Do you think I'm going to let you give up?"

Violently moving her arms, she pushed herself up on the bed. "It's going to take longer than ten weeks for this to heal. That's already a huge chunk of time. I won't be able to make it to the NFR like this," she screamed—actually screamed—so loud that it echoed in the small room.

Narrowing my gaze, I folded my arms over my chest and glared at my client.

"Don't look at me like that." She lowered her voice, moving to sit on the edge of the bed, her face wincing as her leg bent a way she didn't mean. A natural move that anyone would do and think nothing of it, but for Quinn...for me....that move would hurt like hell. She placed her palm on her leg and pressed.

"You're not giving up on this. You've had two PT appointments and one training session with me. This is the beginning of a long journey, and if you give up now," my voice was getting louder and louder with each word, just pulling the memory from my own experience. I gave up. I wouldn't let her. I inhaled, steadying myself. "You'll never get on a horse again."

Quinn's bottom lip quivered. "How..." she began before a small breath left her lungs. "How long did it take you to get back on a horse?"

"Longer than I'd like to admit." I loosened my body, hoping not to come off as a father figure who was pissed. She had a dad back in Montana; she didn't need her trainer coming down hard on her. "But you didn't have as extensive an injury as I did."

She gave a small nod. "It still counts."

"It does. Any injury counts." I sighed, sitting down next to her on the edge of the bed. There were parts of my life Quinn didn't need to know. The extent of what happened in my accident was one of them. "It will work, you just have to keep getting back in the saddle."

Quinn breathed a small chuckle.

"Don't give up on me Quinn." I placed a hand on her shoulder and squeezed.

Her gaze hit mine, eyes wet with tears that refused to fall. She was tough, but I could see little by little this was getting her. She was forcing herself not to break.

"What else did you do? When you had your accident?"

What did I do? Physical therapy, acupuncture, got divorced, lost my friends...

"The same, with added acupuncture," I said instead. "That's not a bad idea, actually. I'll find you an acupuncturist."

"Needles?"

"You scared of needles?" I raised a brow.

She shook her head. "No I just...ok." She slouched. "I'll try anything at this point. I don't want to lose my spot in the NFR."

I smiled. "There's my girl."

"Don't let me give up Cash," she said, softly.

"I won't."

It was dark by the time I pulled back up the ranch. The lights in the kitchen and a few rooms upstairs in the main house were still on. I made my way directly to the stables, knowing very well that Lachlan was most likely already hiding in his cabin near the edge of the property. All I had to do was check on the horses, and then I'd get to do just that.

Hide.

"Your name suits you, doesn't it." I heard Abi laugh as I stepped inside the stable. I slowed my pace not wanting to take her off guard again. "Charming. You are very, very charming."

She stood in front of Charming's stall, his nose right up to her as her hands brushed along his mane. She scratched behind his ears and lightly kissed his nose. He bobbed his head up and down in approval.

I slowly approached her, making sure I made enough noise for her to know I was there.

"He's a great horse," I added.

She stiffened and turned a quick glance at me. "You're making it a habit to eavesdrop on me."

I frowned. "Nah, just here to check on the horses."

"That's—"

"Rhett's not here," I interrupted.

Abi gave me a side eye before petting Charming one more time, kicking herself off the gate to turn to the other horse. It was a new one. A gray speckled horse that was waiting impatiently for her to go to their stall. She bent and picked up a bucket before taking a few steps to the stall's door.

"Rhett's with Kyla. Date night," she added.

"Ah." I raised my chin and took the last remaining steps towards Hook's stall. He was already taken care of and had everything he needed, but he clearly wanted more attention. "So it's not Rhett's job?"

"Not tonight it isn't."

I watched her as she entered the gray horse's stall, giving him a slight pat on his neck before moving to muck out what was there, before she rose up and wiped her forehead with her arm.

"Who's this?" I asked.

She cleared her throat before turning to the horse. "Gemini. We'll be boarding him for a few months."

"I take it the showings went well today?" I asked, leaning up against the stall door, crossing one ankle over the other.

Abi left Gemini's stall and took a deep breath. "What are you doing?" she asked, staring me down.

"Making conversation."

"Why?" She sounded exasperated. Tired. Over everything—and having me here was the icing on the cake.

Too bad for her, I wasn't going to give in that easily. We used to have a strong friendship. We used to be able to talk about anything. And looking at her now, seeing how much she changed in the five years, I desperately wanted to talk to her. I wanted that friendship back. The one I used to hold so close.

"Because it's polite. You're in the stables by yourself. Don't you want company?" I pushed myself off the stall.

"I'm not by myself. There are horses." She bent and picked up a bucket, avoiding my eyes.

"Horses can't talk with you like a human can."

She rolled her eyes. "I'd rather have any other human in this stable with me right now."

"Alright Abi," I said, louder than intended. "I get you don't want me here, but let's face it—I am, for a while so maybe...just maybe, we should be friendly?"

"Friendly?" she parroted. "I don't—"

"Tolerant, then. I'm gonna be around. I'll be in this stable every day while I'm in town. I'm helping Lachlan with things around the ranch, and three times a week I'll be training Quinn. I'm going to be here whether you like it or not," I bit, sounding harsher than I intended.

Abi chewed her bottom lip and gave me a quick nod. Her body relaxed just a fraction as she stepped towards me, that small quiver still in her chin as she chewed on her lip.

"I didn't mean to sound rude," I added, making sure to lower my tone, not liking the melancholy that showed on her face.

"No, you're right. We can be...cordial." She rolled her eyes again after the word slipped off her tongue.

"You'll talk to me?" I raised a brow. She opened her lips to respond, but I quickly added, "Without rolling your eyes?"

She met my gaze, and I grinned, seeing how badly she wanted to roll those blue eyes again. She took a breath. "Well I won't throw any more brushes at you."

I chuckled and lowered my chin. I got a joke out of her. It wasn't all lost. That spark we used to have was still there. The knot in my stomach loosened. "Alright, that's all I ask."

She blinked a few times, her eyes rapidly moving from her shoes, to me, back to her shoes as if she was trying to form the words, thinking about exactly what to say that wouldn't pull her back into our old rhythm. Finally, she gave me a curt nod before bending to drop the bucket on the ground.

"I'm sorry," she finally said, placing both of her hands on her hips. "For throwing the brush at you, and calling you an asshole."

"You called me an asshole?" I smiled, giving her a slight tease.

"Oh, come on, you're not going to pretend you didn't hear that earlier." She pinched her brow as she spoke, her shoulders relaxing as she loosened up.

I smiled again, this time wider. I didn't want to get my hopes up, but I felt as if I was getting her back. Maybe just a tiny bit.

"I did," I admitted as I took a step towards her, "I'm sorry I called you a grumpy cowboy."

She dropped her arms. "Kyla called me out on that, too."

"I like Kyla."

"She likes you too." Her lips twitched, but she stopped the smile before it spread.

Changing the subject, I gestured towards Gemini behind her. "How many horses you got now?"

"Just the four. Your three and this guy. We had two showings that went well. One mare moves in on Friday."

"And Rhett's taking care of them?"

She nodded, but let out a long sigh. "He's supposed to, yes. Lachlan keeps him busy most days, and he still trains because he's planning on returning to the circuit next year. But mainly it's been me."

"What about Wyatt?"

She let out a laugh, and *damn* it was just as perfect as I remember it being. "You know my brother. He's gone right now at a rodeo."

"That I do." I stroked Gemini's nose. Sweeping my gaze around the space, I took in the large stables, mainly spotless despite the few odds and ends that needed to be picked up before Abi called it a night. It was late. Stetson was most likely already asleep, and I knew she would be getting up early. Lachlan was busy on the field, Rhett had odd jobs and Kyla to keep him company, Wyatt was out of town. Who was helping Abi?

"I can help out when Rhett can't," I said softly, carefully looking up at her to see her reaction.

"You're paying us to do that," Abi protested.

I looked at her, noticing again how tired and worn down she seemed. How broken. My heart ached, wanting to reach out to her and comfort her in some capacity. I could do this one thing for her, if she'd let me. "Let me help," I all but whispered.

Our eyes met for the briefest moment, and I swore I caught a glint in there in the blue, something more than she was willing to give. She shook her head lightly, raising her chin high, letting out a sigh before giving in.

"Fine. You can help. But I'm not discounting your rate." She shifted then, walking away from me.

"I wouldn't ask you to," I called after her.

NINE

Abi

To Do:

 -*Chicken coop: gather eggs—breakfast!*
-*Stables: Did Rhett muck them?*
-*Budget sheet.*
-*Feed Pigs: is Margie ready to have her babies?*
-*Stetson: Homework due tomorrow—can Kyla help?*
-*Horse chores: brush all horses, check on Gemini, muck all stalls (Rhett probably didn't).*
-*Showing? Contact Mr. Hubbard.*
-*Meeting with Lach.*
-*Prep land.*

I glared at my to-do list, only skimming the first few tasks before heaving a sigh and folding it back in my pocket. I wish I had time to myself. I'd have to schedule that into this massive, growing list. I laughed at the thought of actually having free time. The only free time I had was when I met Kyla for the sunset, and even then it was thirty minutes.

I cracked an egg and plopped the yolk into the pan, taking great satisfaction in stabbing it with my spatula. My mom taught me to never scramble eggs in a bowl—you scrambled them in the pan. *"Trust me Abi,"* she would say. *"Don't murder it in a bowl before it's had time to touch the perfectly seasoned iron."* When I was little, I loved cooking in the kitchen with my mom. It was a reason I started making breakfasts for everyone, she was there next to me. But now that mom prefers to sleep in—making breakfast became just another task.

What would I even do if I had time to myself? Watch a TV show? Doom scroll? Read a book?

I raised an eyebrow at the thought. I would love to be a reader. On my nightstand, I currently had a historical fiction, the bookmark still sitting in chapter six where it had been for months because every time I went to pick it up, my eyes began to drift closed. Physically reading was definitely not my thing. Listening to an audiobook maybe? I could listen.

The microwave beeped, telling me my coffee was yet again warm as I reached for my phone. There was an app for audiobooks, right? There was always an app. Grabbing my coffee from the microwave, I leaned against the counter, pulling up the App Store, my ears still focused on the scrambling eggs in the pan.

The front door opened, and boots hit the hardwood floor. Moments later, Rhett appeared.

I smiled. I'd gladly take his company while checking off the breakfast task.

"Hey," I greeted him, setting my phone on the counter to grab the carafe for him. He never used the mugs we had here. He always had his Thermos on him and this was probably his second time filling it.

"Morning Abi." He held out his Thermos for me to fill, but instead, I set the carafe down on the counter and gave him a stupid grin.

"When do I ever fill your coffee?" I joked, picking my phone back up.

"I have high hopes that one day you will." He sighed, taking a drink from his Thermos.

"Did you muck out the stalls?" I glanced at him through my lashes, a single eyebrow raised awaiting the answer. I knew what it was, but he said he would.

"It's dark out. I guarantee you the horses are still sleeping."

I rolled my eyes at him, mentally crossing *Did Rhett muck them* off my list and adding an imaginary *NOPE*, before continuing my search for a book app.

"What are you thumbing through?" He motioned his chin towards my phone.

"I think I want to listen to an audiobook," I answered. "I'm trying to find an app."

"Kyla uses a few, and she'll be over soon. She wasn't feeling too well this morning, but she insisted I head over before Lachlan bit my head off."

"Is she ok?" I pinched my brow and looked up at him. I had just seen Kyla the night before and she seemed fine, albeit a little quiet, but fine.

"Yeah." Rhett shrugged his shoulder. "It's been an odd couple of days for her, but she says she's fine. Most likely some stomach bug."

"Stomach bug?"

He shrugged again, raising his Thermos to his lips. "Yeah, it seems to be coming in waves. She was worried she ate something bad last night."

"Stomach bug?" I repeated, turning back to the eggs, moving them around a few times before adding them to the mountain that grew on the plate. "And it's coming in waves?" Was my brother really that dense?

Rhett nodded again, before he turned to the stove to grab a piece of bacon from the pan. "She'll be over soon, and then she can talk to you about books. She's added to my collection that's for sure," he said.

Obviously...he was.

"Oh, I know." I smiled. "I've seen her additions. I love having a book called *The Friend Zone* next to *Rodeo through the Ages*."

"There's also a few cowboy romances; she's told me about a few fictional Rhetts."

I scoffed. "I bet she has." I shook my head, returning my complete focus to the task. More ranch hands would be showing up soon, plus Lachlan, and I didn't need that bacon to burn. "What's on your agenda?"

"The west side of the roof, and a fence out in the south pasture."

"Stetson doesn't have school today—"

"Oh, he let us know. He'll be back on the roof."

I swallowed, and that single thought pushed to the front of my mind. *Is Cash helping today?*

I wanted to ask it aloud, but I didn't want to spark anything. Not that Rhett would question it. He may raise his brow at me, but he wouldn't say a thing.

Shooting that question from my mind, I blinked. I didn't care if Cash was going to be here or not, it wasn't any of my business.

I cleared my throat. "I'll send him your way once he's awake. I bet he'll be up that ladder the second he's dressed. Do you think Kyla will be ok to keep an eye on him once the roof is done? I have a long to-do list today." I forced a laugh. "It's never ending."

"You could delegate some things, you know," Rhett chastised as the front door opened again and more boots hit the floor. Spurs this time too. "And I'm sure Kyla will be fine." He turned to me, narrowing his eyes. "Do you think it's food poisoning, not a stomach bug? Since it's coming and going?"

I raised my eyebrows at him, not even giving him the satisfaction of an answer.

"Morning Abi!" Nick, our lead foreman, smiled as he walked into the kitchen. "What's for breakfast!?"

Nick was a morning person. A loud morning person.

"Morning, Nick. Bacon and eggs."

"Perfect. Where's the boss?" he asked, reaching over to grab the coffee carafe.

Lachlan appeared. "Right here. Get your breakfast and then get your ass out on the land."

Nick saluted. "Yes sir."

"Don't do that." Lachlan narrowed his eyes.

I snorted a laugh. "Come on guys, you know what to do." I patted Nick on the back and passed by the other ranch hands as they filled the kitchen. "I'm going to go check on your wife." I gave Rhett a small hug. "Be careful on the roof."

I left the house, wishing I had grabbed my coat once the chill air flew through my skin. I jogged to my truck, not willing to make the quarter-mile trek to Rhett's cabin in this temperature. I was tricked by the sun yet again. It was the beginning of March in Idaho. It could either be snowing one day or sunny and spring the next. As soon as I shut the door to my truck, I caught Cash's truck from the corner of my eye. He climbed out, gave me a wave and smiled before he turned and went into the stable.

I inhaled, held my breath for a few seconds, and then exhaled through my lips.

He offered to help with the horses and the roof. That's why he's here.

Five minutes later, I was barging in through Rhett and Kyla's front door. The warmth of their cabin greeted me, and I could smell fresh coffee.

"Hey Ky…" I shouted. "It's just me. Rhett said you were sick—"

"Abi?" Kyla's voice came from the bedroom, a slight distress to her tone.

"No, it's Taylor Swift," I teased, heading to the kitchen to get myself a fresh cup of un-microwaved coffee.

"Abi!" Kyla shouted again. "Is Rhett with you?"

"Pretty sure if he was, he would be in that room with you already."

Kyla appeared in the bedroom doorway, her cheeks pink with a wide look on her face. I leaned against the counter, her expression already confirming what I was pretty sure I knew.

"How are you feeling? Rhett said you had a stomach bug...or..." I raised the mug to my lips and looked her up and down. "Food poisoning." I used the cup to hide my smirk.

This girl was not sick. If anything, she was glowing.

"Abi," she sighed. "I um..." She placed a palm to her stomach.

"Kyla..." I urged her on.

"I'm pregnant." Her voice broke slightly as a smile spread across her lips.

I mimicked her smile, trying to keep my excitement down.

"I'm...we're...we weren't even trying. We wanted to go slow."

"Yeah well, someone had other plans." I gestured towards her tummy.

"Rhett will be happy right?"

"Rhett will be ecstatic when he finds out." I took another sip, resting my hip against the island, watching as my sister-in-law began to pace.

"Like really...he will be, right? He wants kids, right? We haven't really talked about that yet. We've been dating, and we've been—"

"You can't really say you were taking things slow because you are married to the man, and he'd do anything for you." I looked at my friend, noticing her roll her lips. Her eyes were wide, and the hand over the stomach was quivering slightly. Panic? Anxiety? I wasn't sure. I handled my own panic differently. I bottled it and moved on. I didn't let anyone see it. But Kyla's anxiety was something she'd been working on not bottling up.

"I promise you he's going to be happy." I set my mug down and made my way over to her, placing my hands on her shoulders and giving them a little squeeze. "Are you happy?"

She let out a shaky breath. "I don't think I've ever been happier."

That's when the tears fell. She beamed and, in an instant, I was in her arms. She laughed as she cried into my shoulder. I could feel how fast her heart was beating. These were happy tears, joyous laughs. Kyla was happy, finally really happy.

"You knew, didn't you?" She laughed as she broke the hug, holding me at arm's length.

I gave her a nod. "Well when Rhett said you weren't feeling well, he jumped from stomach bug to food poisoning. I knew you weren't sick. When did you find out?"

"Just now. The test turned positive when you walked in the door."

"Just now?" I repeated, not even bothering to hide the shock in my voice.

"Yeah, I've been feeling off the past couple of days...and then I put two and two together. I went and got a test yesterday."

"How far along are you, do you think?"

She shrugged her shoulders. "I'm not sure? I'm only a week and a half late. I'm just so sick. Were you this sick with Stetson?" Her eyes widened as she placed her hand on her stomach.

"It's different for everyone," I replied. "I was sick with Stetson, up until my second trimester."

She nodded a sigh, walking past me, straight to the kitchen to grab the mug Rhett left out for her every morning. "Wait." She stopped. "Can I drink coffee?"

"Some, yes." I followed her. "But you're going to want to stay away from lunch meats, shellfish, and it's a good thing you don't keep any of the barn cats in the house."

Kyla looked at her mug. "How much caffeine are we talking?"

"A cup maybe? And when are you telling Rhett?"

Kyla licked her lips nervously. "When did you tell Sylas? How did he take it? How far along were you?"

My heart always paused when I heard his name. I didn't even pay attention to her other rapid questions. Here came those emotions I had to bottle up. I swallowed and inhaled, telling myself it was normal to talk about him, normal to think about him. She just asked me a question. I should be happy to relive the memory...right? It was a good one.

"What does it say? What does it say?!" Sylas basically bounced up and down as we waited three minutes to see if the test was positive or not. "Mi Alma, tell me."

"Sy... it's not ready yet, hold your horses."

"You know Luna would be running around in circles right now if she were me. There is no holding her down."

He bounced on his feet again.

The man may be seven years older than me, but he was definitely a child at heart. His smile radiated through the room as he moved, excitement flowing from his pores. I shook my head and just watched as he danced.

I glanced down at the test. One pink line...then...two. Tears welled before I even could form words.

"Abi, Mi Reina." Sylas stopped moving, his expression changing once he saw the look on my face. His eyes were focused on me. Not on the test, but me. He was reading me. He used his fingers to move a strand of my hair behind my ear, and I finally met his gaze. The tears fell.

"We're having a baby," I cried.

Sylas screamed, squealed more like it. He bent, wrapping his arms around my waist to hoist me off the ground, spinning me in a circle in the small bathroom.

"We're having a baby," Sylas repeated, dropping me to the ground, his lips meeting mine.

I sniffed, and pushed that away. A good memory, yes, but not one I wanted to think about often. Any memory of him still hurt too much.

"We found out together," I finally said. "We had been trying for a few months. He was ready."

Kyla took a deep breath. "Rhett and I are ready...right?"

"It doesn't really matter at this point does it? That baby is going to grace us with her presence whether we're prepared or not."

"Her?"

"I always called Stetson a boy, we never found out the gender, and yet we had a boy. I'll manifest a baby girl. I need to see Rhett as a girl dad." I raised my eyebrows at her and took a long drink of my coffee. "He's ready. You're ready. This is going to be amazing, and I won't say a thing." I reached for the empty mug in her hands. "Now, let's get you a cup of coffee, a shower and over to see Josie."

She smiled and let out a small laugh. "Sounds amazing. Help me plan a way to tell Rhett?"

"Brainstorming Abi, at your service."

TEN

Cash

N*INE YEARS AGO*

I never wanted to run towards a woman faster. Her blonde hair cascaded down her back, looking soft enough to run my fingers through, and her blue plaid shirt hugged her just right. Her jeans were tight, showing off her perfect ass, and her boots and hat topped off the buckle bunny look. I needed to talk to her, and more than that—I needed to kiss her and feel her.

She leaned up against the gate, lifting a boot up to rest on the metal, leaning forward towards the arena. Her profile hit, blue eyes that caught my attention even from several feet away, and a smile that made my knees turn to butter under my weight.

Taking a deep breath and narrowing my eyes, I stalked towards her. She was here for a cowboy and damn. If my chaps and sponsor vest didn't give me away as a cowboy, I didn't know what did.

"Is this your first rodeo?" I asked, my voice smooth as I leaned against the gate next to her. I bit the inside of my lip, wishing I could take back that stupid cliché line. I dropped my chin with embarrassment.

I was Cash Callahan. I knew how to pick up girls. I knew how to be sexy and exactly what the bunnies wanted. So why *the hell* did I start off with that line.

"I mean..." I stammered. "You...look like this is your first rodeo."

I finally looked up, making eye contact with the gorgeous woman in front of me. The expression on her face was comical. She was doing everything in her power not to laugh at me. Her eyebrows were pinched, her lips were forming a tight smile as they held back the laugh. This girl was already getting in my head in more ways than one. I started to question everything I had ever said to a girl at a rodeo. Embarrassment started to seep through my veins, yet I couldn't bring myself to move away from her.

"It looks," she said softly, a pause in her voice as she eyed me, "like this is my first rodeo?"

"Ok, maybe not my best pick up line."

"That's your pick up line?" Her chuckle floated between us, and I couldn't help but laugh with her. It was contagious, and while she laughed, every other sound muted. "That was a terrible pick up line because I mean..." She looked down at herself, a hand gesturing down her body. "Look at me."

I eyed her up and down, taking her in. She looked like she carefully planned her outfit, even down to the mud on her boots.

"No offense, but you look like you dressed up for this, like the other bunnies around."

"Bunnies?" She snapped, her hand flying to her chest. "You think I'm a buckle bunny?"

Ok, this was not going the way I planned. But even as she was beginning to argue, she was still gorgeous. I still wanted to know who she was, and damn, I wanted to kiss her. I could turn this around. I could turn on the charm.

I raised a corner of my lips, giving my best suave smile.

"Nah, I mean..." I moved my body, my elbow raised to the top of the gate, but she kept going.

"You thought I was here just waiting for a cowboy to come and sweep me off the gate and take me to their trailer, or truck, or hotel and then move on to the next rodeo and the next cowboy?" She gave me a coy grinned. "Right?"

"I didn't..." I stammered.

Oh shit. This isn't going my way at all.

"I'll have you know..." she turned towards me, taking one single step closer. I inhaled, breathing in her scent of cinnamon and maple, forcing myself to stay focused on the task: turning on the charm and at least getting her name. She continued, "I was raised on a ranch in Idaho. My family owns a small arena, and we have a rodeo every year. This"—she waved her hand up and down her body again—"is how I dress on a daily basis. I muck stalls. I feed pigs and goats. I milk cows, and more often than not I have some kind of shit under my fingernails. If you are looking for a buckle bunny, I suggest you go find some other blonde who's wearing a tight skirt with her boobs hanging out of her tube top. They dressed up for you, not me."

Oh man...I think I'm in love.

"Nah, I don't want a buckle bunny." My voice came back, smooth as silk as my accent rolled off my tongue.

Her lips twisted as she licked the bottom one, the wet of her tongue turning them pinker, more teasing. "OK then." She cocked her head to the side. "What do you want?"

You.

"Cash!" A voice I knew all too well called my name from the side. It was a new bull rider who I had grown to enjoy having around. Sure, he was a bit eccentric, childish at times, but my rodeo pal, Lachlan, insisted he was the best addition to the rodeo. "I've been looking for you, please tell me you'll be there with Lach while I get on that bull?"

Sylas Acosta.

"You bet," I answered him as he approached, but his eyes weren't on me, they were on *her*.

And as soon as her head turned, her smile widened as she watched him.

"Mi Reina." As soon as he was close enough, he slipped his hand around her waist and pulled her close, knocking her hat off to the side as he kissed her temple. It was then I noticed the ring on her finger. "Have you met Cash?" Sylas slapped my shoulder.

"I was just about to ask him his name." She smiled at Sylas, and her face lit up. Damn—she was stunning. And also very—very—taken. "He thought I was a buckle bunny."

Sylas let out a deep laugh. "You're joking. Abi is the furthest thing from a buckle bunny."

She shook her head and made eye contact with me. "The words buckle and bunny are being said way too much for my liking. Hi, Cash." She held out her left hand, and all I saw was that ring on her finger. "I'm Abi Hartwell."

"My fiancée," Sylas added, kissing her temple once more.

Blush spread across her cheeks.

Well...fuck.

Abi Hartwell. Not only was I checking out and trying to pick up Lachlan's cousin that he had told me about numerous times, but I told Sylas's fiancé she looked like a buckle bunny. And she told him.

I took a deep breath and closed my eyes for a split second before grasping her hand, knowing that as long as Sylas was my friend, Abi would be. This moment would hopefully be forgotten.

"Hi, I'm Cash Callahan."

Present Day

Stetson stomped on the tile a few times with his boot before taking a step back, looking down to admire his work at placing the shingle.

"Looks great, Stet." I gave him a hard pat on the back, just like my dad would do to me, his entire body flew forward. "Just wait until your mom sees."

"Can I fix another one?" The smile spread against Stetson's lips, spreading from ear to ear. *This kid...*

Taking a quick glance around the roof and noticing Lachlan and Rhett had finished the west side, I looked over at Stetson. "Tell ya what, tomorrow we're gonna paint the side of the barn. I need help convincing your cousin that it needs to be red."

"All barns are red." Stetson nodded. "But let me guess, he bought brown?"

"A deep brown," I confirmed. "Wanna head to town with me and get some red paint?"

"Sure!" Stetson shouted. "I'll go ask mom."

"Great, meet me by my truck."

Abi—surprisingly—had no issues with Stetson coming into town with me. What was more of an issue was getting the almost-eight-year-old to pick a shade of red. There was even one called 'Barn,' and he passed it up for a bright, more vibrant red I knew would drive Lachlan absolutely up the wall. I convinced him to get one can of the bright red, white for the trim and a few more of the deeper shades I knew Lachlan would approve of.

One cart full of paint, and a sucker in the kid's hand, we were heading back to Hartwell Hills. Stetson sat in the front seat, watching the world move in the window. He looked so much like Sylas, I doubted I would ever get used to it.

Meeting Sylas was a pivotal moment—for me and my rodeo career. At first it was just Lachlan and me, two cowboys jumping on a bucking horse. Then Lachlan brought in a newbie bull rider who was more eccentric than anyone I had ever met. With both Lachlan and me being cowboys with one goal in mind, he balanced us. Helped us remember the fun of the sport, that it was more than just money and girls. And when Abi began to join in the adventures, traveling with him when she could—that is before she got preg-nant—it was a hell of time. She had four different events to cheer for, and we all took in her shouts.

You could hear her from the chutes, no matter how far away she was. At least, I could.

I could always see and hear her.

Ever since I first met her.

"You think I'm a buckle bunny."

Her words were still ingrained in my mind, that first meeting would always be ingrained in my mind.

Abi was a breath of fresh air when we first met. Her smiles, her laughs, the pure joy she brought to the room. I always loved it when she was around. Even if she was attached to Sylas's hip, I loved the friendship she and I formed. I loved the friendship we all formed.

Then...that pivotal piece was gone.

Stetson jumped from the cab of the truck the moment I popped it in park.

"Hey, you gotta help with the paint!" I called after him, even though he was already halfway to his aunt and uncle.

Kyla bent down and wrapped her nephew in her arms. Rhett gave me a quick nod as I climbed out of the truck.

"Stet!" I began to jog. "Get your ass over to the rig and get the paint."

"Uncle Cash, have you met Josie yet?" Stetson let go of Kyla and stood to run back towards the pasture.

"Is that kid always running?" I looked up at Rhett. "Can you help with the paint?"

"I got it. Go meet that damn cow." Rhett let out a grumble, gently touching his wife before heading to my rig. "Stetson won't shut up about her until you do."

"With reason. That's a great cow." Kyla smiled. She bit her bottom lip and looked at her husband. "Come on, let's get the paint."

My gaze followed to the pasture where Stetson climbed over the fence, jumped down, and ran towards a small brown-and-white cow. I shook my head, tipped my chin, and followed him, stepping up on the wooden fence as he wrapped his arms around the cows neck. She let out a small moo, but my smile faded when I saw a brown horse resting on the field, laying in the small patch of grass. And resting against the horse was a gorgeous blonde. Abi.

It was Luna, Sylas's horse, and Abi leaned up against the horse's stomach, her legs outstretched in front of her. Her chin tilted up as she seemingly took in the sun. The horse didn't mind the weight on her stomach, didn't seem to care at all that Abi was basically using her as a pillow. Instead, Luna turned her head and used her nose to nudge Abi's temple. Abi raised an arm and touched Luna's nose, hugging her, never once opening her eyes.

Years ago, I used to draw. I had dozens of sketch books at home with doodles and random pictures of horses, people, rodeo. It was a hobby I kept only to myself, a part of my life not even Carolyn knew about. And seeing this, I suddenly wished I had a sketch book. I would capture this for her, freeze this moment in time, even though I hadn't picked up a pencil in years.

She was in the moment with the horse, taking the nudges the mare was offering her. I noticed her breathing, long and deep, as she rested. Then Luna shook her head and gracefully laid it down next to

Abi's body once more. Abi moved slightly, adjusting for the horse, as she draped her arm over her neck, her other hand reached up to wipe her face free of something before she laid her head back on Luna's belly.

Abi looked...sad. Even in such peaceful moments, she was hurting.

Hurting from...what?

It took all my strength not to go sit next to her, ask her what was going through her mind, how I could potentially hold some of that for her.

I would only cause more if I did that, even if we were trying to move forward from the past. There were still scars there. She still didn't want me around even if she agreed she would be cordial. I wanted nothing more than to be her friend again.

I could hear Stetson calling, his laughter, but all I saw was Abi and emotions that came with her as she moved. Her gaze followed to where her son was. She inhaled deeply, scratched behind Luna's ear, and then slowly stood. The mare shook her head again, obviously not liking the fact that she was pulled from her nap. Still glued to Abi, I watched as she reached her arms over her head in a stretch before placing both hands over her face. She took deep breaths—one...two...three...before dropping her hands to give her son a large, warm, welcoming smile.

Even through the smile, I saw the pain.

In the back of my mind, I made a mental note to go grab a sketch book on my way home tonight.

ELEVEN

Abi

THE NIGHT AIR HIT my skin as the wind blew by. Why I decided to sit on the porch at eight at night thinking it would be a good way to clear my head was beyond me. The same way I thought sitting with Luna would be a good idea. I couldn't peg what was going on with me today. I just knew I couldn't stop my thoughts. Those memories would creep up, no matter how hard I tried to force them down.

Putting on a smile was easy enough; dinner was actually kind of interesting. Kyla turned down the wine Rhett offered her, saying she was still not feeling the best from this morning, and when a giant steak was placed in front of her, she gagged and ran out of the room. I glanced at my mom, giving her the knowing smile while my brother stood to follow his wife, seemingly still oblivious. I knew Kyla was telling him tonight. She wanted to tell him before announcing it to the entire family, but seeing as my mom picked up on it too, it wouldn't be long before everyone else would.

Cash was there at dinner, taking a seat in between Lachlan and Stetson, deep in conversation about the color of the barn. Stetson was insisting it be red, and he showed Lachlan the swatch he brought home from the hardware store. Lachlan turned that down immediately, promising Stetson that the paint wouldn't go to waste. Every now and then, even in the middle of their conversation, I would catch Cash glancing over at me, his eyes filled with questions I wished he would speak out loud. Even then, I probably wouldn't answer them.

So, after Stetson was asleep, I made myself a cup of decaf coffee and wrapped myself in a blanket burrito. As soon as the quiet hit, everything I was pushing down during the day came creeping back up.

Sylas.

I missed my husband.

I missed the way he would jump when he was excited.

I missed the way he smelled, the way the smell still enveloped pieces of clothing.

I missed his laugh, his voice, his touch.

I stopped the tears before they began again—crying once today was enough—and lifted my mug to my lips. I sniffed, looking at the stars as I adjusted my shoulders, sinking deeper in the cushion. Why did the memory of us discovering we were pregnant come with such pain? It shouldn't still feel this way, should it? I should be able to think about him without getting sad, without crying. I can talk about him with others with no issues, a smile half of the time. Of course, they don't see how I am after we talk. All the tears I hide. But this...this is kind of ridiculous. It's been five years. I should be able to remember these things without breaking down on the inside.

"It's a bit cold out here to be stargazing, don't you think?" the Southern drawl filled the emptiness, and as much as I hated to admit it, I was grateful I was no longer alone. But I didn't move. I simply took another sip of my coffee.

"Ah, well," Cash sighed. "You're wrapped in a blanket and have coffee?" He came in front of me to lean against the railing, crossing his feet in front of him.

"It's decaf," I answered, avoiding his gaze.

Cash let out a laugh. "It's cold." He shivered.

"Hence, blanket." I snuggled into it more. "I am a burrito."

"A burrito." Cash snorted another laugh and then cleared his throat. "I saw you today," he said softly.

I met his gaze, those dark eyes holding those same damn questions.

"With Luna," he finished.

I nodded, pursing my lips. "I take her out from time to time. She's old, and doesn't get ridden much anymore, but we relax."

Relax. That's all he needed to know. He didn't need to know that we took walks a few times a week together. He didn't need to know that I went to her when I missed Sylas the most. He didn't need to know that I cried and cried against her more times than I cared to admit. All he needed to know was that we relaxed.

"You looked relaxed. So did she." He took a deep breath. "She's not *that* old."

"She's pushing fifteen."

He furrowed his brow. "No, she's not. She was a baby when Sylas took her over."

I inhaled. I didn't need to hear his name again today. So, I blinked and took another pull of my coffee. "She was three, maybe four. Lachlan broke her."

"But she doesn't ride anymore?"

I shook my head. "Not much, no."

"Because she doesn't want to or because you don't want anyone to?"

"She just doesn't." I answered, lifting my chin and aiming a challenging look at him. He had a single eyebrow raised, his chin tilted just right as the glow from the porch caught all his features.

I let out a small huff and avoided his gaze once again. Hoping he got the hint that I didn't want to talk about Sylas or Luna anymore, I watched as he sat next to me, leaning his elbows on his knees. The air was still, I could practically hear the gears in his brain turning. Was he calculating what to say, which question to ask first? We both had so many things we needed to say to each other, but neither one wanted to make the first move.

A deep part of me wanted to build our friendship back up, not just be cordial like I originally agreed. Maybe knowing he was next to me to talk about anything and everything was the start. He was here, wasn't he? He was making the effort simply sitting next to me. I was the one who was closing off.

I took a deep breath.

"What color did Lachlan land on?" I asked, breaking the silence that floated between us.

Cash's head turned and his lips curved into a soft smile. "The burnt red. Your son won that battle."

"I think you helped. Barns need to be red, not brown."

"Thank you." He sat up straight, his palms slapping his thighs. "Not sure what goes through your cousin's head sometimes."

I smiled. "He's trying to turn Hartwell Hills into the same colorless void that his life is." I joked.

Cash chuckled, reaching up to remove his hat from head. Placing it on the small table in between us, he met my gaze. "He's doing alright, isn't he?"

Thinking of my cousin and how far he's come, I nodded. "He's better. He'll never be one hundred percent again, but...he's ok."

He chewed on his lips, his gaze staring out into the darkness. "He doesn't let me in like he used to."

"That's Lachlan. He hides from everyone. I have high hopes. He'll get a happy ending."

"You think so?"

"Hey, if it wasn't for me, Rhett and Kyla would have never gotten married, and she would still be in Washington running from her ex. If I can call Rhett's future, I can call Lachlan's." I circled my shoulders, feeling my muscles relax.

"And what about Wyatt?"

"Maybe someday, but for now he's a lost cause. He'll be chasing those girls at rodeos until they turn him down." I shifted, scooching my ass into the cushion even more.

"And you?" His voice was heavy as he spoke.

I met his gaze. What about me? Was that one of the questions burning behind his pupils? Out of all the questions that were running through his mind, this is the one he decided to ask? Besides, didn't I already have my happy ending?

"I got everything I need right here," I lied.

He pinched his brow. "Everything?"

I nodded slowly. "Everything."

He mimicked my nod, before turning his head to look out into the night sky.

"And you?" I parroted his question.

His shoulders raised. "I could use a bit more," he admitted.

"A bit more of what?" I asked, more out of curiosity, actually finding myself enjoying his company.

He shrugged, then with one loud groan, plopped back onto the wicker chair. "More of this." He waved his hand in the air.

"Nighttime porch talks in the freezing cold?" I said, a hint of sarcasm in my voice.

His eyes hit mine, and they told me everything I needed to know. It wasn't just late night talks on the porch in the cold, shivering our asses off. He missed this, probably just as much as I did. He wanted the old times back—everything we used to have.

He laughed humorlessly. "Something like that."

I studied him then. His smile faded slowly as his body relaxed into the chair. A heavy sigh left his nose while his chin raised in the air. I had always thought Cash was handsome. His tawny skin had just the right glow to it, and he was perfectly flawless, especially now with the moonlight hitting him. He closed his eyes and swallowed, his Adam's apple moving. He looked tired, but that didn't take away from the rugged features he carried. His chiseled jawline was lightly dusted with a five o'clock shadow that traveled down his chin, defining his features more. His chest and arms were toned from years of being on a horse, training for strength, and ranch work. Even with layers of clothing to keep out the cold, I could see it. I could remember his hugs. Solid and safe. I always felt safe in Cash's presence.

"So," I broke the silence, finally getting up the courage. "What happened with Carolyn?"

Cash's head flipped, landing with a bob as his eyes rolled at me. "What? Don't you miss her."

I bit my lip and held back a chuckle. "Oh, hell no. She always rubbed me the wrong way, but...you loved her so...we loved her."

He rubbed the back of his neck, turning away from me. "She didn't love me. The moment I broke my leg and I didn't fit that mold anymore, the moment I couldn't..." He stopped himself and took a deep breath, his palm landing on his knee with a smack. "She left. Filed for divorce. I wasn't what she wanted."

"Her loss," I scoffed, even though my mind was circling on his unfinished sentence.

"I don't know where she is now and don't care to find out. She got what she wanted out of the divorce and then left my life. Lachlan didn't lie when he said we celebrated. We did."

"I'm sorry that happened. I know you loved her."

"I don't think I ever really did. I just wanted to feel like I had that...you know." He turned to me. "I would see Lachlan and Hadley, you and Sylas...I wanted...needed that, and Carolyn, she was the first one to really give it to me. Not that it was real."

I hummed. "Well, she never deserved you." Shifting in my seat, I lowered the blanket to my waist, feeling the brisk air through my sweater. "And you're happy? Without her?"

"It's been three years since the divorce was finalized. I wouldn't say they were the best three years of my life, but they were better than when she was with me."

"That's..."

"Depressing?" Cash let out a small scoff, leaning forward in the chair. "Yeah, well..."

"Life goes on, doesn't it? No matter what curve balls it throws at you."

"Is that what you do?" His voice was low, almost a whisper, but it was loud enough to hit all the right nerves. "You just...go on?"

I pursed my lips, and stared into his eyes. That deep brown that I remembered from all those years ago, still holding onto something that he had yet to let go of. I saw the hint of something there when he first arrived, but with a blink that was gone. Now here, our eyes locked, I saw it again. I wanted to reach out for him, tell him whatever he was holding on to, he could let it go. But before I could even move, I forced myself to stop. I didn't think I was ready for that yet.

"Kyla's pregnant," I blurted out, instantly regretting my words. There were other ways to change the subject, and I had to go to that?

"That's exciting," He responded. "I'm sure everyone is looking forward to another little Hartwell running around."

"I'm the only one who knows. Well—now you, and my mom suspects. Kyla hasn't told anyone yet."

"Why don't you sound excited about it?"

"I am. Really, I am. It just…made me remember something."

"What?" His voice was soft as he pressed.

I swallowed. "It just reminded me of when I found out I was pregnant with Stetson."

"God." Cash chuckled, leaning back into the chair, the grin wide as his fingers ran through his short hair. "I remember Sylas freaking out. He was so thrilled. He told everyone, even though you ordered him to keep it a secret for a while. Everyone in that arena knew."

"I was so mad. Superstitions and all. I didn't want anyone to know until we had our first appointment, and he went along blabbing it to everyone." I couldn't help my laugh at that memory of Sylas. I had gotten so many text messages, so many phone calls, all from cowboys and cowgirls congratulating me. It seemed everyone involved in the circuit knew I was expecting—all before even my mom and dad did.

"He was excited. Can you blame him? That man was meant to be a dad."

I took a deep, deep breath. "He was. I think…" I paused, looking down at my feet to completely avoid Cash. "We were supposed to have more kids, you know. Sylas wanted a big family."

He was silent for a beat, but then his voice hit my ears, almost a whisper. "Do you still want more kids?"

"Sure, but…" A hesitant chuckle broke from my lungs. "That's impossible seeing as I'm single and most likely will be forever." I tightened my lips, another wave of regret hitting me. "What about you?" I asked, pushing the topic to him. "Didn't Carolyn want kids?"

Cash's brown eyes jerked towards me, his brow twitching, the expression on his face completely unreadable. The only response I got was a quick shake to his head before his chin lowered. I struck a nerve, one I didn't even know was there.

"Sorry I—"

"It just wasn't in the cards for Carolyn and me, but in the long run, it's better right?"

I heaved a sigh. "Right," I agreed. "We're a pair, aren't we? I feel like we have a lot to catch up on."

Cash nodded, silence filling the space between us. After a few moments, which felt like hours, Cash inhaled sharply and pushed himself to standing. I blinked, bringing my mug to my lips. And it was cold. I scrunched my nose, but swallowed it anyway.

"We do." He chewed on his lip. "I'm around Abs. I never left. My number is the same and I'll answer anytime you call. All you gotta do is call."

"Who you gonna call?" I joked in song, defusing the awkward air between us. Maybe the *Ghostbusters* song would pull me from the stupor.

"I'm being serious. No jokes, no sarcasm." He reached out and lifted my chin with his thumb and forefinger until our gazes met, and his eyes were heavy on me. "I'm here."

He placed his hat on his head before leaving me alone on the porch.

I had one question swimming through my mind. If he said he never left—his number never changed—then why did he ignore all those texts and phone calls? I shifted, reaching in my back pocket to pull out my phone. Scrolling to Cash's name I opened a new text thread. Years later, a new phone had erased all my attempts to contact him years ago, but I still remembered the texts.

Sylas's funeral is on the 17th. I need you there.

Why didn't you come? Cash...I can't do this.

I saw the rodeo last night, I'm worried, what hospital are you in, I'll come. I want to see you.

Cash are you ok? I don't like the silence.

Cash....please...I need my friend.

I can't do this alone anymore. I miss him so much. I can't keep pretending I'm ok.

Swallowing, I typed out a new message.

Me

> Same number? Mine's the same too…See you tomorrow, Cash.

> P.S. I won't admit it out loud, but I'm enjoying you being here. Thank you for tonight.

TWELVE

Cash

Six Years Ago

Storming out of the Hartwells' house was not how I expected to end my evening. I don't think I had ever been this furious at my wife. We had some fights in the past—many, if I was being honest—but with how she just blew up in front of Abi and Sylas, screaming so loud that Stetson woke up, she even shook me to my core.

And all over nothing.

I gripped the railing and hunched my shoulders, willing the pounding in my head to slow. Closing my eyes, I forced air to swell in my lungs. Inhale. Exhale. Deep breaths. Over and over. In and out. They told you to breathe, right? The professionals said breathe. But then again, the professionals never had to deal with Carolyn.

"Hey, you ok?"

Abi's calm voice filled the air, and immediately the pounding lessened. No matter what, she could always take the chaos and turn it calm. Opening my eyes into the darkness, I gave her a curt nod.

She scoffed, calling my bluff. "No you're not."

"How's Stet?" I questioned, deflecting the conversation.

"Sylas went to check on him." She pushed against the railing, crossing her ankles in front of her.

"Divided and conquered who would take care of who huh?" I quipped, sounding more irritated than I should have.

"Well, when Carolyn stormed into the bathroom and knocked a photo off the wall when she slammed the door. We both just took off where we were needed. And I was needed here. Plus, Stetson literally screamed for Dad." She shifted her body to give me a bump, my entire frame moving slightly.

"Ah, so I was second choice," I joked, trying to bring light to the situation.

"You are not, and you know it." She gave my shoulder a light punch. "So...honestly this time. You ok?"

I shook my head. "I'm sorry. We've been fighting more than usual. I just hoped we could make it through one night."

"Fights happen, though I'm confused as to why she was acting the way she was."

I tried to play the night back in my head, starting with Carolyn promising me it would be a good evening. She didn't particularly like Sylas and Abi, but when they invited us over to dinner, I begged her to come. Being with this family made me feel like myself. Smiles came easily here. We got there early, I gave Abi a hug, Sylas got a pat on the back, and I scooped Stetson up in my arms. When Abi disappeared to put Stetson down, Carolyn loosened up slightly, even cracking a few smiles when Sylas told a joke. Once Abi came back, Carolyn made sure to be at my side the entire time, her hand slinking up my shirt, her long nails scratching into my skin.

I wasn't one to mind a little PDA, but when it turned into something more and Carolyn whispering that we sneak off, that was a little too much for me. When I asked her to stop, her switch flipped.

"Of course you would prefer to stay here. Of course I don't come first for you."

Her screams were so loud, so over the top, that I couldn't help but defend myself.

"You know you come first."

"You're different here. You're not the Cash I married.

"You're the one acting different. You're the one touching me as if we were alone, suggesting we go up to their room. Come on Carolyn, have some respect."

"You have some respect. Maybe show your wife *you actually love her instead of—"*

"Come on Carolyn, let's just have a good time—stop doing this."

I knew why Carolyn was acting the way she was. She was claiming dominance, making sure Abi knew I was hers. Even though that was the farthest thing Carolyn had to worry about, she still made it a big deal. My relationship with Abi was deeper than any of my other female friendships I had, but that didn't mean I wasn't loyal to my wife.

"She really hates me that much doesn't she?" Abi asked.

I didn't answer.

"It's fine." She sighed, shifting to face the empty field in front of us. Her shoulder grazed mine, her warmth seeping over me. "But I will be that friend and say I do not like the way she treats you."

"She was just—"

"I know what she was doing. You deserve better than that."

"Abi—"

"I know, I know. She's your wife and you love her. I admire that you're trying to defend her even after all of that." She waved a hand behind her shoulder. "I'm sorry that happened, Cash."

"You don't need to apologize." I wrapped my arm around her shoulder, pulling her into my side. I still loved the way she fit there, and the way her head naturally landed on my shoulder. "I just don't expect another invitation anytime soon."

"You damn well know you are welcome over anytime. No matter what."

No matter what.

This woman didn't know how much she meant to me. How much she made me feel like I was whole from simply being my friend. What started as me accidentally hitting on her turned into one of the best friendships I'd ever had.

I sighed. "Thank you for coming to make sure I was ok." I dropped my arm from her shoulders. "It won't happen again."

The front door slammed open wide, hitting the side of the house with force, making both of us jump. Carolyn stormed past us, only stopping once she made it to the grass. She turned, her platinum blonde hair flipping over her shoulders. A deep hatred that pinged across her face was aimed directly at Abi. She chewed on her bottom lip before turning to me.

"I'm going home," she announced. "You can either come with me or stay here, but I'm leaving." She huffed before turning and bolting to my truck.

"I better go. I need to fix this." I watched my wife leave, taking that step to follow her. "Say goodbye to Sylas for me, okay? Tell him I'll text him later."

"Sure." Abi took a step back, her hand reaching out for the door, which was still wide open. "See you soon."

I gave her a nod and a quick wave, not realizing that would be the last time I would have Abi in my arms.

Present Day

Two weeks came and went in a blink of an eye. Between helping Lachlan paint the barn and getting Quinn to and from appointments and back on her horse, I felt like I missed more than not. Abi and I had shared passing smiles, but no real time to sit and be with each other again, and if I was being one hundred percent transparent with myself, I wanted nothing more. Each night, I came to the stables to hopefully get some time with her, but I was either catching her just as she was done for the night or ended up spending more time with Lachlan.

I thought Abi and I were back on track after the night on the porch. But I had the inkling things were just beginning to circle each other. It wasn't as if she wasn't talking to me—she would say hello and carry on small talk, but nothing like the conversation we had the other night. For a moment there, before nerves got the best of me and I stupidly ended the conversation, I could have sworn there was something there. She bore into me that night, almost like she was digging deep, trying to bring up everything. There were things she wanted to say, things I needed to say, and all I could do was tell her she could call me. It was steps—baby steps—back to the way we used to be. Friends.

And yet—I could almost feel more.

I shouldn't be feeling more...should I?

"You're lookin' better Quinn," I shouted as she passed me on Charming, finally getting into a full gallop but still too nervous to ride Hook.

After a few acupuncture appointments and physical therapy, she still needed the mounting block, but she was more relaxed to run. Next, I'd add the barrels and start the timer—until then I just needed her to get comfortable on her horse again.

Spring had taken over Hartwell Hills, the snow finally gone. The horses that had found a temporary home here were now en-joying the outside with the warmer air. I even caught Nova trotting with Luna one day, inspiring another doodle in my new sketchbook. But Quinn was using Charming again and again. The horse needed a break. Hook spent most of his time outside, relishing in the pasture while Charming worked harder than before. He was a good horse, but she needed to get on the horse that she fell off.

Cranking my neck to look behind me, I watched Abi open the last few stables to lead the horses into the fields. She held onto Hook's lead, as well as the horse that had moved in last week, giving both of them a kiss on the cheek. Making sure Quinn was in her element, I jogged back into the stable, catching Abi right before she made it outside.

"I'll take Hook," I said once I approached her, reaching for the lead.

Abi wasted no time in handing it over to me, her hand still firm on the leather strap. I took it from her, noticing our fingers brush against each other ever so slightly.

"You sure? He loves the pasture. I have a hard time getting him back in the stable at night." Abi laughed, using her now free hand to pet his neck.

"Quinn needs to get her ass on this horse. Would you be able to come get Charming once she's on Hook?"

Abi looked behind my shoulder at the arena. "Sure, but...do you think Quinn wants to get on him? How long did it take her to gallop on Charming?"

"Too long. I gotta get her back on the horse she fell off of." I motioned towards her, pulling Hook's lead for him to follow.

Abi raised a brow. "Okay...I'll be back for Charming."

I gave her a wink before leading the black horse towards the arena. He protested slightly, pulling the reins towards the gate, but gave in with a grunt.

"Quinn," I shouted, opening the arena gates. She turned to look at me. "Dismount."

Quinn slowed, taking Charming over to the mounting block, walking him over the moment her feet hit the ground. Her face faltered as she got closer and closer to me. She knew exactly what I was doing.

"Are you afraid of Hook?" I asked, pointing to the black horse next to me.

"No," she grumbled, avoiding meeting my eyes completely.

"Pretty sure you are. The past three weeks you haven't ridden him once. He's going to become a pasture horse if you don't train with him, too."

"He's not going to become a pasture horse." Quinn reached out and touched Hook's nose, "I'm just..."

"It took me a bit to get back on another horse after my fall, too. At least with barrel racing you can ride your own horse, and Hook"—I held the reins out to her—"is a fantastic racer. Swap out the saddles and mount him."

Frozen, she moved only her eyes, looking from her horse to me.

"Swap out the saddle and mount him," I repeated, making sure to add the tone of voice that got her moving.

Quinn took a deep breath before moving to ready both horses. I stepped back, only feeling slightly bad for making her change horses in the middle of training. Watching her, I leaned against the gate as she took her time talking to her horse, and reassuring Charming he did a good job today. Hook bobbed his head, seemingly ready to go for something more than the pasture.

"You're tough on her." Abi came up behind me, her arms coming into view on the gate next to me. Her eyes were focused on Quinn as she removed the saddle from Charming. "You really think she's scared of Hook?"

"I do. She would always pick Hook over Charming, and now she won't even come near him." I didn't take my eyes off Quinn as she took every piece from Charming and placed it on Hook. "Look at her. She's hesitating."

"And you're just going to watch her hesitate?"

"Yup." I folded my arms and watched.

"I'll say it again, you're a tough trainer." There was a small laugh in Abi's voice.

"She's tougher." I said with confidence, my focus on Quinn not faltering.

Abi shifted on her heels. "How did you get into barrel racing training? I'd figured you would go for something with saddle bronc. That *was* your event." She stepped up on the gate, making herself a little taller than me as her focus stayed on Quinn.

"Yep." I mimicked her action and took the step upon the gate, feeling that twinge of pain radiate up my leg. I sure as hell hoped Quinn never had this residual pain. She didn't need this plaguing her for the rest of her life. I continued, "I thought about it, but to be honest, it may have been harder to become a trainer for that event than anything else."

"Why?"

"I would want to get back on that horse."

"Why haven't you?"

I watched as Quinn ran her palm down the length of Charming's back. Hook was almost ready to go, he just needed the bridle, and Quinn was still hesitating. She claimed she wasn't afraid, but I could see it in her expressions. I could tell by the way her legs buckled once she got near Hook. Her breathing got heavier, and her movements weren't as fluid.

I could see it in her because it's exactly how I was.

Fear.

"Fear." I finally said out loud. "I was messed up after my accident. Took me a long time to get back on any horse once I could fully walk again."

"How long have you been taking training jobs?"

"Quinn's my first client. My only client as of right now. We're in year two."

Abi's eyebrows raised. "And what did you do for the years before training?"

I met her gaze. "Recovered."

She didn't respond to that. She didn't need to. She knew what I was recovering from. Losing Sylas. My accident. The divorce.

"I'm not fully recovered." I stuck my left leg out in front of me. "I still get this shooting pain in my leg sometimes, like just now. When I stepped on the gate, I felt it. It reminds me to go easy on myself. I guarantee you I'll always feel that spark of pain."

"Do you think you'll even ride bronc again?"

I shook my head. "Nope. I miss it, but I can't. So, I immersed myself in other ways. Most trainers don't follow clients to rodeos. Me...I'd follow Quinn to each and every event just so I could still be a part of it."

"How the hell do you afford that?"

I raised a brow. "I was very smart with my money, let's say that."

"So." Abi stretched her arms out, taking a big exhale through her lips before pulling herself back to the gate. "You go to rodeos, and you miss it, but you won't ride. You're still afraid?"

"Terrified." I didn't drop a beat.

She hummed. "Wanna know what I think?"

"I have a feeling you're gonna tell me no matter what."

Abi jumped off the gate. "I think you need to take your own advice and get back on a bucking horse. You know damn well you can do it. You're making your client do it. Take your own damn advice." Walking behind me, she entered the arena. "I'll take Charming out to the pasture," she told Quinn, taking his lead with ease. She gave me a wink, much like the one I gave her earlier, as she passed me.

That night, I found myself knocking on Rhett's door. He answered, an eyebrow raising high once he saw me. He was already dressed in a t-shirt and sweats, basically turned in for the night. Leaning against his door frame he crossed his arms across his chest.

"Hey, sorry to bother you." I scratched the nape of my neck, still not sure about what the hell I was really doing. Abi's words got to me, and they had been ringing in my ears ever since. I had watched Quinn take Hook around the arena. Her back was stiff, but she eventually loosened up, her confidence coming back after a few runs around. When I added a barrel, it was as if she never took a fall.

I needed to take my own advice.

"You're not bothering us, what's up?" he asked, lifting his chin in the air.

"I was wondering if you could help me with something."

Forty minutes later, Rhett, Lachlan, and I stood in the arena with one of the Hartwell's horses in the chute. I pulled my gloves for the tenth time as I watched Lachlan adjust the flanking strap.

My heart was racing. I hadn't done this in three—damn, almost four years. I had ridden a horse, sure—Nova and I were naturals—but getting on a horse that was purposefully trying to buck me off was a different story. I knew the motions. I knew what to do. It was like riding a bike...right? Arm up, legs straight, back loose, shoulders square...but the last time I was on a horse, my posture was perfect, and I still fumbled. Who's to say it wouldn't happen again?

"He's a bucker"—Lachlan looked up at me—"even without the strap. Are you sure?"

"Positive," I answered, hearing the shake in my voice. I was anything but positive. "You got the gate, Rhett?"

Holding onto the rope, Rhett nodded. "Kinda wish Wyatt was here. He could help."

"I'll jump on Onyx the minute the shoot opens. I'll be the pick-up," Lachlan answered. "Wyatt wouldn't be much help anyway."

"I could get on a horse," Kyla, who sat in the stands, called back. She was cuddled in a blanket, her boots untied as if she had just tossed them on.

"No." Rhett pointed at her, a little too defensively. He cleared his throat and lowered his finger as Kyla gave him a smirk. "I mean, you just sit back and relax. You're keeping time."

Kyla waved the small timer she held in the air. "Eight seconds."

"Maybe lower it to six?" Rhett looked over at me. "It's been years since you've done this."

I shook my head. "Eight seconds."

"You ready?" Lachlan asked, stepping away from the horse.

I nodded, exhaled through my rounded lips, and used all my strength to hoist myself over the gate and land on the horse's back.

Instantly he moved, grunting as I pressed my knees into his side. He was not happy we woke him up for this. *Good. He'll buck more.*

"What the hell are you doing?" Abi's loud voice echoed through the arena before she even came into view. I looked up, catching her as she pursed her lips. Her hair was up in a messy bun, she wore black sweat and tennis shoes, and a large sweater covering her torso. Obviously—she crawled out of bed for this—yet she was still beautiful in every sense. And she was going to see me ride.

Nerves ran through my chest. No one answered her. They all just stared, stunned, as if they had just been caught by their mom.

"Taking my own advice." I finally broke the silence.

"Now?" Abi approached the chute. "At ten o'clock at night? You think now is a good idea?"

"Yeah, I do."

She took one deep breath, then dropped her arms to her side. "You're crazy."

"You told me to get back on the horse."

"I didn't mean today. I meant later. In a different arena," she argued back.

"What better place than here, Abs?" I bore into her, silently telling her I needed this, that she told me I needed this. It was because of her I was on this horse in the first place, and it was because of her I wasn't getting off. She knew I could do this. I just had to show myself I could. "Lachlan's on Onyx, Rhett's at the chute, Kyla is timing..."

"Kyla." Abi looked around, her eyes landing on the stand where Kyla sat. She gave Abi a soft wave.

"Don't worry, Rhett is making sure I stay here." Kyla said loud enough for her to hear.

"You need someone else on the chute." She dropped her arms.

"You volunteering?" I asked, gripping my hand on the rope, not even bothering to look at her.

I heard her groan. "Yes. Fine. I'm volunteering."

The moment she reached the back of the chute, she placed her hand on the horse's neck, pulling and moving him back and forth, only gearing him up more.

"Again..." Abi sighed, speaking loud enough only I could hear. "You sure about this?"

I answered her by giving Rhett the nod.

The chute opened, and I used my spurs to move the horse, giving him a good kick, and the minute he was out of the chute, he bucked. And bucked. And bucked. The sounds of the metal gate and Rhett's cheers vanished as the only thing that I could hear was the harsh 'thump' of the hooves hitting the dirt. As if instinct was taking over, my body began to move with the motions. My right hand in the air, my left holding on to the cinch as tight as I could. I tried to focus on the count instead of the massive beast under me that was giving me the ride of my life. He bucked harder than I remember, or maybe it had been that long since I had done this, but he was ruthless. *One...two...three.* He spun, his entire body going to the left. *Four....five...*he spun again, this time flinging my entire body with him to the right, bucking higher than anticipated, and I lost all control and grip on the horse, flying off.

"Oh shit." I heard Rhett's voice and saw a flash of black to my left.

Adrenaline pumped through my veins as I tumbled through the air. I had to land on my feet. If I didn't, this newfound courage to try again was going to disappear before I had a chance to fully embrace it. I hit the ground, both boots digging into the dirt, and pain shot through my left leg. But I was on my feet. At least I didn't land on my ass. I kept my body moving, my legs flying in a full jog as I watched Lachlan grab the cinch and pull the horse back through the arena gates, slowing him down. Once the horse was running in a circle, moving to trot, my pace slowed—but my heart was still racing.

"Cash!" Abi's voice got louder. I turned and saw her running through the dirt towards me.

"Six point eight seconds," Kyla shouted, but her voice was dull, because my entire focus was on the woman running towards me.

"Are you ok?" she screamed as she forced her body to stop, her breath heavy. She grabbed onto my arms and looked at my legs, taking in my body with worried eyes. "You flew and I...damnit Cash." She used her entire body strength to punch my shoulder. She could definitely throw a punch. My shoulder ached, but all of her attention was on me.

"I'm fine Abs, I mean..." I lifted my left leg. "I can feel it but..."

"But what?" She met my gaze. "Do you need to sit, do we need to—"

"No Abi." I grabbed her shoulders, taking her by surprise. "That felt..." I smiled. "Amazing." I swallowed, feeling my heart beat through my chest. I could feel my body shaking, everything was moving so fast and I...loved it. "Absolutely amazing." I said softly before wrapping my arms around her, pulling her to me in an all-consuming hug.

She was stiff, but soon, her arms wrapped around my waist, and she relaxed. She buried her face in my chest and she inhaled, then exhaled a shaky pattern that matched my own. I wasn't sure what was making my heart race more. The almost seven seconds I lasted on a bucking horse...or finally having Abi in my arms again.

Thirteen

Abi

THE ARENA WAS ODDLY quiet after the events of last night. I spent the morning looking at the dirt as if it didn't even happen. It was as if it were a movie, not a real thing. Watching Cash on the back of that horse did all kinds of things to my mind and heart that I didn't exactly want to admit. I was terrified the moment that chute opened. It brought me back to Sylas's last ride, and it felt like I was in that moment. This was a horse—not a bull—but by just pulling on the horse's hair, I felt how tense he was. He was going to buck Cash off in an instant. And the last time Cash was on a horse, it fell on him, causing a complete disruption in his life.

But there he was, on a bucking horse, because I told him to take his own advice. And then—even after only lasting six point eight seconds—the look on his face was nothing short of excitement. He did it. For the first time in God knows how long, he did it. The fear vanished once I made it to him, grasping him in my hands to feel how solid he was. Even though his body was shaking, he was stronger than he gave himself credit for. And the first thing he wanted to do once his feet were on the ground was hold me in his arms.

I was trying to think of anything else other than Cash's arms around me, but I could still feel the warmth he brought to my bones. I could still feel him when I mucked all the stalls. I could feel the butterflies as I fed the goats and pigs. I could feel his warmth, even against the chill of the air, while I worked in the milking barn. I couldn't shake the feeling, but I wasn't sure I wanted to.

"Calving season is going to come up faster than you think," Lachlan said, breaking me from my stupor as he touched a cow's swollen belly. "We need to move all the mamas in the barn."

I gave the cow a kiss on her nose. "And no late calves this year," I added, referencing Kyla's favorite baby cow Josie, who still had yet to be tagged. That cow had become Hartwell Hills' Mascot.

"As far as I know, none conceived late."

"How many calves are we expecting?"

"Close to fifty this year I think..." Lachlan trailed off, dipping his chin before taking a step away from the cow. He rubbed his hand against his Wranglers, flexing his palms before reaching up to remove his hat.

My cousin had never, not once, let himself go in the years that followed his breakdown. He was built and lean, perfect for ranch work, and with the warmer weather hitting Idaho, he had begun to roll his long sleeves up in the field piece, showing off his tattoos on both his forearms. The one arm a cascading Lily of the Valley flowers, and the other showing off feathers. Both held a special meaning for him. I loved seeing them just as much as he did, even if he never talked about them. It still shocked me that he was single, though I knew he wasn't looking, especially after what had happened to Hadley, but still—the guy deserved something.

If I could feel that warmth again, couldn't he? I watched him, his movements smooth as he went from cow to cow. He deserved something other than the hand he was given. His brow furrowed slightly, and that small line in between his brow appeared as he looked from me back to the heifer next to him. Lachlan was focused. Lachlan was determined. And Lachlan needed something to brighten his life.

"Stop looking at me like that," he grumbled as he worked, bringing me out of the stupor that was thinking about something other than the task at hand.

I grinned. "Like what?"

"Like you're trying to set me up with one of your friends."

"My only friend is Kyla and she's taken, so I can promise you I'm not setting you up with anyone."

"Then stop making me a Tinder profile in your mind." He turned his back, giving the cow one final pat before making his way to the next.

I gasped, following him. "That's a good idea, actually. I can just see all the matches you would get."

"Stop it."

"Mama!" Stetson ran into the barn at full speed, his backpack bouncing up and down, the massive amount of keychains he had jingling with every step. I smiled at him, enjoying the sunshine he always brought with him everywhere. "Can I go on a ride with Uncle Rhett? I can saddle up Marsh all by myself."

I nodded, then noticed my brother waltz in the barn behind him. "We won't be out long, just a quick ride around the pastures. Moving cattle tomorrow right Lach?"

"Last year you had a random girl in your bed that you just had to get back to. You're not going to be rushing out on me again this year, are you?" Lachlan said as he bent to accept the hug from Stetson.

Rhett grinned. "Watch it, that 'random girl'"—Rhett air quoted—"Is always in my bed now. But you know I'd still rush out just to get back to her. Come on Stetson, let's go saddle up."

"Be careful," I shouted as both Stetson and Rhett made their way out of the barn. Rhett waving his hand in the air as if to say 'I got this.'

"When are they gonna tell everyone the news?" Lachlan's question caught me by surprise. One of his eyebrows was raised, and both hands were on his hips as he watched Rhett lead my son towards the stable.

"What news?" I acted dumb. As far as I knew, Kyla had told Rhett. She told me he was just as happy as she was, but they weren't going to tell the family until they had their first appointment. They wanted to soak it up for a while, living in their own little bubble.

Lachlan's head tilted my direction, that single eyebrow still raised pretty much to his hairline. "Don't act like you don't know. He hasn't said a word to me, but it's obvious she's pregnant."

I narrowed my gaze and pointed at him. "Don't say a word."

He raised his hands in defense. "I won't, just wondering when he will drop the bomb."

"It's not a bomb."

"What's not a bomb?" Another voice entered the barn, one I hadn't heard in a few weeks. My twin brother sauntered in, a smile on his face as he approached us. His baseball cap was backwards, his blonde hair sticking out in all directions under it, his red plaid shirt unbuttoned and his converse shoes throwing everything off. Nothing about him screamed ranch, he was way too clean.

"Nothing." Lachlan and I said in unison, a mirroring smile forming as Wyatt made a look, a pinch in his eyebrows in complete disbelief.

"When did you get back?" I kept talking, hoping Wyatt would ignore the entire conversation he walked in on. He wrapped his arm around my shoulders, pulling me in for a side hug.

Wyatt was older than me by three minutes, and he was taller than me by almost a foot. We looked almost identical, the same blue eyes, same shade of hair, same skin tone...everything that screamed we were twins. When we were younger, we were inseparable, always doing things together even if it meant us getting into trouble. He was my best friend growing up, then he developed his voice and went into the rodeo world. He was gone all the time in the circuit, announcing at any rodeo who would take him, working his way up to the Utah Days of 47 last year; hoping to get to Las Vegas in a few years. He always put his name in the running, but we never knew how close he got to being chosen.

"Just now." He squeezed a little tighter. "Already saw Stetson and Rhett and had to come in here before I went up to shower before dinner."

"When do you head out again?" I asked.

"Already trying to get rid of me?" He leaned back and looked down at me, pinching his brow. "Come on Abi…"

"No, believe it or not I like having you here."

"I'll be around for a bit," he responded, giving me his award-winning smile.

I smiled back, actually happy to have my big brother around. He may have some setbacks, but I did love having him home. I rested my head on his shoulder and wrapped my arms around his waist.

"Good." Lachlan broke the moment. "We've been working on fixing things up around the ranch, and I could use your extra hands."

I pulled away. "Your idea—boarding horses and using the arena to train? It's paying off. We're already boarding a few horses now." I squeezed his waist.

Wyatt looked amused, but only somewhat. "Glad I'm good for something."

"Yeah well, get ready to work. Cash and Rhett have been helping, too."

I felt my brother stiffen. Cash Callahan was not Wyatt's favorite person, mainly for what happened between us. Wyatt was the only person who saw me break after Sylas died, and he's kept that moment between us, just like I asked him too. But when he saw me needing Cash, and Cash completely erasing me from his life, he took it harder than I did.

"Cash?" His voice deepened.

"Yes, Cash. He's helping and he's using the arena," Lachlan defended.

I patted his shoulder and stepped away from him. "I'm ok with it. Just so you know."

"I'm not."

"Wyatt, just..." I gave a small laugh, remembering what Lachlan had told me. "Put your big boy pants on." I tapped his shoulder again, "Welcome home."

"So..." I drew out the word, sitting next to Kyla that night on her porch. I had a beer in hand, Kyla an iced tea. According to her it was the only thing besides water she could keep down lately. "When are you going to let the cat out of the bag?"

"Soon," She answered. "Now that Wyatt's home, we can tell everyone at the same time. Then there's my mom." Her eyebrows pinched, she added, "And Grace."

"You're not worried about them not being happy are you? I mean, Rhett was ecstatic," I teased, taking another pull from my beer.

Kyla let out a small giggle. "He was. You were right, nothing to worry about with him. My mom may be shocked with how soon it is, and since we're still mending our relationship. Grace will be pissed I didn't tell her first, but..." She shrugged. "I think your mom knows, she always asks me if I need anything or if I want a jolly rancher."

"You aren't very subtle with your morning sickness."

"You try being sick twenty-four-seven," Kyla protested.

"I was. I have some tips I can share with you, plus, it will get better."

"I hope. I don't like feeling sick all the time." She shifted in her seat, placing her palm on her stomach.

"It's temporary." I smiled at her. "I'll write down my tips before I head out. Which is soon. Stetson needs to read me a chapter still, and there's school tomorrow."

"Oh no. Before you head home, we need to talk about last night."

"What about last night?" I acted dumb.

I was distracted by Lachlan planning calving season, Wyatt coming home, and the moving cows into the barn, and it only helped cool the feeling in my body for a millisecond. As soon as the tasks were done and I was back to my normal routine, the memory of Cash's arms around me seeped back. I even hung around the stables for as long as I could, hoping Cash would show up, maybe pull me in for another embrace. But he didn't come in. I texted him, asking if he was planning on coming by today, but like always, no response.

It only added to the confusion. Cash and I were friends, he was Sylas's best friend—I shouldn't be constantly checking my phone to see if he had texted. I shouldn't be wanting...more.

"You know exactly what I'm talking about."

"It was just a hug." I said, trying to even convince myself.

"That was not just a hug. Coming from someone who called Cash an asshole less than a month ago and threw a brush at his head—"

"Kyla." I frowned at her, exasperated. "It was just a hug between old friends. He was excited, I was excited. It just happened."

Before Kyla could respond, her jaw opening to no doubt give the best remark to that, I heard hooves hitting the ground with force as Buckle galloped up to the porch. Rhett was alone, his hair completely disheveled and a look of pure terror on his face.

"Hey Cowboy," Kyla smiled, only to fade once she really saw the look on his face. "What's wrong?"

Rhett looked at his wife and then me. "Stetson and I got separated—"

"What?" I shot up from my chair. "What do you mean got separated?"

Nerves shot through my entire body as my heart rate began to pick up. I could feel my limbs starting to shake as I glared at my brother.

Rhett swallowed. "We went to the lake, rested the horses and then on the way back...we started to race and when I looked back...he wasn't there."

"Rhett!" I screamed, anger bursting through the air. "And you ran back here instead of following the horse!?"

"He knows his way back to the ranch. I was hoping he would come here." Fear streaked across his face as I tried to keep mine at bay.

"He's seven, and that's eight miles of land for him to navigate in the dark! Kyla"—I turned back to her, and she looked just as terrified as I felt—"Call my parents please. Get them on the land."

Kyla already had her phone to her ear before I dashed off the porch, looking at Rhett. "Please get your ass out there and find my son before the sun sets all the way."

Rhett didn't even respond; he kicked Buckle and flew off towards the pastures. My heart raced; panic was setting in, but I had to stay logical. I had to remain calm and find my son.

When I was twelve, I got separated from a group, and it took me a while to find my way back home. I ended up going to the lake and followed the river back to the gardens, but that was in broad daylight. It was getting darker. Though I had taught him the land, that logical side of me wasn't loud enough. My son was missing. He was alone. He was somewhere on the land, without a source of light...

My body began to shake as I watched Kyla pace in the house while she spoke on the phone. The sight of Rhett on Buckle getting smaller and smaller...all I could think about was how helpless I was. How helpless and afraid Stetson must be. I placed my hand on my chest, told myself to breathe, and tried to pull myself together.

Pulling out my phone, I went for the one name I wouldn't think I'd go to in time like this. I would have thought my first instinct would be Wyatt, or Lachlan...anyone but who I chose.

I ran to my truck as the phone rang over and over as I tried to reach Cash.

FOURTEEN

Cash

CHARMING WAS RELAXED, HOOK was chowing down on fresh hay, and Nova was enjoying her nightly brushing. I wasn't concerned when I came into the barn to only a ranch hand mucking out the stalls before the horses came in from the pasture. As much as I wanted to see Abi, it was probably a good thing she wasn't here. I would have wrapped her in my arms again.

That's all I could think about.

All. Day. Long.

Abi in my arms.

Me in hers.

It happened so fast. One minute I was flying through the air, focusing on nothing but the dirt in front of me. The next, she was in front of me, asking if I was okay, and I couldn't help myself. I needed to feel her. Her heart was beating just as fast as mine, but the moment her arms wrapped around my waist, the world slowed. Our breaths matched, and everything made sense.

It wasn't until Rhett's loud 'Whoo-ee' rang in my ear that we came back to reality. She looked at me, our gazes locked for mere moments before she smiled and said, "You did it," soft enough only for me to hear. Then, when Lachlan and Rhett appeared at our side, she quietly left the barn.

But that didn't stop my mind from racing.

I laid in my bed that night, staring at the ceiling, sleep far from happening. Each time I closed my eyes, I felt her arms around me, felt her heartbeat next to my chest, heard her voice in my ear.

You did it...

To try and return my train of thought to normal, I'd avoided the ranch during the day. I could keep myself busy with other tasks, but no matter what I did, Abi found her way into my mind. Even Quinn mentioning her at a physical therapy appointment—just hearing her name—turned my stomach inside out. The jolt of electricity that shouldn't be there was shooting through my arms and legs. And all from hearing her name?

I shook my head and wrote it off as excitement that we were becoming friends again. She was finally opening up and smiling when I was around. It had taken weeks, but maybe the hug was the breaking point. The reminder that we were and always would be friends, no matter what happened in the past five years.

Yeah...that was it. That was the answer.

Then why couldn't I get her out of my head?

I never noticed her scent as strong—cinnamon with a hint of maple. I never noticed the dark blue specks in her eyes until I held her close and our gazes locked. I never noticed the way her lips had the most perfect Cupid's bow. I never noticed the way her breath shook as she inhaled. It caused an entirely new sensation in me.

I wouldn't have noticed those things before. But now she was right in front of me. Now...I could notice those things. I wanted to notice them. I wanted to discover more.

That *more* from before...

Hook snorted—pulling me back to reality. He shook his head and then bobbed it up and down, heavy breaths coming from his nostrils.

"You got your attention," I said to him, turning back to Nova in front of me. "It's her turn now."

Hook shook his head again, completely turning away from me just as I began to hear rushed footsteps coming into the barn, followed by heavy, scared breathing.

"Lachlan! Uncle Rhett!!!" The scream echoed around me.

Tossing the brush to the ground, I left Nova's stall and watched as Stetson ran into the stables, a look of fear on his face. His cheeks were completely flushed as he rushed in. The moment he saw me, he screamed my name, his legs moving faster than before.

"Stet?" I questioned, lowering myself to his level as he bar-reled into my arms. "What the hell happened?"

His breathing was quick, and between each breath, he spoke. "I fell off Marsh," *Oh shit...* "And he took off..." *Shiiit...* "Uncle Rhett didn't hear me fall, and it was getting dark, and I didn't know how far I was and...no one is at the house... where did everyone go?" His body began to shake as he tried to catch his breath. I held him tightly, taking deep breaths to try to calm him. I could feel his heartbeat, rapid thanks to the run and his fear.

"Breathe, bud..." I muttered into his shoulder. "Breathe."

Moments passed, I'm not sure how long exactly, but soon he calmed. His breaths matched mine—in and out, slow and deep. He sniffed and pulled away, tears streaking down his face.

Standing up, my arms settling onto his shoulders, I looked around the empty barn. Buckle was gone, so was Onyx, but other than the few missing horses, everything seemed normal. There was only the one ranch hand when I got to the ranch, and when I thought about it, I hadn't even seen Lachlan.

"I'm sure they're in the house..."

"No," Stetson mumbled, reaching up to wipe some tears away from his face, "I went and looked, no one was there."

"Alright, dude." I reached in my back pocket for my phone. "I'll call Lachlan, someone is around." Lachlan's number was the first in the recent list, tapping his name I brought my phone to my ear.

"Cash?" Lachlan's voice hit my ear, sounding just as scared as the little kid attached to my legs. "We can't find Stetson. He went riding with Rhett and—"

"I have him."

"What?" Lachlan shouted, "Abi!" His voice was faint when he screamed her name.

"He just ran up. How long have you guys been out looking, and why didn't you call me?"

"An hour or so, maybe longer. I figured you were with Quinn, but...where are you?"

"The stables. Stet just came in. He looks kinda beat up."

Bending down, I looked at Stetson, really looked at him. His shirt was covered in dirt, his jeans were torn at the knees and his hat's rim was bent and facing in a direction it should be.

"He said he fell off Marsh."

"He *what!?*" I heard Abi's voice. It was faded, but loud enough to know Lachlan had me on speaker.

"Tell Abi to calm down. He's okay. He just had a tumble. How many times have we fallen off horses?" I reassured everyone, including myself, as I took in Stetson's face.

Lachlan let out a small chuckle. "More than I care to admit. Okay, Abi will come back in the truck. Rhett's on Buckle, and I'm on Onyx, so we will head that way. My folks went out to the lake. Wyatt went out to the grazing field. Kyla's at Rhett's place. Wanna bet who will get there first?"

"Abi. One hundred percent." I pulled Stetson into my side, giving him a comforting hug. "You got a first aid kit here? I'll start patching him up."

"In the tack shed."

"On it. See you soon."

We hung up, and before dashing to the shed, I looked down at Stetson. "You good?"

"I'm never getting on a horse again." He mumbled, tears now slowly rolling down his cheeks.

"I doubt that. I thought you wanted to be a bareback rider like Lachlan?" I squeezed his shoulder, offering some reassurance.

"Not after falling off Marsh." He shook his head, his knuckles raising to wipe a tear away.

"Marsh is a big horse, Stet." I ran my fingers down his shoulders to grasp his hand. "But never say never. Come on, let's get you cleaned up before your mom gets here."

"Marsh ran off." Stetson sniffed. "He knows the way home, right?"

"He'll be fine. If he doesn't show up tonight, I'll go out tomorrow and look for him. It's a big ranch but not that big." I led him to the tackle closet, hoisting him up on the worktable before digging for the first aid kit. "He'll come home, I promise."

Stetson nodded. "At least I didn't break any bones."

Tilting my head, I gave him a grin, "Yeah, that's a good thing. You'll be back on that horse before you know it."

He shook his head. "Nope." He shook his head faster, then watched as I pulled out the hydrogen peroxide. "Well," he finally sighed. "Maybe."

"You love that horse." I placed the gauze on his knee, getting a hiss from him as the sting hit just right. "How did you fall?"

"Something spooked him, and he bucked."

"That's it?"

"Well, Uncle Rhett and I were racing home," he admitted sheepishly.

"Ah ha, there is more to the story." I chuckled, raising my chin to look at him, giving him a smile. I had done some stupid shit in my day, too. I'd given my parents a run for their money. Stetson was just having fun with his uncle.

"Well...don't tell mom. She won't like it, and I'll get grounded."

I raised an eyebrow. "Secret is safe with me, little man."

Stetson nodded then added in a whisper. "I fell off, and Uncle Rhett didn't see. Marsh took off one direction and Uncle Rhett the other. My leg hurt..."

"So, you...." I urged him on.

"I went the wrong way."

"The wrong way?" I raised a single eyebrow, staring at the boy in front of me.

"I tried to follow Marsh...and then it started getting dark...and then I realized how far away from home I was. I ran...but when I got there, no one was there."

"And you didn't see anyone looking for you?"

He hissed again once I added a bit more pressure to the scrape on his knee. "Am I in trouble?"

"No." I said faster than I could even think. "You came here, and that's the smart thing to do. But we may want to invest in a phone for you, or maybe one of those watches."

Just then I heard the crunch of tires approaching the stable. The headlights brightened up the dark entryway, and Abi's blonde hair came into focus seconds later. She bolted from the car, leaving the door wide open and the engine running.

"Stetson!" she screamed, rushing towards the tackle shed. "Oh my God, Stetson. What happened!?" She pulled him into her arms, her entire body shaking as she tightly closed her eyes.

"He fell off Marsh," I answered for him, seeing as he was buried in her hair.

She shot me a look. At first it was full of anger, heat behind her eyes, but then after a few moments they softened. Her lips quivered as she held her son close. She blinked a few times before a single tear fell. Then, taking a deep breath, she closed her eyes tight and pulled her son at arm's length.

"Good thinking coming here," she said, her voice becoming more solid, her back and arms less shaky. Even though tears were forming, they refused to fall. All except that one, single tear.

I had the urge to wipe it away, to take them both in my arms. Abi was scared, an idiot could tell that, but for Stetson, she was pulling herself together. She didn't need to be strong. She could break here, with me and Stet. She could break, and I would be there to catch her.

"I went home…"

"We were all out on the land." Abi's voice shook slightly. "I made everyone go out to look for you. The house was dark…"

"But I saw the light in the stable." Stetson looked at me. "Cash was here."

Abi's gaze hit mine for a flash, less than a second. "He was." She sniffed and turned back to her son. "Come on bud, let's get you home and in a bath and in bed."

"What about Marsh?"

"We'll go out tomorrow and look for him." She helped her son off the table, and gripping his hand tight, led him out of the barn.

"Night, Stet," I said, no longer wanting to be ignored.

Stetson turned and waved to me. "Thanks Uncle Cash."

I waved back, standing frozen in place as Abi left the barn. If it wasn't for the moment our eyes met, I would have thought I was invisible.

Marching into the stable the next morning, I was determined to find that white horse for Stetson. I was on a mission. I would saddle up Nova and not come back until I had that stupid horse in tow. I just didn't expect my mission to be halted by a beautiful blonde, already saddling up a horse.

"Morning," I said to Abi as I approached Nova.

She didn't say anything. She just kept preparing her Palomino horse, aptly named Twinkie.

"Are you going out to look for Marshmallow?" I asked, opening up Nova's stall.

She twisted her lips and nodded.

"Me too."

She hummed.

"We could ride together? Maybe find him faster?" I suggested.

"I'm not stopping you," she grumbled.

Furrowing my brow, I looked over at her. "Are you mad at me?"

"No, why would I be mad at you?"

"Because you're acting like you want to throw a brush at me." I shoved my hands into my pockets and took one step closer to her.

Abi let out a long, loud sigh before she tilted her head and met my gaze. "I'm not mad, I'm just..." Shaking her head, her breath shook.

Her mind must still be reeling from last night, and from the looks of it, she didn't sleep at all. Her eyes were heavy, puffy from crying, and the dark circles that had formed were weighing even on me. Her hair was hanging over her shoulder in a messy braid, and her hat sat lopsided on her head. She was wearing a Carhartt jacket, keeping her warm from the morning air, but easy to carry once the sun beat down on her. She was prepared for an entire day on the back of a horse to make her son smile.

I had the urge to pull her close to me, to take away everything that settled in her chest.

Without thinking, without even telling my body what to do, I took one large step and swooped her into my arms. Just like the other night, she was stiff, but once that first shaky breath left her lungs, she melted into me. The world stilled when her arms wrapped around my torso and she buried her face in my chest. It just felt right, having her in my arms.

I rested my chin on the top of her head. "He's ok," I reminded her.

"I was just so...scared," She stammered. "Rhett was ...terrified. He didn't know what to do or what to say, and then we all left...it was dumb not to leave someone at the house..."

"Hey." I gently touched her chin and pulled her up to look at me. "He's fine, you did the best thing you could do. I'm just glad I was here, that he was smart enough to come to the barn."

Abi nodded, her arms locking tighter around my waist. "Yeah, he's..." She sniffed. "He's a smart kid. He just was so damn worried about that horse."

"He said he's never going to ride again."

Abi laughed then, and a smile escaped her lips. "Yeah, I'd like to see that happen. That boy loves that horse more than anything."

I laughed with her, feeling the tension leave from her body. "He does." I cupped her face in my palms for a moment, wiping away a tear that fell from her cheek. She inhaled, blinking once before she took a step away from me. Foolishly, I let my hands trail down her arms until our fingers brushed. The moment, as much as I didn't want it to be, was over. I returned to Nova, reaching for the saddle blanket that was hanging over the stall. "You could have called me; I would have come out with you. That way your mom or Lachlan could have stayed behind."

"I..." she started, her voice cracking. "I..."

I looked over at her, seeing the pinch in her brow as she was frozen in place, her eyes locked on me. Then, like before, she blinked.

"I must have forgot." Abi let out a deep breath and finished cinching up the saddle. "I'll go get us some water while you saddle up. Be right back?"

I nodded. "Yeah...I'll be here."

FIFTEEN

Abi

MY PLAN WAS SIMPLE. Go find the damn horse. Not find yourself wrapped in Cash's embrace, feel lighter because of it, and then go find the damn horse. Now here I was, riding on Twinkie next to Cash as we looked around the land for Marshmallow. I was angry. But I was calm. I was extremely frustrated. But I was...content? I was mad at Cash, yet I was happy he was here. I wanted to punch him in the face, but I wanted to be in his arms again.

Basically, I didn't know what I wanted or what I felt.

You could have called me...

I did. I dialed his number three times, each time it rang and rang. It didn't even go to voicemail. I sent a text but like the others I had sent, it went unanswered. So, either he had changed his number and he assumed I knew about it, or he was having fun playing off that he wasn't getting my messages. Messing with me somehow.

When he said that I wanted to bite back that I had, but instead, I made up some excuse that I had forgotten. When, in fact, he was the only one I called. I didn't know why I wanted him there, but next to finding Stetson, Cash was the only thing that traveled through my mind. I thought with him helping, with him there, I would have handled the situation better, instead of going batshit crazy and making everyone leave in a car or horse back to go find my son. The night could have turned out so much different if he were with me.

When I saw Stetson with him, my heart lifted a tiny bit. He was safe, with the one person I wanted to be safe with. I had to remind myself that he didn't answer his phone, he wasn't there for me, but he *was* there for Stetson. I couldn't decide if I wanted the anger or the gratefulness. In the end I focused on what was really important: my son. He was more important than anything, so I did what I did best, and I was there for him.

Last night I lay with him close to me, my heart still racing, my mind on Cash.

Why did I want him so close to me all of a sudden?

Was it because of that hug? The first one in years? Because if I'm getting all flustered over a hug, then I really need to get my emotions in check, because I never—*ever*—would have had these thoughts about him before.

"Do you think he went to the lake to find water?" Cash asked, looking over his shoulder at me.

I kicked Twinkie to trot to catch up to him. "Maybe. We're not that far from the lake. But there's still snow around."

"I say we hit up the lake and then follow the stream."

I nodded. Good thing he was thinking logically. My brain was all mush. "Good plan." I turned Twinkie, following towards the lake.

"Where's Stet—" He paused "—son," he corrected himself.

I grinned. "I let him stay home from school. He's with Kyla."

"How's his knee?"

"Fine. Scraped up, but thanks to Dr. Cash last night, he'll survive."

Cash kept his gaze forward, but he smiled, a small chuckle vibrating through the air. "He hated me for cleaning it out."

"He could never hate you," I admitted.

"You didn't hear the hiss he gave me."

"Sounded like a snake, didn't it?" A smile tugged at my lips.

"A poisonous one," Cash mumbled.

I couldn't help but let out a scoff, "I've heard that hiss a time or two."

"Yeah, but you're his mom. You're supposed to get the hisses. I'm fun Uncle Cash." He straightened his back and wiggled his shoulders, showing he was proud to have that title. "I let him on roofs and teach him how to fix shingles. One day, I'll teach him how to ride bronc and before you know it, he'll be riding in the rodeo."

"He wants to do bareback; did you know that?" I raised my eyebrow at him.

"I did. I won't lie, I was hoping he'd choose saddle bronc, but I can see how he wants to take after his real uncle...cousin?" He furrowed his brow. "Lachlan is his cousin?"

I let out a laugh. "Technically, Lachlan is his first cousin once removed, but he's always called him Uncle Lachlan. He wants to be like him. He's seen his past events on YouTube."

"What about his dad's?"

Taking a deep breath, I shook my head. "No. At least...not with me."

"What if he wants to ride bulls? He's gotta learn from the best?"

Bulls. Sylas. Why did he have to bring that up? We were having a good conversation.

"No." My voice was cold and toneless.

He caught my bluntness, and the air grew tense. The subject needed to change, and fast. Sylas was not a conversation I wanted to breach. I didn't even watch bull riding on the TV or during the Fourth of July Rodeo, what makes him think I'd even let Stetson anywhere near a bull? I didn't even like the idea of him riding bareback—hell, mutton busting—a bull. Fuck no.

I clenched my teeth to stop myself from saying anything further. Instead, I looked ahead and tried to will a white horse to appear.

A few moments of silence later, Cash cleared his throat. "So..."

I side eyed him.

"Lach tells me your dad's finally retiring? That the ranch will be yours?"

"And Rhett's, but he wants me to take the majority of it." I swallowed. This wasn't a topic I wanted to think about either. He wasn't helping the 'figure out your emotions' battle I was having with myself.

"I can see why." A sigh left him as he moved on Nova, straightening his back and tilting his head from side to side. "You're invested in this place. I can tell you really love it."

"I do," was all I said.

It wasn't a lie. I loved this land. It was beautiful. The trees were starting to get their leaves, and slowly but surely the green would consume the land. The blossoming trees near the lake would add the light pinks to make the spring shine. Spring time was supposed to bring the sunshine to the ranch, and for the most part, it did. I loved the colors and watching the ranch come back to life around me.

And with the man on the horse next to me, his concentration ahead of him, helping spruce things up, I couldn't wait to see what it would look like. The barn's red paint stood out against the muted colors, and once the fences around it were fixed, it was going to be perfect. Absolutely gorgeous.

But still thinking of taking over the majority of the business, having my name on the title caused my throat to swell and my palms to sweat. I could even feel my heart begin to beat in an unnatural rhythm. It wasn't about the numbers anymore. We were starting to catch up, looking good for this month to actually make a profit with the new horses we were boarding and Cash using the arena, but we still needed more. Sure, I no longer wanted to call David and take that offer we turned down months ago, but there was a lingering feeling in the back of my mind that I hadn't told anyone. I hadn't even admitted it out loud. I didn't know if this is what I wanted. Did I want to be sitting behind a desk all day while Lachlan was out on the land? Not really. I didn't want to constantly stress over the finances until I didn't sleep at night. I didn't want to be in charge. I wanted to...

I wanted to...

"But?" Cash looked at me, his body swaying as Nova moved over some rough land.

"But?" I parroted.

"Your 'I do' sounded like there was a but at the end of the sentence."

"There isn't." My shoulders stiffened. There was a but. A long but. *But...*

"You sure?"

"Yes. I'm sure. One hundred percent." I sighed.

I don't want it. I don't want to own the ranch. I don't know how to break away from it...

"You have that look on your face."

I rolled my eyes, "I don't have a look on my face."

"Don't forget I know you pretty well—"

"Knew," I corrected him.

"And I remember when Sylas would ask you to do something you didn't want to do, or when he was doing something you didn't particularly care for, you would get this look on your face. Not to be a dick, but I've seen it a lot since coming here." His Southern twang made every single word stronger, the slight laugh that sat behind them only making my annoyance grow.

I didn't have a look. And I certainly wasn't wearing any look right now.

"Cash, a lot has changed in the past five years."

"Right, it has, but that look hasn't." He raised a brow, pulling Nova to stop.

Not stopping Twinkie until she was a few steps in front, I looked over my shoulder at him. "You don't know me anymore."

Cash's jaw tensed. "I do though."

Remember when I said I needed to get my emotions in check? That I didn't know what was going on? I wanted Cash near me? I wanted to be in his arms, but I also wanted to punch him in the face?

Right now, it was a punch him in the face moment.

I didn't like how confused I was feeling. I wasn't in control of anything.

"Abs, you don't have to put up walls with me."

"I don't put up walls."

He took a deep breath. "But you do, and you're doing it now." His gaze hit mine, the calming his eyes that settled me after seeing him with Stetson was fading as he bore into me, searching me for something that I wasn't going to let him see.

Dammit...I was putting up my walls.

And he could tell.

Fuck.

I swallowed and shook my head. "Cash...you're seeing things. I'm not doing anything. I'm only looking for my son's horse."

I urged Twinkie forward.

"Do you wanna know how I know?" Cash said from behind me, his voice a little louder to catch my ears.

"Please." I turned Twinkie quickly, coming face to face with him. "Tell me how you think you know me so well that you are positive that I'm wearing a mask, that I'm putting up walls. How Cash, when I haven't seen you in five years? How can you possibly know?" My voice cracked as I attempted to keep my tone civil when all I wanted to do was scream at him.

His stare was deep, unmoving as he softly said, "Because I do it too."

My eyes widened. That's not what I was expecting him to say.

"I wake up every day, and my leg reminds me just how weak I really am. But I put up those walls. I wear that mask every single day, so people don't see the pain. I laugh, I smile, I ignore that voice in my head. You may think you're hiding it, but Abs...I see it. I see you. You don't have to put up walls with me."

His voice was steady, calm, and smooth as he searched over me, like he had the ability to peer into my soul, grasping at everything that I've been feeling. Was he feeling it, too? Impossible. He didn't have anything to grieve over, he didn't have any huge decisions to make. He was simply coasting through life, doing exactly what he wanted to do. What *pain* did he feel?

He called himself weak. Just like it was a huge Band-Aid that he yanked off and opened up for the world to see. Was that only the tip of the iceberg when it came to Cash? If you were to look at Cash Callahan, you would see a cocky rodeo trainer. One who knew what he was doing. One that knew how to talk the talk and walk the walk of the rodeo. He was confident and strong. Suave and sexy. He had his life together.

But maybe those were walls.

I see you. You don't have to put up walls with me.

Our eyes were locked.

He saw me.

I wish I could see him.

A neigh in the distance pulled me from his grasp, causing my shoulders to jerk as I moved.

"Look at that," Cash said, his voice still steady. "Right by the lake."

And there he was, a white horse with a crooked saddle shaking his head.

Sixteen

Cash

"**Y**OU FOUND HIM!" STETSON came running up to us once we got Marshmallow back to the stable, Kyla not far from him. "You really found him!"

"Of course we did. He didn't go far." I swung my leg over Nova and let my boots sink into the ground. Before I could turn, I felt Stetson's arms wrap around my waist, squeezing as tight as he could. Glancing up at Abi, still on Twinkie, I noticed the small grin that brushed her lips.

The ride back after finding Marshmallow had been silent. I probably pushed too many buttons, but I could hear in her voice there was something else there, that I was spot on with my suspicion there was more to her 'I do.' But she needed to know I saw her.

It baffled me that others who lived with her didn't notice anything. Maybe their attention was all on Lachlan after everything he went through, but Abi was still right there. Hurting. Grieving something that still lingered. There were a number of things it could have been—the ranch, Stetson's little stint, loneliness in general. But whatever it was, I didn't want her to hide from it anymore. Especially not from me.

Abi dismounted Twinkie, her smile widening as she saw Stetson's look once he let go of me.

"He was right by the lake." She touched her son's back. "Cash knew exactly where to go."

"Can we go on a ride?" Stetson looked up at me, hope gleaming in his eyes as he ran to his horse.

Raising my brow, I turned to Abi, as if to say, *And he thought he would never ride again.* Abi gave me a slight grin, raising her shoulder as her eyes fluttering closed.

"How about"—I gave my attention to Stetson—"We get him cleaned up, out of his saddle, and see how he feels?"

Stetson's grin widened. "I'll go get the buckets and hose."

Taking Marshmallow's reins from me, he led his horse inside the stable. I watched, turning back to Abi as soon as he made it to the washing stall. Shoving my hands in my pockets, I never broke eye contact with her.

"Are you ok?" The question had zero meaning. I knew she wasn't. There were so many other ways I could ask how she was, but yet I settled with that.

Her shoulders rose and she inhaled, nodding with her exhale. "I'm great. Thanks for your help."

She walked away, opening her arms to give Kyla a hug the moment they met up. Rhett gave me a wave as he let his wife and sister in the house. And I was alone, trying to read Abi as she walked away from me.

"I thought you said you weren't going to ride again?" I asked when I watched Stetson use the mounting steps to hoist himself up on Marshmallow.

"I never said that." Stetson situated himself on the saddle, grabbing onto the reins tightly. He was on the horse, but he was as stiff as a board.

The kid had somehow convinced me to let him up on the saddle after brushing down Marshmallow. A bath could wait. Stetson wanted to ride. So, we were going to ride. Stetson was determined, brushing the horse down and making sure he had plenty of snacks before resaddling him. Even Marsh looked excited to ride, bobbing his head up and down after each step.

"Your exact words were 'I'm never getting a horse again.'" I air quoted.

"Are you going to take a ride with me, or am I going alone?" Stetson looked at me, and at that moment he was his father. His eyebrows raised to the rim of his hat, the smug look on his face one I had seen many times when I had told Sylas no to something. And I had to tell Sylas no a lot.

The resemblance made me laugh. I missed Sylas everyday, but here he was in his boy.

"Oh, I'm going with you," I grumbled. "You'll fall off again."

"No I won't." He glowered at me.

"Give me a minute to get Nova. Good thing I kept her saddle on, and we aren't going to go far. I have a training session this afternoon."

"You'll stay for dinner, right?"

"Sure will. I'll never turn down your grandma's cooking." I hoisted myself up on Nova and looked at Stetson, who was still sitting on Marshmallow as if he had no idea what he was doing. He was holding onto the leather so tight , his knuckles were turning white. "You gotta loosen up." I said, bringing Nova up to his side. "Marsh can tell you're stiff. He can feel your unease—"

"I'm not stiff."

"Stet, you fell off that horse less than twenty-four hours ago. I wouldn't blame you for being stiff, but now, your horse can tell." I rolled my shoulders in demonstration. "Loosen your body, let him know you're comfortable in that saddle."

Stetson copied my motion, watching me intently. I rolled my neck. He rolled his. I arched my back. He arched his. I moved my ankles, then so did he. I dropped the reins and wiggled my arms. He did the same. Picking up the reins I laughed, shaking my head as I urged Nova forward.

"What's so funny? I'm loosening up." Stetson kicked Marsh forward. He moved with a jerk, causing Stetson to stiffen once again. "Whoa, boy."

"Don't say 'whoa.'" I pointed at him, glad that Marshmallow missed the command. "That's his cue to stop right?"

"Yeah..."

"Do you want him to stop?"

Stetson looked at the large horse under him, and then at me, his brows pinched. "Yes." He hesitated. "Maybe. No." He took a deep breath. "I want to ride."

"Then let's ride." I kicked Nova into a trot, hoping Stetson would follow. When I heard the hooves behind me hitting the Earth, I laughed. There was no way this kid would let his horse stand there while I trotted away.

Marshmallow caught up to me in no time, Stetson seeming a little more relaxed.

"There ya go." I watched, slowing my mare down just a fraction, allowing Stetson to set the pace. "Now, where to?"

"The lake?" Stetson suggested, already turning Marsh in that direction.

"Lead the way."

We made it there in record time, running into Lachlan and a few of the ranch hands along the way. We sat and rested the horses while we ate the granola bars I had shoved in my saddle bag, and once those were done, Lachlan wrangled both of us into helping fix a fence that got knocked down during the winter.

Keeping a close eye on the time, knowing Quinn would arrive sooner rather than later, I held the pole as Stetson helped nail the board into it. You would never have guessed this kid fell off his horse just yesterday. He was favoring one leg, that was for sure, but he was running, laughing and working just as hard as if nothing had happened. He got back on the horse and worked double time.

Watching him only made me want to get back to the arena. Maybe another ride was in the cards for tonight.

Maybe I could convince Abi to help at the chute again.

I would want Abi there; she would *have* to be there. Either at the chute when I nodded my head, or when I was jumping off the horse after the eight seconds were up. I knew I needed to see her there. She inspired me that night, she urged me to do something I'd be too afraid to do. And she allowed me to hold her, to feel something I hadn't felt in years. With every single interaction since, even when she wasn't paying much attention to me, I felt it.

In my mind, I was playing out Quinn's timeline. We've been here for three weeks, almost four. Her injury was starting to heal. Her PT was going strong, and with the added acupuncture appointments, her limp was gone. With every training session, she got stronger, and soon she would be back at full speed. We had four, maybe six weeks left of training here before we were back on the road and in the circuit. My to-do list with her was about to get longer, and all I could think were ways I could extend the time here.

I wasn't ready to leave Hartwell Hills just yet. I wasn't ready to leave Abi.

Were these old feelings creeping up a little too fast? Possibly. I wasn't even sure Abi would entertain this—she's been so hot and cold, but I still felt it, and a part of me was hoping she was feeling it, too. Even if it was friendship again, I felt the connection. My chest would swell just with the thought of her. I didn't want to force anything down anymore; I wanted to keep feeling this.

We made it back to the ranch just in time to see Quinn saddling up Hook. I gave her drills to do as I got Nova unsaddled, helping Stetson with Marshmallow as well. Once our horses were settled in the sun with the others, both of us headed back into the arena.

He was my little shadow today.

"You know where you keep the barrels?" I asked him, pushing the gate to the arena open. My boot hit the dirt, forcing my heel back, and a small sting shot up my left leg. I winced slightly. "I only know where one is."

"We have two more. I'll go grab one." He took off to the left, his arm flying up to his head to grab his hat as he ran.

"Who's the kid?" I heard Quinn come up, slightly out of breath and she approached on Hook, bringing him to a complete stop.

"That's Stetson, Abi's son." I took off my hat, rubbing my free hand through my short hair before placing the hat back on my head, raising my chin just in time to see Stetson open up the tackle shed and disappearing inside.

"Abi? I didn't know she had a kid," Quinn questioned, her gaze turning to the shed where Stetson began to make way more noise than I was comfortable with.

"Yeah, I've known that kid since he was born. He's a good one, and apparently..." I saw a barrel roll out of the shed. "He wants to help today."

Quinn laughed. "Alright. Give the kid the stopwatch, and he can time me."

"We're taking it slow today."

"Hell no." Quinn chuckled. "I want to move, so we're gonna move."

"Slowly."

Quinn's chuckle grew as she kicked Hook, shooting him off into a gallop.

"Slow, Quinn!" I shouted.

"Two barrels!" Stetson's voice echoed in the arena as he rolled the two barrels onto the dirt. "I know where to put them!"

"Sure kid!" Quinn came up next to him. "Go for it."

Stetson tipped his hat to Quinn before rolling the barrels in the right spot. Chuckling, I went and grabbed the further barrel, closest to the chute, placing it at the top of the triangle. I motioned for Stetson to come with me back to the gate.. He ran, the dirt flying up behind his boots.

"You roped him into helping you?" Abi's voice sang in my ears as I approached the gate. She stepped up on the railing, her arms folded out in front of her. "I bet he's thrilled."

"It was his idea." The corners of my lips tugged when I saw her smile.

"Oh, I bet. That kid has been begging to come in here with you. First the roof, and now this. He loves this place." She flipped her hair, rolling her shoulders as she moved a little closer to me.

She was biting her bottom lip slightly, holding the smile as her eyes began to search mine for a brief moment before she snapped her gaze away.

I had always—always—found Abi beautiful. Her blue eyes sparkled, and now that I knew there were specks of dark blue nestled there. I had to stop myself from shifting my body close to hers to see them again. The Cupid's bow I noticed the other day was stretched with her smile, but still clearly visible. Perfectly kissable.

Wait...

What?

Did I just think about kissing Abi?

In the many years I've known her, I've only thought about kissing her once...and that was before I knew who she was. That was before Sylas appeared at her side. Sure, I had kissed her temple a few times during hugs, but kissing her...really *truly* kissing her, a knee-weakening, toe curling kiss...that was a thought I knew I couldn't have.

But now, all I wanted to do was lift her chin and kiss her.

Deeply. I wanted to feel her lips against mine. Were they as soft as they looked? I longed to taste her. Did she taste like honey or cinnamon? Would she lead the kiss, or would she let me guide it and take her? Would her hands find the nape of my neck? Would she let me run my fingers through her hair? The biggest question...would I let her go?

Taking a deep, shaky breath, I turned my back to her, leaning on the railing so I could talk with her but not look at her lips. I cleared my throat.

"Rhett hasn't trained in a bit; I thought I'd at least see him on Buckle in this arena once."

I heard her laugh, and my stomach flipped. Yeah, it was a good thing I wasn't looking at her.

"Lachlan is keeping him very busy. He doesn't have time to train. He's taking the year off, but I know he's wanting to get back in next year... He needs to keep up his training."

"I'll get him back on that horse. Speaking of...I was thinking about doing another run tonight, and I was hoping you'd be there. Maybe we can convince Rhett to do a ride after me?" I turned, thinking the moment of wanting to kiss her was gone.

Nope. There she was.

She was so close. All I had to do was close the gap between us, and my lips would be on hers. An entire new door would be open to us, a wall would be broken down. My gaze dropped to her lips, lingering for a moment too long before I flicked my eyes back up. If I didn't know any better, I'd say she was blushing.

I blinked.

I knew better.

Clearing my throat...again...I turned back towards Quinn as she told Stetson how her runs would work.

"I'll be there. Rhett too. I'll have Lachlan grab a calf—or two."

"I would love it if you were there, at the chute again?" I met her gaze, waiting for her answer.

"I'll be at chute." She nodded, her arms stretching out once again before she pulled herself back. Her attention went back to her son. Her eyes blinked rapidly as it was her turn to clear her throat. Not only did I want to kiss her, but I wanted to know what was racing through her mind. "So tonight? Maybe we can even get Lachlan on a horse." Her voice rose.

"Ha," I laughed. "That won't happen."

"Hey, I got you on a horse. I may be able to work some more magic." She shrugged a shoulder. "I'll be in the stable if you need me. I have another trainer coming to look at the space, Wyatt is helping me." She jumped from the gate, her boots hitting with a thud.

"I didn't know Wyatt was back." I questioned, twisting my torso, catching her just in time to see her spin on her heel.

"He got in last night so..." She pointed at me. "I told him to put his big boy pants on, you do the same."

Cocking an eyebrow up, I twisted my lips, folding my arms over my chest. "You know he's the one who hates me right?"

She chuckled. "I say it's a mutual hatred. I know you don't care for him." She took a step towards me and mimicked my stance, her lips twitched as she kept a smile at bay.

We stared at each other, neither one moving as we tried to figure out the other. I was easy to read; I was sure of it. I knew I was looking at her like I wanted more, keeping our eyes locked together. You hear people talk about a tug to the person they love the most. A magnetic feeling that guides you to them and keeps you there, grounds you, and makes everything whole. With the way she was looking at me now, the way I knew I was looking at her...it was there. That pull.

And it was strong.

My gaze dropped to her lips at the exact moment they parted, and a small sigh left her lungs.

"Uncle Cash!" I jumped, breaking the contact to look at Stetson as he ran at full speed towards us. "Miss Quinn said I could keep the time! Can I have the timer?" Stetson was completely out of breath once he made it to me, his hand outstretched for the stopwatch I had shoved in my back pocket.

"Remind her to go slow." I added, handing in the stopwatch.

He took off, heading to the end of the arena where he would meet Quinn.

"He's going to want to do this all the time with you, you know that right?" She paused, my attention fully on her once again. She looked at her boot, the tip of her toe digging into the dirt for a brief second because she flipped her hair, her bright blue eyes hitting me with force. "Hey, um..." Her voice was heavy as she worked through the words. "Thank you, for last night, and this morning and taking Stetson for a ride and just…"

I reached up, using my thumb to gently touch her jaw line, drawing a soft line there. The contact was quick, but warm all the same, and created tingles that were now finding their way up my arm. "Of course Abs. I'm here, you know that. For Stet…for you."

She inhaled a shaky quick breath before she gave me a single nod. "I know, thank you." Then she turned on her heels again. Keeping her chin down, she hurried into the stables, leaving me feeling that zing in my fingers.

SEVENTEEN

Abi

WHAT THE HELL WAS going on?

One minute I was pissed that Cash was calling me out on my walls, the next I was looking in his eyes, studying every drop of brown that was there, hoping he would keep talking. Hoping that I could get some more of *his* walls down. And maybe scoot a little closer to me. So, what did I do? I moved closer to him. The feeling was there even through the light conversation. The butterflies flew like crazy in my stomach, and I could have sworn he was going to kiss me. The way his eyes kept moving to my lips and how his breaths became short and shaky...something was going through his mind that he was forcing himself to ignore. And then he had to go and say he was there for Stetson and me, and then he had to touch me.

One simple touch threw me off. One simple touch sent a buzz through my skin that I felt all through me.

But this feeling shouldn't be here.

He was Sylas's best friend. My *dead husband's* best friend.

With my chin down, I pulled myself into a run. I put as much distance between Cash and myself as I could, heading straight to the main house.

I passed Wyatt as I barreled in the front door, ignoring his, "Hey! I was just heading to the stable," as I said a silent prayer that Kyla was in the kitchen. If she wasn't, I was about to get a run in for the day in the quarter mile to their cabin. Thankfully, Rhett's voice came floating down the hall, followed by a laugh from Kyla.

"I need your wife," I said, almost out of breath, resting my hands on the counter.

Rhett raised his eyebrows. "Hey, Abs."

Abs?

Rhett never called me Abs. I was Sis or just Abi. The only one who called me Abs was Cash.

"I don't have much time, and I need to talk to Kyla," I said again quickly, still trying to catch my breath from my run.

Rhett's lips formed a soft smile, and his jaw moved. He situated next to his wife, getting comfortable against the counter as he crossed his ankles and folded his arms. His expression told me he wasn't leaving.

"You wanna be here for this?" I sternly asked, giving him a knowing glare that I was hoping would cause him to leave.

"Always." He grinned.

Letting out a deep breath, I pretended Rhett wasn't in the room, and I let everything out. "I think I'm spiraling or something because I can't keep my emotions in check when it comes to a certain person who's showed up on the ranch, and I need you to talk me out of doing something stupid and remind me that I hate him."

Kyla's brow raised. "You want me to remind you that you hate Cash?"

"I didn't say this was about Cash," I bit back defensively.

"Who else has shown up at the ranch?" Rhett muttered under his breath.

I let out a long groan. "I really want you to leave." I looked over at him, giving him a silent plea.

Instead, my brother shook his head and wrapped his arm around Kyla. "Not a chance."

Closing my eyes, I held them tight and tried to form the words that were going through my mind. It had been an odd past few days—starting with the damn embrace. A simple *hug*.

"It was when he hugged you." Kyla's soft voice basically told me she was reading my mind. "I knew it was more than a hug between friends."

"And it stirred my brain. I haven't had that kind of..." I trailed off. I didn't want to use the word *love* when it came to Cash. With the way he held me, the way he looked at me, the things he did and said the past forty-eight hours...it almost felt right.

"I give you hugs," Rhett teased, a small pout on his lips.

"You're just as bad as my son when it comes to pouting." I put my hands on my hips.

"Rhett." Kyla glared at her husband.

"I'm just teasing my kid sister." He chuckled, his hand sliding down Kyla's back.

"Now's not the time," she hissed at him.

"Ok, fine. See you soon?" Rhett pushed himself off the counter, kissing Kyla on the cheek and accepting her small nod, before leaving through the back door.

I waited until the door was shut before I let out the breath I didn't know was lodged in my chest.

"Are you ok?" she asked, her voice soft—caring—almost like a mother.

"I'm really tired of people asking me that," I admitted.

"Who else has asked you that?"

"Since Stetson pulled his disappearing act?" I raised an eyebrow at her.

"OK, fair. But seriously, what's going on?"

"Would you believe me if I said I didn't know?"

"Yes," Kyla said simply. "But I think you need to elaborate."

If only I knew how to.

Taking a deep breath, I willed the words to form.

I told her everything. Cash and Sylas being friends, how we met, how he and Stetson were close, and how he was basically a part of the family. I even told her every detail about Carolyn and how she never accepted us though we tried. The entire time I spoke, I circled the kitchen, my hands moving and my breaths unsteady as they both tried to catch up with my mind. It was a rapid fire of information, but Kyla listened. I hadn't told this story in so long, no one really truly knew the details, yet here I was pouring it all out in the open, the weight of it all lifting from my shoulders and being replaced with something else...a different weight. One I still wasn't sure I wanted to feel.

"He was here you know...the day Sylas died." I forced my voice to calm as Kyla's eyes widened, but I carried on, almost like nothing could stop me from word vomiting all over. "When he fell off the bull Cash was the one to call 911, and he was the one who came to the hospital with Wyatt and me. He was the one to tell me Sylas was gone." I inhaled, my hands doing the motion of 'breathe in, breathe out,' before I began again.

"And then..." I placed my hands on the island once more to steady myself and looked at Kyla. "Well, he vanished. He didn't answer any of my phone calls, none of my texts, and he stopped coming by. Suddenly, two of the most important people in my life were gone, and all I could do was pour myself into this ranch and being a mom to stop thinking about losing my husband and my friend. I couldn't be sad. The only one who ever saw me break was Wyatt, and even then, it was once at the hospital. But that's why he's not keen on Cash—he saw the hurt he caused, and he saw how I broke."

"Abi," Kyla's soft voice carried in the air between us. I simply waved her off.

"It's okay. If anything, pretending to move on helped me...move on." I rolled my eyes at myself. "I mean, I haven't because I'm still pouring myself into the ranch, but then when I finally feel like I'm getting a hold of thing, he appears. And Kyla..."

"You hate him."

"Yes. No." I groaned. "I don't know. I love having my old friend back. I want to let him in and go back to how things were. And now, my stomach will flip when I see him, and I'm not quite sure what to do with that feeling. So, I remind myself that he's telling me I can call him, I can text him that he never left, but then I do call him, and he doesn't answer. I text him and he never looks at the message. Then he shows up in the stable right when Stetson needs him, and I can't be mad because he's comforting my son and then he helps me find the damn horse and just knows *exactly* what to say to push my buttons and then he gives me these looks..." At this point I was rambling—no periods or commas needed here. I couldn't stop the words from falling from my lips. I still didn't know how to piece everything together. I never had issues voicing my emotions. Or was that because I never voiced them? I bit my bottom lip to shut myself up. "I want to be mad at him," I said once I finally caught my bearings. "But it's very hard to be. Kyla, I cannot control my emotions right now, and I need you to tell me to hate him so it can go back to normal."

Kyla's eyes met mine for a moment, her brows furrowed as the worried expression took over her face. "Abi, have you ever considered seeing a therapist?"

I jerked back. "That's not going to help me *right now*. I need *you* to tell me to stop."

"I see a therapist, and it helps. She's helped me deal with what happened with David and get grounding exercises. She's even seen Rhett and me a few times and—"

"Kyla," I interrupted her. "I'm not against therapy, I just don't need therapy."

"I'm a firm believer that everyone can benefit from therapy." Her eyes met mine once more, compassion flooding them. "Abi, I can't be the one to tell you to hate him. There's a lot to unpack there—Sylas, Cash showing up, these new feelings—"

I waved a hand in front of her again. "No, no new feelings are there—just—tell me to hate him."

She shook her head. "I don't think I can do that Abi."

"Why not?"

"Because...you're saying things that make me think you don't hate him, that there *are* new feelings whether you like it or not."

"Like..." I edged her on, hoping she'd enlighten me.

"Your stomach flips? You love that he's here. He's there for Stetson and says all the right things..."

I shook my head rapidly. She had a point, one that I wasn't ready to accept. "I just hate feeling this way. I don't like being angry."

"Then don't be mad at him anymore." Kyla leaned against the counter.

"It's not that simple," I muttered.

"It could be. Cash seems like an amazing man. He cares about the ranch, he's helping without being paid. He adores Stetson, and I can tell by the way he looks at you that he missed you, too. Maybe he's not sure how to respond to your messages, or maybe he's just as confused as you are. So maybe....don't be mad at him anymore."

"That simple?"

Kyla shrugged her shoulder. She rounded the island and pulled me into a side hug. "You are the sunshine to the ranch, even if you are hiding something deeper that we are unaware of. You're not one to hold grudges. You're the one who takes the reins and pushes through no matter what. Take the reins here, talk through all these emotions—I'm here if you need to vent—and decide if you want Cash in your life for a while, or for a season. Either way it works...but that stomach flip?"

I rolled my eyes. "I'm trying to ignore that."

Kyla let out a small chuckle. "Which is fine, but it really could be *that* simple to not be mad at him anymore."

Cash stayed for dinner. He sat across the table from me, Stetson settling in right next to him. The entire time, Cash carried on conversation with my mother, asking her if she was looking forward to her retirement coming up, which turned into all the trips she and my father had begun planning, which then turned into when the ranch would get handed down to Rhett and me.

I found it hard to concentrate on the conversation.

My concentration was on the man in front of me. Not on the ranch.

Could it really be that simple to just stop being mad at him? There was too much there to just stop being mad...right? Clearly, I'd have to talk to him first—one hundred percent clear the air when it came to him. Tell him why I threw that brush at his head, ask him why he still hasn't answered any of my messages, ask him why he left, everything would need to be answered before I could just stop being mad.

With how open he was this morning, telling me he saw himself as weak, I knew he would have no issue sitting down and talking with me. It was up to me to find the courage to do it. It had been so long; things had bottled up for so...damn...long. I wasn't even sure how to begin the conversation.

Do you have a minute…I'd like to clear the air here…

Hey so I'm noticing things, and feeling things I didn't before…but so I'm not angry all the time, wanna chat?

Don't take this the wrong way…but…so I don't hate you…can you tell me why you vanished?

Did you mean to just toss us aside?

Nothing seemed good enough. It would have to happen naturally. An 'in the moment' type of conversation.

But there were things that weren't there before. I noticed the way he was looking at me. A soft smile would appear when we made eye contact even for the briefest second. His eyes would trail and linger on my lips before he would return to the conversation at hand, but the moment he could, his focus was back on me. I could feel him even if I wasn't looking, and as hard as I was trying not to look, I always found my gaze flickering back to him.

I had to force myself to not think about those flutters that were growing in my chest.

And before I could do anything—before I could even pretend to acknowledge whatever it was that was 'fluttering' in me—I had to talk to him.

"Quinn seems to be doing better." My mother lifted her wine glass to her lips as she looked over at Cash.

"Yes, ma'am." Cash leaned back into his chair, resting his arm on the back of Stetson's chair. "She rounded the barrels this afternoon and did great, needs to gain speed though."

"She'll be back on the dirt before she knows it. Maybe I'll just have to show her how it's done sometime." My mom chuckled, doing a small dance in her seat. If anyone in Alpine Ridge could show Quinn how to barrel race, it was my mother. "Do you think we can get Quinn and you on the board for the Fourth of July, Cash?" Mom gently set her glass down and gave him a pointed look.

"Quinn, yes. Me? No, ma'am." Cash tilted his head. "I couldn't compete again."

"He did get on a horse the other night though," I spoke up. "He says he wants to again tonight. How about it, Rhett? You up for it?"

"Hell yeah." Rhett shifted in his seat. "I need to get some roping in, too. We can have our own mini rodeo in the arena tonight. Whatcha' say Lach?"

"I'll be the pickup again," Lachlan mumbled, standing up with his empty plates. "Stetson, help me with dishes, and then we can go get the calves if your uncle is thinking he's roping tonight."

Stetson jumped up from the table, grabbing his and Cash's plates right before he went to follow Lachlan into the kitchen.

"I told you, you aren't going to get Lachlan on bareback again." Cash's hushed tone barely reached me over the table.

I gave him a cheeky grin. "I didn't say anything. Rhett did. Don't give up so soon."

Cash raised an eyebrow and leaned back in his seat. "I'll believe it when I see it."

Narrowing my eyes at him, I stood from the table. "I'll get the horses ready," I said softly, handing my plate off to Stetson.

"I'll come with you." The legs of Cash's chair moved against the wood floor and before I had any time to protest, he was at my side, his hand finding the small of my back as he gently guided me from the dining room.

The heat from his palm radiated up my spine and to my neck, a tingle causing me to hitch my breath. Once the night air hit us, my hope was the crisp feeling would take away the warmth from him.

Nope.

I was proven wrong.

Even though his hand had fallen away, his warmth was only amplified.

I could feel him around me, hovering, creating those butterflies I didn't want to admit were there.

"What's the best horse for the wildest buck?" Cash jogged ahead of me, pushing open the door to the stable so I could walk in.

"Hmm," I thought, turning to the ranch's horses. "My guess would be Blaze."

"Blaze?" Cash responded. "Please tell me you're not joking when it comes to his name."

"Nope." I spun on my heel, my braid whipping around to fall on my shoulder. "He's Nick's, technically. Well....we own him, but Nick rides him the most. He doesn't really like when others ride him, so he's a bucker."

"Good. Let's get him riled up." Cash rubbed his palms together, a wry grin forming on his lips.

I eyed him up and down. He began to shift from side to side as I opened the stall, that cocky-ass smile only growing as I stepped into Blaze's stall. The deep gray horse bobbed his nose at me, already angry I was waking him, but he let me slip on the lead. I took two steps back, and he followed.

"Where is all of this confidence coming from?" I chuckled, Blaze puffing some air next to me.

Cash's palm reached out to touch Blaze on his nose, stroking down his white patch. "Honestly..." he sighed. "Not sure. Just...with you here, I gotta get on this horse."

I don't even think he understood what those words did to me. He was so focused on Blaze as he stroked down his nose. But I was frozen. I gave him confidence? Just from being here? I watched as he studied the horse, learning the way Blaze breathed for a few beats. He was focused on the horse, cooing at him and talking to him. Saying things like, "You won't buck me off won't you?" and "You're a good guy...I can tell." All the while Blaze bobbed his head and leaned into Cash's touch. I didn't give this man anything. He already had the confidence.

His gaze met mine, his lips twisting into a smile that formed little wrinkles around his eyes. I blinked away the moment, getting my emotions in check yet again. He may have wanted to kiss me in the arena earlier—but if I wasn't careful—I'd kiss him here.

I cleared my throat, remembering my family was on their way.

Forcing myself to remember I didn't need to feel this way.

I pointed to the tack room. "Can you grab the saddle? Or are you riding bareback?" I changed the subject.

Cash was reaching out his hand to pet Blaze once again, but stopped, frozen in place. He tilted his head and gave me a soft, playful glare. "I do not ride bareback."

"Ah." I lifted my chin, finding myself wanting to play back. I wanted to tease and smile along with him. "Only the insane cowboys ride bareback and bulls."

"Insane," he emphasized. "I'll get that damn saddle. You get the bronc rope."

I led Blaze into the arena, grabbing the few necessary items along the way, catching sight of Cash from the corner of my eye. He had the saddle hung over his arm, the long rope swung over his shoulder, his hat tipped on his head, the bridle in between his teeth. He walked quicker to catch up to me, his eyes glowing once he got closer to Blaze.

"Think I can get a ride in before Lachlan gets here with the calves?"

"You need more than just me in this arena before you jump from a chute, so I veto that idea." I ran my hand down Blaze's neck.

"Oh, come on," Cash groaned.

"Nope, he's not too thrilled we woke him."

"Nah." Cash gave his back a pat. "He'll have fun, we talked didn't we Blaze. The event has to be fun for the animal too, right?"

"First rule of rodeo." I nodded. "You think you got this?"

Cash's eyes flickered to me, the small, soft smile lingering on his tight lips. He gave me a small nod. "You're the one who got me back on a bucking horse, you trying to talk me out of it."

"No, no…" I shook my head, breaking the contact to watch as he laid the saddle on Blaze's back. "Quite the opposite actually. I know you can do this."

His smile grew. "Only if you're there to watch me.

As if it were on cue, voices began to echo around the stables, coming in clearer as my brothers and Lachlan came into the arena. Stetson followed, leading two small calves next to him.

"You weren't kidding when you said we'd do a full on rodeo?" I smiled, watching my son take the calves to the holding pen. "You gonna ride, Wyatt?"

My twin shook his head, shoving his hands in his pockets. "Hell no. I'll open the chute and hype you guys up." He looked over to Cash. "Well, except you."

Cash winked at Wyatt. Wyatt's eyes flinched slightly before he stepped away.

"Ah, the announcer." I smiled. "Big boy pants remember?"

I loved my brother and his chosen career. At least I didn't have to worry about him getting trampled by a...

Nope.

Wasn't going to fall into the memory. I was going to be here and here only.

Cash stayed next to me as Rhett did a few runs, a large smile on his face the entire time. He needed this moment with Buckle. Just him and the rope between his teeth. His best time of the night was an eight point nine, and he took it proudly.

"Alright Callahan." Wyatt's voice dropped. "You're up."

Cash looked at me, his eyebrows waggling as his grin grew, then he made his way to the chute. Following him, I looked around for my son, who thankfully had settled himself on the gate, away from everything. Lachlan mounted Onyx and moved to the side of the arena, ready to be Cash's pick-up man.

Cash climbed on Blaze's saddle. He flexed his fingers a few times, loosening them up before wrapping the cinch around his palm. He shifted in the saddle once more before he stilled. He let out a long, low breath through rounded lips before finally giving the nod. Wyatt opened the chute, and Blaze flew out. Literally flew. He jumped, his hind legs kicked once, and twisted, Cash moving with him for each turn and each jump. Cash's arm never once fell to his side, and his body was positioned perfectly. The look on his face was nothing short of determination. Even the small smile of enjoyment peeking out as he was bucked from side to side didn't take that away.

He said he was weak. He said woke up every morning knowing that his leg would remind him just how much he had lost. He put on that mask, he put up those walls...*weak*. I saw anything but.

I saw him.

He was meant to do this.

The entire eight seconds, Cash was focused. He was shining brighter than I had ever seen him, and once the faint buzzer went off and Cash was able to pull Blaze into a gallop, Lachlan came up to his side to pull him off. I realized I never once had that twist in my stomach. I just loved watching Cash do what he was born to do.

Cash jumped from Lachlan's horse, a slight limp to his first few steps, his eyes locked on me.

If he came up and pulled me into his arms again, I wouldn't mind it.

I would relish it.

But he didn't.

Instead, he walked up to the chute where I stood, his arms wide, his smile wider. His eyes locked on me.

"We gotta get that horse in the chute again," he exclaimed, his shout echoing off the arena walls.

I chuckled. "Told you he was a bucker."

He clapped his hands together and then rubbed his leather gloves against one another. He watched as Lachlan led Blaze back into the chute, and the horse gave a loud huff. And Cash? He was glowing. He was strong.

"You were wrong, you know," I said, catching his attention.

"About what? One more ride? I don't think so." He cocked his grin. "Hey Lach!" He shouted, turning his back to me.

"No, not about that." I reached out to grab his forearm, pulling him back to me. "You most definitely can ride again but...you were wrong."

"Okay, I give up. Wrong about what?" A corner of his lips raised in a smirk.

I couldn't help but smile back at him. "You're not weak. After seeing you on that horse, seeing you here...you're the strongest person in this arena."

Eighteen

Cash

*Y*ou're not weak...

You're not weak...

You're. Not. Weak.

You're...weak...

"You're so weak, Cash, I can't believe this is what's happened...I can't believe I married you..."

I shot up, sweat dripping from my brow as Abi's voice turned into Carolyn's. Abi's words stuck in my brain for the remainder of the week, from the moment she said them, right up until she gave me a soft hug goodnight. *You're not weak.* So why my brain had decided to twist them into the last thing Carolyn truly said to me before she asked for a divorce was beyond me.

Carolyn was the reason I called myself weak. She was the reason I knew I would never amount to anything again.

And she didn't deserve a second of my thoughts.

I rubbed my palm down my face, a long sigh leaving my lungs as I took in the room around me. The dresser with the flat screen TV was in front of me, a small red light in the corner. The desk near the window where my computer and sketch book sat, illuminated by the moon from outside. Twisting, I tapped my phone alive, seeing just how late—or early—it really was.

I hadn't had a nightmare like that in a long time. Starting out with something I was drawn to, something I wanted to be enveloped in. Abi. And ending with that horrible twist of something I wanted nothing more than to get away from. Carolyn.

Flinging the covers off my waist, I climbed out of bed, the cool air hitting my bare chest. I flicked on the light on the desk, seeing my sketch book open on a messy drawing of Nova. Flipping the page, I turned to see the sketch of the mountain range, Luna and Nova mid gallop and finally, Abi and Luna laying in the field, and the other haphazard drawings I managed to get from my head on the paper. I hadn't drawn in a long time, and finding the outlet now had become a comfort. I flipped to an empty page and grabbed the pencil that was next to it, pulling out the leather chair and bringing pencil to paper.

An hour later, I had the ranch sketched up, complete with the wooden post sign. Even in messy pencil scratch, this is one I would frame one day. I dropped the pencil to study to sketch, taking it all in. That's where I wanted to be at this exact moment. There. Hartwell Hills Ranch.

With purpose, I went for my phone, bringing the screen to life. Thumbing through until I found Lachlan's name, I typed out a text.

Me

You awake?

I knew he was. It was just past four. He was up and ready for the day by now.

But no text came through.

He must be sleeping still.

Me

I'm gonna head to the ranch early if you don't mind. Can't sleep…see you for coffee in the main house?

Closing my eyes, I breathed in deep when the first image that came to my mind was…

Abi.

Her smile.

Her laugh as a horse would nudge her as she mucked the stall.

Her arms slipping around my waist.

Her soft voice as she said the words, *You're not weak.*

Abi and I had spent the majority of the week in close proximity with each other. She was always in the stables, focusing on the horses that Rhett was supposed to take care of. She loved it, and even though she wouldn't admit it, I knew it was where she was meant to be. Maybe I was just imagining it, but she wouldn't fake a smile. I began to get the genuine ones. The smiles when Stetson ran in the stables after school were the best. The second ones I craved were the ones only for me, the ones where she would turn and look at me before she left the stable, our eyes connecting for the briefest moment. She would smile, I would mirror it, then she would turn and leave, her son at her heels. I would watch until they were gone, taking the smiles with her.

I wanted—*needed*—to be around her more than anything.

Wasting no time, I tossed the phone on the bed and went through my morning routine. Shower, wranglers, boots, meds, and hat. My mind was focused on one thing and one thing only. Getting to that ranch.

You're not weak.

Her voice still rang in my ear.

I pulled up the ranch in record time. With no cars on the road this early, it didn't surprise me. What *did* surprise me was the light coming from the stables. It wasn't even five. Lachlan was more than likely getting his coffee before coming out. It should still be dark. The main house had its porch light lit, a soft gleam coming from one of the windows, but other than that, it was still.

Something seemed off.

Furrowing my brow, I took one step towards the stables.

Hook was in his stall, popping his head out for a pat once I reached him. Charming was resting, Nova bobbed her nose when I walked by—but my focus was on the blonde, walking in circles around the arena guiding a stunning, black horse around.

Abi looked overly tired. But she walked...and walked...

"Abs." I shoved my hands in my pockets and walked onto the dirt. "What are you doing?"

She blinked, her eyelids heavy. The dark circles that surrounded her eyes became more apparent the closer she came to me.

"Hey." Even her voice was heavy. "You're here early."

"Couldn't sleep. Who's this?" I asked, tilting my head towards the horse next to her. He stopped and started pawing at his
stomach, his back leg raising slightly. "He's got colic." It wasn't
a question. I had seen this—and walked—more horses with colic
than I'd like to count. Poor guy had to be just as uncomfortable as
Abi looked tired.

Abi nodded, her shoulders raising with a deep inhale. "This is
Boone." She patted the horse's nose. "He got here at the beginning
of the week, remember?"

Giving her a slight nod, I took another step towards them. I
did remember him coming in. He was a racehorse, here for a few
weeks for some races. I remembered being introduced to him with
a much longer name, but Boone fit him.

"He started showing signs last night. We had the vet come out,
but he had to order medicine from the city. So...we walk until
the medicine can come." She leaned against him, but his nudge
told her he needed to move. "Lachlan walked him until about
midnight, then I took over."

"You've been walking him for four hours?"

"We take breaks. I don't want to over-tire him, but walking
seems to be the only thing that makes him comfortable." She took
a step; so did Boone. "Come on boy...just a few more hours."

"Abi," I stopped her, touching her arm lightly. Her gaze went
from my hand to my eyes. "You need to rest, let me walk him."

"No, I got it. It's my job."

"Technically, it's Rhett's job." I flashed her a grin, giving her a wink. Amazingly, she smiled back, even if it was a sweet, sleepy, smile. "Let me walk him. You have a boy to get ready for the school day—"

"Kyla said she'd get him—"

"Let me walk him."

Her chest moved as she inhaled, then she handed me the lead.

"Thank you," a soft whisper left her lips.

I pulled her into me, then braved a gentle kiss to her temple. I could feel her lean into me, sighing as her entire weight spread over me. She needed to sleep; she didn't need to be here with a horse.

"Go inside. I'll wait for the vet."

Abi stepped away, her arms folding over her chest. She gave me a single nod before turning to leave the barn.

Lachlan arrived as soon as the vet pulled up, his eyes just as heavy and his morning scruff thicker than normal. His eyebrows pinched once he saw me with Boone, but he asked no questions. He accepted me just as simply as he would any ranch hand.

Once Boone was medicated and resting in his stable, Lachlan and I made our way into the main house where hopefully coffee would be waiting for us. I had been walking Boone for three hours, and my leg was sore. Pain shot in all directions. I'll admit I didn't think about my leg when I offered to take over the walk; my only thought was Abi.

"Why the hell," Lachlan started once we stepped into the house, "did you text me at four in the morning?"

"Because I was awake, thought you would be." I rubbed the back of my neck, forcing my body to keep moving. "It's a good thing I just came. Abi needed the rest."

"I was passed out on the couch after walking that horse for hours, or I would have responded. Abi's probably upstairs since she didn't get much sleep either."

"Wrong." We heard Abi's voice float from the kitchen, "I'm in here...with coffee."

I passed through the threshold of the kitchen, seeing Abi dressed comfortably in sweats and a baggy sweater, her hair in a messy bun. The bags under her eyes were still visible, and she still looked tired, but the smile she gave me lit up the room.

"Here." She poured me a cup of coffee, handing it to me with care. "You must be as tired as I am."

"What about me?" Lachlan grumbled.

"Get your own damn coffee," she replied flatly.

Lachlan's eyes widened and twitched as his gaze met his cousin. "Damn Cash, she must be changing her mind when it comes to you."

"I just have my big girl pants on." Abi lifted the mug to her lips and gave Lachlan a sneer, but the look she gave me was anything but. It was...endearing. And it made my heart jump. "Now, if you excuse me, I'm going to go..." She paused, blinking a few times before she looked over at me. "To the stables."

"The stables?" Lachlan called as she left the kitchen. "He's fine. You don't need to go in there."

Gripping my cup, I gave Lachlan one last glance and left, catching Abi just in time before the door closed behind her.

"You should go to bed." I caught up to her quick enough, my strides longer than hers. I found myself at her side faster than expected. But still, I would run after her.

"I spend almost every morning with Luna," she said. "I'm sure Boone is okay, and Rhett assured me he'd muck out all the stalls, but—" She paused. "Luna needs this time just as much as I do."

Staying silent, I stepped next to her, taking a sip of my coffee.

"And you're following me why?" she asked, turning to look at me, that small smile on her lips.

"You need time with Luna, I need time with you."

She hummed. "Okay, I won't mind the company. I may fall asleep, so..."

"That's totally fine. You can even use my shoulder as a pillow."

Walking into the stables, Abi did a quick check on Boone, happy to see him resting, before turning to Luna's stall. She opened it and let me pass before she did. Luna stood in the center, her ears perking up when she saw Abi walking into the stall.

"Ah, Rhett's been here." She took in the cleaned stall, fresh hay on the sides and water in the trough. One less stall for her to muck. "Wanna grab that blanket for me? We can sit on the hay."

The blanket she motioned to was hanging over the gate. I grabbed it and laid it on the floor, moving my body to lean against the wall. Abi was scratching under Luna's ear, the mare happy to have all the attention in the world. She kissed her nose, both of them looking more peaceful than anything, before Abi came to sit next to me. Our shoulders touched as she settled, taking the last sip from her mug.

"Thank you again," she finally said, "for taking over for me."

I nodded. "Did you get any rest?"

"A little, then I helped Kyla with Stetson and couldn't go back to sleep. So, I watched from the living room. I saw the vet come and knew you'd want coffee."

"You made a fresh pot of coffee just for me?" I leaned slightly, looking over at her, faking shock.

She nudged me. "Don't start expecting it." She giggled.

A giggle. Abi giggled. It was a sleepy giggle, one that pulled at the corners of my lips. How can I hear that sound again?

"Never." I nudged her back. "Thank you."

She hummed again, looking up at Luna. The horse moved then, taking a few steps before kneeling down, laying on her side with her head resting on Abi's lap. Abi began playing with her mane. Her fingers threaded through the dark black hair. She seemed at peace here with Luna, even if she was tired beyond all reason. The more I watched her interact with the mare, the more sense it made.

"You don't care that Rhett hasn't been mucking out the stalls, do you?"

She shook her head, her hands running through Luna's mane. "Not in the slightest."

"You like it in here," I stated.

Softly, she nodded again. "I love it here." Her head hit the gate with a bang. "The stables are probably my favorite place on the entire ranch." She shrugged her shoulder. "I've always loved being around the horses. I spent most of my time growing up in here."

"Getting in everyone's way?" I teased.

"Hell no." She looked shocked that I would suggest such a thing. "I was mucking stalls. I was feeding the horses. I was giving them baths. I was riding them, breaking them. I was walking colicky horses all night long. I barrel raced—"

"You barrel raced?" I asked, taken aback that in the years I'd known her I hadn't known that.

"Not professionally, just for fun. I was the flag girl at some rodeos, though. Smaller ones mainly."

My imagination drifted to Abi in her teenage years, spending all of her time with her favorite horses, dressed to the nines as she waved the flag for the national anthem, maybe even entering into Miss Rodeo Idaho. I smiled at the thought. Even if it was all made up, not really knowing who Abi was before I had met her that day at the rodeo, I could see it.

"What are you thinking about over there?" Abi's voice pulled me back to reality. I turned to see her, her neck tilted away from me, both her eyebrows raised.

"You as Miss Rodeo Idaho."

Abi let out a loud laugh that echoed through the stable. Luna lifted her head slightly but laid it back on Abi's legs.

"I would never pass as Miss Rodeo Anything. Miss Rodeo Has-the-Most-Manure-Under-Her-Nails maybe." Lifting a hand Abi looked at her fingers. "I can never keep them spotless."

I looked at her hand. "Do you remember when we met?"

"Oh." She dropped her arm back on Luna's mane. "When you thought I was a buckle bunny?"

I scuffed, "No—"

"I clearly remember you hitting on me."

"How could I not? I saw a beautiful woman standing alone, only my pickup line was terrible."

"Didn't you say something like, 'Is this your first rodeo?'" She mocked my accent, turning to look at me.

Any fear that I had said the wrong thing drifted the moment I saw the blush hit her cheeks. I tilted my lips into a smile. Chuckling breathily, I broke her gaze and looked at her hand. I gently slid her palm in mine, turning to hold her fingers to take in the delicate features, even if she claimed she could never keep them spotless. "You told me, and I think your exact words that day were, "More often than not, I have some kind of shit under my fingernails.'"

"Well, I do." Abi's laugh was light, but fun. Her fingers moved against my skin, slowly wrapping around my own, taking in the moment just as I was.

Me and her, just us. There were no distractions of the ranch to take us from each other, and I had the deepest urge to kiss the pinkish tint that still lingered on her cheeks, and then her lips.

"You look good with that shit under your fingernails," I finally said, almost a whisper.

"I'm not sure if I should take that as a compliment or..."

"Definitely a compliment. You're not a buckle bunny. You're not a rodeo queen or a spotless girl who thinks she knows what it takes to run a ranch. You get your hands dirty. You muck the stalls, you ride and break them, you care for the horses and the ranch. You raise your little boy to be just as strong as you. You're absolutely amazing, Abi. The shit under your fingernails just proves it."

She inhaled, her lips parting softly.

I could kiss her, right here, right now. No one to stop me, nothing to ruin it. And I wanted to. I could almost feel her lips on mine...

Reaching up, acting on pure instinct, my fingers lightly brushed her chin. Her skin was warm even in the chill of the barn, and soft...just as soft as I'd imagined. The specks of blue in her eyes, that perfect Cupid's bow of her lips...

She blinked; her eyelashes fluttered as she took a deep inhale. Moving the weight of her body, she rested her head on my shoulder. Did she know I wanted to kiss her? For the second time in less than a week? She had to have known. She looked as if she wanted me too. Next to me, I felt her body rise and fall with each breath she took. I kissed the top of her head, resting my cheek against her hair.

"Thank you, Cash," she whispered before her breathing slowed, and she drifted off to sleep.

And as I rested my head against her, my body leaned up against the wall, Luna with us, I finally fell asleep too.

NINETEEN

Abi

Five Years Ago

The hospital was too bright. There was way too much white. Even the chairs were white. The stupid painting on the wall of the sunset on the beach had way too much white in it. Where were the blues? The oranges and pinks that came with a sunset? All I saw was a white blur.

My teeth clenched as I sat in the waiting room, Wyatt next to me, his fingers laced with mine as we waited...and waited...and waited. Cash was sitting across from us, his elbows resting on his knees and his face buried in his palms. Rhett had taken Stetson, thank God. He didn't need to be here for this.

I squeezed Wyatt's hand and leaned my head on his shoulder.

You're okay...Mi Alma...

The last words Sylas said to me before the paramedics came still rang in my ears. The sight of him was still ingrained in the back of my mind. The look in his eyes as that glint left him, the blood on his shirt, the soft lulls his breath took, the light slowly leaving him. I would never ever be able to get this out of my head.

You're okay...Mi Alma.

"Mrs. Acosta?" I heard my name, and I instantly sat up. The doctor who had been with Sylas gave me a sorrowful expression. Quickly turning to Wyatt, squeezing his hand tighter, I shook my head knowing there was absolutely no way I could talk to the doctor, sinking down into my chair some more.

Wyatt let go of my hand, looked over to Cash, and they both stood. Fear in each and every one of their steps as they walked towards him. The doctor looked at me, then to Wyatt—nodding before continuing to talk. I saw Wyatt freeze, his back stiffened and then Cash...

He turned and hunched his shoulders, his hands reaching out to the chair in front of him. His grip was so tight on the white plastic that his knuckles blanched. He dropped his head and began to take long, deep breaths.

I needed one of them to come back to me. Even though I knew what was said, it wasn't real until I heard it with my own ears. It couldn't be real.

Wyatt nodded as the doctor left, and he turned to Cash, gently resting his hand on his back while his gaze met mine. Wyatt's eyes were wet with the tears he was trying to hold back, his cheek flushed.

Then—a howl filled the waiting room as Cash snapped, Wyatt's arm jerking back as the chair Cash was white knuckling lifted in the air and flew across the room. It hit with a bang, the echo filling the vapid space as everyone who waited turned to look at Cash.

His fists were balled at his sides, his breaths shallow as he held his eyes tight. Any fear he had from before as he sat and waited was replaced by anger. I had never seen him like this, and now, not only did my heart cry for Sylas, it cried out for him. I was tempted to jump up and pull him in my arms, cry on his shoulders, and let him scream and throw all the chairs he wanted, but my body was frozen. My entire world was being thrown across the room, just like that damn chair.

"Sir..." A nurse said, approaching Cash with caution.

"He's fine"—Wyatt held out a palm to her—"I'll get him out."

"Leave me alone," Cash bit over his shoulder, his gaze landing right on me.

His brows met in the middle as his body tensed. He took ten steps towards me, but his expression didn't soften. Stopping in front of me, his chin lowered.

He stood stone still, looked me directly in the eye, and said, "He's gone."

Toneless. Lifeless. As if it was just everyday news that he needed to share.

He's gone.

Then Cash turned and stormed out of the hospital.

The entire world stopped. The white room turned black, and the last thing I remembered before I crumbled were Wyatt's arms tight around me as he let me fall apart.

Present Day

My alarm clock blared, the familiar sound pulling me from the rest. Crawling out of my bed, my feet hit the cool hardwood floor. I knew today was going to be hard when I went to sleep last night. Today I'd have to face it again.

Five years ago today, I lost him.

Flinging a blanket around my shoulders, I lightly stepped to my dresser, my eyes instantly finding our wedding photo on my dresser. I would never move that picture. It allowed me to see him every day, it always brought a smile to my face. Except for today. Today, I held back the tears.

Today I just wanted to see his bright smile as he turned to face me in the bed. I wanted to hear his voice telling me I deserved five more minutes of sleep. I wanted his finger tips touching my hips, his lips on my forehead. But...I sighed and touched the frame lightly...a photo would do.

It was early still. Not even Lachlan would be up yet. The house was silent, every move I made was amplified. I quietly made a pot of coffee with the glow of the oven light, the drip, drip, drip of the coffee maker sounding so loud in my ears. With the coffee in hand, I settled on the couch, my eyes focused on the rolling hills of Alpine Ridge as a slice of color popped against the dark sky with the rising sun.

Lachlan's rig showed up sooner than I thought, giving me a good idea as to the time. I had been sitting here for a good two hours now, my coffee long gone. I watched as he plopped his black hat on top of his messy hair, sulking up to the door. He knew what today was. He would come in, give me a hug, and then start his day. It's the same thing he did every year.

He opened the door, gave me a nod and waited for me to stand. I walked into his arms. He squeezed, letting me linger there a few moments, his warmth bringing more comfort then he knew, before he finally let me go.

"I made coffee," I whispered.

"Thanks Abi." He kissed the crown of my head, dropping his chin as he turned.

Instead of following him into the kitchen, I went back to my room. Throwing my hair into a braid, I dressed for a ride. I woke Stetson up with a kiss to his forehead, his eyes fluttering open softly. He smiled when I reminded him that today he didn't have to go to school. His smile grew wider when it hit him. He always looked forward to today. For him it was a different experience, and he loved it every year.

"Are we going to see Daddy? Can we take Luna?" he asked in a whisper.

I nodded. "Yeah, I'm gonna go saddle her up. Get some breakfast and meet me in the stable?"

"Ok, Mommy." Stetson wrapped his arms around my neck and pulled me close, tugging at my heartstrings.

The moment I walked into the stable, Luna peeked her head out of her stall. She knew, too.

"Hey girl," I cooed as I slid my hand down her nose. "Wanna go for a ride?"

"A ride?" That low, Southern drawl sang through the hollowness of the stable, and a small smile spread on my lips. "On Luna?"

He was here. My chest began to swell.

Cash walked up to me, his gait seamless as his arms moved in sync with his steps. He wore a tan cowboy hat today, complete with his wranglers and denim button down. My stomach did that small flutter as he got closer, almost helping me forget what today was.

And then it dawned on me. He should be there, too.

"Yeah..." I hummed, turning back to Luna. "I think today calls for a ride."

"What makes today special?" he asked, raising a hand to scratch behind Luna's ear.

Instead of answering him, I asked, "Do you have a training session this morning, or does Lachlan have plans?"

"There's always plans," he answered, leaning his body against the stable door.

"Cancel them for the morning," I said sternly, dropping my arm to my side.

He furrowed his brow. "Why?"

"Well, today..." I took a deep breath. "Today's the day Sylas died. And every year, Stetson and I ride out to visit him. And..." I took a single step towards him, lifting my chin to look him dead in the eye. "I think you should come with us."

Cash swallowed, his eyes widening as his Adam's apple moved. Then, slowly, he nodded.

"I'll come."

TWENTY

Cash

THE RIDE TO THE cemetery was silent. Not even Stetson made a single noise. The only sound was the hooves hitting the ground. It wasn't silent in my head, though. And I couldn't turn my brain off.

How did I forget what today was? How did it not cross my mind that I lost someone so important to me five years ago today?

I pretty much wiped that day—and many that followed—from my memory.

The day of his funeral, I watched as Rhett, Wyatt, Lachlan and three others carried the coffin from the building to the car. And then I left. No one even knew I was there. I didn't even cry. I wouldn't let myself. I was so mad that he was gone. I was so mad that Carolyn didn't care. I was so mad that I missed so much trying to fix something broken. I was so mad at everything, and there was nothing I could do to change it. He was gone...and that was that.

The moment I drove away, Carolyn in the passenger seat scrolling on her phone, not saying a word, I knew my life wouldn't be the same.

Now here I was, heading to the cemetery with Abi, Stetson and my racing thoughts. On the one hand, I was honored she asked me to come. On the other, I was terrified. I hadn't let myself think of this.

Abi was riding Luna with ease. Her hold on the reins was loose, as if Luna knew exactly where she was going. Stetson would kick Marshmallow into a trot, then slow him back to a walk when he went too fast, his back going stiff as if the memory of his fall took him over. The two of them led the way, each moving at their own pace. But I kept back, moving Nova softly through the flat terrain.

I watched them, my heart fighting to feel the warmth that was growing.

I wanted to be here with them. I wanted this moment.

But...

I didn't belong here.

Watching the two of them only reminded me of the way I failed them. I had left, unable to handle the fact that my best friend was dead. I left Abi sitting on that hospital chair, all alone after I told her he was gone. I got in my car and tried to break the anger that had taken over.

I wasn't there for Abi.

I wasn't there for Lachlan, or Rhett...the entire Hartwell family...

I wasn't there for Stetson...

I never got to say goodbye to any of them.

I failed them. In so many ways. And I never got to talk to Abi about it.

I was going to be coming face to face with the man I considered a best friend, and then what? Would I stand there and just stare? Would I ask for a private moment? Talk to him? How dumb would it be to talk to a piece of stone? I could technically talk to Sylas anywhere—he would hear, right? That's what people say? But I never did. So why would I start now and have that moment of weakness when the people who I loved needed me to be strong. Pushing down every single emotion that was running through my veins, I straightened my back, donning the mask I always wore. Abi wouldn't see me break today.

Stetson kicked Marshmallow into a gallop, bursting ahead of us as the cemetery came into view. Abi slowed Luna and looked over her shoulder, her eyes hidden by the shadow of her hat.

"We come here every year." She said it loud enough for me to hear. I nudged Nova, coming right up to Abi's side.

The shadow faded and I saw the emotion in her eyes. She swallowed. "We each take turns talking to Sylas, basically letting him know what's been happening. Stetson talks a lot, just a warning." Through the sadness, she smiled.

"And you?" I choked out.

"Everything we say is private." Abi broke eye contact. "I never ask Stetson what he said, and he never asks me. It's our moment with Sylas...you know. Sometimes Stetson gets animated, and he talks a little louder than he means to, so mainly he talks about Marsh and the ranch. Sylas knows all about Kyla." She gave a small chuckle. "And me, well..." she took a deep breath. "I just like to be with him."

"Do you talk?"

She nodded. "Sometimes."

"Mom!" Stetson screamed, waving his hands in the air. He was already off Marshmallow, the horse tied to a nearby tree. "Can I go?"

"Yeah, we'll be right there," Abi shouted back.

Stetson didn't even wait; the kid took off running, and Abi and I fell back into silence. Together, we dismounted and tied Luna and Nova up to separate trees, then began the walk to Stetson. He was already sitting on the ground, his hat on the top of the stone. With my eyes trained on him, I didn't notice Abi until I felt her fingers against mine. Her palm slid in my hand as if it was something she did every day, a natural feeling of the two of us coming together. We walked in sync as I squeezed her hand. And she squeezed back.

Abi stopped me to give Stetson his time, and her body came close to mine. Her opposite hand found my forearm as she drew me close to her, the warmth of her body colliding with the frozen chill that circulated through me. She rested her head on my shoulder, just like the other night at the stables, and we waited. We stood, watching Stetson as he spoke, laughter and shouts coming from him. Abi would let out soft laughs, but her head never left my shoulder. Her warmth never left my body.

Finally, Stetson stood and ran back to us. Abi lifted her head, and didn't let go of my arm.

"That was a lot to catch up on." He smiled.

"I bet," Abi said softly.

"Your turn, Uncle Cash." Stetson looked at me.

My eyes widened. "Me?" I looked down at Abi. Tears were welling up in her eyes, but she didn't let them fall. Instead, she gave me a nod and dropped her hands.

"It's been a while, right? Go talk to him." She ran her hand down my back, giving me a gentle push forward.

Sylas' stone was a long rectangle, reaching just to my waist. A soft gray that still looked new, as if five years had nothing on it. The words *Sylas Acosta, riding bulls in the sky* were etched into the gray surface. Below his name were the dates, and below the dates, the engraving of a bull rider mid jump. It suited him. I half expected to have a stupid saying on it, something he would have laughed at himself. I took a quick look at the back of the stone, semi shocked to see it empty.

"What," I whispered, feeling odd enough just being here. "No witty remark to get the last word?"

I touched the top of the stone before glancing over my shoulder at Stetson and Abi. Abi stood with her arms around Stetson's shoulders, his body leaning into her. She gave me a nod and a reassuring smile.

"I feel weird doing this," I admitted, "talking to a rock...but here we are. You must be so pissed at me." I laughed, deflecting from the real emotion that wanted to break through. "I bet you're wondering why I'm even here. Why in the world am I pretending like everything is okay when I haven't been here for five years. You would probably give me a lecture. Tell me I was being a complete idiot, and that I needed to get my act together. Then you would laugh, call me some stupid nickname in Spanish, and then we'd ride. I miss those rides. The ones where we would take Stetson and build a fire and roast marshmallows. We would drink and talk about stupid shit. You remember those? I should take Stetson out before I leave and do that. It's warming up enough. Plus, the fire will keep us warm."

I glanced behind my shoulder again. Abi and Stetson had moved, their backs to me as they walked hand-in-hand back to the horses.

"He's a good kid, you know. He helped me with the roof on the stables, and we picked out a color for the barn. Lachlan fought us, but it's red. He fell off his horse a while back, but he got right back in the saddle even after he said he wouldn't. You would be proud of him. I sure am. And Abi...damn Sy if you could see her now. She's amazing..."

I stopped. The pit in my stomach grew.

There were so many things I could say to him now, but only one thing crossed my mind. Only one thing I needed to get off my chest and into the open. But forming the words was a lot harder than thinking them.

Before I could stop them, tears began to well in my eyes, and being here...with just Sylas...I let them fall. I sniffed and blinked through them.

"I'm sorry." I finally spoke, my own voice gravely as the pit in my stomach grew bigger. "I'm sorry I left her. I'm sorry I left Stetson. I'm sorry I..." I inhaled, "I'm sorry I..."

I fell, my knees unable to carry all my weight as I held onto his stone for support. Resting an elbow on my knee I dropped my head, and I cried. I cried as silently as I could, letting every bit of guilt and pain flow through the tears and onto the ground. This was a lot harder than I thought it would be. Opening up, even to a stone—to Sylas—was the one thing I never saw myself doing. And now, breaking down and coming to terms with every single fucking emotion that was flowing through my skin...I couldn't take it anymore.

The guilt.

The anger.

The fear.

The loss.

I thought of Abi.

The love.

Everything hit like a ton of bricks.

"I'm sorry I wasn't there to help her through this. I'm sorry I let other things control me enough to not see what was right in front of me. I'm sorry I never said goodbye to you. I miss you...I missed everything so much, and I want to go back to that. I want to feel that again. It feels so good to be back at the ranch. It feels like home. It feels like I could belong here with them, with her. I know I left, and I fucked it up, but I'm here now, and I want to make everything better. Starting with Abi. I want to make this right. I can see why you fell in love with her. It's hard not to. Ever since the first time I saw her, there was this small flicker—this spark she ignited. And that never went away.

"Did she tell you I hit on her? You know I would have never admitted this while you were alive. I would have never acted upon anything, and now I'm feeling like a shit friend for more reasons than just forgetting that today is the day you died. I probably shouldn't be feeling this way about your wife, but Sylas, I'm falling for her, every day. I want her near me. I need to feel her there. She gives me the courage and strength to get through all of this. She needs it too—I can see it, and I think...I think I can love her just as much as you did.

"I want to make her smile again. I want to take away her pain...

"I want to love her."

TWENTY-ONE

Abi

WHEN CASH CAME BACK to the horses after his moment with Sylas, he wrapped me in his arms and buried his face in my shoulder. He inhaled, grounding himself before pulling me back to arm's length. His eyes were red with tears, but he gave me a soft, comforting smile. The comfort I wanted five years ago, I was getting now. He needed this just as much as I did.

The ride back from the cemetery was lighter than the ride there. I could cut the air with a knife on the way there, but back, we talked, we laughed, we smiled. Cash didn't trail behind us like he did on the ride out; he kept Nova right next to Luna, and we talked about Sylas. We brought up memories of when he first started bull riding and how he would celebrate even though he lasted two seconds on the back of a bull. He was always celebrating, no matter what.

"I would like to think he would want us to celebrate today," I finally said. "Not mope around thinking about how he's not here."

"That's exactly what he would want us to do," he answered, his tone uplifting. "I should call Quinn and cancel today."

"I wish I could. Sadly, the ranch doesn't stop."

My time with Sylas was like it always was, with one simple exception. I told him about the ranch, about Kyla and Rhett expecting their first child, how Lachlan was still fighting any sort of happiness that came his way, and about how Cash was back in my life. And how I was confused about it, but ultimately, I wanted to chase those feelings.

"I'll always love you," I told him softly, reaching out to run my fingers along his name, "nothing will take the way I feel about you away, but I can't deny this."

The time spent at the cemetery with him only solidified that more. It felt right having Cash there. As if he should have been there all along. I was still confused—I was still nervous—but I didn't want to ignore what was growing any longer.

Quinn was at the ranch when we arrived, ready for her training session. Cash dismounted, and I took charge of the horses while Stetson ran back into the house. Cash trailed his fingers down my arm as he walked past, his demeanor changing into work mode.

I watched as Quinn rode, Hook taking each turn with stride, a smile on her face with each round of the barrel. You would have never guessed she fell off her horse the way she was riding now. She lit up the entire arena once Cash called out her time, each ride getting faster and faster. And Cash was shining just as bright.

He clapped and smiled as she zoomed past him, whooping loud enough for her to hear, and once she dismounted without using the block, he ran over and scooped her up in his arms, congratulating her on beating one of her fastest times. I couldn't help but smile as I watched.

Watched him.

And damn....there were those butterflies again.

I still had so many things I wanted to ask him, but I also just wanted to forget about it and move forward. Twice now he had almost kissed me, and twice now I had almost let him. Having him next to me the day in the stables, his body keeping me grounded at the cemetery, his breathing keeping me calm while Stetson was talking to his dad. I could still feel the pressure of his body next to me.

I just needed to talk to him.

But not today. Today was the day we were celebrating Sylas, not bringing up ghosts of the past.

The past week, I had been spending every spare moment in the stables. Stetson was helping with a few tasks Lachlan had managed to add to his own growing list, and Cash had stuck around. I wasn't sure if he was hanging around to spend time with me or to help on the ranch more, but I wasn't complaining about it. I liked having him here. I liked the connection that was growing between us, and I found myself beginning to crave it.

But because of that craving, I hadn't looked at the books all week. I had to catch up before seeing my dad and brothers. So after grabbing another cup of coffee, I went into my office to try to distract my mind, even if just for a fraction of the day.

An hour later, I was answering emails about another potential boarding and a bull rider interested in seeing the arena for training.

"Ok," I whispered to myself, pulling up the calendar on my computer. "Boone is here for three more weeks, the Jackson's horse leave in ten weeks…" I mumbled. "We have three stalls left. That's good. That's great."

"What's great?"

I looked up from my laptop to see Cash leaning against the door frame, his hands in his pockets and hat perched on his head. He cocked a smile, and my stomach flipped.

"Another horse."

"You're gonna have a full house soon."

"We only have three more stalls, but I'm assuming Hook, Charming and Nova won't be here for much longer." I looked up at him through my lashes. "Quinn's doing great, she's going to be back on the circuit in no time."

He nodded, chewing on his bottom lip as he pushed himself off the door frame. "Yeah she's…" His voice was hesitant, almost as if he didn't like the news he was about to deliver. "She's doing great. Her physical therapist says maybe three more weeks."

"Eight weeks on the dot."

"Yeah. Not gonna lie, I was hoping for ten." He flopped into the chair across from me.

"Well," I swallowed. "You're welcome to come train here whenever she needs an extra push."

Cash raised an eyebrow, his eyes boring into me.

You could talk to him now, I thought. *Just get it over with. The sooner the better. Just ask him why…*

Why he didn't come back.

Why he's still not answering your phone calls and texts.

Why he looks like he's going to kiss you at any moment.

I opened my lips to talk, but Cash broke the silence before I could.

"I'll probably take you up on that, especially since Stetson told me I can't leave."

I widened my eyes. "He didn't give you a ring or anything did he?"

He chuckled. "A ring? No. But there's a story there."

"There is. Ask Rhett." I sighed, trying to find a way to bring the conversation back—either to the important topic, or something different.

"I will." He leaned back, his arm slung on the back of chair.

The room grew silent as we looked at each other, the tension growing thicker as I battled in my brain whether or not to talk to him. I had said not today, but he was here, staring at me as if he wanted to say something. As if his mind was running just as fast as mine was. We could get it all out right now, end it and move on. All I had to do was start the conversation.

"Cash—" I began, but he spoke at the same time I did, stopping me from finishing.

"Thank you," his voice was soft. "For letting me go with you today. I really...really needed that time."

I gave him a smile. "Thank you for coming, you belonged there," I responded. "Do you think he would hate that I'm working today? I mean we'd said we'd celebrate."

"There's plenty of time for celebrating. He'd understand you have a ranch to run. You said it yourself, the ranch doesn't stop, but Sylas would probably come in here and pester you."

"He would. He always made sure to pester me."

His lip twitched. "How would you celebrate today?"

If I could spend any way celebrating today it would be with Cash, a beer in hand, sharing everything we could remember. We each had so many stories we could bring up, some the other probably didn't know. I could only imagine what I would get out of Cash. Bring Lachlan into the mix, and it would be a party. The perfect way to remember Sylas.

Sighing, I met his eyes. "With you."

His eyebrows twitched as a shaky breath left his lips.

"I um..." he began. "I know it's supposed to be private but—"

"Abi—" Rhett appeared in the doorway behind Cash, pulling his attention from me. "Dad wants to meet with us."

I sighed and stood, shutting my laptop before scooping it up in my arms. I passed Cash before stepping out of my office. "We'll talk later?" I asked.

Cash gave me a nod before I left him standing there.

"I knew it!" My mother clapped, basically leaping from her seat. The entire table's attention went over to her and watched as her hand covered her lips. "I hate to tell you Kyla dear, but you weren't very secretive."

"I thought I was being very discreet," Kyla admitted, touching her stomach with her hand.

She and Rhett had just dropped the news of their pregnancy, and as much as I adored my sister-in-law, she wasn't as discreet as she thought she was. I smiled and laughed at her, turning to Cash—who'd chosen the seat right next to me for family dinner. He was leaning back in his chair, one elbow resting on the back of my seat. He was so close; I was surrounded by his scent. Leather and amber enveloped me. I even caught myself taking deeper breaths before stopping myself.

"Sweetie," my mom continued, "you could barely eat a meal without getting sick, and when you stopped showing up for family dinners all together..." She cocked an eyebrow and tilted her head to Kyla, giving her that knowing 'I had you figured out' look all moms had.

"The red meat was making me really sick." Kyla sunk into her chair, leaning into Rhett. He laughed at his wife and kissed her temple as he wrapped his arm around her shoulder. "I'm only about thirteen weeks along. We just had our first few appointments, and everything looks great, so...it was time to tell everyone. Only Abi knew."

"And me," Lachlan muttered. Everyone turned to him. Kyla's jaw dropped. He stood, taking his plate with him. "What? It was obvious."

"Does this mean I'm going to have a cousin?" Stetson asked, leaning across the table. "Can I teach him how to ride Marshmallow? I promise I won't let him fall off when he gets spooked."

"Who says it's going to be a boy?" Rhett mimicked Stetson by leaning forward. "Maybe it'll be a girl?"

"Then I'll teach *her* how to ride Marshmallow. My baby cousin needs to know how to ride a horse."

"And they will." I yanked on Stetson's arm, pulling him into my side, giving him a hug. He grumbled and groaned as he tried to get away from me. "I promise as soon as that little baby is big enough, he or she will be on a horse. Maybe even mutton busting?" I looked at my brother.

"You know it." Rhett nodded as he took a bite of his roll.

"Well," Wyatt shouted, his voice carrying over the table. "I say this requires a celebration."

"A celebration?" Kyla repeated. "Isn't the baby celebration enough?"

"Nope. I say we head to The Steel."

"Ah," I lifted my chin to look at my twin. "Because that's the perfect place for a pregnant woman to go."

"No, let's go!" Kyla stood quickly. "I can drink a Dr Pepper. I didn't drink coffee this morning so..."

"Water." Rhett grabbed her hand and pulled her back for a kiss. "You can have water."

She chuckled against his lips before she grabbed her plate. "Abi, join us?"

I looked over at Cash. "Whaddya say? Shall we go celebrate?"

"I'm invited?" Cash asked, raising his brow.

"Of course. Hell, call Quinn." Rhett answered for me.

"Can I come?" Stetson piped up.

"Nope." My dad spoke up this time. "How about you and I watch a few rodeos and then head to bed early."

"You sure dad?" I asked.

"Yes, yes, go." My dad waved us off.

"But I want to go to The Steel," Stetson whined.

"Maybe when you're older, I'll take you." Cash grabbed onto Stetsons, shoulder and squeezed.

"Promise?" Stetson smiled, looking up at Cash.

Cash raised an eyebrow. "Promise."

My heart flipped a tiny bit. Did this promise give good indication he was considering staying? "He'll hold you to that." I stood. "I'm going to go get changed. I probably shouldn't go to the Steel looking like I've been spending all my time in a barn. Oh, wait." I locked eyes with Rhett. "I have been."

"I'll go check on the horses so you can change. Wyatt—" Rhett grumbled as he stood.

"I will start the cars." Wyatt jumped, ready to move. I chuckled as my brother bounded out of the room before meeting Cash's gaze once more.

TWENTY-TWO

Cash

I T HAD BEEN A while since I had been to The Steel, even though Lachlan and I said we would go. This was the first time I walked through the doors since the last time with Sylas. That was six—damn—maybe seven years ago. It looked exactly the same down to the hats on the rafters. Kyla ran to the corner booth, dragging Rhett behind her. Quinn gave my shoulder a pat and then headed to the bar top, to wave down the bartender. Wyatt slipped past me, steps behind Quinn—hopefully to buy the first round—and I walked smoothly to the booth and slid in after Lachlan.

The Steel smelled like cheap beer and burgers, the sound from the grill getting heavier once a waitress opened the doors, carrying the source of the smell.

"And why did you tell us at dinner?" I asked, watching as the burgers floated by me. "You could have told everyone before, and then we could have come here to eat."

"Well, we weren't planning on coming here." Rhett leaned back and pulled Kyla into his side. "I had other plans." He nuzzled his nose into her hair.

"Which can still happen." Kyla kissed him. There was no denying what she was referring to. Her cheeks were deep red by the time she turned back to me, her eyes beginning to search the room. "Where's Abi?"

I twisted around, looking towards the front door. She rode with Wyatt, so I was surprised to not see her after he made his way in.

"Bathroom maybe." Lachlan looked over to the bar where Wyatt was now eyeing a group of girls, not ordering drinks. "How long is it going to take him?"

"Well, did you really trust Wyatt with drinks?" Kyla began to scooch from the booth. "I got it. Cash, whatcha' drinkin?"

"Just whatever is on tap."

"I'll get you the local brew." Kyla smiled.

"Hey Ky..." Lachlan held up his hand.

"I know, I know." She tapped the brim of his hat, reminding him to remove it. "Coke with a shot of whiskey. Be right back."

I stood with the goal of helping the pregnant lady with the drinks, when I was instantly stopped in my tracks.

Abi was at the bar, standing next to Kyla, the brightest sparkle in her expression. I hadn't seen her since she had left the table after dinner. She went to change, and when I saw her last, her hair was still in the messy bun, and the tips of her boots were covered in mud, but now...

Dark leggings hugged her thighs, and brown boots reached almost to her knee. A blue button down shirt was knotted at her waist, a white tank top peeking through. Her messy bun was now in a perfect mermaid braid that hung over her left shoulder. Her blue eyes shone brighter than any other in the place, and she laughed as Kyla ordered, the sweet sound floating through the crowd even here to me.

She was radiant.

I couldn't look away.

I was stunned, and my bones melted. Thank God the booth was right next to me because before I knew it, I was sitting back down.

"And why are you looking at my sister like that?"

Rhett's question pulled me from my stupor.

"I'm not," I snapped, my defenses rising. *I totally was...*

"Yeah, you are," Lachlan agreed. "You have been now for weeks."

"We've all caught on." Rhett shook his head, leaning on the table.

"Caught on to what?" A softer voice rang in my ears.

And that was Abi, standing at the front of the table, her eyes locked with mine.

"Nothing," I said, my voice heavy.

Abi lifted her chin, motioning for Lach and me to move over so she could weasel her way in next to us. She placed a shot glass in front of Lachlan and a pint in front of me. She had her drink in her hand, an Arnold Palmer she probably spiked with vodka—that was her drink, always. I swallowed as I watched her mouth touch the glass, the clear lip-gloss making her lips look even more plump and perfect in this lighting.

I cleared my throat and glanced at Rhett. He was safer, I wouldn't get all flustered looking at him, but his eyes were focused on me, his eyebrow raised almost to his hairline as he pulled Kyla in close.

"You may have to go save Quinn." Kyla let out a small laugh. "Wyatt is working his way down the bar, and I swear he's had eyes for her since he got back."

With that statement pulling me from my Abi-fog, I whipped my head to the bar, relieved when I saw Quinn talking to somebody other than Wyatt. "He talks to her, he dies," I grumbled, lifting my glass. Sure, Quinn was 'just a client', but she was young and didn't need Wyatt Hartwell making moves.

"Ha," Lachlan barked. "She'll turn him down."

"I love how it was his idea to come here, yet he's not celebrating with us," I pointed out.

"Nah," Abi chuckled. "He just wanted a designated driver."

"But he drove?" I raised a brow, finally taking a swig of beer.

"Most likely he'll leave his truck here, or I'll drive him home," Abi remarked.

"Who wants to bet he leaves with..." Rhett leaned forward, his eyes searching around The Steel. "Her." He pointed to a blonde that was currently giving Wyatt *the* look.

Furrowing my brow, I turned to Abi. "Didn't know The Steel was a tourist spot."

"It's not," she replied. "People from the city come here for the experience."

I rolled my eyes and turned back to the table. Lachlan's shot glass was empty, and he was now sipping the Coke Kyla had brought him. Kyla had water with lemon, and Abi was already half done with her Arnold Palmer. Then there was me with my beer still full, only the one sip missing, when I normally would have chugged down the first half in five minutes.

"So," Abi began, leaning across the table to Kyla. "Names. Tell me names."

"Well, if it's a boy…" Rhett began.

"Nope." Kyla put her hand over his mouth. "We're not telling until they are born."

"What! Everyone had a say in Stetson's name," Abi protested.

"You named him after your favorite hat," Lachlan piped up.

"I did not. Besides, a Stetson was Sylas's favorite hat. I wanted to name him something different, something Sylas's Latina mom would approve of, but no. He wanted to go *country* like his dad did while naming him. Sylas isn't exactly a traditional Hispanic name." Abi chuckled, most likely enjoying the memory of her husband. "So we compromised. Stetson Alejandro Acosta. Martina protested once we told her the name, she wanted us to flip it. Alejandro was her father's name."

"See." Kyla pointed at Abi. "The way you said his mom protested. I don't want anyone judging our names before they are born, and yes, we've picked them already." With the same hand she had pointed at her sister-in-law, Kyla rested her chin on her fist, narrowing her eyes at Abi.

"Once Rhett's tongue gets a little looser, he'll let us know," Lachlan said smoothly.

"In that case, come on Mr. Hartwell. Let's go play pool." Kyla grabbed her husband's forearm and dragged him from the booth.

"She's going to beat his ass." Abi moved to the other side of the table, her gaze meeting mine in an instant.

I felt my knees shake again. I couldn't get over how stunning she looked, how absolutely perfect. If I thought there was something going on before—those times when I almost kissed her, those times when I did touch my lips to her skin—looking at her now there was one hundred percent something going on with me and this woman. Saying it out loud to Sylas's grave this morning just made it more solid, more true. I wanted to push Lachlan out of the booth, wrap her in my arms and kiss her senseless. I wanted to taste the lemonade on her tongue and feel her skin under my fingertips.

Yeah...everyone most definitely caught on to the looks I was giving her. There was no hiding them now as we held each other's gazes.

Lachlan elbowed me slightly. "This is awkward as fuck. I'm going to go play darts." His elbow hit deeper in my side, forcing me out of the booth. I stood and watched as Lachlan left. And now, Abi and I were alone.

Did the air with us get that thick that fast, or was Lachlan just being polite and letting me have a moment with her?

Abi lifted her half empty glass to me. "To Sylas?"

I clinked her glass. "To Sylas."

"Do you think he would be happy Kyla shared the news today?" Abi asked, a slight tilt to her. "You know he loved having the attention on him."

I nodded, "One hundred percent. I think as long as we are celebrating something, he'd be happy. He knows we love and miss him. He would be thrilled to know that we were drinking to a pregnant lady. He'd drink more just for her." I leaned my head back, hoping to pull off the same kind of enthusiasm Sylas would have had.

She smiled. "He would have been. You're right—that man just wanted to party for everything."

"Stet got his enthusiasm. After helping me with Quinn's practice, he was jumping, asking me when I could get him on the back of a bucking horse."

"Oh God," Abi grumbled. "He loves the rodeo. He wants to do it all."

"Kid asked if we could watch my old rodeo videos."

"I think seeing you in the arena the other day gave him that idea. He's absolutely enamored with you."

"Enamored?"

"Extremely. When you leave, the kid will lose it."

"Enamored," I parroted once more, the word ingraining itself in my mind. Then—stupidly, I didn't think before I spoke. "Wanna know who I'm finding myself enamored with?"

"Let me guess, Stetson? You love him just as much as he loves you," she asked, leaning back in the booth.

I laughed, lowered my chin, and shook my head lightly. "No, not Stetson." I lifted my gaze. "You, Abi."

She froze, and her lips slightly parted as she tried to find the words. So far, I had called her beautiful, almost kissed her—twice—and now I was basically telling her I was falling for her. Saying it out loud to Sylas this afternoon was only the beginning. Now that he knew, all that was left to do was let her know exactly what was on my mind. Her. Always her.

"Was that too forward?" I asked, making sure my tone was strong, confident. I had to be confident here, especially if I was really going through with this. I didn't want to tiptoe around this anymore. I didn't want to question how I was feeling.

Dammit, I *knew* how I was feeling—and all of me thought she was feeling it too.

She shook her head and moved fast, her fingers going to her drink. I narrowed my gaze and watched as she picked it up and chugged the rest of it down.

"Hey," I said, reaching across the table to take her hand.

Her fingers floated around mine, and she inhaled, pulling her hand back to her lap. "Wanna play darts?"

She stood, leaving her empty glass on the table to join Lachlan and the dart board. I slipped from the booth, grabbing her hand again before she could get any closer to her cousin.

"No, I wanna dance." I spun her close, stopping for a brief moment to allow myself to feel her against me, before I led her to the open area where other couples were already dancing. I saw Rhett watching us as I wrapped my arm around her waist, pulling her closer to me once more, her warmth spreading over me. To my surprise, her hand squeezed mine as her other reach up and sat softly on my shoulder. She fit against me like a glove, like she was meant to be there.

Two pieces to a puzzle.

"You don't dance," Abi whispered.

"I dance." I pressed my check to her temple, thankful that a slow song started the moment I got her on the dance floor. Some female country singer rang in my ears, my senses filling with her cinnamon and maple fragrance. "I just never danced with you."

"Well." She hummed, raising her chin and arching her back to look at me. "You're not missing much. I'm not a good dancer."

"That's alright, I'll lead you."

She shook with her inhale, her body stiffened. She was trying to relax into my touch, to let me take the lead, but I could see her fight response was taking over. I swallowed, and once again pulled up that courage.

"Sorry," I mumbled.

"For?" she asked, lifting her chin.

"If I'm being too..."

"Forward?" She parroted my apology from moments ago. "You're not," She said simply.

"I'm not?"

"Could *I* be for a moment?" She raised her chin, the questioning look on her face throwing me for a complete loop.

What's going on inside that head Abi Acosta? "Be my guest."

"What happened between you and Carolyn? Why did she leave? Why did you...celebrate?"

I raised my eyebrows, completely off guard. There were too many reasons to go into. One—I wasn't what she wanted; I no longer belonged to that upscale life she craved. Two—we weren't good for each other. We never were. I settled, trying to find the same happiness that Sylas had with Abi. Three—my accident changed more than just my ability to compete in the rodeo...and, well...that reason was better left unsaid.

"That's a complicated answer, one I'm not sure we have time for."

"No holding back Cash. You can tell me anything." I felt her fingers brush against the nape of my neck as her eyes bore into me.

"Anything?" I smiled. "In that case, can I be more forward?"

"How?" Abi raised a single eyebrow.

"By not holding back."

"And what exactly are you holding back?"

"Everything." I said softly, just loud enough for her to hear. I was holding back more than just my past with Carolyn. I didn't want to talk about the past in this moment. I wanted to be present with Abi.

She arched her back slightly. "Everything?"

I gave her a single nod and flattened my hand against the small of her back, pulling her even closer to me.

"I've always thought you were beautiful, gorgeous, *stunning*." I swayed us, my eyes locking with hers. "Even when you're deep in a stable, mud on your shoes, and shit under your fingernails, you're the most gorgeous person in the bar. No woman would amount to you. Ever. I consider myself lucky just to be dancing with you now."

She let out a soft laugh. "Next thing I know you're going to tell me you were jealous of Sylas."

I took a deep breath. "I won't lie and say I never had some feelings when it came to you." I let out a small chuckle with my breath. "Hell, I hit on you." Abi rolled her eyes at me, her head turning to the side. Using my thumb and forefinger, I gently brought her attention back to me. "But you and Sylas, that was love. I was never ever jealous of him. You belonged with him in every sense of the word. I was jealous of the next guy. The guy who got to comfort you when you felt alone. The guy who kissed away your fears and laughed when you were happy. The guy who spent time with you in the stables, who watched you flourish after losing so much. I was jealous of the man after Sylas."

She stopped swaying, forcing me to still.

"There was never a man after Sylas," she said nervously, a slight shake to her voice.

"I didn't know that. After Carolyn...after that whole disaster...I would think of you, that maybe...I could come and show you how much I cared for you. But the thought always hit me that you were already happy with someone else."

"I..." Abi stumbled. "I wasn't."

"You could have been. You could have had any guy, though none of them would have deserved you. You're perfect Abi, in every way. I've known that since the first moment I saw you, and I've wanted to show you that. From the second I saw you again, after years...I knew those feelings I've carried...they've never gone away. But I was never going to be deserving of you. So, no." My eyes began to search her, noticing the way her lips parted and the way her chest rose with each breath. "I was never, ever jealous of Sylas. I was jealous of that guy who was going to be next. The guy you deserved."

"The guy I deserve," she repeated, before she rose, and her lips crashed into mine.

TWENTY-THREE

Abi

CASH'S FINGERS THREADED THROUGH my hair as he pulled me deeper into him. His kiss was just as I imagined, just as intoxicating. I let out the softest sigh, and Cash took the bait, sliding his tongue in to meet mine, sending a shock wave through my entire body. Everything was pushed from my mind as I began to float, and this kiss was the only thing keeping me grounded. I clutched the nape of his neck. I gripped his shirt, becoming greedy with him. He couldn't get close enough, even though our bodies were flush against one another. I needed more of him.

Everything around me faded as Cash's fingers slid under my tank top, his calloused fingers only adding to the current that flowed between us. He broke the kiss for a second, allowing both of us to get some air before he claimed me again, this time his palm against my back, as the desire got thicker, stronger—flooding me.

I was drowning.

And I didn't want to come up for air.

This felt right; this felt so good. *He* felt so good. His body against me, his hands on my skin, his lips dancing with mine. Everything felt so...so...

No.

Not tonight...

My senses returned in a rush, the loud noise from the bar hit me like a ton of bricks and it suddenly hit me *who* I was kissing.

Cash.

No.

I broke the kiss, the sizzling desire of the moment before still buzzing in my veins, but no, no, no...

I moved faster than I planned, pushing him away to arm's length, feeling my entire body shake and heat rise in me. This wasn't what I was supposed to be doing with him. This wasn't supposed to feel so right. I had so many things I needed to do first, so many things I needed to say. We needed to be friends again. I wasn't supposed to *want* him. Not tonight, not like this.

"Abs," he groaned as he stepped back into my space, his hand lightly touching my elbow.

I met his gaze. He was breathing rapidly, most likely just as quick as I was. His eyes were heavy, and his lips...

I dipped my chin, ignoring the urge to kiss him again.

No.

"No..." I whispered. "This....I can't..."

I couldn't form the words. I wanted to kiss him, but I wanted to yell, to scream. I wanted to wrap myself in his arms and just....

Forget.

But the urge to scream was louder.

I used my weight to push him, watching as he stumbled back a few steps before I turned and stormed through the crowd, determined to leave this feeling. Everything about it could stay right here in this dingy bar. I couldn't do this.

"Abi!" I heard Cash shout, but his voice was faint as the shivers from the kiss were replaced with shaking.

He said he didn't deserve me.

He said he thought about me.

He said he cared about me.

He was saying all the right things to make me forget what we needed to talk about, everything that happened and I wouldn't—couldn't—just forget.

"Abi!" His voice was stronger now that I was outside, the chill hitting my face, taking the heat away. "Abi stop!"

"No." I shouted over my shoulder, my anger rising.

"Don't put up these walls, Abi."

I felt his hand grab my wrist, yanking me to a stop, spinning me to look at him.

"Don't—" he began.

"No, you *don't*. You don't get to ignore me for five years, erase me from your life, and then kiss me like that. You don't get to tell me I can call you and then never answer your phone. You don't get to do this to me, Cash," I screamed, pure rage falling from the same lips that kissed him, that still—for whatever reason—wanted to kiss him again. I let out a loud groan, lifting my head towards the sky as I cried, "This wasn't supposed to happen this way."

But it was...and it was happening in the wrong way. I didn't want to scream at him, I didn't want to push him away, but it burst. Like a volcano, it all came flowing from me, nothing stopping it.

"Abi, I..." Cash's voice was calm as he stood there in shock. His arm stretched out, wanting to touch me. Comfort me?

"Why did you leave?" I burst through the tears. "Why? The last thing you ever said to me was that Sylas was gone. And then you turned and walked out of that hospital, after throwing a fucking chair. You didn't answer my phone calls, you ignored all of my texts. You didn't come to his funeral. You were gone. Like we...like I didn't even matter. When all I needed was my friend." Tears slid down my cheeks, my eyes drowning. I couldn't even blink them away fast enough. My heart was beating rapid fire. My breath was heavy and I just couldn't control it. "I needed you, Cash. Stetson needed you. But we weren't good enough. You were gone...just like that..."

"I was mad!" he shouted.

"Do you think you're the only one who was mad? My husband *died,* in my arms! And then his friend—*my* friend—left. I'm sorry Cash, but I have more reason to be pissed than you do." My shouts were so loud, most likely everyone in The Steel could hear me, and I didn't care one bit.

"You have every reason to be mad, but try seeing it from my point of view. Sylas was my best friend, and I missed so much because I was trying to be a better husband to someone who didn't even matter. I went to see him for thirty minutes because that's all she would allow, and in those thirty minutes, he died. The anger...the fear...it just took over." He took one step towards me, his hands finally moving enough to grasp my shoulders. "I told you he died. I saw you break. I saw the light leave your eyes and I..." His breath shook. "I knew I couldn't do anything. I was afraid to hold you. I was afraid that I would lose you."

I struggled against him, punching his shoulder. "But you did. You made it happen. You're the one who left me. You're the one who walked away. Did you ever consider that I couldn't lose you? That losing you along with Sylas was the last thing I needed?"

"I didn't think—" He fought back, gripping onto me tighter. "I couldn't Abi. I went to the funeral. I sat in my car and couldn't get out. I couldn't see Sylas that way. I couldn't see you that broken again when I couldn't fix it. I just."

I snapped in his face, making him flinch back. "If you say couldn't one more time..." I barked, my voice echoing against the walls of The Steel, the night air carrying it further than I intended.

"Abi, listen to me. I'm sorry. I never meant to leave you. I didn't know if you really wanted me there or not. If I'd known. If I'd had any inkling that you wanted me by your side, I would have been there—"

"You should have been there anyway!" I screamed, using my fist to try to push him away, but he held me. His eyes locked on to mine as he watched me cry, each and every tear coating my face with more anger and fear than before.

"I should have. I should have...but..."

"But what? What was more important that kept you away from us?"

"I wasn't good enough..." His voice fell. "You told me today that I belonged at that cemetery when I was telling myself I didn't. I failed you; I failed him, and Abi—" His tone began to rise, louder and louder with each word. "I can't fail you again. I don't want to, *ever*, leave you again. I'm trying to start now to make it up to you."

I felt my bottom lip quiver, tears still falling. I could still feel the anger surging through me, and the pounding in my heart vibrated so strongly that it felt as if it were going to come crashing through my ribs. He failed us. He knew he did. He admitted it. And he wanted to fix it. He wanted...me.

"I never knew you needed me. I never heard from you. I thought you wanted me gone." His voice shook.

I shook my head. His hands were firm on my shoulders, helping ground me. Chewing on my bottom lip, I reached up and grabbed his neck, feeling his hair under my fingers. I just needed to feel him, to make sure that he was here. "I never wanted that. I wanted..."

"I wanted you in my life." Cash rested his forehead against mine. "I never left you, even though I wasn't here...Abi...I..."

"Abi?" Kyla's voice pulled me from Cash's semi embrace. "Are you ok?"

I took a step back and folded my arms. I looked at Cash, then back at Kyla, giving her a nod. "Yeah but..." I tried to talk, forming any words that would make the most sense. "Cash and I need to head back to the house."

I turned without another word and walked to Cash's truck. Sitting in the passenger seat, I ran my hands down my face and watched Cash say goodbye to Kyla before walking with purpose to his truck.

He climbed in, his face solemn as he stared at the steering wheel.

"This conversation isn't over," he said. "Not by a long shot."

Feeling the tears starting to well, I nodded, and he drove us back to the ranch. In silence.

Cash held my hand as he led me to the porch of the main house. The lights created the perfect glow as we each took a seat on the swing. If it were any other time, it would be romantic, but I was still crying, and Cash's palm had grown sweaty in mine.

I wasn't sure where to start. I had been avoiding this for a while, ignoring the feelings that were creeping up in my stomach, and look where that got me. I had gotten good at hiding my true emotions in front of people. I'd become the master at making people think I was fine and happy when every day I forced myself to be that way. No matter how hard I may try to deny it, Cash saw it. He saw moments I didn't think anyone saw. He saw me. He wanted to make it right somehow.

And I blew up at him.

"I'm sorry—" I started.

"I'm sorry, Abi," he said at the exact same time.

I furrowed my brow and tilted my head. "What are you sorry for? I'm the one who started this."

Cash swallowed, his Adam's apple moving as he clenched his jaw. "For leaving. I never meant to make you feel like I didn't care."

Biting my bottom lip, I took a deep breath. "How else was I supposed to take it? You were gone."

He didn't answer. He lowered his chin so the rim of his hat hid his eyes.

"My husband's best friend, who I thought I was friends with, too...disappeared. I tried to call; I texted every night and even left you a few sobbing voicemails. Not once did you return my calls. Then, I saw your accident. I lost Sylas that way. I couldn't lose you too, even if you wanted nothing to do with me." I shifted on the swing, my fingers still laced with his. I rubbed my thumb on the back of his knuckles and noticed as his eyes found our joined hands. "So, I called, texted and called again...and silence. That's when I decided to stop. That's when I let go of the idea that you were still there."

"Lachlan and Rhett came to see me." He sniffed, raising his chin just enough that I could see tears on his cheeks. He was crying, and I had the sudden urge to wipe them away. But I kept still. "I wanted to ask about you...but—"

"You couldn't." I repeated the word he had used so many times in the parking lot. Couldn't. Couldn't. *Couldn't.*

"I thought I had lost you already."

"Well." I squeezed his hand, and then let it go. "You kind of did."

His eyes met mine for the briefest moment, but a wave of grief flooded him as he looked away from me.

"Why didn't you come back? If you wanted to, why stay away?"

"You're not going to like the answer," he murmured.

"Try me."

"Carolyn." He looked at the darkness, still avoiding me. I held back my eyeroll. Now was not the time for that. I tightened my lips and waited for him to continue. "We had that fight, remember?" I nodded, remembering the day clearly. "And after that, Carolyn and

I had a long talk. She said I wasn't choosing her, that I would rather be with anyone else. I tried to make her a priority. But that meant less time with my friends."

"I knew that," I muttered, still hating the fact that I lost him before Sylas died.

"Then, after Sylas died, it was her in to get me out. She took my anger and molded it. She said so many things to keep me away, and I, still wanting to be the perfect husband for her, believed her. I tried going to the funeral. I sat in my car and watched Lachlan, Rhett, Wyatt. They carried the casket to the grave, and I couldn't help but think I was supposed to be there, too. I was just..." He trailed off, turning his head away from me to look into the darkness.

"Mad." I finished his sentence.

He nodded and turned back to me. "And Carolyn...she was good at manipulating me. She said if you wanted me there, you would have called. If I was wanted at all...you would let me know. And when I got silence, I believed her."

"But I did call you," I interrupted.

He shook his head. "I swear to you, Abi, I would have been here if I knew. I assumed Carolyn was right. That because the link between us was gone...you didn't care anymore."

"The link? Sylas?"

"She said with him gone, the friendship we had was pointless. There wasn't anything there to hold onto anymore."

I muttered under my breath. "That's the furthest thing from the truth."

"It made sense. It was as if the entire Hartwell family was done with me. I didn't hear from Lachlan for a long time, maybe two or three months after the funeral. I finally called him, and we reconnected. Come to find out Wyatt had told him about the whole chair thing, and he was respecting you. But, having him back in my life helped. Carolyn didn't like that. Then, I had my accident, and she left." He swallowed, the pause in his voice making me think there was more to the story, but I'd take what I could get right now. He was opening up, and I wanted to hear every word. "After she left, the rest of the story had to come out. She wasn't happy for a while. I couldn't give her what she wanted anymore—that lavish lifestyle. I was broken, and she made sure I knew that."

"You're not broken." I placed my hand on his leg, gently moving my fingers against the denim. "Carolyn was a..." I stopped, pursing my lips. I didn't want to talk negatively right now. I shook my head. "She can't be the only reason why you stayed away."

Cash's eyes searched me. "You said you called, texted?" I nodded to his questions. "I never *ever* got a call or text. Nothing. I was pretty sure that after I didn't show up at the funeral, you were done with me." He licked his lips, taking a deep breath before meeting my gaze once more. "Like I said...I failed you. I knew I did I just didn't want to think about it."

"Why didn't you call me?" I asked, my voice shaking.

"Well, how I saw it, not only did I lose my best friend, but also my wife, and then you. Like I said, I was pretty sure you were done with me."

"I wanted to be," I admitted. "I was hurt."

"I don't blame you for feeling that way, but Abi...I never ever meant to cause you any kind of pain. I wasn't lying in the bar. I hate myself for making you think that, and I am so...so sorry."

His apology struck me. Where, weeks ago, I would have screamed 'too little too late' in his face, now all I saw was him, and the pain he was trying to let go of. He lost Sylas, he lost Carolyn, and...me. For a while he even lost Lachlan and Rhett. This wasn't one sided, this wasn't all on him or all on me—we both made mistakes. It was time to right them. I tightened my lips and slowly reached out for his hand once more. He watched as our fingers intertwined, his thumb moving against the back of my hand in slow circles.

"I was in a dark place after Carolyn left me," he choked out. "The physical therapy and months of healing...I did it all by myself. I missed you. I wanted to reach out. I wanted to hold you and just...have you. But then I would remember what Carolyn said. That I was weak, that no one would want me after I had lost everything I was. And I convinced myself that no matter what I did, you wouldn't want me the same way I wanted you. I had to convince myself you were happy."

"I wasn't. I haven't been for a long time," I whispered. Admitting it for the first time out loud to someone felt scary. Cash's eyes met mine. "I'm not *alone* by any means. But... I don't have that one person anymore. He's been gone, and the one..." I slammed my eyes shut, stopping the tears before they could fall again. "The one person who I wanted to lean on left. I was alone."

"I'm here now. And, Abi..." Cash shifted, his hand raising to cradle my face. "I'm sorry I ever made you feel like I didn't care. And I know that I'll never be able to make it up to you. But I want to. At the cemetery..."

"We don't need to talk about the cemetery." I leaned into his touch.

"I said goodbye to him," he continued. "I told him I wanted to care for you. I told him I wanted to watch Stetson grow, and I wanted to...God Abi I want to figure all this shit out and—" Lowering his chin, Cash shook his head, a heavy sigh leaving his lungs. "Be there for you. Always."

I swallowed, feeling my heart skip a beat. "We both have some things to atone for," I whispered, taking him in. "Five years of miscommunication we have to work through. Five years of lies, and loss and heartbreak."

"I'm willing to if you are. I meant every word Abi. I've always had feelings for you. And I refuse to lose you again. I may not be deserving of you now, but maybe, if you let me, I can be."

"What are you saying?" I asked, almost terrified to know the answer.

"There's something here, and I think—hell, I know—if we work through this, we can find what it is."

"I've been trying to avoid it," I said softly, shifting my body to face him more.

"Avoid what?" His voice was soft as he moved. His hands went from my neck to glide over my knees until our fingers twined together. The contact sent that same spark through me, and those butterflies filled my stomach again. They flew like crazy, up and down and twists and turns. All because of a single touch? No, because of him.

"These..." Damn, what I was about to say was stupid. I shot up from the porch and leaned on the railing, keeping my back to Cash. "I sound like an idiot," I muttered. "These stupid butterflies."

"Butterflies?" I heard him as he stood, his heels hitting the wood, and then he was next to me. He didn't reach out for me, he just stood and waited. Looking at him, I saw everything in his eyes. Every emotion, every touch, every kiss that could be mine. If I just let it.

"Abi..."

"No more holding back with each other. There's more that needs to be said. I know, but..." I inhaled. "I can feel this too."

"You held me that night. The night I jumped from the horse before the eight seconds was up." I nodded as he spoke, remembering the way my heart felt when I saw him fly through the air. All I wanted to do was wrap him in my arms. "I've wanted you in my arms every moment after that, and I've wanted to kiss you numerous times. This...whatever this can be..."

"I think I want it," I finished for him. "But again..."

"No holding back," he finished for me, his fingers tracing my jaw.

This was happening. Him. Me. Us. Nothing left between us as both of our walls came crashing down.

TWENTY-FOUR

Cash

I COULD STILL FEEL Abi's lips on mine, even hours later. I lay in my bed, my eyes focused on the ceiling, my mind running through the entire night. The dinner, the dance, the kiss, the confessions. She was feeling this, too. Butterflies, she called them. The same knots I had in my stomach were twirling in hers—and she wanted to go for it.

She wanted me as much as I wanted her.

The conversation we started wasn't over. As she said, five years of miscommunication. There were still so many things we needed to sift through in order to make it truly work, but I wanted this. I wanted to have her, fully...not halfway, and if that meant opening up then fuck it. I was going to open up.

The one thing that sat unsettled in my stomach was the phone calls and text messages she claimed to have sent in the past five years.

I told her she could call me, that I would answer. But I never received anything.

Grabbing my phone from the charger, I thumbed through my missed calls, then my texts. Nothing. Absolutely nothing from Abi's number or even an unknown number. That's didn't make sense. I would text her before, and nothing had changed on my end.

Taking a gamble, I went to my settings and clicked on something I never had before. *Blocked Contacts.*

Being on the road constantly, talking to as many people as I had, I never blocked anyone. Not even Carolyn. But fear rose as soon as I saw the only name on the list.

Abi Acosta

"Fuck." I shot up, quickly tapping her name to unblock her. No wonder why I wasn't getting anything—but how?

A quick Google search told me I wouldn't get any texts, but voicemails may still come through.

I left so many voicemails of me sobbing...

A moment went by, but then notifications came through, and there they were. Messages from the last few weeks blew up my phone.

Missed Call: Abi Acosta

Voicemail: Abi Acosta

Missed....missed...voicemail...missed.

She had called me.

Not wasting a single moment, I opened the first voicemail...which according to my phone was left when Stetson went missing. Abi's voice filled the dark space.

"Cash. Come on. You told me I could call you. Stetson. He's...he 's....he went riding with Rhett and Rhett's back but not Stetson, and Cash, I'm scared. I'm trying not to want you here in this moment, especially since you said I could call you and text you and you haven't answered a single one but...Stetson is missing, and I don't know what to do. He knows the land...I shouldn't be as worried as I am...but...dammit Cash, answer your fucking phone! Please."

"It's been over an hour, and I can't find him. If you get this, please come to the ranch. I...God I hate to admit this...I need you here."

"Cash...I just...wait...you're calling Lachlan..."

Her voice died down and the room fell silent.

I didn't sleep.

I just heard her voice in my head.

The sun was just rising as I pulled up on the ranch. I sent Lachlan a quick text.

Me

Any tasks for me today?

Lachlan

I got a few I could use your help on. Let me know when you're here.

Locking my phone, I took in the sight of the stables in front of me. It looked better than when I arrived weeks ago. The new roof had really made a difference, and the barn in the background shined the deep red. There were still things to fix and do while I was able to help, but first...

How the hell was I going to explain to Abi that her phone number was blocked? Would she believe me when I told her I wasn't sure how it happened? After last night, I had high hopes she would, but then again...she even said there were still things to hash out, and me not even attempting to call her for these five years was most likely the top of her list.

There were a lot of 'I should haves' or 'I could haves' during this. They fell on both of us. But that saying 'the phone works both ways' didn't add up here. She *had* called, she *had* texted. I was the one who vanished.

How the fuck was I going to explain this?

I didn't even have an answer.

The soft light that came from the stable told me she was there. Turning off my rig, I grabbed my hat and slowly made my way inside. Hook bobbed his head up and down once he saw me, and Charming popped out munching on some hay. Nova was near the back, and Luna...she was with the person I wanted to see.

Abi was hunched over, her hair in a messy ponytail that was flopped over her shoulder. Her Carhartt jacket covered her back, her boots had that signature mud on the toes. Even mucking out a stall—she was gorgeous.

She stood, taking a deep breath before she turned, taking a jump into the air once she saw me.

"Holy shit, Cash..." she said breathlessly, and I couldn't help but smile. "Say something next time."

"I just got here." I opened the stall as she started to make her way towards me. "How did you sleep?"

"Not bad," she said, the ghost of a smile lingering. "You?"

I shrugged a shoulder. "Listen, I..."

"Nope." Abi stopped me, a hint of a smile on her lips. "I haven't had that much coffee yet so, before we start the day with 'Listen, I need to talk to you' how about..."

I reached out and grabbed the edge of her coat, pulling her to me. With ease, almost as if she had done it every day, she slipped her arms around my waist, nuzzling up next to my chest. She hummed as she melted into me. I kissed the crown of her head, taking her in, enjoying the brief moment I would have before telling her a hard truth and potentially pissing her off even more. For now, I just needed to have her here.

"Good morning." I lifted my chin slightly, and Abi arched her back to look up at me.

"Morning. Sorry I smell. I got up early because I have a showing today, and I didn't shower. I need to get Stetson ready for school after this and...well...you know how it is." She let me go, taking a step back, holding her arms out to the side as if showcasing herself.

Absolutely magnificent—in every way possible.

"I told you, you're the most beautiful woman in the world, shit under the fingernails and all." I moved towards her once more, using my fingers to grab her coat. "Come here."

She let me pull her towards me, and once she was close enough, I cradled her face in my palms.

"Are you going to kiss me?" she asked, almost a whisper.

"Can I?"

She nodded slightly, and then I dipped my mouth to hers. I could taste the slight hint of coffee on her lips, I could smell the cinnamon on her skin, and once she deepened the kiss, I breathed her in. I could get lost in her. No matter what was happening, this right here would bring me back to life. Abi. Her kiss. Her scent. Her taste. Everything about her made me whole.

Her hands ran up my chest, pulling warmth the entire way until her fingers locked at the nape of my neck. She hummed and her entire body relaxed, I had to move my hands to keep her up right. I smiled against her lips, loving the way she let out a breath of air. My arms tightened around her waist.

"I just had to stop you from melting," I muttered against her, giving her a small kiss.

Shaking her head, she dipped her chin. "Well, it's been a while since someone kissed me like that."

"Like this?" I lifted her chin with my forefinger and thumb, taking her mouth in mine again. She hummed as I gently licked her bottom lip with my tongue, smirking as her lips parted for me.

Holding her tight against my body, I could feel each and every breath she took, every deep inhale that was followed by a sigh, our lips barely leaving each other's. Her fingers caressed my hair, they gripped at the collar on my shirt and tickled the skin at the back of my neck. Enhancing the spark between us.

A throat being cleared stopped us mid moment. Abi pulled away first, her hands sliding down my chest as she tilted her head to look behind me. Secretly loving the blush that spread across her cheeks, I twisted, keeping one hand on her waist, to see Lachlan standing in the center aisle. His arms were folded, baseball cap on backwards, and one eyebrow raised higher than I've ever seen.

"Hi Lach." Abi's voice was heavy as she licked her lips, fully stepping away from me.

"Hey." I turned back to her, remembering the entire reason for my trip to the stable. "Have lunch with me?"

Her eyes danced as she bit her bottom lip. "Okay." Taking a breath, she snapped herself back to reality. "I need to get Stetson ready for school."

Her eyes met mine once more, before she took a single step past me, past Lachlan, and finally left the barn.

Lachlan was a statue, his full attention fixed on me. "What was that?"

I shrugged. "A ruined moment thanks to you." I shoved my hands in my pockets, casually walking up to him like he didn't just catch me making out with his cousin. "What's on the docket today?"

His eyebrow raised higher—if that was even possible. "Do you know what you're doing?" he asked, completely avoiding my question.

"Yeah."

"Does she?"

I looked back at the main house, just in time to see Abi pull open the screen door, vanishing inside.

"She's a big girl Lach," I quipped, remembering his 'big girl pants' bit the day I arrived. I looked over at Lachlan, "If you raise that eyebrow any higher you're going to get it stuck that way."

"Just...be careful there. Abi hasn't let anyone close to her—like this—since Sylas."

"I'm aware. I haven't been close to anyone—like this—since Carolyn."

"Abi's different, Cash. Don't screw this up."

I pinched my brow, not quite ready for the *don't hurt her* speech.

My phone dinged, the vibration pulsing as I pulled it from my back pocket. My eyes twitched and a smile pulled on the corner of my lips.

Abi

> It's a long shot to text you…but lunch? Meet me at 12:30.

"Oh." I looked up at Lachlan. "There is no way I'm screwing this up."

I typed out my reply faster than I think I ever have.

Me

> It's a date.

Shortly after noon, once Lachlan and I had managed a few tractor repairs, I jogged into the stable. The spring sun was beginning to beat down on the farm, any trace of snow long gone, but that chill was still in the air. Flowers would be blooming soon; the cattle would need to be moved, and before we knew it calving season would begin. More things to keep the Hartwell's busy. Another excuse for me to have this time with Abi now.

As soon as I got to the stable door, Abi appeared—the messy ponytail replaced with two braids, a cowboy hat perched on her head. She wore boot cut jeans with a brown jacket half zipped to show a pink shirt underneath. And yet still just as vibrant, stopping me in my tracks. In her hands were two reigns, Luna and Nova, saddled and ready to go.

She flipped her braid off her shoulder, and her gaze locked with mine.

"Oh, hi." She smiled, "I thought we could take the horses and have a picnic."

"A picnic?"

"You said lunch. I um..." She handed me the reins. "I made us sandwiches, and Luna's saddle bag has snacks and water." She cleared her throat and turned to my horse. "And a bottle of wine."

"Wine? We have to talk and you're bringing wine?" I raised an eyebrow, smirking down at her.

Her lips twisted. "It's a white wine."

"And that makes a difference?" I chuckled, stepping forward closer to her. I smelled the cinnamon again and had to force myself not to kiss her, over and over. "I have something to tell you," I whispered.

She smiled, her free hand reaching out to my arm, her fingers trailing down to my hand. "Then let's go to the lake and talk."

TWENTY-FIVE

Abi

"I WAS..." I TRAILED off, taking in what Cash had just told me. "Blocked? You blocked me?"

"No," he hastily replied. "I didn't. I don't even know how to block a number."

"It's not hard." I arched my back away from him, using my palms to keep me upright on the blanket I had spread out by the lake.

The grass was damp, but the camping blanket I stuffed in Luna's side pouch before meeting Cash kept us dry as we sat and ate lunch. Cash wasted no time in starting the conversation, even creating a small buffer by giving me a kiss before we set up the picnic. He knew what he was doing. Making me swoon before starting the talk. We needed to finish what we started last night; we had to get this all out on the table, but I honestly didn't expect to hear what he told me.

I was blocked on his phone. Well, that explained why he only responded to me today.

"I promise you"—he leaned forward slightly, moving his legs to rest his elbow on his knee—"I didn't. I meant what I said by you could call me, I just thought you didn't want to. But then..." He swallowed. "I heard your voicemails."

"Which ones?" I inhaled, nervous that he finally heard every single one. The drunken ones, the ones where I was crying and sobbing, and then the ones where I told him I was done with him.

"Stetson was lost..."

"Oh, ok." I let out a breath of air. *Phew.* "Those ones are nice."

"Nice?"

I rolled my eyes. "Nicer. I may have left some pretty mean ones there towards the end. Well, when I thought it was the end."

"Abi, I'm sorry. It was never an end..."

"But it was. I know I said this last night, but you just vanished. I was pretty certain I would never see you again."

"I fucked up."

"You kinda did."

"You tried to call me, and text me, and I didn't even try once."

I tightened my lips. I had two ways I could take this. I could get up, mount my horse, and tell him I never wanted to see him again, basically rip up those big girl pants that Lachlan told me to put on, or—if I meant what I said last night—I could take a deep breath and think about what I really wanted from this. From him. From us. Take us, whatever we were, forward. Not stuck. We could go around and around this all day. It would be never ending. But that was just pointless.

There's no way I could walk away from him.

"You swear you didn't block me?" I lifted my chin and inched closer to him.

"I didn't block you." He met my gaze. "I don't know how you got blocked. I had the face ID on my phone. I had passwords that only me and—" He stopped, his eyebrows pinching as a look of realization hit him. "Shit." He mumbled, running his hand down his face.

"What?"

"This is a stretch..."

"Just tell me," I sighed, wanting to hear his words.

"Carolyn." Cash looked out to the lake. "She knew my passwords to my phone in case something happened. She carried it while I rode...she...I bet she..."

"You think she blocked me? Why just me? Why not Lachlan and Rhett and Wyatt and..." I let out a long sigh, allowing the dots to make sense. "Did she really hate me that much?"

"Abs..." Cash exasperated. "She really did. It could have been her."

I shrugged a shoulder. "There's no use in pointing fingers. It's not like she's here to defend herself, but..." But what? What did I want to say? It made sense, and I could once again overreact her or... "I just don't think I care."

Cash pinched his brow and turned to me. "What?"

"I don't care. If you say you didn't block me, then I believe you. It happened and it's over and..." I shifted, reaching for my phone. I pulled up his name and typed out a quick text.

Me

It doesn't matter.

His phone dinged, and his eyebrows raised. "Did you just text me?"

I smirked. "Maybe."

He pulled out his phone and read the message, looking up at me once the three words hit him.

"It doesn't matter." I shrugged a shoulder. "Does it hurt? Sure. Do I want to punch you a little bit? Yes."

"Ouch," he muttered.

I scooted closer to him. "But it really, truly doesn't matter. We need to go forward, right? I could be mad and scream and throw a brush at you, but if we want this"—I waved my hand between us—"what would that do other than take us back to five years ago? There's absolutely no point in letting this linger. I want to move forward, don't you?" I reached out and gently touched his cheek, cupping his face in my palm. "Do you want this?"

A moment passed before he nodded. "I can't get you out of my head, Abi. I want this. I want you."

He rested his forehead on mine, his dark eyes pulling me to him. As much as I hated to admit it...I couldn't get him out of mine either. I swallowed my pride and ran my thumb along his jawline. Lifting my head from his, I gave him a soft smile.

"Don't let this get to your head." I grinned. "I can't seem to get you out of mine either."

His lips met mine in a sweet, soft kiss, one that barely felt like a whisper against me. His thumb traced the path his lips had touched, the sparks his lips caused only amplified by the calloused pad of his thumb.

"Call me, text me…every day," he muttered. "I will answer. I will come to you."

I silenced him with another kiss.

"You're going to get sick of me," I whispered into him.

"Impossible."

Me

Stetson is demanding you come to dinner.

Cash

I'm with Quinn. Tell him I will be there as soon as I can.

Me

He won't like that answer.

Cash

He won't, or you won't?

Me

Smart ass.

Cash

I told Quinn I'd stay for this appointment. She's hoping to get the clear to go back to the arena. I'll come to dinner right after I drop her off at her hotel.

Me

Bring her to dinner.

Cash

You sure?

Me

Absolutely. You know we have more than enough space.

Cash

Alright. I'm sure she'd love to get a few rides in tonight.

Me

You wanna ride?

Cash

When do I not.

"Abi?" Lachlan's voice pulled me away from my phone, reminding me that I was very much in my father's office, sitting next to my brothers with my dad at his desk, Lachlan up against the windowsill like he was the last time we had a meeting like this. "Who are you texting?"

"Wouldn't you like to know."

He raised an eyebrow, giving me the sign that he knew exactly who I was texting. I chewed my bottom lip.

"Ok, sorry." I locked my phone. "Phone down." I clutched it in my hands, feeling the small vibration from another text.

Rhett shook his head and chuckled.

I semi-hated these meetings with my father and brothers; they seemed so formal. Last time I sat in between Wyatt and Rhett, we went over the financials and Dad reminded us of his retirement plans, and since this was the third follow up with everyone, we all assumed he had some bigger news.

"Numbers?" My father sighed, standing up and leaning on his desk. "How are we looking?"

"Better," I said with a smile. "The line is going up. We still need a little more, but with spring here, it should be easy. We have every stall full in the stable, I've been showing off the arena to more trainers, and Cash is still renting the arena."

"When is Callahan done with the space?" Wyatt asked, shifting in his seat.

"Um...as soon as Quinn is ready to be back on the circuit, but I told him he was welcome back to use the arena as much as he needed or wanted to." I looked from Wyatt to Lachlan, and then finally to my dad.

"That's a great idea, like a permanent slot. Doesn't he live in Montana, though?" Dad folded his arms.

Lachlan nodded. "He still has his house there, but he travels around with rodeos. Having him here permanently would be great, especially if and when he takes on more clients."

"But would we charge him?" Rhett questioned. "I mean, he's always been around...it doesn't really feel right, does it?"

"And he's been helping out around the ranch. Not sure if I could have gotten the roof fixed, the barn painted, and the fences up before calving season with just us. Having Cash around has been nice." Lachlan agreed.

"I won't charge him," I said. "He's been helping a lot, and Rhett's right...I don't feel right charging him." I looked at my phone on my lap. "But I don't know if he's going to be staying."

"Talk to him, see what he says. Maybe we can offer him a discount instead of not charging. We still need to make the money." My dad gave me a nod. "Keep doing what you're doing, putting these offers out there. It's working. And Lach" —he turned to my cousin—"the place really does look great. Now—"

"Ah, the reason for the meeting!" Wyatt clapped his hand and rubbed his palms together.

"Your mom and I are heading out soon."

"Officially retiring?" Rhett leaned forward.

Our father nodded. "I want to draft up the new title before we leave, so here's my suggestion. Lachlan has fifty percent of it already, and after talking to him, thirty percent to Abi, fifteen percent to Rhett, and the remaining five to Wyatt."

"I don't need any of it, Dad." Wyatt leaned forward in his chair.

"You'll want enough to build a house on in the future, I guarantee it."

Wyatt shrugged. "Maybe one day so..." He nodded, agreeing with him. "Yeah, I can take that five percent."

Rhett and I locked gazes, and then he softly said, "I can live with fifteen percent."

I pinched my brow at him. He deserved more than fifteen percent. Rhett took a deep breath, the life draining from his face. He didn't like this either, and from what I was gathering, neither of us was going to say anything.

Dad smiled. "We're planning on a trip to Europe in the beginning of May, so I'll draft up a new title and have it ready to go before we leave."

"You'll be back for the Fourth?" Rhett asked, referring to the Fourth of July Hartwell Rodeo, the one rodeo of the year where this town went all out. Rhett was going to ride, Wyatt would announce, and Lachlan would set up the fireworks. Me? I'd make sure my son didn't die from riding a sheep and maybe...

I smiled.

Maybe convince Cash to make his comeback.

"Most definitely. You know we wouldn't miss that for the world. We have a few places planned to go this year, but home for the Fourth of July is exactly where we will be."

"Perfect." Lachlan pushed himself off the windowsill and slapped Rhett's shoulder. "Come on Rhett, we have more to do today."

Rhett stood, giving me one last glance before following Lachlan out the door.

I looked at my dad and attempted to give him the best smile I could.

Once it was just him and I in the office, I unlocked my phone to read the text from Cash, feeling a small flutter in my stomach. These damn butterflies.

Cash

Because I'm new to this…what's your coffee order?

Me

My coffee order?

"Abi?" This time it was my dad to pull me out of my texting stupor.

"Hmm?" I hummed, raising my brow, once again ignoring the buzz in my hand.

"Did you hear me?"

Shit.

"Sorry…no. I was talking to"—I looked at my phone—"Kyla."

He shook his head. Dad could always tell when I was lying. The look on his face, one eyebrow slightly raised, his eyes boring into me, that simple smirk growing as he tried to read my face. I did my best to keep myself composed, even though the buzz in my hand was happening again. Cash really wanted to know my coffee order, didn't he?

"I asked if you were okay with this?"

"With keeping the numbers up? Yeah, I can do that, that's easy."

"No, the percentage we want you to take."

"Oh." I paused. "I mean...sure?" I shrugged a shoulder, the *sure* coming out in the form of a question rather than a statement, which I was sure gave him the indication that I was indeed not okay with it.

I still had no idea what I wanted when it came to the ranch. I loved it, that was evident, but did I love it enough to make it my entire life?

"Abi?"

"Yes, Dad, I'm fine with it," I said. Maybe if I said it enough, I'd believe it. "Rhett and Lachlan seem on board..."

"You don't seem to be on board. You were quiet today."

I sighed, letting my shoulders drop as I tried to find the exact words to say.

"I'm just a little overwhelmed. I'll be fine once the numbers are consistently going up. Speaking of"—I stood—"I need to make sure we have enough and place that feed order before dinner. Are we done?"

I could tell he didn't believe a word I just said. "Yeah...We're done."

"See you at dinner, Pops."

TWENTY-SIX

Cash

IT WASN'T LONG BEFORE the entire Hartwell family made their way to the indoor arena for an impromptu rodeo. Quinn simply asked if we could get in a few rides before she headed back to her hotel, and Lottie jumped on that idea. Before I knew it, Stetson grabbed my hand and yanked me towards the arena.

While Kyla and Leo made themselves comfortable behind the gates, everyone started moving. I was almost tempted to suggest we head to the Hartwell Rodeo Arena, but they were in the zone setting up right here at home. Rhett and Lachlan wrangled a few calves, Abi prepared the horses with Quinn, Stetson and I rolled the barrels out onto the dirt, and Wyatt plopped a cowboy hat on his head and hoisted himself up on a gate, locking his ankles in the railing—ready to announce anything he could, even if it was just his family in the arena.

I couldn't help but notice his eyes focused on Quinn. He had tried at dinner to talk to her, maybe threw out some pickup lines, but Quinn seemed to have no interest in the playboy rodeo announcer, even rolling her eyes at him a few times. I found it comical that he was trying so hard, knowing that Wyatt was one who could pick up any girl at rodeos, and he was having trouble with Quinn. That didn't stop him, though. Every time she passed, he would say something to try to get her attention.

"Maybe." Quinn finally turned to him. "If you would get your ass off the gate and saddle a horse, I'd be more inclined to talk to you."

Wyatt pinched his eyebrows, and I swear I could see his breath stop. I couldn't help but burst out laughing. Abi used the back of her hand to slap my chest, pulling me back to the hustle of getting ready for a ride.

Rhett was up first, using a few different calves to rope, trying to beat his time over and over—each run ending with him bounding to the gate to give Kyla a deep kiss. Kyla's face was becoming permanently red. Wyatt even got off the gate to rope a calf. Even if his time was seventeen point two seconds, he still tossed up his hands like he owned the sport.

"Stick to announcing!" Rhett called from the gate as Lachlan led the calf into the opposite end of the arena.

Wyatt gave his brother the middle finger before giving Quinn a wink, raising himself back on the gate. "Who's next? I'd love to see the barrel racers." He turned to Quinn, waggling his eyebrows.

She shook her head, giving him the most epic eye roll I had ever seen before she turned to Stetson. "Ready little dude?"

Stetson looked up at Quinn and nodded his head vigorously. He ran out on the dirt and moved the barrels to where she pointed, and once he was back to us, he turned and stepped on the gate, his eyes fixed on Quinn as she rode Charming to the back door of the arena.

"Too far. Turn," I muttered under my breath, and as if she could hear me, she spun Charming. "Get up speed..."

Quinn used her legs, a motion that just weeks ago would have caused her to wince, but today, she was moving with ease, just like second nature.

"That's it." I smiled once she took off and rounded the first barrel, her back straight, her ponytail flying behind her.

She rounded the second, Charming's tail barely clipping the barrel's side as he passed, and she sped up to the last and third, racing back to the opposite end of the arena before she made Charming halt. The dirt flew up around his hooves, and he reared up, Quinn holding on with her legs.

"And that's Quinn Compton, the barrel racer who is going to take the world by storm with her eighteen-point two time." Wyatt shouted across the arena, drawing out her name.

Kyla clapped, and Quinn did a small dance on Charming before leading him outside of the arena to go again, and again.

"She looks like she's ready to get back on the circuit." Abi leaned into me. "How much longer do you think?"

I wrapped my arm around her shoulder gently. I wasn't too sure how she felt about affection in front of her family, or what they knew about us at all. This was still so new, but having her near me, I couldn't help but want to hold her.

I watched Quinn round the first barrel on her second ride. "Her doctor gave her an all clear at her appointment today." I quirked a smile. "I can start planning her rides."

"Shouldn't she do that? Or an agent?" Abi's brow furrowed.

I shrugged. "I'm happy to help her out this season. Last year, she did it all on her own, so she needs the support. Next year though, if I take on more clients—"

"Oh!" she shouted. "We were actually talking about that today." Abi stretched out her arms on the gate, forcing my arm to drop. "You could train your other clients here…if you'd like. We wouldn't charge you."

I jerked my head towards her. "You're serious?"

She nodded. "I mean, as long as you keep helping around the ranch, we won't charge you."

"Ah," I threw back a laugh. "There's the catch."

"Quiiiiiin Commmpton," Wyatt hollered. "And now, giving us a special show, coming back after a few years off the circuit…"

Abi looked at Lachlan, hope seeping from her eyes. He just trotted along on Onyx, not even registering what Wyatt was saying.

"Don't get your hopes up," I whispered to Abi, who instantly hit me with a side eye.

"…Lottie Hartwell!" Wyatt used his hands to extend his voice as everyone—and I mean everyone—cheered. Leo was the loudest as he stood, hooting and hollering as we all focused on the arena entrance.

Lottie flew in, her form perfect on the back of her horse, Opal, as she came up to the first barrel. They turned, Lottie following the horses' twists as if they were one being. The second barrel came just as easy for her, and Opal didn't miss a beat. At the last barrel, Lottie's smile grew as Opal gained speed and turned, Opal's tail whipping around as she took the turn with ease. The dirt was worn, but Opal didn't even falter. Like they had been doing this for years. They didn't even come close to touching a single barrel. Once Opal was back on the straight path, Lottie raised herself up on the stirrups, her arms high above her head like she was a trick rider, her dark hair now a complete mess as she raised her chin to the ceiling.

"And that," Wyatt shouted, "is how it's done!"

"Fourteen point nine seconds!" Kyla shouted into the arena, waving the timer in the air.

"Damn," I muttered. "I need her to train Quinn."

"That felt so good." Lottie sighed as she and Opal trotted up to us. "I haven't done that in years."

"Amazing as always, Mom!" Abi cheered. "Cash just said you need to teach Quinn."

Lottie smiled. "I'll be more than happy to do that again! Quinn can observe and learn a few things." She cocked her head with a grin.

"Mommy!" Stetson called, running up to Abi. "Can I try that! Please!"

Abi looked down at Stetson, before giving me a quick glance. "You want to barrel race?"

Stetson was vibrating with excitement. "I can, right? It's not just a girl sport! Cash can show me!"

"I'm down." I pushed myself off the gate, sliding my hand along Abi's shoulders. "Quinn, how's Charming with kids!?"

Quinn came up to us, Charming lightly bobbing his head. "Little man wants to ride? Oh, I'd love to see this. Charming can do one more run." Quinn swung her leg over Charming's body, slipping off the saddle and stepping to the side, allowing Stetson to slip his foot in the stirrup to easily lift himself up. Charming took a few steps, getting used to the new weight.

"Hold up..." Abi stopped us. "Let's get your helmet."

Raising his hands above his head, Stetson cheered.

"Alright Stet, your posture is the most important thing," I began, pulling up the stirrups to fit his feet.

"Not too stiff, not too loose," Quinn added. "You saw your grandma, right? Perfect posture."

"And it's a tight turn." I walked to the other side, adjusting his foot there. He grabbed the reins and nodded, taking in each and every word, his eyes wide.

"Really tight. Charming may take them faster since you're so light." Quinn took the helmet from Abi and handed it up to Stetson, who quickly buckled it under his chin.

"Choose left or right first..."

"It doesn't matter which." Quinn reached up and checked his helmet, knocking on it with her knuckles after making sure it was secure.

"Then go to the opposite side." I patted his knee. His head was moving from me, to Quinn, back to me.

"Turn around the barrel, and make sure you don't touch it." Quinn pointed at the barrel.

"Then to the front."

"Then to the back. I'll meet you there." Quinn smiled at Stetson before jogging to the end of the arena. "Come down here to get a good speed going!" She waved her arms in the air.

"How fast should I go?" Stetson looked down at me, his entire face beaming with pure joy. This boy was made for the rodeo.

"As fast as you'd like. Remember..." I raised a single brow.

"Posture. Not too stiff, not too loose. Left or right, hold on tight." Stetson bobbed his head as he recited each thing Quinn and I had told him. Crash course in barrel racing. "Where will you be?"

"Where do you want me?"

Stetson hummed. "By Mommy." Turning my back, I looked at Abi. She leaned against the metal gate, her arms crossed over her chest. "She doesn't like it when I practice mutton busting, so she won't like this either. But she'll smile if you're next to her." Stetson whispered.

I grinned. "She sure does, but I'll go keep her company. Now, go down by Quinn and round these barrels."

With a loud "Yeah," Stetson kicked Charming's sides and rounded the corner to where Quinn stood. She gave him some final instructions before pushing Charming off as Stetson kicked his side. Then he was off, Charming probably going a lot faster than Stetson intended. At first the shock took over, but once Charming rounded that first barrel, and he headed towards that second, I'd never seen that boy smile so big.

"That's it," I muttered.

"You're going to get him hooked on this. He'll be the first male barrel racer."

"Hey, men can race barrels, and it's better than saddle bronc." I nudged Abi's shoulder.

She teased. "He's taking after his Uncle Lachlan, remember?"

Stetson rounded the third barrel and made his way back to Quinn, who clapped and jumped as he slowly brought Charming to a stop.

"Can I do that again?" Stetson hollered.

"Go again!" Leo screamed back at his grandchild. "I gotta film this!"

"Make sure you send me everything, Dad!" Abi cupped her hand over her lips, and Leo gave her a quick thumbs up before setting up his camera to catch every single move of Stetson's second run.

"He's a rodeo natural. He's going to want to ride bronc next, you know that right? I wouldn't be surprised if he asked if he could do that tonight." Folding my arms, I leaned against the gate, looking down at Abi.

Her eyes met mine, and she smiled. "He's going to after watching you. Speaking of which..." I wiggled my eyebrows at her, and then without breaking my eye contact Abi shouted, "Stetson, I think it's Cash's turn to get on the dirt!"

"YES!" Stetson screamed, jumping off Charming. "I want to pull the chute!"

"I'll help him." Rhett jogged to the chute, making it right before Stetson did.

"Wish me luck." I reached down and squeezed Abi's hand for reassurance.

"You don't need it," she said as she squeezed back.

I made it to the chute and looked out on the dirt. Lachlan, Kyla, and Quinn had moved the barrels off to the side. Stetson and Rhett stayed by the chute, and I waited until Lachlan was on Onyx to be my pick up man to lower myself onto the horse. He started moving the second my legs wrapped around him, ready to get out of the small cage and let loose.

I grabbed the cinch, instantly wished I had my cowboy hat on—you know, for the full effect—then looked at Rhett. He smiled and looked at Stetson.

"I think he's gonna nod." Rhett said to his nephew.

"Nod Uncle Cash!"

I nodded, and Rhett and Stetson opened the chute. The ranch horse, aptly named Moose, blew out of the chute, flying into the air. I could hear the cheers from Lottie and Leo, Abi too, as Moose turned left, then right, and flew higher in the air. I kept my hand up, my back straight and my focus on his weight under me. He moved and jerked, almost forcing me off his back a few times, bucking higher than Blaze did the other night. But then I heard the buzzer, the eight seconds were up. I tightened my legs and lowered my arm, grabbing the cinch with both hands and geared him into a run. Lachlan showed up at my side, matching Moose's pace perfectly. I let go of the cinch and reached for Lachlan as he dragged me from the saddle. I jumped, my feet landing on the ground for a split second before I took off towards Abi.

"You're getting better and better with each ride, before you know it, you'll be—"

I stopped her, gripping her face in my hands and pressing my lips to hers. Since she was in mid-sentence, it was all too easy for me to slip my tongue inside to dance with hers, sending chills down my spine. So much for PDA. She melted into me again, and she hummed as I kissed her, tasting her, our hearts beating more rapidly with each swipe of my tongue. I could see why Rhett did this after every ride. The pure rush from the ride was exhilarating, and then having her in my arms, her lips against mine, kept the adrenaline pumping, but this time it was all Abi.

Her hands gripped onto my arms, holding me steady against her, and once I broke the kiss, she let out a soft sigh.

"Hey now," I heard Rhett's voice as he came up from behind us. "That's my bit."

"I can see why," I breathed, leaning down to give Abi one last kiss.

"MOMMY!" I heard Stetson squeal. "YOU KISSED UNCLE CASH!"

I chuckled and looked back at Stetson, who stood right in the middle of the dirt, his jaw dropped as he watched us.

"Sorry Stet," I said, my hands lowering from Abi's face to her arms. "Is it ok if I kiss your mom?"

"Does that mean you'll stay longer, because if it means you'll stay longer you can kiss her." Stetson brushed a hand in the air, as if waving off what he just saw, running back to the gates, "Can I open the chute again if Uncle Cash goes!?"

Abi rubbed her lips together and then blinked herself back to reality. "I'm going to have to talk to him..." she said, her voice soft and breathy. "If he's ok with us kissing, he should probably drop the uncle."

I laughed and raised my eyebrows. "Should I ride again?"

She nodded, a twitch to her lips. I casually walked back to the chute, giving Rhett a look, and then took a quick inventory of how that kiss was taken by Abi's family. Wyatt looked anywhere but at me, her mother was smiling, her dad was getting his camera ready (most likely to film another ride), and Kyla had a huge grin on her face and was mouthing something. I turned and looked at Abi, whose smile matched Kyla's and she was mouthing something right back.

That shot up my ego just a twinge. Abi and Kyla were acting like teenagers, all over my kiss. Yeah...I was definitely kissing her again after this ride.

I rode three more times, lasting eight seconds each time, and kissing Abi after each one. Nothing like the first kiss, but after having her family take zero note of it, I couldn't stop myself. Stetson even squealed each time, at one point screaming, "Gross!" It wasn't until Abi took him away for his bedtime that I pulled them both into my arms for a hug, loving the way they both felt against me. Nothing could take this feeling away, not even watching them walk out of the stables. Pure bliss was etching into my body.

"Hey, Callahan."

I scanned the arena, seeing Lachlan and Rhett already in the stables taking care of the horses, Quinn was talking to Kyla, Lottie and Leo were re-watching videos on his phone. The only other person who could possibly be next to me...

Wyatt stood in front of me, his arms folded, his baseball cap slightly perched to the side, and a look of extreme anger plastered all over his face.

Okay, maybe Wyatt could erase that feeling. I rolled my eyes and lowered my chin. "Yes, Wyatt?"

"What the hell was that?"

"What was what?" I pretended to look stupid. Here was the brother's protection speech. I was honestly expecting this from Lachlan after the small warning he had given me prior but knowing that Wyatt would rather talk to anyone else but me, I was shocked he even approached me.

"You know what," he grumbled.

"Alright, then, what was with you hitting on Quinn?"

"I didn't suck face with her like you did with my sister."

"Suck face?" I parroted. "I kissed her, I didn't 'suck face' with her. Pretty sure that's what you do."

He shook his head. "I don't like you."

"That's fine."

"Stay away from Abi."

"I don't think that's up to you."

His glare deepened. "You hurt her once. I was there for it. I saw every second of it after Sylas died. I saw how long it took for her to get over him, and over you. Over losing who she thought was a friend. You can't just waltz back into her life and expect to replace Sylas. No one can do that. No one will ever fill that hole for her. You don't know what she does to stop it. You shouldn't have come back here—"

"You done?" I interrupted, not wanting his words to get to me more than they already were. Abi knew I wasn't wanting to replace Sylas. Just by seeing everyone's reaction to our touches and kisses, no one felt that way either. But Wyatt...turns out he wasn't done.

"Just stay away. Quinn's better, so get off my property, and stay the hell away from my sister."

I chewed the inside of my cheek, stopping myself from saying anything to defend myself. If he wanted to give me this speech, he could, but it didn't change a damn thing. Wyatt's jaw tensed as he held my stare, and when I didn't respond, he gave me a single nod and turned his back, heading to his dad with his chin down. The entire time I watched him walk away, I thought about the next time I would have Abi in my arms again.

TWENTY-SEVEN

Abi

"A ND THIS," I SPUN, my arms wide, a smile on my face as I looked at the bull rider who followed me into the arena, "is our training arena."

Oakes Ashford, the bull rider currently leading the standings, shoved his hands in his pockets and tensed his jaw as we stepped into the arena. His Wranglers had dirt around the boot, and a fancy belt buckle showed off his winnings. His black hat was perched on his head, his longer, dark hair sticking out in all directions under the rim. His jaw clenched; the only thing missing was a piece of straw sticking out between his teeth. Showing off the stables for potential horses was easy, but Cash was still the only one using the arena...and this was Oakes Ashford. I was a little intimated.

"It's small," he grumbled.

My smile fading, I tried to keep my confident look on my face. "We hold small rodeos here often, just the other night in fact. I can assure you it's big enough for bulls to train. Rhett has done a lot of training here—"

"That'll be me." Rhett came around the corner as if he were summoned, appearing behind Oakes with his signature tan cowboy hat and blue button down on. "We've met." Rhett approached Oakes' side and held out his hand.

"Rhett Hartwell." Oakes shook his hand, a large smile spreading across his lips. I mimicked him, hoping to sell him with kindness, especially now that Rhett was here—he could help. "You won the NFR last year. Congrats."

"And you're leading the boards this year." Rhett tipped his chin.

Oakes wiggled his eyebrows. "All the way there. Your sister was just showing me around the training arena. I'll be sticking to the western circuits this next year and looking for a place to train away from the city. When I saw this ad, I had to come check it out."

"It's a great space." Rhett mimicked Oakes's stance, feet apart, hands on his hips, jaw tense. "You can ask Cash; he's been training Quinn Cambell here."

"Callahan?"

Rhett nodded. "The one and only. He and Quinn should be arriving soon for a session. You're welcome to watch and see the space in action. If it can handle barrel racing, it can definitely handle bulls."

Oakes's stoic glance turned into a smile, where he began to chew. Apparently, he had gum in his mouth this entire time. I sighed, relief swimming through me. At least the clenching of his jaw was justified.

"I can stick around." Oakes turned to me. "Any chance I can try out the space?"

"Sure." I grinned. "Why don't you and Rhett stay here, and I can go grab Lachlan. I'm sure he will be more than happy to bring a bull."

Oakes tipped his hat. "Make it wild one, yeah?"

"You got it." I gave him a thumbs up.

Rhett took a step towards me. "I can help."

I spun on my heels. "Nope, I got it. You show Oakes around." I winked at my brother, he winked back, and left the arena.

With a skip in my step, I ran to the bullpen, where thankfully Lachlan was ready and waiting for me. He had already seen Oakes pull up and figured the famed bull rider would want a practice ride. He pulled in the biggest bull on the ranch—perfectly named Hulk—and was already moving him to the training grounds.

When I appeared and scratched the bull behind his ears, skipping back again to let him through, I noticed Lachlan's eyes on me, a single eyebrow raised.

"What?"

He shook his head softly. "Nothing."

"No, what is it? You're looking at me funny."

"Abi...you're skipping."

I stopped and looked at my mud-covered boots. "I'm not..."

"Yeah, you are. Oh...and look." He tilted his chin back towards the arena "Cash just pulled up."

I felt my heart jump—literally jump—in my chest. It took all my strength not to run...well, skip towards him. It was weird to feel this way. To have this excitement fill my body. There was no more questioning what I was feeling. No more denying it. Not after he kissed me in front of everyone, even getting my son's stamp of approval. Whatever was here, I was going to keep it and hold on to it. So, yeah...I started to skip back to the barn.

Cash stepped out of his rig, placing his hat on his head, his forearms free with the warmer weather. He turned to the other truck that was coming up behind him—Quinn—and once she was parked, his eyes met mine.

"Hey Abs." He smiled, his smooth Southern accent filling every vessel in my body. My jog got faster, and in my head, I saw myself wrapping my legs around his waist, kissing him senselessly as his hands roamed my back, allowing those butterflies to take complete control.

It was only then that I remembered I had a potential client in the arena and should probably not maul him in front of them. I slowed and simply reached out for his hand. He responded by threading our fingers together.

"Were you skipping?" He raised a single eyebrow, lowering his chin to look me in the eye.

"You know what?" I pulled my hand away, taking a step back. "I was just..."

"Excited to see me?" His grin turned wicked.

I rolled my eyes. "Okay fine, yes. I'm excited to see you, but we also have a potential client."

Quinn came up behind Cash. "Is that Oakes Ashford's truck?" She used her thumb to point behind her back at the bright blue truck that was parked near the stable.

Oakes' logo, a white outline of a bull rider mid jump on it, a fancy O and A in the empty space, was painted on the side of the truck. Everyone who was following the rodeo knew that logo, Quinn included. I looked at Quinn, answering her question silently.

"Ok, it's his truck, but is *he* in the arena?" She lowered her voice, leaning in.

I gave her a nod.

"Oh my God." She stood up straight as a board. "He's leading the boards."

"And he wants to watch you train, so…"

"What!" She froze.

"Quinn." Cash's voice lowered as he looked at his client. "Keep yourself together."

"Oh, I am. I'm gonna show him the best ride." Quinn marched forward with determination, stepping into the barn.

We both watched her, standing by the entry way as Cash brushed his hand down my arm, his fingers weaving through mine again. He lifted my arm, bringing the back of my hand to his lips, his body facing me. I could feel the blush reach my cheeks.

"You were so excited to see me—"

"Oh, come on." I rolled my eyes again, leaning into him.

"You skipped."

"I ran enthusiastically."

His lips cocked a grin, and he bent his head, giving me the sweetest kiss.

"Go out with me Abi," he whispered against my lips.

"Go out with you?"

"On a date."

My heart jumped again. "Like a real date?"

He nodded. "A real date. One where I plan it, pick you up, and pay for everything...I kiss you goodnight..."

"I like the sound of the last detail." I raised myself on my tippy toes, brushing my lips with his once more. "When?"

"Tomorrow night."

"Saturday night?" my eyes widened. Saturday? A busy night in town? Really...a Saturday? "How about Wednesday?"

"No, tomorrow." He nodded. "Go out with me."

I licked my bottom lip. "Okay...I'd love to."

"Perfect. I'll pick you up tomorrow at seven. Dress warm." Cash jerked his eyebrows once, brushed my nose with his thumb, and then left me standing in front of the stable, the butterflies rising in my chest.

A date.

Cash asked me on a date.

A real one. And I said I'd love to.

I haven't been on a date since...

"Well, shit," I muttered, booking it to Rhett's cabin.

Kyla opened the door before I even had a chance to knock. I basically ran into her house, doubling over with my hands on my thighs, heavy breaths leaving my lungs.

"Is there a reason why you're heaving in my living room?" Kyla asked as she tilted her body, her long brown hair falling to the side as she leaned to look at me.

"Cash..." I breathed, standing up with one hand on my hip, the other brushing my hair back. Why I thought it was a good idea to wear it down was beyond me. "He uh..."

I looked at Kyla, her eyes wide and eyebrows high, waiting for me to finish my sentence.

"He asked me on a date."

She smiled. "Okay...and?"

"A date, Kyla."

"I heard you."

"A date."

"Do you need to sit down?" She moved to the side and presented the couch to me. Without even thinking about it, I rushed past her and plopped on the leather couch. Kyla sat calmly next to me, one leg fitting under her nicely as she made herself comfortable. "You good?"

"I don't know." I closed my eyes and took a deep breath, holding it for a few seconds before finally letting it out through my lips. "I mean...my heart is racing..." I admitted.

"Well, you did run here." Kyla chuckled.

"I'm just...nervous?" I put my hand on my chest. "Cash asked me out on a date."

"After the way he kissed you last night, I'd hoped he would." Kyla smirked as she leaned her torso towards me. "Why are you nervous?"

I blushed at the memory of our kiss, giving her a shy look before turning back to the table in front of me. I pulled my legs up to my chest, creating that barrier, trying to wrap my head around why I was acting this way.

I closed my eyes tightly and tried to make myself form the words. Turn these feelings into tangible thoughts I could digest. I liked Cash. I liked the way I felt when he was around. I loved the way his lips felt against mine, the way my stomach churned when he touched me. I loved the sound of his voice, the comfort he brought. So why was I nervous about a date with him?

I sighed, forcing the tears to stay back. I would not cry over this again.

"I haven't..." I finally said. "I haven't been on a date since Sylas."

"That's understandable." Kyla shifted. "I mean, you loved him."

"Love. I love him." I corrected her, narrowing my eyes.

"But wouldn't he want you to be happy? Wouldn't he want you to go on dates?"

"Believe it or not, we never had the 'if I die while riding bulls, I want you to date my best friend' chat." I took another breath, the air leaving my mouth. "Cash was Sylas' best friend."

"Does that sit funny with you?"

"I mean...kind of. But...no." I shifted, moving to sitting cross-legged on the couch. "Cash was always there, and if I'm being honest...if Sylas knew, he would...approve?" I hunched my shoulders, furrowing my brow. "It doesn't make any sense."

"No, it does. It's weird. Forbidden almost. Now, I'm not the best person to ask for advice here, because well...I didn't know Sylas, but with the way Cash kissed you last night, in front of your entire family…" She touched my shoulder, squeezing slightly. "No one seems phased by the fact that he was connected to Sylas. He knows you, and he obviously has feelings for you. You need to decide if you can move on from it. Having that connection to Sylas may make your and Cash's relationship all that stronger."

"But isn't it fast? I mean seven weeks ago, I was avoiding the man and was pissed he was here."

Kyla let out a soft laugh. "I'm not one to talk to about timing either. I knew your brother for twelve days, and I married him, and here we are not even together for a year yet and we're expecting our first baby. Life moves fast Abi; you have to decide if you wanna run with it or not."

I chewed on my bottom lip, taking yet again another deep breath. "I like him. I like that he's here."

"But seven weeks ago…"

"I was mad, I resented him in a way."

"Well yeah, you didn't make the man a bologna sandwich." Kyla chuckled.

I gave her a friendly glare. "But," I continued, "we've talked. We…we want to try this."

"This being…"

"Us."

She smiled. "And you're worried about a date…because?"

"And we've come full circle, I haven't been on one since Sylas."

Kyla stood and held out a hand. "Lucky for you, Rhett and I have been going on plenty of dates, and I have dresses that are starting to be a little to snug—"

"You are not showing yet."

"In the chest area." She pulled me off the couch, giving me a cheeky grin. "Let's find you something amazing to wear so when he picks you up, he will melt and never want to leave your side again."

"He said dress warm."

"Good thing I have plenty of long sleeve dresses that will go perfect with your boots."

TWENTY-EIGHT

Cash

I REMEMBER MEETING CAROLYN, and then showing up on our first date. Which was the exact opposite of what was happening now. My first date with Carolyn was at a bar, she was dressed in a skin-tight, red tube top, her breasts basically popping out, makeup caked over her already flawless skin, and she was holding a drink the entire time. It ended with us hooking up in the bathroom.

This was different. I was doing this right. I couldn't mess it up. I found the perfect place to spend the evening with Abi, knowing it would give us the first date experience and that it would end with a kiss on her porch when I dropped her off, asking for a second date. And a third. And a fourth.

I took each step up to the main house as if they were new, because they felt new; even though I had taken them plenty of times in my life—never with this purpose. My boots clunked against the wooden porch, and I breathed deep, raising my finger to the doorbell. I never rang the doorbell, but that's what you did picking up your girl for a date. You rang the doorbell, and you talked to her parents. You agreed on a curfew and then went along your way. Granted, we were both adults, so a curfew wouldn't make a difference...but I rang the doorbell anyway.

I was put off a bit when Wyatt answered the door. His face was blank, stoic as he looked me up and down.

"I'm supposed to talk to your father, not you." I smiled, hoping he'd catch the tease.

"Dad's out," he voiced toneless.

I smirked and gave him a quick nod. "Can I see your sister?"

His eyes narrowed.

"Wyatt! Cut it. Let him in." I heard Abi call from the back of the house.

With a heavy sigh, Wyatt stepped aside. I tipped my hat and entered the house, wishing I had just opened the door instead of ringing the doorbell. Abi was in the kitchen, setting up Stetson at the table. She moved, flawless as always, but with a purpose.

"Stetson, I'm cooking you what you like—"

"Nope." He folded his arms.

"Stetson..." Abi stopped, raised her chin and grumbled. She inhaled, her chest rising and falling, slowly lowering her chin to look at me.

Our eyes met, and suddenly the fact that Wyatt was standing with his arms folded watching my every move, didn't matter.

Abi was mesmerizing, wearing a lavender, long sleeve, knee-length dress that cinched at her waist. If she spun, the skirt would flow out. The sleeves were a different fabric, thinner and flowy around her arms. Her tan boots, mud free, only complimented everything. Her hair was half up, half down, waves falling over her shoulders. The natural makeup she wore only made my heartbeat faster.

"Abi...you..."

"I'm late." She sighed, interrupting me, frustration spreading across her face, "Stetson is being stubborn even though he gets to hang out with Uncle Wyatt all night."

"I don't want to hang out with Uncle Wyatt," Stetson spat.

Abi's expression was close to defeat. She took a step towards me, her fingers brushing my forearm. "Give me just a second, okay? I'll be ready to head out soon. I just need to get him settled. He's not used to me going out."

"Where's Kyla? I thought she would be the first to step up to the plate to babysit." I asked, looking around the kitchen hoping the newest addition to the Hartwell family would materialize. It would definitely make it less awkward than Wyatt standing there.

"Date night." Abi sighed again.

"Yeah, and I'm not staying here with Uncle Wyatt." Stetson stood up and walked over to his mom, keeping his arms folded.

"Oh, come on, bud. We can watch *Bluey* and stuff." Wyatt walked up to Stetson, fluffing his hair with his hand.

"I'm too old for *Bluey*, Uncle Wyatt," Stetson grumbled.

"What's *Bluey*?" I asked, raising my eyebrow, catching Abi's gaze.

"A cartoon he's definitely not too old for. I find myself watching it after he goes to sleep, Chili is the most relatable cartoon character,"

Abi said quietly, then turned back to her son, "Stetson, I'm begging you...let me have this night."

He turned to look at her, giving the most perfect seven-year-old glare. This kid wasn't going to give up this easily. Just seeing the stern look he was giving Abi told me that no matter what we did or said, he wasn't going to approve of his mother going on a date.

Abi gave me another apologetic look. "I'm sorry. I talked to him about the date, and he was okay with it until he figured out that I wouldn't be here. The kid loves to hang around others when I'm home, but take me out of the house—"

"And he's not happy. He's a kid, he just wants his mom around. I get it."

"Maybe we should reschedule?" Abi raised a shoulder in question, her brows furrowing as she waited for my answer.

My breath hitched, I definitely didn't want that to happen. Lightly grasping Abi's hand, I felt her warmth. Then—like a light bulb, the thought hit me.

"I have an idea," I said, squeezing Abi's hand. "Stetson, why don't you come with us?"

Abi and Stetson both jerked their heads to look up at me.

"What?" Abi breathed.

"Really?" Stetson shouted at the same time.

"Yeah." I cocked my shoulder up. "It will be fun."

Stetson spun and faced Abi, his arms dropping to his side, his glare gone and a smile now spreading. "Can I!?"

"Are you sure?" Abi leaned into me; her voice low. "I don't want him to think he's getting away with acting like this."

"He'll know he's not, and of course. One hundred percent. But we have to leave now before it gets too crowded." I replied, not once breaking eye contact with Abi.

Her eyes twitched as a smile grew. "Crowded? Where are we going?"

"Stet." I touched the top of his head. "Go get your boots, coat and hat. We're going to the spring fair."

"YES!" Stetson shouted before he took off running.

Abi watched as he bounded up the stairs. "You're sure?"

"Absolutely. You *and* Stet? The night just got better." I stepped forward, taking her in now that I really could. Even with the frustration that still lingered, she was still absolutely perfect. "Abi..." I reached up and lightly touched her hair between my thumb and forefinger. "You look breathtaking..."

She smiled, closing her eyes softly as she closed the gap between us.

"Wyatt, you may want to leave because I'm going to kiss your sister now."

"Oh, please," I heard him grumble. "If I'm off the hook, I'm heading to The Steel."

I kissed Abi before Wyatt was out of the room, slipping my tongue in between her lips as she sighed. She placed her hands on my chest, her weight leaning into me. She hummed, breaking the kiss, her lips forming the smile I had grown to crave more and more.

"Absolutely astonishing," I whispered against her lips.

Her eyes fluttered open. "You look handsome as well," she whispered, still breathless. "Kiss me again."

"As you wish." I brushed my lips against her, teasing her slightly. "Let's go."

Stetson ran in front of Abi and me, taking in everything the Alpine Ridge Fair had to offer. Abi's fingers were threaded through mine as we stepped together. It was the first night of the fair, so the crowds were thick. Stetson would turn every now and then to make sure we were still by him, not losing us for a moment. He begged for a ride on the twirl-o-whirl, where Abi and I joined him willingly. Her laughs filled the seat as the motions threw her into my side, her hand gripping onto my thighs.

"The Ferris wheel next!!" Stetson screamed once we were stumbling off the ride. "Please!"

"Stetson," Abi laughed. "You gotta let me catch my bearings. I'm not twenty anymore."

"Come on, Mom!" he shouted as he waved us along.

"We're coming, Stet, we're coming." I hollered back.

"Funnel cakes!!" Stetson screamed, his trajectory changing once he saw the food truck.

"And he's forgotten about the Ferris wheel. Do you regret inviting him along?" Abi asked, her body pressing into mine as she wrapped her hands around my arm.

"Not even a little bit." I kissed the top of her head. "This may not be the date I envisioned, but I wouldn't change it in the slightest."

"Hmm." Abi leaned her chin on my shoulder. "He'll hopefully crash after this."

I laughed, leading Abi towards the funnel cakes.

"Dates are supposed to be sitting in a low light restaurant, eating cheap-yet-expensive Italian food while we talk about our favorite things and colors and what we like to do during our free time." Abi smiled.

"Well, for one..." I gave her a smirk. "You don't like cheap-yet-expensive Italian food. You prefer corn on the cob with a grilled hamburger. Your favorite things include Stetson, the stables, and long rides ending with a nap by the lake. Your favorite color is purple, and in your free time..." I stopped her and pulled her into me. "You spend it with Luna."

"I do love that horse." She smiled. "It's been five years, and you still know those things about me. I hate to admit that I don't know those things about you." She clenched her teeth and hunched her shoulders slightly, her cheeks red with embarrassment.

God, she was adorable. I grinned. "I love a bratwurst, grilled preferably. Favorite things include reading, rodeos, and you. Green is my favorite color, and in my spare time...I like to draw."

Abi's eyes widened. "Draw? You draw?"

"Not very well, and I haven't in a long time. Actually, I just bought a sketchbook a few weeks ago. I've doodled in it."

Her jaw dropped slightly as her smile widened. "Can I see them?"

"I'll bring it to the ranch tomorrow."

She rolled her lips and stepped back, her hands trailing down my arms to find both of my hands. "What do you draw?" she asked, her body spinning to walk back towards the food truck. Stetson was already in line, standing with his hands in his pockets, stance wide, his hat perched on his head...a true cowboy in the making.

"Horses, bulls, barns...things like that. Again, Abs, they aren't very good."

"I doubt that." She pulled me closer. "What's something you've drawn recently?"

One of the last things I drew? Her and Luna in the field. Taking a deep breath, I decided to be brave. "A couple weeks ago, I saw you and Luna out in the field, just resting."

"Yeah, we like the time together." She smiled, lifting her chin.

"I drew that. It's messy and..."

"You drew...me?" Her voice dropped, her eyes seeming to fog.

I nodded. "I draw what I see."

After the soft smile left her lips, a sigh following, she raised herself on her toes and kissed me. Her fingers locked on my nape as our mouths moved together flawlessly. Sparks flew between us as we got completely lost in each other. I could kiss this woman for the rest of my life if she'd let me.

"Mom!" Stetson called. "We're next!"

Abi chuckled. "Come on, Cash. He may lose his mind if we don't get him a funnel cake."

We caught up with Stetson and ordered funnel cakes with lemonade, easily the best fifty-four dollars I've ever spent. Once they were gone and Stetson was fully sugared up, we went to watch the rodeo. Stetson cheered for the bareback riders, and complained it was too late to sign up for mutton busting. Once the barrel racers began, I started watching all their maneuvers. Stetson clapped and cheered for each girl.

"Quinn should have signed up for this one." Abi shouted over the screaming crowd. "*You* should have signed up for this one." She nudged me.

I let out a laugh. "It's one thing in your arena back home, not here."

"Not yet," Abi whispered. "But it could happen."

"I won't say never...just...I need some more practice rides first."

"More rides." Abi rested her chin on my shoulder.

"Uncle Cash!" Stetson shouted, catching my attention.

I turned to the boy sitting at my side. "What's up, Stet?"

"Bulls are next! Can we stay? Mom never lets me watch the bulls."

Taking a deep breath, I looked at Abi. Her eyes were heavy on her son. She twisted her lips, and her jaw tensed. She didn't watch the bull riders, even when Oakes did his practice run before finally signing on to train, she stayed out of the arena. She hasn't outwardly said why, but I knew the reason. The last time she saw a man on a bull, the rider died. I could imagine how hard this could be for her, and I didn't want the night to end with this feeling. Her eyes looked up at me and sighed, a silent plea in her look.

"Nah bud, let's head—"

"We can stay," Abi interrupted me.

"Yes!" Stetson fist pumped.

"You sure?" I whispered

She nodded, leaning her body into me. I kissed the top of her head, proud she decided to overcome whatever ate at her with me by her side. I squeezed her hand for reassurance before turning my eyes back to the dirt.

"If you feel like you need to—"

"Nope," she stopped me, "I'm good. I'm excited for this." Her lips touched mine in a feather of a kiss before she took a deep breath and settled to watch the bulls.

The announcer riled up the crowd, and when the first bull left the chute, the loud music blaring overhead, I felt Abi stiffen. Her hand on my arm tightened, the pressure building as she watched each ride. Her eyes followed each rider, her breath letting go once the bull was off the dirt. My gaze was on her the entire time she watched the event, her lips moving with encouraging words that only she could hear, muttering under her breath with 'come on, come on, yes!' and counting down until the eight second buzzer went off. Joy and thrill filled her eyes, as if she had forgotten how much she loved this. And I was here to witness her remember. I kissed her cheek again, pulling her attention to me.

She gave me a look of freedom before bending slightly to look at her son. "Having a good time, bud?"

"Can I be a bull rider?"

"No," Abi and I said in unison.

He furrowed his brow. "Bare back?"

Abi smiled, reaching over me to touch her son's cheek. "For now, let's stick to mutton busting."

Stetson smiled, and then without missing a beat, "And barrel racing! Can we get ice cream?!"

The drive back to the ranch was silent. Stetson was fast asleep in the back. Abi weaved her fingers through mine again, and I relished in the feeling of how well they fit together. Every now and then, I'd raise her hand to my lips, kissing it gently before placing them back on my lap. The butterflies Abi mentioned several times grew in my stomach as we got closer to the ranch. I didn't want this night to end.

It was a high, being with her...being with Stetson. The night didn't go exactly as I planned, but having Stetson there added to the perfection that was our first date. His excitement and energy only seeped into us as the night grew longer, and before we knew it, his sugar high had ended. I carried him to my truck, his arms draped over my shoulders as his head fell on my chest, soft breathing coming from him as we walked. He was out like a light, allowing me to give Abi another kiss before she stepped into the passenger seat.

The moment I parked the truck in front of the house, Stetson jolted awake. He grunted and blinked a few times, another groan leaving his lungs.

"We're home..." He yawned.

Abi twisted in the passenger seat. "Yeah, bud. Why don't you head inside...I'll be right in to tuck you in. I need to talk to Cash."

He nodded. "Thanks for letting me come, Uncle Cash. I had a lot of fun. Sorry I was a grump before, Mom."

Abi smiled. "It's okay. Thank you for coming with us."

"Night, Uncle Cash."

"Night, Stet. I won't keep your mama too long."

Stetson hummed, leaving the truck and lazily walking up the steps and into the house. Once the door was closed, I turned to Abi.

"I really...really loved tonight." I said softly, lifting my hand to cup her cheek. "Even with Stet—"

Abi moved, faster than I could comprehend, as she climbed into my lap, her hands settling on my shoulders as she positioned herself on top of me. Shocked, I placed my hands on her waist. Her hips moved, creating a reaction in me that most likely wasn't appropriate for the moment...but the second her lips crashed into mine and she pushed into me, the moan that left her throat told me she didn't think it was inappropriate.

"Holy shit, Abi," I whispered, my hands slipping from her waist to her shoulders, moving her hair to the side.

"You amaze me," she said breathlessly, her hands clasping on my neck.

"I amaze you?" I raised a single eyebrow, reaching down to shift the chair back, giving her a more comfortable position. She shifted, and my eyes fluttered closed.

"Don't get cocky," she grinned.

"Abi, how can I not get cocky with you straddling me?" I teased, leaning forward to take her lips.

"I'm serious." She kissed me gently. "You amaze me. You just spent the entire night with me and my son, simply because he was throwing a fit about me being on a date...which I was already nervous for—"

"You were nervous for our date?"

"Stay on topic." She leaned back and pointed at me. I locked my eyes with hers and gently kissed the tip of her finger. "You didn't have to invite Stetson. You didn't have to spend that amount of money on rides and funnel cakes and a rodeo. That wasn't your plan."

"It wasn't, but everything about it was perfect in its own way. I loved everything about tonight, Abs, and I hope we can do it again."

"Again? You want to go out on another date?"

"Hopefully many more dates." I brushed her hair from her shoulders. "Being with you and Stet, it was the best night of my life."

She inhaled, her chest moving up as her eyes bore into me. "Cash..." Her hands cradled my face, her thumbs gently brushing my lips. "Kiss me."

I wasn't sure who moved first, but our lips met and fire ignited. My hand cupped the back of her head, holding her to me. Our tongues danced as the kiss grew deeper, the fire only growing, as she began to move her body against mine. Her hands glided up my chest, to my neck, then back down my chest again. Abi explored. Her fingers wandered my body, as if she was studying every aspect of me through the fabric.

If there were any walls left between us, they were gone now. I'd never felt this way with a woman before, and I had had plenty of women, but with Abi it was more passionate. We moved with each other seamlessly, completely in sync from the way our hips circled and our breaths matched moan for moan. Our lips even knew exactly what the other needed, but light nips and gentle swipes of our tongues—I had never been kissed like this. There was no thinking involved. Abi was made for me.

Arching her back slightly as she looked at me, desire flooded through her eyes, her lips perfect and plump. Running her hands to my shoulders, she tilted her head, giving me perfect access to kiss her neck.

The same soft moan fluttered through the air once my lips met her skin, and she shivered. She pressed into me, both on my growing erection and into my chest. I licked and sucked on her neck, not even thinking about how far I was taking this. Her neck rolled, forcing me to stop, but not for long once her lips met mine again, a kiss so deep—so electrifying—I couldn't contain myself. I ran my hands down her arms, moving to her back.

"Cash," she breathed. "I...I..." Her hands trailed up my chest, gliding back down once they reached my shoulders.

"What is it, Abi?" I asked, kissing her again and again. "Tell me what you want. It's yours, no matter what it is."

"I want..." Her fingers played with the buttons on my shirt, not actually undoing them, but playing with them. Teasing them. I could feel her fingertips hit my skin as she played, the chill from them alone making the heat in me grow.

"Abi..." I rocked my hips, showing her exactly what I wanted. She let out a moan, only making me harder as she moved against me.

"I want you to touch me," she whispered.

TWENTY-NINE

Abi

KYLA LOOKED LIKE I had just dropped a total bomb on her front porch. Her mouth was open, her eyes were wide, and her hands were frozen in front of her. I chewed on my bottom lip, instantly regretting telling her the story of what happened in Cash's truck.

We ended the day with a few drinks—non-alcoholic for Kyla, a little alcoholic for me—on the front porch, the chill from winter still lingering in the spring air. It was warm enough that we were fine wearing light jackets, the spirits in our drinks—well at least mine—helping keep us warm.

"Well…" she finally burst. "Did he touch you? Please tell me he touched you."

"He started to—" I hesitated. "But we didn't go far…clothes stayed on."

"Why did you stop?" she urged, her voice an octave higher than normal as she lurched forward on her chair, her eyes nearly bugging out of their sockets.

"Well...I remembered something, and it forced me to put a stop to the moment."

"What could have been so important that you stopped it?" She slapped her thighs.

I slumped my shoulders and looked at her. "I don't know, maybe the fact that I started my period yesterday morning."

"Oh." Her entire body slumped dramatically. "Yeah, that would kill the mood."

"Oh, it didn't kill the mood...we just...toned it down." I raised my glass to my lips.

"Toned it down?" she parroted.

"We slowed the touching; we slowed the kissing. It was...more intimate, not frantic. Like his body knew exactly what my body wanted. And then...he walked me to the door, kissed me goodnight and left." I swooned at the thought. The moment his fingers began to find my skin under the dress, finding their way to my underwear, I jerked at the memory of my cycle starting. I hadn't had to think about it with regard to something like this in the past five years, and I definitely didn't plan on straddling Cash in his truck. But he was understanding. He helped smooth the fabric of the dress, he kissed the bare skin on my shoulders and helped me climb out of his truck, kissing my temple the entire way to the front porch. "He was a gentleman." I said softly, replaying the night in my head.

"He seems like he would be." Kyla smiled. "And...did you talk to Stetson? Having a relationship with a kid doesn't seem like it would be easy?"

I nodded. "Last night when I tucked him in. I told him I really liked Cash. No more 'Uncle Cash.'" I air-quoted.

"I don't think the kid would mind if someone else stuck around. He really likes Cash, too; I think we all do." She gave me a small side eye, her lips stretching into a smile when she saw my reaction. "Where was he today? I didn't see him?"

"Mainly out with Lachlan. He's roped Cash into doing more projects around the ranch."

He came early in the morning and found me in the stables. After a few kisses, he helped me finish my morning chores before Lachlan carted him off onto the land. He appeared briefly when Quinn showed up for a few rides, giving me more private moments before, yet again, Lachlan stole him away from me again. He kissed my cheek, whispering that he'd see me for dinner, but when he and Lachlan didn't show up for dinner, I tried not to read too much into it. Sometimes the land took over and you ate the protein bars you had packed. Knowing Lachlan and his never ending to-do list...that's exactly what happened.

"We have a bull rider signed up to use the arena." I changed the subject, still feeling the heat in my cheeks. "Oakes Ashford."

"Rhett told me. He seems like a decent guy. Maybe a bit cocky."

How can I not be cocky when you're straddling me.

My cheeks flushed hotter.

I cleared my throat and nodded. "He can be. I'm glad Rhett and Cash showed up, because I wouldn't have been able to sell the arena on my own. I think his first booking is tomorrow. Cash said he'd come and help."

"Cash is pretty much done with the arena, right?" Kyla leaned back into her seat, raising her tea to her lips. "Quinn is healed or what not?"

I nodded. "Her first rodeo back is this coming weekend. Cash is heading out on Thursday."

Kyla stayed silent, rolling her lips as she studied me.

"What?" I asked.

"Is he coming back?"

"I hope so, but I also know he's set on helping Quinn for the year. Next year, he's going to take on more clients."

"And use the arena?"

"I offered it."

"And Rhett says you're supposed to sign the new deed tomorrow."

I froze, having completely blocked that from my task list. *Sign deed to Hartwell Hills* was so down on my to-do list...even though it should be one of the top things. Even though everyone agreed to the way it was going to be split—it seemed completely asinine to me. I didn't even know if I wanted thirty percent.

"I'm not going to lie," Kyla started. "Rhett's a little upset about how your dad is splitting the ranch."

I met her gaze. "Why didn't he say anything when we met with him, then. I mean...I could tell, but he didn't speak up."

"He knows how hard you work and ultimately, he's not done with the rodeo. Having a baby doesn't change the fact that he wants to compete for a least one more year, maybe two if I can travel with him, but this ranch...he loves it. He doesn't want *just* fifteen percent." Her voice dropped, moving from my moments with Cash to defending what her husband wanted and needed.

"I know I..." I stumbled. "I don't know if I want to take what's being offered."

"So, why aren't you saying anything?"

"It's hard when my dad is looking at me for all the answers. I know this ranch inside and out. I may not be on the land every day like Lachlan is, but I know the inner workings. Rhett doesn't. Lachlan knows them to an extent, but if I stopped handling those books..."

"Maybe someone else could. If you don't want the majority, what do you want Abi?"

What did I want? I hadn't thought about what I actually wanted in a long time. The last time I remembered actually starting to pursue something I wanted was Sylas, finally reaching an age where I didn't think the 'age gap' between us would matter. I was an adult, and I went after what I wanted. Him. Asking him out was simple enough. I walked up to him and Lachlan five days after my eighteenth birthday, standing in front of him until he finally locked eyes with me.

He had been working at the ranch for four years prior and I had *always* had a crush on him. I was too nervous to even talk to him, so I would hide or run when I saw him come up. But I watched him. I watched as he and Lachlan would ride, I watched as he worked on simple tasks, I watched as he stopped to wipe the sweat from his brow, I watched as he learned to ride a bull...I was always looking...but never talking. Until I finally knew the age gap wouldn't bother him, or at least I knew it didn't bother me.

I asked him out. As simple as that. Told him I wanted to get to know him and that I thought he was...I believe my exact verbiage was...damn sexy. I remember Lachlan bursting into laughter, but Sylas said yes. Maybe out of pity, but we were rarely apart after that. He started calling me nicknames in Spanish, *Mi Alma, Mi Reina*...and together—we fell.

He was the last thing I really truly wanted for myself.

I didn't have that luxury now. I wasn't able to think about what I wanted.

I had the ranch to worry about. I had Stetson to prioritize. I had my parents' looming retirement. I had a deed to sign...

I had Cash.

Cash.

I inhaled, opening my lips to speak, "I'm not sure, but I do know one thing I'm starting to want."

The next morning, after getting Stetson off to school, I walked with a purpose, determined to find and take something I wanted.

Cash was in the stables getting Nova ready for a ride when I found him. I leaned up against the gate and watched him for a moment before clearing my throat, gaining his full attention. He looked up at me, his smile growing the moment he saw me on the opposite side of the gate. He came towards me with the perfect amount of swag, and I just took him in. Once he was close enough, his lips met mine, and he breathed me in.

"Good morning." I smiled against his lips once he pulled away.

"Good morning," he repeated in kind, his eyes still closed from the kiss.

"Did you know—" I started right off the bat, his eyes opening to look at me.

"Wait," he stopped me. "I brought something I want to show you."

I stepped back as he opened the gate to the stall, his hand gently brushing my arm as he stepped behind me to the tack bench. I didn't notice the black book there when I came in, but when he picked it up, I had a feeling it was his sketchbook. The drawings he told me about on our date. He approached me, his eyes glued to mine as he handed me the book. Gracefully, I took it from him.

"Is this?" I asked, even though I knew the answer.

"My brand spanking new sketchbook. Bought it a few weeks ago." He folded his arms and watched me open it to see the first sketch of a profile of a horse.

My jaw dropped. "Nova."

For being a quick pencil sketch, he was able to capture her perfectly, down the pattern on her nose. Flipping the page, I saw a mountain range, another horse with trees behind them, two horses galloping and then...

I couldn't believe what I was seeing. He told me he drew me and Luna, but what he didn't tell me was he drew Stetson at Sylas's grave. It was a sketch—rough pencil lines and shading—but it was clear as day he had spent time on it. Stetson was kneeling, one hand resting against Sylas' name, his hat upside down on the top of the stone. Not wanting to look away from the drawing, I covered my lips with my fingers, telling myself I would not cry.

"Cash...I..." I muttered, hearing the crackle in my voice as I tried to form the words. "I love this. Can I have it?" I looked up at him, noticing how his eyes were hyper focused on me. With a single nod, he bent down and kissed my forehead.

"It's yours," he whispered against my skin, sending shivers down my spine all the way to my toes.

"You are amazing. These are amazing," I turned back to the horses, nervous to see the sketch of me and Luna, but I went back to the one of Stetson. "I can't believe..."

"You wanted to tell me something?" he interrupted, reaching up to take the sketch book from me. I let him take it, and he pulled it to his chest.

I swallowed, trying to remember why I had come in here in the first place. "Oh...right..." I blinked before looking up at him. He had his arms folded around the sketchbook, giving me his full attention. "Right before Sylas died, Stetson and I were going to travel with him for the summer. We were going to go to every rodeo, every gathering, every fairground...we were going to go..."

"Everywhere," he finished. "Yeah, Sylas told me about that. He was excited for it."

"I was too. I wanted to see him shine. Before Stetson was born, I would travel with him but, not to the extent we were planning." I searched his eyes. "I was really looking forward to the summer. Stetson's first time seeing big rodeos, bigger names. It would have been amazing."

Cash grinned at me, sincerity flowing through his expression.

"But then he died." I said, matter of factly. I couldn't keep that part out, that day changed my entire life. "And I couldn't go to rodeos like that anymore. I could watch them, and go to smaller ones like we have here, or the one we went to the other night...but I never watched the bulls. I would always think of that time we didn't have."

"Well then, we have to get you back to more rodeos. You love them. I know you do."

"Well...that's why I'm here."

He chuckled. "Okay."

"You're leaving on Thursday, getting Quinn back in the circuit?"

He nodded.

"Let me come with you."

"To rodeos? Even though I'm not riding?"

I nodded. "Just to be with you, travel, see the things I wanted to see with Sylas. But instead...see them with you. I know it's not far from here. Maybe just for the weekend? I can come and we can spend some time together. I can be the support groupie for Quinn."

"Groupie?" He raised a brow and gave me a smirk.

"Well, she doesn't want buckle bunnies hyping her up so..."

He laughed, and his hands found my belt loop, pulling me close as I spoke. "I think a groupie will be better, don't you think?"

The soft chuckle still lingering in the air, Cash spoke. "I'd love to have you on the road with me Abs, but..." He lowered his chin, his perfect straight hair line coming into my view before he raised his gaze to me again. His tawny skin had a tint of blush to his cheeks, and his dark eyes moved as he searched for the words to say. "I don't want to replace a moment with Sylas…"

"You're not." I slid my arms around his waist and pulled him to me, his arms opening up for me. I loved the way his body felt against mine. "Last night, Kyla asked me what I wanted, and I could only think of one thing. Time with you."

He raised an eyebrow. "You're serious?"

"Absolutely. I don't get to think of things I want…but I know I want this." I tugged him closer. "I just need to make sure to handle one thing…well two…"

"Stetson?"

"I'm going to ask Rhett and Kyla if they can watch him for the weekend. Quinn only has a few rides, right? We'll be home…"

"Tuesday."

"I'm sure Stetson would love to be with Kyla for four days straight."

"The other night, he complained about you leaving for a few hours." He reminded me.

"Well, to be fair, that was because he was going to be with Wyatt. Wyatt's fun for horse lessons, but his idea of babysitting is scrolling on his phone while Stetson watches a movie. If he were with Kyla, he would have jumped on that and shoved us out the door. You asked Rhett about the ring right?"

He raised an eyebrow in confusion. I let out a small laugh, taking it he didn't ask Rhett about Stetson's little proposal.

"Anyway, that's beside the point. I want time with you," I reiterated. "Let me come with you."

Using his thumb, he lifted my chin to him, giving me a whisper of a kiss, but it was enough to make me melt. His arm tightened around my waist.

He let out a soft chuckle. "I just had to save you from melting, again."

I relaxed into him, simply not caring what his answer was. I was content in his arms like this all day.

"Come with me. I would love to have you there for every moment."

"Every single moment?" I asked.

He nodded. "Every one."

I hummed and gave him a soft smile, but then my mind went back to the sketchbook that was now resting on my back. I twisted my arm and miraculously grabbed a hold of it, slipping it from his hands.

"Hey..." he protested.

"You'll get it back." I gave him a sly smile, stepping away from him and clutching the book to my own chest. "Maybe."

Still a little melty after my brief yet perfect moment with Cash, I floated into my dad's office, giving one soft knock before I came into the room.

"Abi. Hi, sweetheart."

"Hi, Dad." I took a few steps into the office and stopped right before his desk. I shoved my hands in my jean pockets, my thumbs tapping on my belt. "I um..." I stammered. "I have a favor."

"Sure."

"We were going to sign the deed today...right?"

He smiled. "I have it right here." He raised the stack of papers held together by a clip, and his smile grew. "I just need to call our lawyer, and give Lachlan and your brothers a call—"

"Can we possibly...wait to sign it for another week or two? I know you and mom want to head out but there's no rush...right?"

"Well, not technically. We just want to make sure all our ducks are in a row before we officially retire." He dropped the stack of papers and leaned against his chair, his eyes narrowing at me. Dad knew me. He knew me well. He was trying to read my mind, and his gears were turning.

"I just..." I took a deep breath. "Cash invited me to go to a few rodeos with him and Quinn and well...he makes me feel..." Lowering my gaze away from my dad, I exhaled. "I...I want to enjoy this time, so..."

My dad gave a soft smile, understanding showing in his eyes. "We can push it until you get back. How does that sound?"

I smiled. "Thanks, Dad."

"How is Cash?" He asked, folding his arms over his chest.

"He's good...great actually. I think he's going to stay on as a permanent trainer here, once he brings on more clients of course."

He hummed. "That's just fine, I actually like having the guy here."

I tightened my lips and gave him a curt nod. "I like having him around. He was always a breath of fresh air. It's good to have him back."

"I really...really like having him here."

THIRTY

Cash

STETSON HOISTED HIMSELF UP on the fence, locking his boots on the railing. He'd followed Lachlan and I out onto the land after he got home from school, and once the conversation turned to Abi leaving with me this coming weekend, Stetson got quiet. Once we got back to the ranch, and he still hadn't uttered a word, Lachlan raised his eyebrows at me, and left me alone with the little dude. Stetson didn't speak until Lachlan was out of ear shot, and then he folded his arms against his chest, leaned against the railing, and turned to me.

"When are you leaving?" he asked, his voice as low as it could go for a seven-year-old.

"Thursday," I answered, making sure Nova was tied up to the post before leaning against the gate next to Stetson.

"And mom's going? Like for sure, for sure mom's going." His head nodded each time he said 'for sure.'

I narrowed my gaze at him, offering a small smile. "Yes. She told me she'd talk to your aunt and uncle to see if you could hang with them for the weekend."

He gave me a curt nod. My heart was kind of breaking here. A part of me screamed to invite him along, to make it a family affair, but the louder part of me desperately wanted time with Abi. The time we spent together these last couple weeks had been nothing short of life changing. She made my body light up when I was around her, every single emotion flooding my veins. The way my heart was drawn to her, wanting to spill every little thing about me, about my life, my past. I wanted to be known by her, and I knew she felt the same way. She was breaking down her walls more and more, and the time alone could be a good thing for us. I felt like I could be myself around her. There was a man I *used* to be and the man I *wanted* to be, and with her I was more like the man I wanted to be more than ever before. With her...I was better.

There wasn't any more *pretending to be cocky* or *fake smiles* when she was around. With myself—or her. She had gotten really good at hiding her pain, but Abi was flourishing. I could see it, and if I could, I bet everyone else could, too. Including her son.

"Okay, let's be real here, man to man." I gently punched Stetson in the shoulder, his small body moving with the soft impact.

"Man to man?" he parroted, squaring his shoulders.

"Man to man. Do you remember the other night when we had that rodeo?"

"And you kissed Mommy. And then you took Mommy on a date."

"Yep, it's no secret that I really like your mommy."

"And she really likes you. She told me."

I raised an eyebrow. "She did?"

He pursed his lips and nodded quickly, loosing up his body to grab ahold of the railing he sat on. "She told me I shouldn't call you Uncle Cash anymore; she said now that you guys are kissing it's kinda weird."

"When did she tell you that?"

He met my gaze, almost hesitantly. "After the fair, when she came to tuck me in. She told me she wanted to keep you around, but I had to want you around, too."

"Well, do you? Want me around?" I asked.

Stetson narrowed his eyes as he studied me. Nerves shot through my stomach while I waited for the kid to speak. I wasn't sure why this little man was the one sending my stomach in knots, but here I was, my breathing getting very unsteady as I waited for him to finally break the silence. He had to be accepting of this just as much as we were. I suddenly wanted his approval more than anything.

And his silence was killing me.

He nodded, and the nerves settled, a breath of air leaving my lungs.

"Well, yeah. You're fun. That's why I'm sad I can't go with you and mom to the rodeos. I can miss school for a few days. I'll be good, I promise."

I chuckled. "Stet, I have no doubt you would be. You're an amazing little dude, but I think your mom just needs the time alone."

"But she won't be alone," he grumbled.

"Okay, okay, let me rephrase this. She wants time with…" I paused, taking him in, "me."

He made a look of disgust, which just made me chuckle. "So she can kiss you?"

Laughter broke through my throat. "I hope so."

He scrunched his nose, shifting his weight slightly on the railing.

"Is that okay?" I asked, hesitation filling my voice. "I want to be more than friends with your mom, and that means I want you to be comfortable with it."

"Like her boyfriend?"

"Yeah," I huffed a small laugh, "like her boyfriend. Your mom makes me really happy; she makes me laugh, and she makes me want to be a better man. I want to keep her—and you—if you'll both have me."

"You want to take her to the rodeos to ask her to be your girl-friend?"

"Something like that."

"And I'll get to stay with Aunt Kyla?" His voice rose, and a small smirk spread across his lips. Excitement finally started to take over.

I gave him a nod.

"I guess I can stay with them, but you have to come back as my mom's boyfriend."

"Does that mean you'll keep me around?"

"Yeah…I'll keep you around." He nudged me with his elbow, and I wrapped my arm around him, pulling him off the railing into a hug. He hugged me back, nuzzling his nose into the crook of my neck.

Not only was I falling for Abi, but I was falling for Stet too.

"Oh wait." He pulled away from me. "I have a project in school. I need to interview someone for it. About their job and what they do. Can I interview you?"

"Sure bud, when is it due?" I looked down at him, giving his back a quick rub.

"Friday."

I laughed, dropping him to the ground, shaking my head at the way his seven-year-old brain was working. "And you thought you could skip a few days of school."

Me

I have you signed up for three rodeos this weekend. Saturday afternoon, Sunday evening, and Monday night. How you feeling?

Quinn

Ready. It's been a long eight weeks.

Me

Find more and sign up. You have a lot of money to rack up.

Quinn

(Saluting emoji) Yes, sir.

Shaking my head, I tossed my phone to the bed. Shutting my laptop and tossing it to the side, I plopped down on my bed, my head hitting the pillow with a thump. The hotel's comforter was soft against my skin, cool and welcome against the heat from my bare back. Lifting my arms I placed them over my eyes. I had left the Hartwell's ranch shortly after Stetson interviewed me for his project, just in time to give Abi a quick kiss goodbye.

Stetson's questions were flowing through my head.

What made you want to ride saddle bronc?

What was your childhood like?

What was your favorite part about your job?

If you could change anything about your life what would it be?

The one about my family and childhood was an easy enough answer, and the kid seemed to be excited to learn about my upbringing. Growing up a mixed race with a Black farm hand father and a Caucasian farm owners' daughter—they were a cliché really—wasn't easy, but my parents worked together to give me the best life possible. Because of my father, I learned skills around the farm. Because of my mother, I started riding horses. She was a breakaway roper, and my grandfather rode bronc. Their love for the rodeo only amplified it for me. Taking saddle bronc to the next level with rodeos was easy. It was a thrill. Favorite part about the job...the travel and the people I met.

What would I change?

The slight twinge of pain in my leg brought me back to that night, that ride that changed my life completely. It's the one thing I would change...to an extent.

I don't remember much of the ride itself; I remember drawing the horse's name, saddling up, and grabbing the cinch as tight as I could. I nodded, and the chute opened, and the horse flew. Higher than any horse I had ridden before. It was the adrenaline I craved, and even though the horse went up, my weight shifted just the wrong way, and his back hooves slipped. He landed on his shoulder, and his entire body went limp after that, landing directly on my left side. Everything happened in slow motion from that moment on.

I swear I could still hear his spine and neck cracking.

His neck and back had broken, he died on impact, and his entire weight was on my center. I couldn't move. I was stuck. And pain was radiating everywhere.

I could still hear the crowd release a loud 'ooohhh' and the announcer trying to calm them as best as possible until the emergency responders could come and lift the horse, guide him off the dirt, and then place me on the stretcher. By the time I was in the ambulance, I had lost consciousness and woke up hours later in the hospital room. Carolyn was there, and the first thing she said when I opened my eyes was, "*Well, I guess this means you're out for the year...*"

No *Thank goodness you're awake,* or *How are you feeling.* All she was worried about was the rodeos I'd have to cancel. She didn't grasp my hand to comfort me; she didn't cry or give me a kiss. She just opened her phone to call my agent to cancel rodeos. No emotion from her.

The surgeries to fix my broken femur and knee kept me in the hospital for a few weeks. I rarely saw Carolyn. I did everything alone. When the physical therapy started, the slow progression I made—the two steps forward and five steps back—only proved Carolyn right. I was weak. Follow-up appointments became a monthly occurrence, and the one Carolyn decided to attend with me, changed my life forever.

So...I guess, if I could change anything but still end up right where I am, it would be to erase the fall. Erase the fall, erase the injury, but have this life.

Taking a deep breath, ignoring the pain, the slight buzz of my phone forced me to pull my arms down. I expected Quinn, but Abi's name popped up with my notifications, and the simple text brought a smile to my face.

Abi

> I hear you talked to Stetson. That was quite the bed time story.

I replied instantly, hoping she was seeing those three little dots with anticipation.

Me

> I did, accidentally let it slip you were coming with me.

Abi

> Accidentally huh?

Me

> Well, I was telling Lachlan and he overheard.

Abi

That makes more sense. He told me I had to become your girlfriend.

Me

He basically told me I had to come back as your boyfriend.

Abi

That sounds weird…being 29, I didn't think I'd ever have a boyfriend again.

Me

Boyfriend. I like the sound of that.

Abi

This weekend will be your trial period, I guess.

Me

Trial period!?

Abi

We'll see how I feel after.

I laughed. Only she would say something like that. Before I could respond, the dots began to dance again.

Abi

My feelings won't change.

I grinned.

Me

Mine never have.

THIRTY-ONE

Abi

IT HAD BEEN FOREVER since I'd been in a larger rodeo arena. The Hartwell Arena had nothing on this—and this was considered tiny. The stands were starting to fill. Slowly but surely, the people came, and just by looking at them, you could tell who was here for their first time, and you could easily spot the girls that were here for the cowboys.

I caught a glance of Oakes Ashford, who tipped his hat at me before following a group of men, winking at the group of girls who were off to the side. They giggled so loud, I could hear them from where I stood. Shaking my head at them, I drew my attention back to the arena. The groundhog was out, dragging the dirt once more before the events began. The two announcers were looking over their call sheets, getting ready to carry excitement. Pulling out my phone, I snapped a picture of them and sent it to Wyatt.

Me

> Wish you were in that box. How's Stet?

I hit send before I even registered that I called him *Stet*. For a fraction of a second, I considered editing the text.

Wyatt

> I'm headed to Colorado. Get your boyfriend to change Quinn's schedule. Stetson was as happy as could be with Kyla this morning going to school. Rhett said he'll take him out on the land.

> By the way, you called him Stet.

Abi

> Don't get used to it.

Wyatt

> Never.

Rolling my eyes with a light smile on my lips, I pocketed my phone and turned back to the dirt. Cash was with Quinn and her horses, leaving me alone to take in the sights. After Sylas's accident, I never went to a rodeo arena without Wyatt, or at least someone from my family with me. Last year, during the National Final Rodeo—The NFR—Kyla and Wyatt shoved me between them, the two of them creating energy that seeped into to me. But like always, I 'had to go to the bathroom' once the bull riders came on. Kyla was with Rhett by that time, and Wyatt was more than willing to go talk to the announcers. At the Hartwell Rodeo, I was always with Stetson and my parents. I never had a moment to sit and watch, to look and to just remember how much I loved this.

And I *loved it.*

I had a small suspicion that being here would bring up upsetting memories, pulling me back into that melancholy pain of losing Sylas. Taking a deep breath, I took in the smells. Closing my eyes, I took in all the sounds. Raising my chin to sky, I let the sun take over my skin, filling my entire body with warmth. Instead of sadness, all I could feel was how right it felt that I was here.

Rodeos ran in the Hartwell blood. My mother was a barrel racer, my father was a team roper. Rhett and Lachlan started our generation off with their events, even pulling Wyatt in against his will. Though he didn't compete in a livestock event, he loved the rodeo just as much as the rest of us. Me? I would barrel race for fun, but my joy came from the stands, right where I was. I loved to watch. Adrenaline came in different ways. For Rhett, it was jumping off his horse and getting the calf. For me, it was watching them.

A part of me wished that Cash was competing today. Or that he'd compete in general. The way he was at home, I could see it in his eyes that he loved it. He deserved to be on the board, making a comeback. I convinced him to get in the saddle again. Maybe, just maybe, I could convince him to get on the board again. He could start with small rodeos—smaller than this one—and work his way up. He would tell me his leg hurt too much, or he was too old, but I knew this was the life for him.

And I wanted to see it.

"Well, if it isn't Rhett Hartwell's little sister."

A deep Southern accent drew me from my sun. I turned to see Rhett's friend, and fellow tie-down roper, Zeke leaning against the railing. I smiled. I had known Zeke for a while now; he had been roping alongside Rhett since he started his career, and even though I hadn't seen him in a long time, my smile grew when I met his eyes.

"Zeke!" I stood from my seat to wrap my arms around his neck. "I didn't know you were going to be here today."

"I thought Rhett was out for the season. What brings you here?"

"He is. I'm actually here with Cash." I pulled away from him, taking him in. He hadn't changed one bit.

"Callahan?" He raised his eyebrows in question. "He's competing?"

"No." I tapped the rim of his hat. "He's training Quinn Compton."

"Aw, man. I would love to see him compete again."

"Me too. Maybe you can help me convince him."

"I'm on it." He placed his hands on his hips, giving me his award-winning smile. "I know just where to find him."

"Hopefully getting Quinn set up."

He gave me a single nod. "I guarantee you he's over by the bunnies that rally up around the trailers before the show."

I pinched my eyebrows. "Why would he be over there?"

"Abi, come on. You know the guy. That's where he was all last year." He tilted his head at me, the grin on his lips shifting to a cocky 'you know what I mean' smile.

I raised my eyebrows. "Well I hope he's not over there..."

"Wait." He stopped. "You came with Cash. Are you guys together?"

"It's still new," I replied, feeling the blush tint my cheeks. "Very new..."

"I never would have put the two of you together."

"Neither would I honestly." I shrugged my shoulders, forcing the blush to stay down. "I should probably go find him. He said we'll watch from a certain area."

"Oh, of course, I'll walk with you. Families, trainers, agents...all the important people watch from the ground, don't know why you insist on higher up." Zeke placed his hand on my shoulder.

I shrugged and gave him a smile. "Better view."

He returned my smile, nodding in agreement. It was true, sitting higher let me see the entire arena, not just the chutes.

"Listen, we all go out after events. We'd love to have you and Cash join us? I can try to convince him to get back on the board."

"Oh, maybe. I'll ask Cash—if I see him before the event starts."

Zeke laughed. "Even then, drag his ass out."

"Ok, okay. I'll have to find you after."

"Please do."

He began to talk about his family, catching me up on his wife and kids. I was shocked to learn he had four kids now, and that his wife was happy being a stay-at-home mom. They would come to events closer to home, but mainly it was just him on the road. If Cash ever got back into this world, I didn't want him to do this alone. I wouldn't want to only attend certain events. I'd want to come to all of them.

"You still at the ranch?" Zeke asked, and I rolled my eyes slightly. *As if I'd be somewhere else.*

"Yup...my parents are retiring soon actually. We're splitting it between the three of us—"

"Abs, there you are!" Cash came jogging up to us. "Oh hey, Zeke." He came to a stop in front of us and reached forward lightly to touch my hand. "You found her for me, she wasn't at the stands."

"She was settled higher up like always."

"Taking it all in." I took a single step towards Cash. "It's been a long time since I've been in an arena like this. The one at home is nothing compared to this."

"You coming to Days of 47 this year? You remember that arena—right Abi?" Zeke asked, referencing the biggest rodeo the state of Utah put on. If I remembered correctly, Kyla called it a TARDIS...bigger on the inside.

I looked over to Cash, who was wearing the most perfect smile as he lightly shook his head. "By that time, I'm hoping Quinn doesn't need her trainer booking her events."

Zeke let out a laugh. "Girl needs an agent if she can't handle her own bookings. I told Abi we all go out after, and I've been tasked to convince you to compete again."

Cash pulled me close to him, his hand finding the small of my back as he looked down at me.

I smiled. "What? We'd both love to see you compete."

He shook his head. "Nah, I'm retired."

"Too bad, man...too bad." Zeke shrugged his shoulders he turned back to me. "I tried Abi."

"Not hard enough." I elbowed Cash gently in his side.

Zeke laughed, shaking his head as his smile grew. "Find me after, okay? Come out with us and let loose a little."

"Let loose. Ha, sure." Cash agreed, giving him a pat on the shoulder as he walked past. "Let me guess," he whispered as soon as Zeke was out of ear shot. "He told you I was by the trailers, so you had to come find me?"

"He did say you were there, but that's not why I wanted to find you." I faced him, wrapping my arms around his middle. "Thank you for letting me come. I'd forgotten how much I loved the rodeo arena."

"You're welcome." He titled his chin up, his eyes still firm on mine. "I was near the trailers though."

Rolling my eyes, I moved, using my fingers to pinch his sides, feeling nothing but firm muscle. "I bet you were."

"Not for the bunnies. That's just where Quinn was."

"Uh huh...sure..." I stepped back. "Let's go get a drink before it starts."

"Yes, ma'am."

Once the rodeo started, I started beating myself up for staying away for so long. The one we went to with Stetson was fun...but my focus wasn't on the event. Then I was hyper-focused on Cash and Stetson and how much I was in love with being with the two of them. But here, I was immersed in the events. Jumping and cheering when a roper got a good time. Booing when a barrier was broken, and sending Kyla videos of the mutton busting to show Stetson.

When the barrel racing started, Cash's demeanor changed completely. He studied each rider, focusing on where they turned, how they handled their horse and their body language as they rode. I even caught him counting out loud, stopping right when the buzzer went off. When Quinn came, he furrowed his brow and sat up straight on his seat. She held his entire attention, and she didn't even know it.

She burst through the gate, hitting the first and second barrel with ease, then moving towards the third, curling around it like a knife spreading frosting and then she raced back to the entrance. Her smile filled the entire arena. She was back. The eight weeks she took working with Cash had finally paid off. He pumped a fist and turned to me, shouting.

"She's in second."

I cheered loudly in his ear, clapping even louder.

"I take it you're having fun?" he asked, leaning into me.

I kissed him, taking him completely by shock. "I am. Thank you."

He kissed me again, deeper this time, his hands cradling my chin as our lips danced against each other. The spark was radiating through my body, heat traveled everywhere, and I knew Cash could feel it as his fingers threaded through my hair. I hummed against him, breaking the kiss and placing my forehead on his.

"I'm having the best night of my life," I admitted, remembering him using those exact words with me. Every night with him was becoming the best night of my life.

"That's setting the bar high."

"You can break it," I smirked, giving him one last chaste kiss.

THIRTY-TWO

Cash

THUNDER CRACKED OVER US just as we stepped into the lounge at the hotel. Abi's entire body jumped as she scooted closer to me. I laughed, pulling her flush to my side, kissing her temple, not caring who saw or who would comment. I should have known the comments would come right away.

"Whoo-ee!" Darren—another tie down roper who Zeke was closer to—whooped. "Tell me Callahan, how did you rope Rhett's little sister?"

I rolled my eyes at the level of maturity coming from the cowboy following Abi and me.

"He didn't *rope* me," Abi protested. "Technically...I roped him."

"It's true, she did throw herself at me first." I looked down at her and wiggled my eyebrows, remembering the first hug she gave me after my ride.

"But..." Abi pulled away from me, her hand sliding down my arm until our fingers intertwined. "That's not the topic for tonight...right? No one wants to hear about our relationship."

"Not gonna lie," Zeke began. "I kinda do."

"Come on, Callahan." Quinn came up from behind me, patting my back as she made her way into the lounge. "Let's get some drinks and then off to bed. We gotta head to Montana early tomorrow morning so we can't—"

"Man." Darren wrapped his arm around Quinn. "You're just as uptight as Rhett was. Relax, Compton. You're with the big boys now."

Quinn grimaced and shrugged him off. "First Wyatt, and now you."

"Wait...Wyatt?" Abi spun her body around to look at Quinn. "Please tell me my brother didn't make an ass of himself?"

"Oh, he did." Quinn barked a laugh. "At The Steel, the same night you kissed Cash."

"I need the entire story." Abi grabbed Quinn's arm and pulled her to a couch, as me and the guys made our way to the bar top. I kept my eyes on Abi the entire time, wanting to be right next to her and Quinn, rather than at the bar top with some tie down ropers.

I ordered our drinks, listening to Zeke and Darren laugh and talk as they tried to pull me into the conversation, but my eyes were on Abi. The smile that was spread across her lips as she listened to Quinn tell her story made those butterflies begin to flutter in my stomach. She was happy, genuinely happy. She wasn't faking that laugh or smile, that was all her. I recognized that smile from years ago, when her life was exactly the way she wanted it to be. And now—here with me—the joy that seeped through her was real.

She told me she wanted to live these moments with me, that I wouldn't be replacing times she could have had with Sylas, she was making new memories, new dreams and desires...with me.

"So really, how did you snag her?" Zeke asked, leaning on the bar top as soon as his drink was in his hand.

I turned back to him quickly. "Thought we said that wasn't up for discussion."

"Nah, Abi said it. Not you. Abi is occupied, and I want to know how that happened." He gestured towards Abi. "I mean, everyone knew you had a thing for her—it was clear as day. Pretty sure Sylas even knew."

"I never would have acted on it. Sylas knew *that*, too." I gave him a side eye.

"True, but then she stopped coming around after Sylas passed. No one blames her, and Rhett let us know she was doing okay, but seeing her now..." He looked over his shoulder at Abi. "She looks happy. I take it that's your doing, so...how did you land her?"

The bartender dropped mine and Abi's drinks in front of us, nodding his head once as he took my card to pay. Handing me the slip back, I signed my name quickly and slipped my card back into my wallet, all the while trying to figure out how to tell Zeke how I got so lucky to 'land' Abi. Grabbing both drinks, I stood from the stool.

"First of all," I started, "I didn't 'land' her. She wasn't a prize to win. Second," I met his gaze, "she brought me back to life, and…well." I looked at her just in time to see her laugh. She caught my gaze, and her smile softened. "I helped her smile again."

Leaving the guys at the bar top, I walked over Abi and Quinn, my gaze never once leaving the woman I was in love with.

In love.

How long did it take to fall in love with someone?

Did it matter?

Looking at Abi, I knew it didn't and never would.

I had been in love with her for a long time.

Handing her the drink, I bent to give her a slight kiss before taking the seat next to her. I leaned back on the couch and rested my arm on the back, giving her the chance to sink into me if she chose.

"Quinn was telling me about Wyatt's fail." Abi pivoted to face me, lifting her drink to her lips. "It's comical because, well…"

"Wyatt doesn't fail." I finished her sentence.

"Oh no." Quinn laughed. "Someone has to tell him no. He's too cocky. He's too…"

"Full of himself?" I asked, pretty much a mumble under my breath.

Abi turned her head, her braid flipping to her other shoulder. "It's true, but harsh. Wyatt will figure himself out one day. Until then, I'm glad Quinn turned him down."

"You know he told me to stay away from you, right?" I took a drink.

Abi laughed. "Yeah…he wasn't too thrilled when I told him you asked me out." Just then, Abi's phone rang on the table in front of her. Kyla's name appeared on the screen, and she shot forward. "It's probably Stetson. I'll be right back." She reached for her phone as she stood. "Hey, Stet."

I blinked, watching as she walked away. She called him *Stet*.

"Okay I gotta know, why does Wyatt hate you?" Quinn asked, leaning forward.

"We used to be friends, but he is not too fond of the way I treated Abi." *With every right...*

"Which is..." she pried.

"Nothing we're not trying to fix."

She smiled and plopped back in her chair. "You *are* a big softy."

"Only when it comes to her," I replied.

Abi turned to me and gave me a wink before turning her back again. I gave her a moment of peace to talk to Stetson, loving just watching her interact with him, but soon she bounded towards me, holding the phone out.

"He wants to talk to you now, then bedtime," she said, waving the phone in my direction.

"Bedtime for all of us." Quinn stood. "I'm going to head to my room. We have a long drive tomorrow. Night Abi." Quinn gave Abi a quick side hug as I took the phone from Abi's hand. "Night Cash."

I gave Quinn a quick nod before I put Abi's phone to my ear. "Stet...shouldn't you be in bed?" I asked.

"Are you mom's boyfriend yet?" he asked, his voice so full of enthusiasm I was certain the people on the other side of the lounge could hear it.

I chuckled and looked at Abi. She shrugged as if she knew exactly what he asked.

"I'm getting there, bud. Don't worry."

"She told me she had a lot of fun and took a lot of pictures. I can't wait to see them. Keep her smiling. She needs to smile more. Also, she likes those iced tea drinks, the ones with lemonade in it. Get her one of those and you will be her boyfriend for sure." He talked rapidly.

"You giving me dating advice?" I questioned, raising my eyebrow.

"Well, you need it," Stetson said flatly.

I winced. "Ouch, dude...ouch."

"What? It's what Uncle Rhett said."

I heard a faint *hey* come from the background, and I could just picture Rhett sitting next to him as Stetson called him out, only causing me to chuckle.

"Just make sure you come back as her boyfriend. Remember, she's not a flower person either—"

"I know, I know. How did your project go?" I asked, changing the subject as fast as I could. I didn't really want dating advice from a seven-year-old.

"It was so good!" he shouted. "Everyone wants to meet you, so I told them they could come to the Hartwell Rodeo this July Fourth. They can see you ride."

"Stet, man, the Fourth of July Rodeo is..." *Not something I'm ready for.* I glanced up at Abi who was shaking her head quickly. She mouthed 'no, don't tell him no' as her hands met my thighs. "That sounds like fun."

Abi pursed her lips and squeezed my thighs. I wasn't sure if it was pity in her eyes or disappointment--I just knew that rodeo in particular was too close for me. Riding in an empty arena was one thing, but in front of people…I didn't want to disappoint Stetson if I ended up hurting myself.

"Awesome!" He shouted. "I knew I could get you on the dirt again. I'll mutton bust, Uncle Rhett will rope, and you'll be the lead saddle bronc rider. This rodeo is going to be the best one."

"Stetson." I heard Rhett in the background, his voice faint but very, very clear. "It's bedtime, little dude. Say goodnight, and we'll call them tomorrow."

"Okay, Uncle Rhett!" Stetson shouted, not moving the phone away from his mouth. "Tell Mommy I said goodnight, and Cash?"

"Yeah, bud."

"Come back her boyfriend!"

I laughed, tempted to salute even though he couldn't see me. "Yes, sir. Sleep well, and we will talk tomorrow."

"Bye!!" The phone went dead. Lowering it, I looked at the black screen and handed it back to Abi.

"Wow." She took her phone from me. "He didn't even want to say goodnight to me?"

"Guess not. He was too excited about making sure I was your boyfriend. I'm supposed to get you an Arnold Palmer, and make sure you are smiling."

Abi raised her drink, flashing me a sexy smile. "You're on the right track. You even spiked it." Her laugh floated through the bar as she leaned in for a kiss.

Downing the rest of my drink, I ignored the sting from the whiskey as it hit my throat. "The rodeo though…" I said, my voice heavy.

Abi took my empty glass and stood, grabbing her half-empty glass from the table. "We'll talk about it, but...I'm sure Quinn is right. We have an early morning tomorrow...so..." she grinned.

"Yeah, let's head on up."

We said goodnight to the guys, threaded our fingers together, and then made our way up to our room, my body nowhere near tired yet.

"Can you call down to the front desk?" I heard Abi shout from the bathroom.

I sat on the edge of the king-sized bed, removing my boots and kicking them to the side, furrowing my brow at her request. "Um...why?"

"Well, you need a sleeping cot."

I stood, folding my arms over my chest. "Excuse me?"

"There's one bed."

She appeared from the bathroom, sticking her toothbrush in her mouth. Her hair was let down, covering her shoulders. She had removed her plaid, button-down shirt, leaving just her tank top on. Her jeans still hugging her every curve as she leaned against the door frame.

"Yeah...and?"

She tilted her head, raising a brow.

"Come on Abi, we're adults."

"You planned this," she mumbled through her toothpaste.

Truth be told, I made the booking for the hotel before Abi asked if she could come on the trip. I just didn't change it once I knew she was coming. The idea that Abi would be sleeping beside me, in my arms if she let me, set my entire body on fire. Nothing needed to happen to make this night a perfect night. I just wanted to be with her.

I inhaled and stood, taking the few steps towards her. "You caught me."

Shaking her head, she spit the toothpaste into the sink and washed her mouth. "I can't believe you," she muttered, a smile sneaking through.

"You absolutely can believe me." I leaned against the door frame and crossed my arms. "So no, I will not be calling the front desk."

Running her fingers through her hair one last time, she stood up straight and looked at me, "Well fine then. Just so you know, I snore."

"Snoring would have been an issue even if I was on a cot." I pushed myself off the door frame and followed her to the bed. "Hey." I chuckled, grabbing the belt loop of her jeans. "Come here."

She fell back into me, her hands sliding against my arms as I wrapped them around her waist. She leaned her head to the side, a soft sigh leaving her lungs once my lips touched her skin there.

"I'm teasing," she admitted, making my heart skip a beat. "If there were two beds in here, I'd plan on sleeping next to you."

"Well, that's good. I promised Stetson something," I whispered.

"Oh yeah...what's that?"

"That I'd come back as your boyfriend." I kissed her shoulder again.

"We've had this discussion before. This is your trial period, remember?" She turned her body to face me, lifting her arms to rest on my shoulders.

"I think I passed the trial period."

"Really, what makes you say that?"

"A few reasons...one, pretty sure when I saw you with Zeke, I felt a small surge of jealousy."

Abi's chin tilted up as she laughed. "You were not jealous. Plus, he's married. And—how is that a justifiable reason?"

"Two," I ignored her comment, "Sitting next to you at the rodeo was the best experience I'd ever had. Three, I can't stop thinking about you, even when you're twenty feet away. And four..." I took a deep breath, swallowing, trying to keep the words from staying down, not sure if it was time to really tell her how I felt. They were fighting to get out, and I was going to let them win the battle. "I'm falling for you."

Abi froze, her hands sliding down to my shoulders, resting on my chest. "What?"

I fumbled. "I just...you know I've always had feelings for you. I never would have acted on them...ever. But now...I can't not tell you how I feel. And with everyone asking me how I managed to 'snag' or 'land' you—all I could think about was how I was the one who didn't deserve to have you, and yet here you are. After everything I've done, you're giving me a chance, and I knew these feelings were stronger than anything I've ever felt in my entire life. Abi...I'm falling. Harder and harder with each touch, each kiss. Every time I have to save you from melting...Abi I'm falling in love with you."

Those words hung between us as her breath quickened. I could hear her heart thump, thump, thump in her chest as she searched me.

"Cash I..." she whispered, breaking her gaze.

"You don't have to say anything. Hell, I wasn't planning on saying anything. I just...I couldn't keep it in any longer." I interrupted her, tightening my hold around her waist.

"Cash I..." she tried again, looking up at me, her eyes hooded over as she searched my own. "I forgive you for everything that happened, for all the things we both could have done better—I forgive us, and Cash..." She swallowed. "You do deserve me. We deserve each other."

She kissed me then, soft, slow, tantalizing. I began memorizing the way our lips fit together, the way she tasted of her minty toothpaste, a small lingering of the drink she had on the tip of her tongue. The wave hit us both as we drank each other in, repeating the same touches, the same kisses and the same urgency. I took a step back, not breaking contact, and sat on the edge of the bed. Situating herself to straddle me, she began to work on the buttons on my shirt, revealing my skin inch by inch. Her porcelain fingertips danced against my darker skin, sending shock waves through my entire body until I moved to help her remove it fully, tossing it to the ground.

"Will you be my girlfriend?" I asked, kissing her gently.

She hummed against my lips. "I'll be whatever you want me to be, as long as I can call you mine."

"Yours?" I repeated.

"Mine."

Before she could lean to kiss me again, I played with the hem of her tank top, slipping my fingers under the fabric to feel her. She shook with each breath but slowly raised her arms. I slipped the tank top over her head, her hair falling like a waterfall over her shoulders, leaving her torso bare in her jeans and bra.

"God, Abi," I groaned, pulling her towards me to kiss just above her breast. "I've never seen a more perfect woman." I licked up her neck, feeling myself getting harder with each move she made on my lap, of simply having her in more ways than I thought. "Fuck...I can't wait to..."

"Cash," she stopped me, grabbing the nape of my neck to lift me up to her, "It's uh..." she hesitated.

I could feel her shaking, her entire body shivered under my fingers. She bit her bottom lip, but met my gaze.

"It's been a while since...well..." She shuttered. "I haven't..." She moved to cover herself with her arms, her body almost folding over, her breath hitched and she bit her lip.

"Abi," I whispered, kissing her sweetly. "I'll take care of you." Carefully, I pushed my fingers under her bra strap, watching her reaction as my calloused fingers touched her soft, perfect skin. I slowly unclasped her bra, my hands gliding past her arms to leave her completely bare in front of me. With the same care as before, I cupped her breast in my hands, slowly rubbing my thumb over her nipple, wanting to kiss and suck them, holding back as much as I could. I didn't want to rush this. I wanted to give her everything she needed, everything she wanted. I moved one hand to her neck, pulling her closer to me to kiss and lick her skin. She gasped and arched into me.

With one motion, I scooped her up, standing and turning to lay her on the bed. I ran my hands down her stomach, bending to kiss in between her breasts, down her belly button. She shuttered again, her breathing shaky as she let out a soft moan.

"Cash...I..."

"I have you Abi." I kissed right above her navel. "I'll take care of you, if you trust me."

"I trust you," she whispered. "Cash I...I trust you."

Slowly, I undressed her completely, standing at the edge of the bed to undress myself, my gaze never leaving her as she let her eyes wander all over my body. Her focus on me lit me up, creating sparks and a fire in me that I hadn't felt before. Sex with Carolyn was just that...sex. There was never this level of intimacy that I was feeling with Abi's eyes on me. I couldn't help but think about what it would be like once her hands explored again, just like the night in my truck, but deeper this time. With every intention of becoming one with her, I inhaled, standing in front of Abi completely bare as she took me all in.

"Oh, God," she finally sighed, her breath shaky. "Cash...you're beautiful."

She sat, her hands finally finding the most sensitive parts of me. My head falling back, I let her find her way, her skin feeling exactly how I imagined. Tingles flew up my skin as her fingers touched every place she could reach. I let her explore until I couldn't hold myself back anymore. I kneeled over her, my lips finding the skin on her shoulder as we touched, teased and kissed until she finally met my gaze.

Lowering her back on the bed, gently placing her head on the pillow, I kissed her—raw and deep.

I love this woman.

"Abi," I muttered against her lips.

"I'm yours Cash, please I..."

"I have you Abi."

Our worlds came together, and Abi gave me the one thing I never thought I could have. Her.

THIRTY-THREE

Abi

I woke to Cash's lips peppering kisses all over my back. He would lick a spot, then kiss, then move to a new area, repeating again and again and again until I stretched against him. His knuckles trailed along my side until they reached my neck, moving my hair before his lips found my skin.

I wasn't lying when I told him it had been a long time since I had been with someone. Sylas was the man I lost my virginity to; he was the last one to see me so vulnerable, but with Cash, there was nothing but complete trust. The way he moved against me, his hands finding all the right places to send sparks through my skin, his tongue tasting every piece of me...just thinking about it made my skin sizzle. I couldn't remember the last time I had experienced a night like this. And it was Cash who gave it to me.

And he had said he loved me. My chest swelled just at the memory of him saying those three small words. I didn't expect them to fill me like they did. Love? Already? In the back of my mind, I was telling myself to protest it, tell him it was way too soon for any of those kinds of emotions—but it felt so good to hear him say them, and it felt right to want to say it back. Even though when I started, I choked...but there would be time for that. I knew there would be.

Lifting my arm over his head, I stretched before turning to my back, relaxing as I wrapped my arm around his neck, pulling his lips to mine.

"Good morning," he whispered against my lips. "Did you sleep well?"

"Hmm," I hummed. He wrapped his arms around me and held me as close as he could. His skin was warm, his body soft and comforting, yet hard in all the right places. "I did. What time is it?"

"Early still. You've only been asleep for a few hours."

"A few hours." I arched my back slightly, as much as he would let me. "You woke me up?"

"I couldn't wait anymore." He kissed me.

"For? Don't we have to leave pretty soon? Quinn was pretty determined that we had an early morning." I squirmed, but his arms tightened around my waist, stopping me.

"We have plenty of time." He bent his neck, kissing my bare shoulder.

I giggled. "Cash, we don't."

"Oh, but we do."

"Cash Callahan." I laughed, trying to be stern, but absolutely loving the way his body was responding to me, the way mine was responding to him. I could already feel the heat building. "How about..." I pushed him playfully, trying to peel myself away from his arms.

It was a struggle to even pretend to want to be away from him. I could spend all day in this bed, letting Cash do whatever he wanted with me—whatever I wanted to do with him.

"We spend all day here," he finished for me, basically reading my mind.

"I wish we could." I let my head fall back onto my pillow, imagining spending all day in bed with him. I had never ever done that before. I never had the chance, but with him...now...complete euphoria.

"Perfect." He turned, keeping one arm holding me to him. "I'll call Quinn—"

"Cash!" I squealed, moving to stop him, climbing on top of him in the process. "As much as I'd love to stay here, and make love to you over and over—"

He closed his eyes and dropped his head on the pillow, letting out a soft moan, "Yes, please."

I giggled, "Well, I was going to suggest we take a shower, and then meet Quinn at the stables to get the horses and head to Montana."

His eyes fluttered open. "That's probably what needs to happen. Why are you always so responsible?"

"If I'm not, who will be?" I leaned over him, kissing him deeply before rolling off the bed. "Come join me." I teased as I sauntered into the bathroom.

Eventually, we checked out of the hotel and followed Quinn to the next rodeo. As Cash popped the truck in park, I took in our surroundings before his hand cupped my cheek and pulled me to him for a kiss, reminding me that he was mine. My lips still buzzing from his kiss, we jumped from the truck to the back side of the arena, the side not many people saw. Hundreds of livestock waited for their chance to play—after all, they had to have fun at this, too. I stopped to scratch a few horses behind their ears, giving them all the love they deserved. Once we reached Quinn's trailer, we caught her just in time to see her lead Charming out of the back, her turquoise button down the perfect choice for tonight's rodeo. Quinn looked elegant in the best way possible for a rodeo gal; even her boots had a slight shine to them.

"Nope." Cash let go of my hand to take the lead from her. "No way. You rode Charming last night."

"Yeah, and we got a seventeen point six, so we'll be repeating that again tonight." Quinn reached for the lead, snatching it back.

"On Hook."

Quinn eyed the black horse in the trailer. She had gotten used to him at the ranch, but this being a different setting, I could tell she wasn't quite sure how the horse would react to the crowd. Taking a deep breath, she looked at me and then back to Cash.

"Fine." She gave in. "But if I fall—"

"You won't."

"—You're paying for my medical bills." She gave Cash a pointed look as she aggressively shoved the lead back to him.

"Yeah, yeah, good thing you have health insurance then, huh?" Cash chuckled. "Come on, let's go get you checked in. Abs"—he turned to me, kissing my temple—"stay with Charming?"

I gave him a sweet smile and nodded, taking the reins from him and reaching up to scratch behind the horse's ear. I watched until Cash and Quinn were out of view before giving Charming a big smooch on his nose. The horse, as calm as he was, leaned into my touch.

"Awe, bud, I'm going to miss you when you aren't living next to Luna. I bet she'll miss you, too." I fished in my pocket for a peppermint, thankful it's become a habit to carry them, and laid it flat on my palm. "She likes you; I know she does."

He harrumphed, his head bobbing as he sucked down the candy.

Looking down the hall, trying to catch a glimpse of Cash and Quinn, I felt warmth spread through my heart. The only thing missing from this moment was having Stetson run after him. I could see it clearly. Me, hanging by the trailer making sure the horses we brought were taken care of. Cash and Stetson—most likely hand in hand—running to get Quinn, or maybe in the distant future, Cash checking himself in. I'd wait for them, making sure Cash had everything he needed for a ride. Joy radiated through my body as I pictured it, as I realized that more than anything, I wanted it. I wanted Stetson to be here with us, and I wanted Cash in our lives.

The ranch was only a portion of my life, not all of it. Maybe tonight, after feeling Cash inside me once again, I would ask him for his advice on it. He knew I loved the stables, the horses and some of the work that came with the ranch, but I could also tell him my new desires, my new dreams...and he would support me. He would help me through this, guide me to make the right decisions. For us. For my family.

Family.

I could feel the heat rushing to my cheeks. Did I really see Cash as a part of my family now? It hadn't been very long, but maybe Kyla was right. Maybe life moved fast, and you had to follow it.

I could feel my heart dancing at the thought. This is what happiness felt like, wasn't it? This is what it was like to feel whole again.

"I don't believe it." A high, almost shrill voice caught my attention. "Abi Hartwell?"

Hartwell?

That made me turn.

Holding tightly to Charming's lead, I twisted my torso, coming eye to eye with the one woman I never wanted to see again. Carolyn Callahan...well, the former Carolyn Callahan.

"Carolyn," I stated, my back stiffening. I forced a pleasant look, a smile I knew was fake. She didn't deserve even a fake smile, but she didn't need a scowl either.

She looked exactly the same, maybe a little more Botox to her face, but her hair was just as blonde and straight, falling over her shoulders. A long, thin nose lengthened her face, leading right to her bright red lips. Her deep plunge neckline dress made her stand out more than anyone else, seeing as it was bright pink, and two long necklaces drew your eyes to her breasts, and under...a rounded belly, being cradled by her hands. Next to me—jeans, boots, a blue t-shirt and my hair tied back into a ponytail—Carolyn looked like a supermodel—ageless. Looking down at my hands, I noticed my fingernails were cow-shit free.

"I didn't think I'd ever run into you at another rodeo." She gave me a fake smile.

"Why not?" I asked, still trying to find my bearings. What do I say here? Do I be polite or slap her across the face for the way she treated Cash? I settled with crossing my free arm over my waist, gripping my forearm as I squeezed Charming's lead.

"I come to all my husband's events. I see your brothers from time to time, but never you." She tilted her head, rubbing a circle around her belly, as if to draw attention to it.

"Funny." I fully faced her now, tilting my head, mirroring her. "They never mentioned seeing you."

"No, they wouldn't have." She laughed with a tension she was sure to deny. "I mean they don't speak to me, I just see them." Her laugh got louder.

I did not miss this laugh.

I hummed, feeling my lips pull into a sneer. If Lachlan were here, he'd remind me to put those big girl pants back on. "I see congratulations are in order." I motioned to her very pregnant stomach. "How far along are you?"

A slight blush ran across her cheeks, and she looked down and stroked her swollen belly. "Seven months. It's our third."

"Three kids. Wow." I faked my enthusiasm, glancing over my shoulder to see if Cash was coming back. It may be for the best if he didn't. He didn't need to know she was here.

"How many do you and Sylas have now?"

Excuse me...*what*?

I twitched. "Come on Carolyn, you know Sylas passed."

"Oh, that's right." Her face contoured, her eyebrows furrowing, and lip puckered out. "Must have slipped my mind."

"Slipped. Your. Mind? Carolyn, you were there the day he had his accident." My voice began to shake. She knew damn well he was gone, and she was just trying to rile me up. Why? I hadn't figured that part out yet. It was just her nature.

"Abs." I heard Cash's voice from behind me, but I didn't take my eyes off Carolyn. Her expression went from fake remorse to shock once Cash appeared at my side. Her eyes locked on him, and her jaw went from being slightly open to the widest, fakest smile I'd ever seen. Cash touched the small of my back. "Carolyn." He said sternly, any and all enthusiasm gone.

"Oh, I should have guessed." She laughed then, the shrill sound carrying on through the back of the stands, echoing as if to mock us. "How long have you two been together?"

"Don't see why that matters." Cash's fingers moved on my back, finding my waist to pull me close. "Congrats by the way." He gestured to her stomach.

"It's her third." I repeated, looking up at him, just in time to witness the anger fill his face. He wasn't hiding anything now.

"Third?" Cash looked shocked, almost, until he gave a small laugh. "How old are your kiddos?"

"Jada is two and Peter will be four..."

"Four?" He questioned, his body jerking with the word, a shock to his voice that even caught me off guard.

"Yes, Cash. Four. You knew I always wanted children." She glared at him, then bounced to me. "Anyway, I'm sure *you two* must have other children besides Steven running around."

Steven?

"Who?"

"She means Stetson. She always called him Steven, even though I corrected her every time and no, Carolyn...you know...we..." Cash began to stumble. I turned to him. Why was he stumbling? The relationship was new. We just became official last night. Why would the concept of kids make him stumble?

She hummed. "Well..."

I turned to Cash, placing my hand on his chest, feeling his heartbeat faster. He met my gaze, his jaw tense. "I'm going to go walk Charming around, I'm sure he doesn't want to be in the trailer anymore." I leaned up on my tip toes and gave him a sweet kiss, and then gave Carolyn one last nod. "I would say it was good to see you..."

"Wonderful to see you Abi. I'm sure we'll see each other again before the event is over."

I smiled, looking at Cash for reassurance, and once he gave me a nod of approval, I clicked my tongue and began to lead Charming out to the field, taking one last glance at the man I was falling in love with and the woman who broke him.

THIRTY-FOUR

Cash

"LET ME GUESS," CAROLYN said, taking a single step towards me as soon as Abi was out of ear shot. "You were fucking her before the ink on our divorce papers was dry."

"Your oldest kid is four!" I shouted. Trying to contain myself I took a step back, my hands forming into fists, looking down at my boots. Why did Abi have to leave me here? I could really use her by my side right now. But for as uncomfortable as I was, I could only imagine how Abi felt. "Four? Carolyn?" I breathed.

"Almost four," she corrected me.

"We've only been divorced for three." I shoved my hands in my pockets. Realization hit me like a ton of bricks. "That means…" I trailed off. She had been cheating.

And she was pregnant when she left me.

And I had no idea.

I must have been so distraught, so upset that I refused to see that my own wife was cheating on me. I don't remember seeing any change to her appearance or health during that time—but then again, the only thing I was really focused on was my own grief.

I heaved a sigh. "Don't even mention my relationship with Abi when you were *fucking* someone else before we even had divorce papers." I looked up at her through my lashes, trying to swallow my anger.

She narrowed her eyes and inhaled, her hand circling her swollen belly.

"And who's the unlucky guy?"

"Curtis Roster."

"Roster?"

I knew the name; I knew his face. I wouldn't consider him a friend, but he and I had gone out for drinks a few times. A bull rider. Still riding. High standings this year. He had all the girls chasing him at one point. Money. Fame. Good looks. Not broken from a riding accident. He was everything she wanted. Of course, she had gone for him, and of course he would have taken the attention. Never pegged him for a guy to steal another man's wife, though.

"You cheated on me with Curtis Roster? Was this before or after you blocked Abi from my phone?"

Carolyn shook her head, her lips a tight line before she finally said, "I was tired of competing with her. Even when you were in that hospital bed, all you talked about was how you wished Abi would call or come see you—never mind the fact that your *wife* was right next to you."

"She'd been trying to reach me before my accident." I glanced behind her quickly, fast enough to see Curtis with a small boy on his hip, a smile on his face, coming up to us. "You blocked her way before that."

"I don't remember when I did that..." She hummed, no idea that her husband was coming up behind her. "But like I said, I was tired of competing."

"There was never a competition with Abi."

"Of course there was. It was one of the reasons why I left you." She tilted her head, putting her hands on her hips. "Wait...does she even know the real reason why I left you?" She snarled.

The real reason? I didn't fit into her mold anymore. I couldn't give her what she really wanted. I could give her the money, the fame, the name in lights...and I couldn't give her—

"Who did you leave?" Curtis's voice came up from behind her, making her jump slightly before he kissed her cheek.

"Mama!" The young boy reached out for Carolyn. Her demeanor completely changed as she turned to her son. She bent and picked him up, giving him a quick kiss to his check.

"Me. Remember?" I tipped my hat at him. "Hey, Curtis."

"Oh..." He stiffened. "Hey Cash."

"Carolyn and I were married, don't you remember? And she hated my friends, she was always creating drama where there didn't need to be. Does she do that with you?" I wasn't holding back with Abi anymore, so why hold back here? I swallowed, took a deep breath, and let it all out. "Carolyn was competing against one of my friends who she had no reason to compete against. But I guess I should thank you, because if she hadn't slept with you while I was out for the count—you remember my accident, right?—I would have never found Abi again."

Curtis blinked, his arm instinctively reaching out for Carolyn.

"Yeah, well...I..." Curtis stumbled, his eyes searching the air around him for a response.

"Curtis, baby..." Carolyn turned to her husband. "Why don't you take Peter and Jada up to your box. I'll be right there."

"Isn't this rodeo a little low grade for you Roster?"

Curtis smiled. "Nah, Cash...you know how it is. I have to get those checks, gotta rack up that prize money to get to the NFR. No rodeo is too small or too big."

"Curtis..." Carolyn reiterated. "Here. Peter, baby go with daddy."

Curtis reached for his son once more, kissed Carolyn and then gave me a nod.

"Good to see you, Cash." Curtis shifted his son on his hips.

"Wish I could say the same." I narrowed my eyes.

Curtis just stood there, a vacant expression on his face.

"Curtis." She snapped.

"Right, right...meet you in the box." He turned finally, leaving Carolyn and me by the trailer again.

"Well, that was awkward," I admitted. "Did he know we were still married when you started sleeping with him?"

"Yes," she admitted, her face whipping right back to me, her hair flying. "But he knew I was planning on leaving."

"What happens if he gets into an accident? Bull riding is a lot more dangerous than saddle bronc."

"He won't," She clipped.

"I didn't think I would either." I shoved my hands in my pockets. "For his sake, I hope he doesn't. For your sake...I hope you get what you deserve."

I turned, catching a small glance at Abi with Charming in the field behind the arena, and my heart stirred. I hated that anger was flowing through me. Anger in seeing Carolyn after years. Seeing her with kids, knowing that she created one of them while I was close to giving up.

Does she know the real reason why I left you?

I hated that *that* was a reason why.

Of course she would bring that up. Twice. Stopping, I closed my eyes tightly, forcing the words not to sting. That small fact had never bothered me before now. Not that I didn't want to have a family. I never thought I wouldn't be able to.

My accident stopped more than my riding. The prospect of me giving any woman kids was pretty much ripped away. It wasn't a known fact; it wasn't a 'Cash Callahan you can no longer have children' type thing...but the chances of it were slim. After my surgeries, the doctors discovered what had happened and told us that little tidbit. They went into specifics, but mainly it landed on complications from the fall and injuries sustained to my body. That's all that Carolyn heard. I couldn't give her a baby. That made me even weaker in her eyes.

I remember when I was told. I nodded, not really caring in the moment that another surgery was needed, that medication would be added to my daily routine, because kids were so far from my radar. I wanted to ride. I wanted to compete. I remember looking at Carolyn, thinking did I even want kids with her? Did I want kids at all? If I was honest with myself, back then, the answer was a resounding no.

Now?

I wasn't broken anymore.

I took one last glance at Carolyn as she shimmied away and then shut the trailer door, locking it from the outside. The anger still festered deep in my bones, but as she got further from me, it lessened. And the moment I started walking towards Abi, it all but evaporated.

And then it was replaced.

But not with what I wanted it to be replaced with.

Fear.

It was always more fear.

That fear would never leave me, would it?

I was certain now, especially after last night, that she was my future. I'd keep her as long as I could, but I also knew that she and Sylas planned to have a big family. They had all the S names picked out and were even planning on trying for baby number two right before he died. She wanted that family, and I would give anything to have one with her...

But would this coming to light put a damper into what we were growing together? Would it be a deal breaker for her?

I leaned against the fence to the field, watching as she led Charming in circles, the horse bobbing his head with happiness. Abi smiled and mimicked his movements slightly. I chuckled, watching her bob her head in unison, and when she stopped, he turned, nudging her with his nose. Once Abi saw me, a sweet smile spread across her lips. She tilted her head before turning back to Charming. The sun hit her just right, and she glowed.

That smile. That glow. That was my future.

I could only hope I was hers as well.

THIRTY-FIVE

Abi

I COULD SEE CAROLYN up in the announcer's box, two kids with her, her pink dress making her stand out more than the other people that surrounded her. I was trying hard to not let the presence of Cash's ex-wife get to me, after all it was my hand he was holding onto, my lips he was kissing, but it still irked me the way she acted.

Who the hell acts like that? She knew Sylas had passed; she was there the day it happened. She came into the arena when she decided that Cash was taking too long. She saw me holding him. She was there when he was loaded up onto the ambulance. She knew very well that he was gone.

Then there was the 'how many kids do you two have' statement. What the *hell?* I hadn't thought about having more kids in...well...since Sylas died. He and I wanted more, sure, but I was happy and content with Stetson. Especially if Cash was willing to join us, I would have everything I needed with just them. When I asked weeks ago if he wanted kids, his answer was 'it wasn't in the cards.' I assumed that meant she didn't want children. I know the subject of kids has ended many relationships—but was it their reasoning? I hadn't pried into the matter of Carolyn since we danced, since our first kiss. He talked about her a few times, then there was the possibility of her blocking my phone number...but I had decided that in the long run that didn't matter. I wanted to move forward with him. Thinking about Carolyn wasn't moving forward.

And now Cash just seemed tense. Even though his hand was laced with mine, and every now and then he would reach over and kiss my temple, there was still a barrier that wasn't there before. I wasn't sure how to break it, and I was blaming the platinum blonde up in the box.

Thankfully, the tie down roping event was able to pull my attention from the pink dress in the arena to the dirt.

"I wish that was Rhett," I leaned over and told Cash. "He shouldn't have taken the year off to date Kyla. They could have gone on rodeo dates."

Cash squeezed my hand, his jaw tight, lasered focused on the arena. I watched him, studying his eyes as they moved, following the cowboy, then the calf as it was free...then up to the box? Was he looking for Carolyn?

"Maybe next year we can travel with him while he goes out. I mean, I know he's talked about not participating in as many, but it would be fun. And maybe we can bring Stetson along?" I smiled, hoping to catch his attention, resting my chin on his shoulder.

He nodded, keeping his focus away from me.

"Do you think your name will be on the list next year? You've been doing great back home."

Home. I let it slip. I called Hartwell Hills home. I referenced our future, twice now, and he still focused on the event in front of him.

As much as I hated to admit it, I could tell that confrontation with Carolyn rattled him. I hadn't asked what they were talking about after I had left; they didn't talk long. Long enough to get under his skin. I just had to pull him back somehow.

Reaching up, I rubbed on his arm. "Hey." He took a breath and turned to me. "It's almost time for the barrel racers." I smiled.

He returned my soft smile, leaning in to give me a chaste kiss. His eyes began to dance as his smile grew. It wasn't my smile that I had grown to search for in crowds, but a vacant smile.

"What's going through your head?" I asked, reaching up to touch his cheek.

He chewed on his bottom lip. "Nothing." Lifting his hand to the nape of my neck, he pulled me to him, kissing my forehead lightly. "I'm just"—he kissed my lips—"here."

"Are you?" I tilted my head, narrowing my eyes. "I said three things just now. What did I say?" I responded, making sure my tone was teasing.

"You wish that was Rhett." He pointed his chin towards the dirt. "You want to bring Stetson here next year, and you want me to ride." He met my gaze. "You're right. I think it's dumb that Rhett took a year off. I saw Kyla last year in Utah, she was enjoying traveling with him. Stetson would love to travel next year so...we'll make that happen."

I smiled. He saw us in his future—that confirmed it, but then his next statement made me crinkle my nose: "But, I don't think I'll be competing again."

"You could, you know."

"I would need way more training."

"Then you train. You have an entire arena at your disposal."

He raised a single eyebrow.

He opened his mouth to say something, but the vibration in my pocket drew me away from him. Kyla's photo shown on my screen. I smiled and glanced at Cash.

"Stetson, it's a FaceTime." I slid the bar, the *whoop* showing my son's eager face. "Hey, Stet."

"Mama, what rodeo are you at?"

I looked over at Cash. He leaned in and looked at my son. "Billings Round Up," he answered for me.

"Uncle Rhett!" Stetson turned his head from view.

"I heard, I heard." Rhett's voice boomed in the background. "Aunt Kyla is checking." Rhett leaned on the couch behind Stetson. "Who's leading tie down?"

"Zeke so far." I answered my brother. "I was just telling Cash I wished you were here."

"That makes two of us Abi!" Kyla's faint voice came through the phone.

"Next year. Make sure you say hi to Zeke for me." Rhett's smile shone through the screen. You could tell he missed this.

"If I see him." I gave him a wink.

"When are you coming home?" Stetson turned, making him the complete focus of the screen.

"Two more sleeps, bud." I answered. "Tonight, then there will be a day on the road, and then I'll be home."

"Cash too?"

I looked over at him, and he gave one single nod.

"Cash too." I confirmed.

Stetson gave me a wide smile, his eyes lighting up.

"Found it. Tell your mom we'll call her back." Rhett said faintly.

"Okay, Mama! I'll talk to you soon." Stetson's hand waved in front of the screen.

"Bye bu—" Before I could finish, the screen went dark. I shoved my phone back into my pocket and looked over at Cash. "I guess he was done talking."

Cash's eyebrows furrowed, and his free hand came to our joined ones. His thumb rubbed mine, and the slight pressure sent shivers through my arm. I thought about his hands the night before, that same thumb teasing the most sensitive parts of me. I could distract him from his thoughts, at least for now. It wouldn't fix everything, but it could bring him back into the moment.

I kissed him, forcing his lips apart with my tongue and slipping it inside, instantly feeling the warmth seep through me. I knew he could feel it too—the way his body relaxed, his jaw moving seamlessly with mine, whatever was causing him to tense was lifted, if just for a moment. The feeling that Carolyn had taken away came rushing back. The hope of a future with him was clearer as we kissed, as his hands cradled my face. Everything just made sense with him, and nothing could change that. It would take more than an ex-wife to pull him away from me.

He broke us apart, ending it with a sweet kiss to the tip of my nose.

"Thank you," he whispered, barely audible over the cheering of the crowd.

I hummed, wanting to kiss him again. He moved, shifting his hips as he reached into his pocket. His brow pinched as he unlocked his phone.

"Rhett is texting me…"

I kissed his temple as he bent to read the text before turning my attention back to the arena for a split second, but his chuckle pulled me back.

"Scratch that. It's Stetson."

"Stetson?"

He titled the phone to me.

Rhett

> I stol Uncle Retts fone. Are you moms boyfren yet?

I laughed at the grammar, and then looked at my boyfriend. "Well, you gonna answer him?"

He kissed me lightly before typing back his response.

Cash

> *Yeah, bud. I am.*

"Quinn Compton! Born and raised here in Montana, she's here to show us what she's got after taking a fall a couple of months ago. That didn't slow her down. Rounding the first barrel with ease, and look at that turn on the second and off to the third." The crowd cheered as every move Quinn made was narrated. "From what I'm hearing, this was the horse she took a tumble on—Hook I believe. But look at that! Seventeen point six seconds for Quinn Compton." The announcer spoke fast—faster than Wyatt on a good day—and I tried to keep my eyes on Quinn but damn...she was fast.

Looks like all that training with Cash paid off.

I jumped, almost hitting the people in front of us, and Cash...

He sat, his body still tense. He was watching, but he wasn't celebrating.

"Hey..." I sat down next to him. "Did you see?" I squeezed his knee. "Quinn...she came in first."

"Yeah." He smiled. "I saw. I...I..." he stammered, standing up. "I'm going to go meet her by the trailer to congratulate her." He kissed the crown of my head and started squeezing past everyone. "Meet us by the trailer?"

I nodded and watched him leave. It made me think that the kiss we shared just moments before didn't mean as much as I thought it did.

My head started to swim. What did Carolyn say to him that jogged him so far from me? Barely hearing the announcer and rodeo clown talk about the bulls, getting everyone ready to hype up the riders, I stood and shimmied past everyone, starting to jog once I made it to the clearing. Without thinking, I went directly to her.

"What did you say to him?" I asked the second I opened the door to the box.

There were several families there, not just Carolyn and her two kids, but she instantly turned, her eyes lightly rolling when she saw me.

"Nothing." She groaned. "Now if you don't mind—"

"I do mind because whatever you said to him got in his head, and now he's having a hard time enjoying the rodeo." I walked closer to her, standing in front of her to block her view of the bull riders.

"My husband is up next and if you think—"

"No, Carolyn. I couldn't care less if you miss your husband's ride. What did you say to him?"

Glancing to her kids, who were engrossed at the event below, her eyes narrowed the second she turned. "I asked him if you knew the real reason why I left him. The fact that you're up here, intruding on my time with my family, proves to me you don't."

"The real reason?" I asked, lowering my voice. "Just tell me, and we can go back to hating each other."

She shook her head. "I'm not getting into this with you. I've managed five years without seeing your face, and it was a glorious five years. Now, if you don't mind, I would like to watch my husband ride."

"Curtis. Roster." The announcer shouted, making his name last way too long as the rock song blared over the speakers, the voice louder in the box with the speakers right there, not being drowned out by any cheering from the crowd. "Two-time NFR champion.

Making the money everywhere he goes. Standing high in the United States and the Western Circuit. Riding Mad Horn...a bull that gets just as high of points as the rider..."

"Excuse me, Abi." Carolyn put her hand on my shoulder and pushed me aside.

I turned towards the edge of the wall and watched as Curtis Roster, Carolyn's husband, rode the bull for eight seconds, jumping off in time and throwing his hands up in the air, giving a victory pose. He pointed up to the box and blew a kiss. Carolyn dramatically caught it. Once he was back behind the gate, she turned back to me.

"You may want to talk to him before you decide if you want to be in a relationship with him." She spoke quietly. "I don't know what he's told you..."

"We've only been back in each other's lives for nine weeks. Someone blocked my number."

She breathed a laugh. "Yeah, that was me. I'll admit that. But Abi...you're going to want to talk to him."

THIRTY-SIX

Cash

ABI MET QUINN AND me at the trailer, her smile widening as she wrapped Quinn in her arms. She congratulated her on her run before she lightly brushed my arm as she headed to help with the horses. She spoke calmly to them as she hooked them in and made sure they were safe, giving them each a kiss on the nose before closing the trailer, making sure my client knew the way to the stables.

"Yes, *Mom,*" Quinn teased.

Mom...

Abi grinned. "Speaking of mom, we should probably call Stetson before it gets too late." She turned to me. "Come on, you know he'll want to talk to you too."

Saying goodbye to Quinn, we pulled out of the arena before the crowds, turning the opposite way of Quinn to our hotel, my hand wanting to hold Abi's the entire drive. She called Stetson, giving him a run down about what happened at the rodeo, then handed the phone to me for a quick goodnight, and once she hung up she faced the window. Looking out at the twilight sky, she played with her fingers, twirling rings that weren't there. I moved, slowly at first, but then her hand moved, too—her fingers brushing mine until they were threaded together.

Instant comfort. Instant relief.

Pulling up to the hotel, our contact broke only briefly until we found each other again, never once letting go. When we made it into the hotel, she pulled me to her, her body pressing against mine.

"Cash," she said in the crook of my neck.

"Abi." I stopped her, arching my back slightly, lifting her chin with my forefinger. "If I had known Carolyn was going to be there—"

"I really don't care about Carolyn," she interrupted, her fingers brushing my jaw line.

"Neither do I."

That was the absolute truth. I was always worried that if I saw her, feelings and memories would come back and I would fall back into where I was, but I couldn't care less about Carolyn and her three kids...her cheating and everything that happened. What I cared about was right here in my arms.

"Do you remember when we danced?" I asked, running a lock of her blonde hair through my thumb and forefinger. "When you kissed me."

Her answer was a kiss, a soft chaste one against my lips. "Yes. The night we stopped holding back."

"You asked me what happened with Carolyn."

"Cash, I don't care what happened with her."

"I think there's bits and pieces you need to know."

She swallowed. "Tell me."

My breath shook as I took a deep inhale, watching as her eyes danced as they searched me.

"Tell me," she repeated, her hand reaching up to caress my cheek.

"Abs." I lifted her, feeling her legs wrap around my waist as I walked up to the bed, taking a seat on the edge, my hands sliding up her back. "I'm happier than I've ever been with you right now, and I'm terrified that what I'm about to tell you is going to change everything."

She shook her head, stopping to kiss me gently. "Can I tell you what I pictured today? When you went with Quinn, right before Carolyn showed up?"

"What?"

"I saw you, and me..." she paused, a slight smile spreading across her lips. Her cheeks blushed as she lifted a hand to gentle touch my hair, her fingers moving to the nape of my neck. "And Stetson. At rodeos together, traveling, at the ranch riding. You two together. The three of us. Together. You hand in hand with him. Us...as a family."

"A family?" I whispered, my voice shaky.

She nodded. "I'm in this Cash, if you are too. Carolyn can't scare me away."

I licked my lips. "She can't but...what if..."

"No what ifs. Tell me."

I took a deep breath, focusing on Abi's blue eyes as they pierced into me. She was giving me no reason to believe she would leave me now. She was giving me everything, all over again. I swallowed, and began, "Carolyn and I weren't good for each other. From the moment we met until the second she ran out of the doctor's appointment—"

"She left you at a doctor's appointment?" Abi snarled, her eyes turning from love to hatred.

I nodded. "Stay with me."

Abi placed her hands on my shoulders and closed her eyes, giving me a nod.

"I tried to fill a void. She wanted a lavish rodeo lifestyle. She wanted the buckle bunny life forever, and she thought that she would get that with me. I was that life for her, until I wasn't anymore. I thought I loved her, or I wanted to believe I loved her. I think she wanted to believe she loved me, too. I wanted what you and Sylas had—but if I'm being one hundred percent honest, I wanted it with you. I would never have done anything, you and Sylas...you two were—"

"We're not talking about Sylas and me," she stopped me. "I know you wouldn't have even considered trying to take me from him. You knew you didn't stand a chance." She smiled, trying to break the tension with a tease.

It worked. I chuckled, shaking my head slightly. "No...but I tried to duplicate it. With the wrong person. Carolyn was manipulative, she gaslit, she cheated, she tried her hardest to pull me away from you, and I hate to admit it worked for a time. But then my accident"—I met her gaze—"took more away than just my career."

"Your leg." She touched my leg softly. "I know you still feel pain."

"I do. But it's manageable. I do acupuncture and physical therapy stretches for it. I take care of myself...but...if it were just my leg..."

"What else is it then? What are you beating around the bush for?"

"I can't have children," I blurted out. No more *beating around the bush*. "The doctors told us details, but it came down to the injuries I received from the accident. The pressure from the horses' body was on me just long enough to crush my left side. I had to have so many surgeries; you've seen the scars on my femur and knees...but I also had to have repair surgeries near my groin and abdomen. I wish I knew the terms they used off the top of my head, but...the chances of me having children are slim to none. Not gone...but...slim. I take daily medication for testosterone levels, and I stick to physicals each year...and nothing has changed. Having my own just isn't in my future."

Abi's jaw grew tense as if she were chewing on her cheek. "And Carolyn, when she found out..."

"She walked out of that doctor's appointment, took the car, and then one week later filed for divorce."

"She really is a bitch, isn't she? What did you ever see in her?"

"At first...a good time. I was the one who tried for more. Like I said at *first*...it was good, but she wanted to have children. She wanted to have that name. And she went and found it."

"But...you told me she didn't want kids?" Abi asked, her brow pinching.

I twisted my lips, "No, I said it wasn't in the cards, not that she didn't want any. She's always wanted to have a family. I just couldn't give that to her."

"You said she cheated?"

"Her oldest is almost four. We've only been divorced for three years. So, she either was pregnant when she asked for the divorce or got pregnant shortly after. With Curtis Roster's kids."

"The bull rider?"

I nodded. "She got the lifestyle she always wanted."

"I don't get it. Is that what she meant?" she breathed, shaking her head as her back slumped.

I furrowed my brow and trailed my hands down her back. "What do you mean?"

"After you left to go find Quinn..." She hesitated. "I could tell you were upset. I could tell something was off. You weren't paying attention to the rodeo, and when Stetson called, you just were kinda...meh." She shrugged a shoulder. "So, I went to her box and asked her what she said to you. She told me I needed to know the real reasons before deciding to have a relationship with you. Was she meaning the no kids thing?"

No kids thing? She made it sound so casual, so...*not* a thing.

I nodded, leaning my forehead against hers to feel her. "She put it in my head. When she asked how many kids we had, she knew we didn't have any. But then I started thinking, if I could have a family with anyone it would be you. I would have a million kids with you if I could."

"Whoa...slow down...a million?" She arched back, her beautiful laugh filling the air between us.

Pulling her back to me, I smiled. "You know what I mean. If I could have a family with anyone, it would be with you. The way I feel about you, Abi, isn't going to fade away any time soon. I've carried feelings for you since the moment I saw you, and now that you're my girlfriend"—I smiled at the word—"there's things I want to think about that I never did before. I never truly thought about having kids with Carolyn, but with you...Abi...I want that. But I can't give that to you. And if you are seeing me and Stetson and you as a family...then...well...is that a deal breaker? Do you still want me if I can't give you a bigger family? I know you and Sylas talked about having more kids, I know—"

She pressed her lips to mine, taking me in as her hands wrapped around the nape of my neck. Her tongue teased my lips, forcing them to open to welcome her in. As much as I wanted to take over and devour her, I let her lead. This kiss was sensual, as if she were learning the way my mouth fit against hers. This kiss was filled with love.

Love.

I love this woman.

"Cash." She pressed her forehead to mine. "You not being able to have children is the last thing I'd ever consider a deal breaker. I have Stetson. I have you. What more could I want?" She shifted, pressing herself to me more. "I'm the happiest I've been in five years when I'm with you."

"Need I remind you that you threw a brush at me."

"I haven't done that in weeks." She punched my shoulder lightly.

"You threw it out of love."

"Sure, we'll say that." She smiled. "I do feel something for you Cash, I never expected this...but as soon as I stopped fighting it...I found myself falling for you. Kids or no kids in our future...I fell, and Cash...I crave you."

"Crave me?" I raised an eyebrow, seeing the desire flood her eyes as she bit down on her bottom lip.

Her fingers trailed up my arms to my shoulders. "I want you in so many ways. I want every inch of you."

THIRTY-SEVEN

Abi

CASH'S LIPS WERE HOT on mine as he kissed me, his fingers dancing on my spine as they worked their way up my shirt. My skin tingled, my insides melting completely as his hands moved to my front, working on the buttons of my shirt. Last night was an almost terrifying experience. I hadn't had sex in so long, and my nerves told me everything that could go wrong. Cash took those nerves and threw them out the window with every kiss, every pulse, every touch. And tonight, it was as if we had been doing this for years. His lips knew just where to go, his hands knew the right amount of pressure to put on me, and our bodies moved flawlessly together.

The chill of the air hit my skin as my shirt fell to the floor, his lips finding my collar bone as he worked on my bra strap.

"Abs, you...you are...dammit, Abs...you have no idea what you do to me," he whispered in between kisses.

"You know," I moaned as his tongue trailed up my neck. "You are the only one who calls me Abs."

He stopped and looked at me with heavy eyes. "Do you want me to call you something else?" He raised a single brow. "I've never been one for nicknames."

"No." I shifted, moving my hips against him, feeling his hard length through his pants. "I love it when you call me Abs."

Tilting his head back, he moaned. "Fuck Abs."

"Just like that." I stood, taking a step back to remove every stitch of clothing I had on as he watched me. Unlike last night, I didn't cover myself. I let him take me in, his gaze gliding up and down my body, before I fell down to my knees in front of him. I played with his belt buckle, the entire time our eye contact never broke. My hands felt along his strong thighs as I slowly pulled his Wranglers down to his feet, tracing the scar on his left leg, silently wishing I could have been there when he got hurt. I wouldn't have left him alone. He would never be alone again.

I kissed his scar, feeling his skin twitch under my lips. He fell backwards on the bed, his back hit with a thump, his hands still laced in my hair. I could take him right here, having him completely naked in front of me, but I crawled over him, my tongue and lips teasing as the shock went straight through my body. We had all night, but like I told him—I craved him.

I kissed up his abdomen, searching out all the other scars he mentioned. How had I missed them last night? Each scar I found received a kiss before working my way to his lips, claiming him. The heat pooled as I felt his cock touch my most sensitive area, a gasp left my lungs.

"You want me." He stated, not a question. "I can feel it."

"Yes." I whispered, kissing him hard, making him know exactly how much I wanted him.

"Abs." He moved, one swift solid motion bringing me to my back. "I don't think I've ever wanted anyone as much as I want you."

"Show me," I begged, my hand tickling down his chest to his length, finally guiding him to me. "Show me how much."

With the simple plea, he growled, and his fingers, his tongue, his body showed me exactly how much he felt, how much we craved each other, and how perfectly we fit. How we molded and breathed as we both shook and exploded at the same time. The intimacy that flowed through us only proved that we both felt it, that this was right—and there was nothing between us. No regrets, no walls...just us.

After, when we were both spent, our bodies still shaking, I lay in the crook of his arm, my fingers trailing the lines of his chest. We hadn't moved from each other, keeping the heat alive between us. He was a gorgeous man. His skin was the perfect tawny color, his eyes deep and endless as he stared into me. He had the most defined jawline, and the small amount of facial hair he had didn't hide it. He was tired—I could see it in the way he breathed—but his eyes, as they searched me, told me he wanted so much more.

Reaching his hand up, he gently moved my hair from my forehead, kissing my skin.

"Let's stay here," I whispered, kissing his chest. "Like this, all night."

"All. Night." He reiterated. "We have all night."

I hummed, scooting even closer to him, my legs tangling up in the sheet even more than they were. "Not just all night, every night. Every day." I closed my eyes, feeling the sleep willing to take over.

Cash's heartbeat picked up, and his fingers trailed down my spine.

"Every day?"

"Mmhmm." I tilted my chin to look at him, already finding his eyes locked on me. The beating of his heart and his stare reminded me of the topic I still had to bring up. I wanted him every minute of every day, by my side—and even though I was pretty sure I had made my decision when it came to the ranch, I still had no idea if that's what he wanted. Hartwell Hills was home. I didn't want to leave it; I just didn't want to own it. "Okay..." I moved, sitting up in the bed, tugging the sheets with me.

His hand dropped to my leg, his thumb beginning to draw slow sweet circles on my skin. "So much for staying like that all night."

"Well, I have something to talk to you about."

His eyebrows raised.

"You know my parents are retiring."

He nodded.

"And you know they want to give me the majority of their half of the ranch?"

He nodded again.

"Where does that leave us? If I take it?"

"If you take it? I thought it was already decided?"

"I don't want it. Not the percentage they are offering."

There. I admitted it out loud. I didn't want the ranch.

He shifted, raising his arm to place under his head, tilting it just so to give me his full attention. "What's on the table now?"

"I would have thirty, Rhett fifteen and Wyatt five. Lachlan still has his fifty. That's not changing."

"And you don't want thirty?"

I shook my head. "No."

He brushed my hair from my face. "Why not? You're brilliant at running that place, I've seen you. Lachlan would probably lose it if you didn't run it next to him."

"Lachlan will survive," I grumbled, slouching into him.

"He would but...I'm still confused why. Abi...your life is Hartwell Hills."

"That's just it. My life was never supposed to be the ranch." I sighed, feeling the tension boil under my skin. I swallowed, sniffed and looked at Cash, deep into his eyes to find the courage. "When Sylas died...I didn't grieve. I did the only thing I knew how to do. Be the best mom I could be to Stetson, and work on the ranch. I trained with my mom on the finances, soon taking over for her completely, and I took over Sylas's jobs. The animals, the horses, the supplies, the schedules...everything he did became my job, and I had to do it well. I had to replace my dead husband while also mourning for the same dead husband, and all I wanted to do was..."

I stopped, and let the tears well up.

"Cry," Cash said, taking his thumb to brush away a tear that had already fallen.

"I didn't cry. I didn't budge. After his funeral, I picked myself up and did what I had to do. No one really knew what I was feeling because I got so good at putting on a happy face but...I know if I take

the ranch, I'll have to keep pretending and I can't do that anymore."
I sniffed, raising my hand to wipe away the last tear that fell from my
cheeks. "I don't want my life to be the ranch. I want this life. I want
to travel with you and Stetson and come to rodeos and just...be here
with you." I sighed. I looked at him, his single eyebrow raised, his
mouth a thin line that was still somehow kissable. His chest rose and
fell calmly. I placed my hand on his chest, feeling for his heartbeat.
Seconds ago it was fast, but now, it was steady. "But I don't want to
leave the ranch. It is home."

"We won't leave it."

"We?"

"You think I'm leaving you now? If you're at the ranch, so am
I."

I chewed on my bottom lip. "I hate to admit I don't even know
where you live."

"Montana. I have a place in Bozeman, but I'll sell it."

"You'd be willing to move to Hartwell Hills?"

He gave me a single nod, his hand that kept my leg warm moving
to cup my face. I leaned into his touch.

He kissed me sweetly. "If that's where you are, that's where I am.
Remember—I was thinking of taking on extra clients. You did offer
the arena to me before. You'll still have some sway in what happens
to it right?"

"Sure, but..." I chuckled. "I don't want to own the majority of
it. Rhett should have it. He loves that ranch more than anything."

"And what do you want?"

"The stables." I said, absolutely no hesitation to my voice and
my heart skipped a beat when Cash grinned. "When we took on

boarding horses, Rhett said he'd do the job. I was already running the finances, the stables, the goats, the calves—all the animals. Lachlan was always out on the land, so he didn't have time to take that job on, neither did I, really. Rhett did, so he offered. But how many times did you actually see Rhett in the stables?"

"Never. Well—maybe once." Cash huffed a laugh.

"It was always me, and I loved it. I like taking care of the horses. I like sitting with them and walking with them when they are colicky. I love brushing them, bathing them—I even enjoy mucking out the damn stalls. I don't want to be in charge of the numbers anymore. I want to focus on the animals, mainly the horses, but I can still work on the livestock. I could even manage the arena bookings, if they keep coming. I would be more than happy to keep doing that side of it. Just as long as we can still attend rodeos."

"Most trainers don't go with their clients."

"You enjoy it." I narrowed my eyes at him, my hand falling to his chest.

"I do. I've always loved the rodeo scene. I especially love it when you're here." His hand ran up and down my back, creating those tingles I was beginning to love so very much.

"I would have to plan things accordingly, but it could work—if Rhett agrees."

"Seems to me like you know exactly what you want. You just need to talk to Rhett when you get home."

I nodded. "My dad wants to sign the deed when I get back. We were supposed to sign it before I left, but he agreed to let me have this weekend."

"What about your parents? What are their plans?" He shifted and scooted up slightly on the headboard, raising his arm over his head.

"Traveling. He talked about buying a small house in town or building a smaller one close to the lake. My mom does love the lake."

"And the main house?"

I shrugged. "If they'd let me, I'd still live in it. It's home. I don't want to leave it. Hell—I'll agree to still make breakfast for the ranch hands."

"And me?" He raised a brow. "Us?"

"Well..." I shifted moving close to him. "I'd hope you'd move in with me. That is, if you want to."

"How many times do I gotta say where you are, I am?"

I leaned against him, cuddling close as his arm wrapping around my shoulders, his lips finding mine as if a magnet pulled us together.

"You're serious?" I whispered. "You'd uproot your entire life for me?"

"Abi....you are my life. I'm not uprooting anything. I'm planting myself where I belong."

The following morning, our bodies were still humming from desire and lack of sleep. I sat on the edge of the bed as Cash showered. Our bags were packed, and Quinn had already texted, telling us she would wait for us at the stable.

Me

I need to talk to you when I get home. Leave a spot open for me on your busy schedule?

Lachlan

Everything ok?

Of course that's what he would say first. My grumpy ass cousin was still caring.

Me

Yeah, I just figured something out and need to talk you.

Lachlan

I can guess what it's about. We don't need to talk, I approve.

Me:

You have no idea what it's about.

My phone rang in my hand seconds later.

"Texting is fine," I sighed into the receiver.

"You don't want the ranch," he said instantly.

I swallowed. "Not thirty percent of it."

"You don't need my approval, you know, but I get it, and well...I approve."

"I don't need your approval, but you approve. Make it make sense Lach." I shook my head, seeing my cousin clearly in my mind.

He was most likely out in the field already, his hat blocking most of the sunrise—guaranteed he didn't shave.

"You won't be going anywhere though, right?" he asked, his voice heavy.

"No, I just need to talk to Rhett...and Dad. We'll be back tonight so I'll catch Rhett before he and Kyla settle in, then Dad in the morning."

"Need me there?"

"I mean, not if you approve already." I chuckled. Imagining my cousin leaning against a fence shaking his head at me.

"I approve of all of it, not just the ranch you know."

I looked at the bathroom, just in time to see Cash walk out, towel around his waist. He gave me a cheeky smile before leaning down to his suitcase, pulling out his Wranglers and a small orange medicine bottle. "I would keep him even if you didn't approve of that." I smiled, keeping my eyes on the man I loved the entire time. Cash winked, shaking the medicine above his shoulder as he disappeared back into the bathroom.

"Oh, I know. Just know I'm putting the man to work."

"Not if it goes the way I want it. But...I'll need to talk to the new owner first."

I could basically hear his eyeroll. "See you tonight, Abi."

"Bye, Lach." I grinned to myself, the blush rushing to my cheeks.

THIRTY-EIGHT

Cash

W E MADE IT BACK to Alpine Ridge in record time, but well after the sun had set. We called and said goodnight to Stetson, giving in to letting him sleep in the main house, promising him breakfast in the morning, and then the cab of the truck finally sat in silence. Throughout the seven-hour drive, we never once stopped planning our future together. The plan was simple: I would spend the night here and then in the morning, leave for Bozeman. I'd put my place up for sale and hurry back to Hartwell Hills. Home. Abi would talk to her brothers, Lachlan, and her dad, and the steps to make the ranch Rhett's would take effect.

"We'll have to hire someone," she mentioned at one point. "I handled all the finances. I'll need to teach someone how to do that. Wyatt and Rhett are both useless there."

"Lachlan?" I suggested.

"No, he's on the land. He doesn't have time to look at numbers. We may have the extra wiggle room to hire someone."

I could practically hear the gears in her head turning, trying to come up with all the plans, but once that goodnight phone call was made, her mind cleared. She laid her head back on the seat and looked at me, a sweet smile on her lips. There was a different kind of calm to her that I hadn't seen before. The past ten weeks, all I had seen was stress and sadness in her eyes, the happiness only breaking through when she was around her family and, most recently, with me. But this look, this time, all I saw was contentment.

"What are you going to do with all your free time?" I asked her as we pulled onto the dirt road leading to Hartwell Hills.

"Ha, free time. What's that?" she joked, her head rolling to look out the window. "My task list won't change too much."

"Well, since you won't be working the books anymore, and you'll delegate other tasks to ranch hands and new employees—"

"Okay, okay, I get it." She inhaled. "Maybe I'll read."

"Read?"

"Yeah, a few weeks ago I was in the kitchen just thinking if I didn't have to do this...I could read. I haven't finished reading a book in...well, since before Sylas died." Her eyes widened at the realization. "I would read."

I reached out and threaded my fingers through hers, bringing her knuckles to my lips. "We can make one of the rooms in the house a library, fill it with all the books you could ever want."

She chuckled. "Ha...I don't need a library. Just a bookshelf."

"I'll make that happen."

I pulled up to the house, the porch lights the only indication there was life. Darkness took over the ranch, everything was so peaceful and quiet and...

"It's perfect," I said aloud.

Abi leaned forward, her body completely shifting in the seat until her lips met mine. Last time we were parked in this spot, she climbed in my lap and kissed me until all thought left my brain. Tonight, this kiss was pure and simple, a promise of something more.

"Let's go inside."

Our hands met again once we were out of the car. We left our bags in the bed of the truck. The house was dark as she unlocked the door, locking it behind her once inside. She led me up the stairs, opening the door quietly to peek at a sleeping Stetson before leading me to her room.

She turned on the bedside lamp, giving a soft glow to her bedroom. A blue quilt sat on the queen bed, pillows lining the white barn-style headboard. A salt lamp lit the corner, and a perfect soft glow illuminated the photos she had hanging on the walls. There were photos of Stetson, her horses, Luna and Sylas...and their wedding photo.

He held her from behind, his face nuzzled into her hair, his smile still visible even though his attention was full on her. Sylas wore his dark hat and a dark suit with a blue flower popping out of the chest pocket. Abi's hair was down, wavy over her shoulders, her head turned to face him. Her eyes were closed, complete serenity settled on her expression. Her dress was stunning, elegant against the fall backdrop. They were perfect, in love and happy. I lifted my fingers to touch the frame, taking in Sylas. It had been far too long since I had seen a photo of him. Even now, I was grateful it was here.

"It wouldn't be weird if I kept that...right?" She whispered, her arms wrapping around my waist from behind, her chin resting on my shoulder.

"It would be weird if you got rid of it." I lightly touched the gold frame, taking in Sylas's wide smile. "I miss him. A lot."

She spun until she faced me, nuzzling her head in my chest. "Me too, but..." She rested her chin on my chest. "I'm so happy he brought me you."

"He brought me huh? Not Lachlan?"

"Lachlan made the call, but Sylas pushed us together. I'm sure of it." Lifting up on her tiptoes, she kissed me lightly. "I have something to show you. They aren't done yet, but...come here." Her fingers trailed down my arm until she pulled me to her vanity dresser.

Sitting on the top dresser were four framed drawings. A mountain range, two horses mid gallop, Stetson with Sylas's grave, and Abi in the field with Luna. She framed my sketches. Every single one that I had drawn during these weeks here at the ranch.

"Abi..."

"I want to hang them in the stables. I want to see them every day." She rested her cheek against my shoulders, her palm gliding around my waist.

"I...Abi I..." No words, there were no words to describe the emotion that swelled in my chest, and by the way she was looking at me, the way the tears were also forming in her eyes, she felt it too.

"Come on," she whispered, pulling me away from the frames. "Let's get some rest."

We undressed—me keeping my boxers on and Abi putting on a loose t-shirt—and climbed into her bed. She cuddled up next to me and kissed my chest lightly before her body relaxed completely, her heartbeat and warmth lulling me into the deepest sleep I've ever had.

Sleeping in was not in Abi's routine, and she made sure I was up before the sun as well. She woke me up with kisses all over my bare chest. We kissed until I couldn't hold back, and when we made love, we were filling voids we didn't know we had, coming together in more ways than one. I was hers, and she was mine.

We showered quickly, Abi fitting me into her daily routine as if I had been here every day. She even reminded me to take my medicine. She let me wake Stetson, saying he would be ecstatic to see me instead of her, and she was right. He opened his eyes quickly, wrapping his arms around my neck and pulling me in for a hug. I lifted him from his bed, ignoring the sting in my leg, and carried him downstairs where Abi already had a coffee mug full and waiting for me. The things she would need to make breakfast were already lined up; the only thing missing was the eggs.

"Mommy!" Stetson leapt from my arms and ran to his mother, wrapping his arms around her legs. "I missed you, Mommy."

"I missed you too, bud." She leaned, giving him a kiss on the crown of his head. "Eggs and bacon for breakfast?"

"Pancakes?" He asked, raising his chin.

"Eggs and bacon for breakfast?" she asked again, pretending she didn't even hear his request for a different breakfast. "Go to the coop and get them for me?"

He let her go and turned to me. "Come get the eggs with me, Cash?" he asked as he slid on a pair of rubber boots over his fuzzy pajamas.

"Sure thing, Stet. Let's go." I grabbed my hat and slipped my boots on, giving Abi one last wink before we stepped out into the new day.

"So," Stetson skipped. "You're here to stay now, right? You're Mom's boyfriend?"

"I am." I smiled at the admission. "But there are steps to take."

"Like what?" he asked, opening the chicken coop's door and taking a small step inside.

"Well, I gotta sell my place..."

"Can I come? It's almost my spring break."

I smiled. The idea of Stetson with me in Montana actually sounded like fun. "I'll ask your mom. We also have to make sure your grandparents are okay with me moving in."

"To my house!?" Stetson asked, his eyes wide as he reached and grabbed an egg, handing it to me gently.

I chuckle. "Yeah, in your house. Is that okay with you?"

He nodded rapidly. "I'd love that. We can go on more rides and get on the roof some more. You'll teach me more things, right? I really want to learn bareback riding."

"Not saddle bronc?" I raised an eyebrow.

He scrunched his nose and shook his head. "It's cool watching you do it, but bare back seems more..."

"Dangerous?"

He furrowed his brow, trying to think of the perfect word to use. "Invigorating?"

"Invigorating?" I parroted. "Where did you learn that word?"

"School." He shrugged a shoulder. "It makes you feel strong, full of energy. And I have a lot of energy Un—" He looked at me, stopping himself from saying 'uncle' I cocked a grin. "Cash."

"Ha, that you do. I'll teach you what I know, maybe get you trained to do junior rodeo once you get in high school, but"—I grinned, reaching up to rub his hair—"We'll have to convince your mom."

Stetson tightened his lips. "She doesn't like the idea of me riding in a rodeo. Not after what happened to Daddy."

"Can you blame her?" I raised an eyebrow as he handed me another egg.

"No, but I wish she'd let me. Like when you ride, she's always smiling. With me, she's scared."

"She just worried about you, but"—he handed me another egg, so I had seven eggs in my arms—"you should have seen her at the rodeos. She loved it, and she wants you to travel with us."

"Us?" he questioned, his hand midair with an egg ready to be dropped.

"Us. Before your dad passed, you were supposed to travel with him, remember?"

He pinched his brow, and twisted his lips. "A little? I remember some things."

I huffed. "You were young. That's ok. But you were going to travel to rodeos with him during the summer. She wants to do that again, with me...and you. The entire summer going from rodeo to rodeo. Watching Quinn and seeing Wyatt make an ass of himself. She's even talked about getting me back on the boards—"

His eyes widened, so did his smile.

"Don't get too excited. I'm not there yet. We'll get you signed up for mutton busting at all these rodeos we go to. You'll start to train if you really want to, and before you know it, you'll be riding bareback just like your Uncle Lachlan."

He smiled. "Maybe saddle bronc won't be too bad."

I shook my head, looking down at the now ten eggs cradled in my arms. "Whatcha' say? Do you want to travel with us?"

"More than anything. We can leave tomorrow. I know Uncle Wyatt has some rodeos lined up. We can go with him!"

"Pretty sure you have school tomorrow."

He walked past me, leaving the coop, not a single egg in his hand.

"Eh, it's ok. I can skip a day or two."

I laughed, shaking my head as I followed, carrying the eggs with care as we made our way back to the house.

I threw my last bag into the back of the truck. Nova was in her trailer and ready to move. She was content as could be, but her eyes looked towards the stables. Abi shut the trailer door, locking it before handing me the key. We had just finished breakfast, saying a quick hello to Leo and Lottie, and avoiding any tasks that Lachlan may give me by saying I needed to start the trip back home. Abi grasped my hand and pulled me to the stables where she kissed me for the last private moment between us.

"You should just keep her here," she suggested. "She and Luna love each other and well, why cart her around when you're coming back?"

"I don't know when I will be back. I'm taking her so we can ride." I placed my hands on Abi's shoulders, squeezing gently before she stepped into me.

"I don't like that you don't know when you'll be back."

"A couple of weeks tops. I gotta get everything packed up and…shit…Stet asked if he could come along."

"He has school, so as much as he would like to start all of our adventures…"

I kissed her, the pure thought of our future together making my heart beat faster. Our adventures called louder than I wanted to admit. If I could leave my place in Bozeman the way it was, I'd never go back.

"Couple weeks tops." I repeated, listening to her sigh. "You have to talk to Rhett and your dad."

She slumped into me. "I wish you could stay for that talk."

"When's it happening?"

She turned to look at Rhett's house in the distance. "As soon as I can't see your truck anymore." She leaned into me, her arms wrapping around my waist. Our gazes met before she pressed her lips to mine, breathing in so deep as she kissed me. "I love you, Cash," she whispered against me; almost so low I couldn't hear it.

My heart stopped, literally skipping a beat before I processed what she had said. I knew she loved me, this past weekend proved that, but the words hitting my ears, creating my entire body to warm and melt in her arms. She loved me, she *loved* me. Moving my hands to tilt her head to me, I kissed her again, slow and smooth, tasting every inch of her and memorizing it. "I love you, Abi. More than anything."

"Come home soon," she murmured. "I don't have anyone else to throw brushes at."

I laughed, kissing her again. "I'll be home soon. I love you. I love you. I," I kissed her, "love," I kissed her again, deeper this time, "you."

She hummed, taking a step back from me, watching as I got in my rig...and slowly left Hartwell Hills Ranch.

THIRTY-NINE

Abi

I WALKED THE QUARTER mile to Rhett's cabin, praying that he was still there since he didn't arrive for breakfast at the main house. I stuck my hands in my pockets, running through the conversation in my head and what I would tell him. Down to each word.

I think you should take the majority of the ranch; I know Dad thinks I should get it, but I don't want it. This is your life, your home, you love this place more than anything...Your heart is this place. My heart is with Stetson, with the stables, with the rodeos...with Cash.

It was all going to go smoothly, a quick conversation that would end with us gathering Lachlan and Wyatt, and meeting my dad in his study to sign the deed. Then I'd wait patiently for Cash to come home and start my life over again. It was all going to go...

"Hey Abi—" Rhett flung the door to his cabin open before I even got a chance to take the first step. He had his Thermos in hand, ready for his day. And here I was, about to block it.

"I don't want the ranch," I blurted out.

I squinted my eyes and stomped my foot in my head. So much for running through each and every word on the walk over.

"I'm sorry...what?" he asked, his voice unsteady.

I took a deep breath, licked my lips, and then looked at my brother. He was dressed for work—his tan hat perched on his head, his Wrangler jeans already covered in dirt, and his shirt tucked in with the sleeves rolled up. Behind him, Kyla leaned on the door frame, still wearing a nightgown, a small bump finally forming on her belly. She saw me and smiled.

"Can we talk?" I ask, going back to my brother.

Rhett nodded. "Yeah, porch or inside?"

"Inside. I have a feeling you have more coffee, and I could use some." I bolted past him, giving Kyla a knowing look before I helped myself to their kitchen.

"Is this a conversation we need Lachlan for?" Rhett asked, lightly closing the door behind him.

"Nope. He knows." I grabbed a mug, grabbed the carafe, and poured myself a fresh cup of black coffee like it was whiskey instead. This wasn't even a bad conversation. It was a good thing. I knew what I wanted, I was giving Rhett what he wanted, and we were going to move away from it. I was making it out to be a bigger deal than it really was.

"And was that Cash who left just now?" Kyla chimed in, running her hands on Rhett's shoulders as he took a seat on his kitchen island.

"Yup. He'll be back." I took a long gulp of coffee; actually thankful it had time to sit before I burned my throat.

"Okay, we're starting over. You don't want the ranch?" Rhett asked, his eyes meeting mine with a small hint of hope resting behind the blue.

I nodded. "Nope. I do not want that much of the ranch."

Kyla's tight lips formed a smile. "I'll let you two talk." She kissed her husband on the cheek before vanishing into their bedroom.

I looked at my brother. "You need it. Not me."

"Dad has a point," he began. "You know the ranch's numbers inside and out. You know the horses' schedules. You know when to feed the animals. You know—"

"Everything, yeah I know everything there is to know about Hartwell Hills but Rhett...I don't want to know everything. I don't want to be the go to person." I slumped, rolling my eyes at myself.

"Abi...why not?"

I had already told this story once. May as well tell it again.

"I had nothing else when Sylas died. I had nothing except the ranch and Stetson. I didn't want to be a depressed, grieving widow, so...I poured myself into what I had. Now...years later I'm miserable, finally discovering what I want again, falling in love and speaking up. I don't want to do this for the rest of my life." I could feel the tears coming, just as strong as they were the night with Cash. "I know what I want, and I need to get you on board before we talk to Dad."

He pinched his brow. "Falling in love?"

"That's what you focused on?" I set my now-empty coffee mug on the counter with a thud.

Rhett chuckled. "Okay, let's circle back to that. What's your proposal?"

"You take forty. I'll take five, and Wyatt can have his five."

"Forty? You think Dad will give me forty percent?"

I nodded. "All I want is the stables." I stood up straighter, confidence flowing through me. "I want to take care of the horses. I want to handle the indoor arena and the rental of that. I want to muck the stalls, and I want to spend the majority of my time there. Rhett," I breathed, finally pulling in all the air, "this ranch means more to you than anything. Your list of priorities goes: Kyla, baby, ranch, tie down. In that order." I clap my hands together with each thing on his list, Rhett's eyes growing wider with each one.

His jaw closed, and he gave me a simple nod. "True."

"You deserve to own the majority of the ranch. Not me. Your heart is in it, mine never really was."

"The stables?" He raised a single brow.

I nodded. "All I want is the stables."

"And this...falling in love?"

"I love Cash." I smiled, the mere memory of him sending a blush to my cheeks. "He's going to sell his place in Montana, but...he'll be back. Sooner rather than later, I hope. Stetson freaked out when I told him he couldn't go with him."

Rhett's lips tipped up in a smile as he nodded, taking his hat from his head and placing it up on the counter. "You know the whole weekend, all that kid talked about was Cash."

I blushed, pure joy flowing through me as a small smile formed on my lips. "Have you seen those two together?"

"Not often enough, but if Cash is coming back...I'm assuming you two are going to hunker down in the main house?"

"If Mom and Dad say we can. If not, we can always buy a place in town, and then I'll come take care of the horses every day."

"Bull shit. You know you're not moving out of that house." He laughed, standing up from the island. I watched him walk around the counter to me. "I'm pretty sure if he doesn't move in, they will wonder what happened this weekend, and Stet has already been going around telling everyone he's your boyfriend." He wrapped his arm around my shoulder, pulling me in for a hug.

"Stet?" I smiled. "Everyone's calling him Stet now?"

"He told us he liked it when Cash called him Stet, and asked to be called Stet."

"That's what..." I whispered softly. I had just gotten used to the idea of me calling him Stet. I loved that he loved to be called that, all thanks to Cash again.

"Sylas used to call him; we know. And we know you haven't been calling him that for years. We've all called him Stetson to keep you smiling." He pulled me closer, offering up more comfort.

I wrapped my arms around his waist, giving him a tight hug before letting him go and taking a step away. "I demand everyone call him Stet now."

"You got it boss." Rhett saluted.

"Nope." I pointed at him. "Not the boss. You are. Call Lachlan...let's go talk to Dad."

Rhett grabbed his hat and began to follow me.

"Are you not going to say goodbye to Kyla?" I asked him, reaching for the door handle.

"Oh shit...yeah. Wait for me?" Rhett let me go and then bounded into his bedroom, basically running into Kyla once he opened the door. "Ha, you snoop." He scooped her in his arms and gave her a kiss, Kyla humming against him.

"Come on Rhett!" I shouted. "We've got a deed to sign."

"Fifty." My dad handed the pen to Lachlan. "Forty." He looked at Rhett, who nodded. "And five and five. You sure about this, Abi?" My dad asked, looking from me to Wyatt, and then back to me.

After talking to my dad, he had his lawyers draw up another deed, giving Rhett the majority of the land, and me the two hundred and fifty acres surrounding the stables. Wyatt had the same acreage I did—but he was just there to sign his name. To him, it didn't matter. We all were getting exactly what we wanted, including Rhett taking some time next year to compete in rodeos. According to him, he wasn't trying for the NFR; he just wanted to keep doing what he loved for the fun of it. Kyla was on board with his decision, excited that she would get to travel with him and their baby and spend time at home on the ranch. The best of both worlds. Everything was how it should be, and Dad was asking me if I was sure.

"One hundred percent." I smiled, watching as Lachlan signed the new deed, handing the pen over to Rhett. "Just make sure it says I get the stables. I want a fancy sign."

"There she is." Lachlan shook his head, placing his hands on his hips, a smile growing on his grim façade.

"What do I get?" Wyatt asked, taking the pen from Rhett.

"You get to keep the apartment above the bunk houses and have no real responsibility when it comes to Hartwell Hills," Lachlan grumbled.

"Deal." Wyatt slashed the line on his double T name and handed me the pen.

I leaned down and signed, dropping the pen on the deed the moment my name was done. God this felt good. Relief in pen form. "What should we name the stables?"

"How about 'the stables?'" Lachlan quipped.

"No...we have to find a name because I want a sign." I glared at my cousin. "Oh, and whoever you hire to do the numbers...I'll train them."

"You better." He patted my shoulder. "Happy for you, Abi."

I gave him a smirk, watching as all the men excluding my dad left the office, leaving me and Leo Hartwell alone.

"Are you sure you're okay with five percent?"

"Dad." I cocked my head to him, a twitch at my lips.

"One hundred percent." He parroted me from earlier.

"I do have a question for you though?" I inhaled, clasping my hands together.

He raised an eyebrow.

"Cash. I um...well..." I chewed the inside of my lip. "He's going to move here. With me. And Stet."

He smiled, his eyes beaming. "Your mother and I are going to build a house next year, by the lake."

I smiled. "She would like that."

He nodded. "She's always wanted a house out there. Plus, this place is too big for us. It belongs to a family."

A family...

"Well, a family may not be in our future...but...with Stetson we are one."

"If you look at the deed, we switched the house to your name and eventually...Cash's? I expect the house will be in good hands, but Abi..." He sighed, standing up and leaning his hands on his desk. "This house has always been the gathering place for the ranch hands in the morning. Even before you were born—"

"I know. I know. I said all I want in my name is the stables, but I'll be happy to keep my morning routine the same. Just add another person in the mix."

"He's a good man." He hummed.

I blushed. "I know." I walked over and gave my dad a hug, holding him tight. "Thank you, Daddy."

He kissed the crown of my head before letting me go, giving me one last smile before returning to the newly signed deed.

I left his office, a warm feeling building in my chest, only growing when I pulled out my phone from my pocket, instantly texting Cash.

He responded right away. Not even giving those dots a second to live.

I chuckled that was his reaction was the same as my cousin's.

"You're blushing."

I looked up, coming face-to-face with my twin. Wyatt leaned against the wall, his arms folded and baseball cap backwards. His narrow eyes and heavy breath told me he was annoyed, and that I was about to get a lecture.

"Yeah, and?" I sneered, shoving my phone back into my pocket.

"He's really moving here?" Wyatt pushed himself off the wall, wrapping his arm around my shoulder.

"I take it you stood here and listened?" I began to walk down the hall, Wyatt having no choice but to follow me. "Yes, he's moving here, so get used to him."

He groaned, "If he hurts you..."

"He won't."

"If he dies..."

"He won't."

Wyatt tilted his head back and exhaled. "So I have to get used to him?"

I sighed. "Yes Wyatt, please? I really...really..." I licked my lips. "I love him."

He stopped, bringing me to stop, too. I turned to look at him. His blue eyes concentrated.

"I haven't heard you say that in a long time." He muttered, a crack in his voice when he spoke the last few words. Out of all the people, Wyatt saw everything—and now he could see this part, too. "I'm just trying to protect you."

I walked to my twin, wrapping my arms around his waist and breathing in his smokey scent. He held me back, his chin resting on the crown of my head.

"I know, and I love you for it. You were there when I needed someone, but Wyatt—"

"You love him?" He interrupted me, arching away slightly to look at me.

I nodded. "Very much so. It's different with him. It's like a new beginning. Don't get me wrong, I'll never—ever—forget Sylas. I can't compare them. Sylas was my first...Cash is my future."

"Your future?" Wyatt repeated softly.

I could feel the heat rush to my cheeks as the small smile spread across my lips. Nodding, I leaned back into him.

"Okay, then...I guess I'll accept that and...get used to him. Maybe I'll be nice to him, too."

"That will throw him off. Please, I do love him. Don't scare him away." I pulled away, "Plus, he'll be training Quinn here more."

His eyes twitched. "Wait, really?"

"Ha Wyatt...you can look but don't touch."

"I won't."

"How come I don't believe you?"

"Not sure, Abi. I'm a respectful guy."

I glared at my brother, still not believing a damn word that came out of his mouth.

FORTY

Cash

THREE WEEKS LATER

The town of Alpine Ridge never looked so appealing than it did right now. Driving down this main road had a different feeling to it now. Even though for the past three months I had lived in the motel, the feeling of home was stronger.

I was home.

Home.

Putting the house up for sale in Bozeman went smoother than I thought it would. It hit the market yesterday, and my agent was keeping me up to date on everything. I was relieved I didn't have to be present for a sale to go through, and I knew it already had several people looking at it. All my things were out and either in my truck or being shipped here. Abi's parents, thankfully, told me I could move in right away even though I offered to rent a place in town. They wouldn't have it. Leo told me he was relieved I was there to watch over his daughter and grandchild while he took Lottie traveling. I responded that Abi could very well take care of herself—but I was honored and grateful all the same. They accepted me as a part of the family.

Hartwell Hills came into view, and my body grew restless. The entire seven hours in the car had nothing on this feeling. My legs were itching to move, and my thumb kept tapping the wheel. She was too close; I could feel her. The constant phone calls, Facetimes and texts weren't enough to curb the want I had for Abi, even if we had done more than I expected we'd ever do over the phone. But I was going to have her in my arms, and this time I was never going to let her go.

The main house came into view, but I turned my rig off to the stables, knowing that's where Nova would be living for the rest of her life. Getting her settled was the second task on my to-do list. The first was kissing Abi.

I pulled the truck to a stop, my eyes landing on the family standing in front of the stables. Lachlan stood with his arms folded across his chest. Wyatt was next to him with his baseball cap on backwards, and Rhett gave me a wave. Abi was next to them, her hands on her hips when her head turned at the sound of my breaks. She didn't even hesitate; she broke out in a run and was jumping into my arms the second I stepped out of the cab.

"You're home," she said as she buried her head in my neck, her legs wrapping around my waist.

"I'm home," I whispered, breathing in her cinnamon scent.

She raised her chin, taking her mouth with mine in a deep kiss.

"I missed these lips." I kissed her again.

She hummed against me. "I've missed all of you."

"Okay, stop!" I heard someone bellow. Looking behind her, I saw Wyatt holding his arms out, a look of complete annoyance on his face. "I said I'd get used to you, but I don't want to see that every day."

"Shove it, Wyatt. I haven't kissed him in three weeks." Abi jumped from my arms, her hands sliding down to my fingers.

Wyatt rolled his eyes at his sister but gave me a nod. A nod of acceptance, possibly?

"So...what are we doing?" I asked as soon as we were in front of the stables. All of us men and Abi stood staring at the entrance, studying the brown wood that already looked weathered. I raised my eyebrows. Well, at least it had a new roof.

"Your girlfriend is demanding a sign for *her* stable." Lachlan didn't even look away from the blank space above the door, "and we're trying to figure out how big to make it."

"The bigger the better." Abi smiled. I chuckled, pulling her closer to me, stepping behind her to wrap my arm around her shoulders.

"What's it gonna say...*Abi's Stable*?" I asked, a light chuckle imagining a large, outlandish sign that didn't fit Abi's personality at all. But hey...she wanted it big.

"No..." Abi leaned over, looking over her shoulder at me, a pinch her brow, annoyance plastered all over her face. I pursed my lips and raised my eyebrows, ready for another brush to be thrown my way later. "I named it."

"She sure did." Rhett chuckled.

She spun in my arms. "I want to paint it. Light brown with a cream trim—as much as I enjoy the weathered look, it does need an upgrade. And since people are searching for it now, I want it to be official."

"So..." I kissed her cheek. "What is it?"

"*The Nova Luna Stables and Indoor Arena.*"

"We have a design." Lachlan finally looked at me. "And we're trying to figure out how big to make it fit above the entryway."

"Nova Luna?" I let Abi go, taking a step towards the stables, visioning the name on the building with the wood freshly painted just like she described.

"The design has the name behind a crescent moon, the moon has little rays coming off it. I'll show you...I love it." She smiled, pulling out her phone to show me a design. I leaned over her shoulder. It was just as she described. The perfect logo for her stables.

"But I had to incorporate the two horses of the man that I loved and the man I love now, the two horses that—"

I interrupted her with a kiss, my hands cradling her face as our mouths moved together.

"I love you," I murmured against her lips.

"I love you," she repeated, her free hand grasping onto my wrist.

Looking to Lachlan, I gave him a stern glare. "You make that sign as big as you can get it."

He saluted, begrudgingly, before grabbing Rhett by the elbow to usher him off. "Welcome home by the way," he called, giving me a wave.

I chuckled, "When do we start painting?"

"That's our project." Wyatt slapped my shoulder. "Abi is certain it's a way for us to"—he rolled his eyes and furrowed his brow before he gave me a once over—"bond."

I raised an eyebrow. "Don't look too excited about it." I laughed, raising my arm over Abi's shoulder.

"CASH!!"

The shrill of my name caused the three of us to turn, just in time to see Stetson barreling towards us. Abi stepped aside, knowing very well he was coming for me and me alone. The kid flew—literally flew—into my arms, almost knocking me to the ground.

"Hey, Stet," I laughed, catching my balance.

"Did Mommy tell you we named the stable!? Do you have Nova!? Can we go riding!? Can I help paint the barn!? I promise I'll do a really good job! Uncle Lachlan had me paint a few fences out in the field, and you can't even tell where I painted and where he painted. Are you going to teach me how to ride a bucking horse? Mom even agreed I was old enough now! I'll be eight soon!" Stetson was talking at rapid speed, so fast I could barely keep up.

I blinked and set him down. "Whoa Stet...one question at a time." I ruffled his dark hair, "Did you really tell him I could teach him to ride a bucking horse?" I turned back to Abi, only to feel Stetson's arms wrap around my leg. I held onto his back, enjoying him there.

Abi shrugged a shoulder. "He wants to take after the men in his life. Better he learns now."

"Come on!" Stetson tugged at my legs. "Let's get Nova and ride!"

"Dude, he just got home." Abi laughed, reaching for her son to pull him away from me, but Stetson just whipped around, making sure he was on my opposite side, away from his mother.

"Yea, he's *home.*" Stetson shot a glare towards Abi. "So let's go for a ride."

I looked at the love of my life and shot her a smile. "I'm yours tonight, I promise. But..."

"Yeah, yeah." She waved us off. "Go for a ride."

"Um...Mom..." Stetson grabbed her hand. "You're coming too."

Abi beamed, reaching for my free hand as the three of us went to saddle up our horses. And there, hanging next to the door, were my sketches, all with a small silver name plaque that read *Artwork by Cash Callahan* underneath them.

Family dinner was hectic. I managed to catch Leo and Lottie on their final family dinner before leaving for Europe, and the topic of conversation was the gender of Rhett and Kyla's baby. It was a fifty-fifty split between boy or girl, and even though Kyla knew, she wasn't telling anyone. Life moved on as if I had been at the table for years, except now I could drape my arm around Abi's chair, touch her hand or thigh, and give her small kisses whenever she smiled, and she was smiling a lot.

I tucked Stetson into bed, promising him I'd take him to school in the morning, before sneaking out with Abi to the stables, settling in Luna's stall. We sat, our backs to the gate, our legs touching, her head resting on my shoulder. Much like the day after she walked a colicky horse for hours, except this time our hands were entwined, and I was still pressing small kisses against her temple every chance I got.

"Do you like it?" She hummed, lifting her head from my shoulder. "The name of the stable?"

"I love it." I kissed her again, for the millionth time since I arrived. I would never stop kissing her. "Nova Luna—it fits."

"Do you think Sylas would like it?"

I laughed, envisioning exactly what he would say. *I love it, Mi Alma, but...Luna is a much better horse than Nova...*

"He would be mad Luna's name wasn't first."

She sighed, leaning into me. "He would. He'd even throw a nickname in there to get me to change my mind."

"Funny. I was thinking the same thing." I rested my cheek against the crown of her head, "Luna Nova?"

She grunted. "Nope. Nova Luna. It sounds better."

Luna kicked at the ground next to Abi, moving the hay under her feet until she gently lowered herself to her side, resting her head on Abi's lap. Abi scratched behind her ear and the horse let out a puff of air.

"Well..." Abi sighed. "We're here for a while."

"I don't know about you, but I'm here forever."

"I like the sound of that."

"Forever?"

"Forever."

Abi lifted her head, her lips meeting mine in a chaste kiss. "I love you Cash Callahan."

I urged the kiss deeper, showing her exactly how much I loved her.

FORTY-ONE

Abi

J ULY 4TH – *Hartwell Hills Rodeo*

Okay...why was I nervous? Since Cash had moved to Alpine Ridge, I had been to plenty of rodeos, seen him ride in our arena numerous times yet here I was, sitting next to Kyla, my knees shaking as I watched the sheep dash across the dirt to open up the Hartwell Hills Rodeo.

"Will you chill?" Kyla leaned into me, her arms cradling her now swollen belly. "You're acting like you've never been to a rodeo before."

I forced my knee to stop, shooting my friend a glare.

"I'm telling you, it's better when you're down there so he can kiss you after." She motioned her chin towards the chutes.

"He's not there. He's with Stet now." I motioned towards the gate of kids lined up for mutton busting. Spotting Cash was easy enough; he was the only one wearing a white cowboy hat. He turned to Rhett, who stood behind him, and laughed, his smile brightening up the entire arena. My heart fell to my stomach. I love him.

"Saddle bronc riders are first...and isn't—"

"Yes, I know." I interrupted her.

"So, my suggestion is get your ass down there and be there when he's done."

I shook my head. "I want to watch from here."

"You'll go crazy." She sang 'crazy' almost to say, 'trust me.'

Shaking my head harder, I looked at Kyla. Last year I was down with Stet, trying to calm a different kind of nerve as he got ready to hold on for dear life. This year I was forcing myself to stay seated and enjoy the show—but my mind and body weren't having it. I turned my attention back to Cash and Rhett, Cash patting his shoulder briefly before turning back to my son. He said something to him, Stet nodded enthusiastically, and then Cash kissed the top of Stet's helmet and left them there.

I watched as the white cowboy hat moved through the crowd, getting a glimpse of his chaps as he pulled on his gloves, making his way to the chutes. This rodeo was his return to saddle bronc, and he was probably just as nervous as I was. He had trained hard for this in between training his clients, his own physical therapy sessions, and acupuncture appointments, not to mention becoming the man of the main house. His life changed in more ways than one, and tonight he told me it was his way of putting everything that had happened behind him. Even though he'd been with us for months, this night was the start of his new life.

"I don't plan on going big. No more huge rodeos, but I'll ride when I want to, and watch when I want to," he had told me this morning over breakfast. "I may be 'coming back' but I still want my life here."

He kissed me then, slow and deep. A promise to give me the life we both wanted.

I swallowed, closing my eyes to remind myself to take in the moment. I'd support him, and we'd watch the fireworks together. I didn't need to be down there like Kyla said; I needed to watch him shine from here.

"Mutton. Bustin'." My twin's voice radiating through the arena forced me to open my eyes. "Those kids gave it their all. Looks like first place goes to—"

"Excuse me, I need to talk to my girl." I heard Cash's voice right next to me, causing me to jolt to the side, almost smacking him in the face.

"You should be down there." I leaned back into Kyla, pointing at the chutes, shock in my voice, but the excitement that gleamed in his eyes distracted me.

"Nah, I have time. Your brother has to do the Anthem, the prayer and then the flag girls. Come here." He grabbed my hand and pulled me from my seat, giving me a wink as we left the stands.

I gave Kyla a look, not really wanting to be saved from my boyfriend, but not wanting him to be late for his ride. "Cash, you need to be getting ready."

In one motion he swung our arms, pinning me to the back of the metal seats.

"I'm not ready until I kiss you."

I looked at him, his eyes heavy as he searched me. His white hat perched on his head, a thin sheen of sweat already on his tawny skin, a dark blue button up shirt, covered by his vest. His Wrangler jeans that hugged him in all the right areas, and his new chaps he had made specifically for tonight. White leather, with gold and blue accents, blue fringe hanging off the sides. But the best part, a blue A and an S sat on his left leg, right above where I knew his scar sat. An A for Abi...an S for Stetson. My heart melted just looking at it. This man was glorious. And he was mine. And right now, he needed a kiss.

I leaned in, closing the distance between us with a kiss. He drank me in, his hands gripping my waist as his tongue explored. We had kissed so many times since finding each other, and each one was different. No kiss was the same, and we loved to find new ways to make each other weak.

"Now I'm ready," he murmured, kissing the tip of my nose.

"You're supposed to kiss me *after* you ride." I said breathlessly, the feel of his lips was still on mine, my eyes still closed, hoping he would take it as a sign to kiss me again.

"Nah, that's Rhett's thing." He chuckled. "What have I been doing before every training session, before every ride I do?

I blushed at the memories, "A kiss."

"For luck." He smiled, kissing me again. "That's more important than a celebratory kiss."

The roar of the crowd brought me back to life. In the time we had been here, Wyatt had led the Anthem, introduced the sponsors and said a starting prayer. Now, it was time for the saddle bronc riders. I caught Cash's eye. Damn, that was a hell of a kiss.

"You need to get out there."

"I do."

"Go, eight seconds."

Giving me one final kiss, he nodded. "Eight seconds." Then he was gone, running off to the chutes.

With heat in my blood, I returned to my seat, finding it occupied by my son, holding a small trophy. My heart swelled as I pulled him closer to me.

"I was worried you were going to miss Cash."

"Never." I tapped the brim of his hat. "Second place. Not bad, little man."

He beamed, holding his small little trophy with pride. "Not bad for my last ride."

We celebrated Stetson's eighth birthday a few months ago and he had officially met the age limit for mutton busting. Now he was ready to move on to bigger livestock sports. As much as my stomach still twisted, he was determined to follow in his dads—and now Cash's—footsteps.

"Look." My dad, who had returned from his trip with my mother in Europe for the rodeo, caught everyone's attention. Even the people sitting next to him. "There he is." He pointed to the chutes. My eyes followed, and I saw Cash lower himself onto the horse.

"Do y'all remember a few years back, a huge saddle bronc name had an early retirement," Wyatt's voice boomed over the speaker, "and he all but disappeared from the scene? He went on a different road than most, taking on clients and training barrel racers. In fact, he trained the one and only Quinn Compton who we will see later.

But tonight is about his return, his comeback to the sport he loves more than my own sister."

I laughed, loving that Wyatt and Cash's relationship was mending itself. Painting the stables and hanging the sign together really forced them to accept each other.

"And back on a horse that loves to buck...I present to you...the one and only...Cash Callahan." Wyatt rang out his name as the crowd cheered.

I didn't notice Cash nod, I just noticed the chute fly open and the horse jump out. Cash's arm was raised high in the air, his chin low, his body moving in motion with the horse. And that horse moved. One...two...three...four. Cash's arm swung back and forth; his hat flew off his head. The horse tilted to the side, all four legs off the ground. Five...six...seven...The buzzer sounded and Cash pulled his body tight, reaching for the synch to bring the horse into a gallop—the smile on his face only showing how much he loved the ride.

I shot up from my seat, hearing Kyla mutter something like, "Told you, you would want to be down there." I bolted down the metal stairs to the fence. I watched as the pickup men grabbed Cash, pulling him from the saddle and dropping him to the ground. His face winced slightly, telling me the pain was still there, but the thrill was stronger.

"He still has it folks! Cash Callahan pulling in an eighty-nine to start the night!"

The crowd cheered as Cash threw up his arms. Giving them one last wave, hyping up the crowd even more than they already were, he raced to grab his hat. Stepping up on the gate, I leaned forward, hoping to catch his eye before he left the dirt to let the other riders go, but he didn't notice me. Instead, he waved his hat in the air and went back to the chutes. He would help the other riders, even riling up the calves for the ropers. He would watch the barrel racers with pride as Quinn showed every rider how it was done. The nerves in my stomach settled as I watched him, finally where he belonged.

After the rodeo, when the sun had set and the crowd dispersed to get the best seats for the fireworks, Cash, Stet, and I stood in the middle of the dirt. Cash's arms around my shoulders, holding me close to him, my arms draped over Stetson, making sure he was pressed to me. The fireworks boomed overhead, the three of us watching in wonder as our life together truly began.

EPILOGUE

Cash

"**C**ASH!" ABI SHOUTED FROM the kitchen. "They're going to be here soon, right? I mean the hospital's not that far away?"

I stepped into the kitchen, watching as Abi frantically ran from side to side, putting plates on the counter, taking her famous baked mac and cheese that she somehow had time to make out of the oven, getting the drinks from the refrigerator—her mind moving a million miles a minute.

"Abs?"

"Have you seen Grace? She said she would make it here before them."

"Abs?"

"Wyatt's with Stet. They are feeding the horses before everyone gets here."

"Abs…"

"Mom and Dad are setting up the cabin for them."

"Abs." I stepped in front of her, lightly touching her shoulders. She met my gaze and let out a long breath as her eyes fluttered closed.

"I'm going crazy, aren't I?"

I shrugged a shoulder and then brought my forefinger and thumb up to her, showing just a pinch. "A little." I kissed the tip of her nose.

When I first moved into the Hartwell Hills main house, Leo Hartwell pulled me aside. I had known this man for a long time, but if I would have said my heart rate didn't pick up, it would be a lie. I was moving into *his* home. I was dating *his* daughter. I was—for all intents and purposes—taking over while he took his wife around the world. I had to remind myself that he didn't carry his shotgun everywhere, and this was not one of those talks. I had never talked to Carolyn's dad; he didn't even say hello to me at our wedding. Leo though...Leo was a man who I respected, and I would shut up and listen.

"She deserves more than five percent of this place," he began, *"but I can see where her heart is, it's with you and Stetson. She may not think it, but she's the center of this home. Her mother and I have just been living here...she's been shaping it. This home is the heart of the ranch, it always has been. I trust you with it, I trust you with her. Give her the life she wants, the life she needs. Give this home the life it needs. The life you* need. *You belong to this family, Cash—love it."*

And love it, I have.

During the first few months of living here, I trained. I built back up my stamina, and then after the Fourth of July, Abi, Stet, and I traveled in the Western Circuits with Quinn and Wyatt, my name finally back on the boards. I had won more than I lost, and I was loving every second with my new family. Not even seeing Carolyn again could ruin it. During that time, I talked to more cowboys who hoped to have their shot in the circuits. With training gigs in my future, it looked like fall and winter were going to be spent back at home.

With me training Quinn, two saddle bronc riders, one bareback rider and three other barrel racers, home became busier—but we wouldn't have it any other way. Every morning, we wake up together, make breakfast for Lachlan and the ranch hands. Abi would start in the stables, and I'd prepare the arena. My clients would show up, and Abi would give their horses the care they deserved. Basically, the Nova Luna Stable and Arena was home to the most spoiled horses in Idaho. Once the day was done, we would eat dinner with Lachlan, sometimes Wyatt, sometimes Quinn if she were in town, but mainly it was just us three. The house had grown calm in the season.

But now with a new addition heading our way, I could see Abi worried about the calm being stripped away. Grace had flown in a few days ago, Kyla's mother was due any minute, and Leo and Lottie were making sure Rhett and Kyla's cabin was one hundred percent ready for the new baby. The house was going to become chaos soon, and even though Abi was the grounding force of the home, the fact that people were encroaching on what has become our space, was getting to her.

"A little?" she repeated. "More than a little. Do you even think anyone will eat the mac n cheese?" she pointed to the dish sitting on the kitchen island.

"Once the newness has worn down, yeah. They will want to eat...especially Kyla. She loves your mac n cheese."

She inhaled again. "Okay. This is fine. I'm used to people in this house."

"Not recently."

She stepped into me. "True. It's just been us in this little bubble, hasn't it?"

"I like our bubble."

"Me too." She leaned in closer, her arms wrapping around my waist as she let out a deep sigh, melting into me.

So much in fact, the small box that sat in my pocket was burning a hole through my sweater. I knew the moment I came back to Hartwell Hills that I was going to marry Abi. I had just been waiting for the right time to propose. My thoughts went from the Fourth of July Rodeo, stupidly having it in my pocket while I rode, to a rodeo on the road, to Thanksgiving dinner—but no time felt like the right time to ask her. I had to remind myself that we didn't need a ring or piece of paper to prove we loved each other.

The front door opened, pulling our attention from our bubble to Grace—who was carrying way more bags than she should be—barreling through the front hall. Lachlan stepped in behind her, closing the door, keeping his chin down.

"I told you I'd beat them here." Grace smiled at Abi. "I got all the basic supplies..."

"Pretty sure they got all of that already?" Abi raised up on her tip toes, pulling on the bag to peek inside.

"Well, now they have more." Grace beamed, looking at the pile of baby supplies that now littered the kitchen island. "You can never have too many onesies. I guarantee you that baby is going to poop through all of them."

Lachlan cleared his throat as he passed us, his eyes avoiding Grace completely. "An Uber just pulled up, too. Kyla's mom I'm assuming?"

"Oh, okay." Grace looked at Abi. "I'll go greet her. The dinner smells delicious. Kyla will be excited."

Abi gave a soft smile, her body relaxing. "Thanks, I bet she will be."

Grace gave Abi's shoulder a squeeze before turning back to the front door, opening it only to have to step aside to let Wyatt and Stetson in. Wyatt slipped off his hat, took an inventory of the room surrounding him, and looked at his twin. Wyatt came up to stand next to his sister, stealing a noodle from the mac n cheese before opening his mouth to speak. Stetson, however, beat him to it.

"Mommy!" Stetson bounced. "They're here! They're here!"

"Wait, what?" Abi turned to her brother, who gave her a single nod.

Abi didn't even hesitate. She rushed to the door, flinging it open and letting the cool air inside. I followed, placing my hand on the small of her back, delighted to see Rhett, opening the back passenger door to let Kyla out, then pulling out a car seat next.

Abi gasped and covered her mouth with her hand. "I can't believe she's here," she whispered.

Kyla had given birth early yesterday morning to a perfect baby girl. As much as everyone wanted to rush to the hospital to visit and meet the baby, Rhett had requested they keep it just the three of them, but now that they were home, I could see the love flooding them. Kyla set the car seat down on the coffee table and slowly pulled her daughter from the car seat. Rhett's hand never left his wife's back as he watched his baby do the infamous baby curl. Her hands were by her ears, her back arched, the perfect restful expression on her face once she settled herself into the crook of Kyla's arms.

"Everyone"—Kyla smiled, her cheeks glowing with so much love as she looked at her daughter—"this is Poppy."

"Poppy Grace Hartwell," Rhett added, kissing Kyla's temple.

After a few moments, Poppy was passed from Kyla's mother to Grace and then finally to Abi. Tears welled in her eyes as she took in her niece, her tiny fingers wrapping around Abi's. She walked over to me, slowly, her lips in the perfect 'o' and she cooed to Poppy. Seeing Abi hold this small baby pulled at my heart, tugging it in ways I've never felt before. I took a deep breath, trying to stop this new sensation.

"She's beautiful," Abi whispered, a tear falling from her cheek.

"She is. You did good, Rhett." I looked up at my friend, noticing how crackled my voice was.

"Nah, it was all Kyla." Rhett chuckled.

"Well, you helped." Kyla smiled, kissing her husband's cheek.

"Look at her." Abi looked up at me, her voice still soft. "Can you imagine..." she began, her eyes drifting back to the baby.

No...I couldn't...

Suddenly—the sensation made sense.

"Excuse me." I kissed Stet on the crown of his head before leaving the room.

Not knowing quite where to go, I went to the stables. I could brush and prepare Nova for the night, even though she was most likely already settled in, but at least the time with her would allow me to think.

The longer Abi and I tested fate by not using any method of birth control only proved to me that having a baby of my own with her was completely out of the question. And seeing her, holding a perfect baby girl, only made me want that more and more.

The box in my pocket burned hotter.

Abi had told me months ago that I was all she needed. She had a family with me and Stetson, and that was enough for her. It didn't matter that we couldn't expand and fill this huge house with more kids. Little miniature versions of myself and Abi, our skin tones blending together perfectly. That would never happen. We wouldn't be the ones greeted by family and fresh mac n cheese as we came home from the hospital. It would never be real.

I licked my lips. It was more than that.

That feeling of being a father...

Thawp.

"Shit..."

A sharp pain hit the back of my head, a grunt leaving my lips as I looked on the ground to see...a horse brush.

Holding the back of my head, I turned and saw Abi, standing next to the open tack shed, her hands on her hips.

"You just threw a brush at me," I grumbled, attempting to keep the smile that so badly wanted to come out away.

"It was the only way to get you out of your head," she teased. She put her hands on her hips and waited for me to come to her. I took a few steps, still rubbing the back of my head.

"I think you drew blood."

"I threw it harder last time and you didn't bleed."

I snorted. "You should be inside."

"So should you. Your niece is in there." Abi pointed to the house. "So why the hell did you come to sulk out here?"

"I'm not sulking."

"There's only room for one brooding cowboy on this ranch Cash Callahan, and I hate to tell you that Lachlan owns that title." She smiled, bringing back yet another memory from what seemed like so long ago. I couldn't help but grin. I grunted and looked down at my boots, closing my eyes tight.

"What's wrong?" she asked, her arms sliding around my waist.

"You look beautiful holding a baby," I whispered.

"Do I?" She raised a brow.

I nodded. "I know you don't care but...I'll never be able to give you that. I'll never get to feel what Rhett feels...I'll never..."

"You came out here to sulk about not having kids?" She arched her back. "Are you comparing our perfect life to Rhett's?"

"Well..." I twisted my lips. "When you put it that way, it sounds childish. I'm not meaning to...I just...want that. With you. And seeing you hold a baby made me remember just how impossible it is."

"Impossible?" Abi parroted.

Lowering my chin, I nodded.

Abi moved, catching me off guard as she began feeling my body, her hands moving rapidly as they began to rummage through every pocket. Her hair moved from side to side as she put her hands everywhere, and I mean *everywhere*.

"What are you..." I watched as she pulled the pockets inside out.

"Yes!" Abi cheered, pulling out the small box from my pocket.

I raised my eyebrows and looked at the box. I bit the inside of my lip.

"You've been carrying this around for months, Cash Callahan." She waved the box in front of my face.

"I..." I stammered. "Have..."

"I have something to ask you, but I need you to ask this first." She grabbed my wrist and put the box in my hand. "My answer is yes so..." She urged me on with her fingers. "Go ahead."

"You're taking over your proposal?" I raised an eyebrow, keeping my chin low.

She nodded. "Yep." She popped the P. "Because I have something for you, and I was going to wait until Christmas because I was hoping you'd ask me then, but...you are dragging your feet."

I barked out a laugh and spun the box in my fingers.

"So...ask me." She took a step back, creating distance between us. Clasping her hands behind her back, she gave me a small twist with her hips, a sexy smirk coming with it.

I narrowed my eyes at her.

"Don't make me throw another brush at you."

"Marry me?" I said instantly, closing the gap she created between us. "Marry me Abi Acosta, let me be your husband and love you forever."

She kissed me. "Yes, yes...Cash...yes."

I opened the box, revealing the white gold band with a single diamond. Abi watched as I placed it on her finger, chewing on her bottom lip before wrapping her arms around my neck.

"I love you," she whispered.

"I love you." I kissed her, relishing in the moment that Abi was and always will be my forever.

Breaking the kiss, Abi arched her back slightly. "My turn." She inhaled, her breath shaky. She pulled away, new tears welling in her eyes. "I was talking to Stetson the other night and I...well we..." She swallowed and glided her hands down my chest. The diamond caught the light from the stables and glistened, drawing her attention for a second. "Stetson wants you to adopt him."

I widened my eyes. Sure, I thought about it, but I never wanted to replace Sylas for him. I never wanted to strip that away just so I could legally be his father. I loved that little man as much as I loved Abi. The three of us made a family, and I could feel my heart swell with just thinking about being his dad. I just searched her eyes, completely speechless.

"Say something," she finally said.

"I don't...I don't know what to say."

"He calls you Dad when he's with me, but he's nervous about calling you Dad to your face. He wants to. He really wants to. You mean so much to him, and when I asked him, he got so excited. It was his decision. He wants you to be his father." Her voice was soft, and when I failed to come up with words she filled the void. "So, none of this you won't ever be a dad bullshit because you already are one. You have a little boy who loves you more than you know, and he wants to call you Dad. You are his dad, Cash."

I opened my lips, finally, but she stopped me, placing a fingertip on my chin. "I know what's going through your mind. You're not replacing Sylas. You are only filling his world with more love. He loves you. I love you."

Tears fell from my eyes, harder and faster than I expected them to as I reached to cradle Abi's face, bringing her to me in a deep kiss. This sealed everything, making my entire life whole. My family. My fiancée...my wife...and my son.

I broke the kiss and leaned my forehead against her. "I'd be honored," I whispered, relishing the way her lips came to me once again.

ACKNOWLEDGEMENTS

When I first typed 'the end' on this novel, I wasn't sure how it was going to get to this point. This book sent me through the wringer. It crushed me. There were so many times during drafting, revisions, editing—I almost quit. The imposter syndrome was strong, and I wasn't sure how I was going to break through it. Now, months and months after draft one was completed, after multiple revisions and time spent away from it...dare I say...I love this book? Abi and Cash's story made me believe in myself in more ways than one, but without the help of many, *many,* people I would have never gotten here. This story wouldn't be in your hands without these amazing people that have been in my corner since I first started this novels journey.

My husband and kids—thank you for dealing with the messy house. Thank you for letting me watch countless movies with you with my laptop on my lap. Thank you for the support and words of encouragement as I cried over these words over and over again. When I first started this novel I told my husband about it in the middle of Texas Roadhouse and he hung on my every word—that night will always stick with me. Thank you, my love!

Jessee. No words can express how much I love you. This novel is here because of you. You read the first messy draft, you helped me brainstorm things again and again and you gave me the courage to push and do this. You listened to me cry and work out kinks, you were there through it all. Thank you for all your words and encouragement and your refusal to let me quit. You're a pivotal piece in my author journey, my best friend who I can't wait to see again. (How many days until Montana?) I adore you.

Kate. Oh Kate. I think second book syndrome hit us both hard, but we got through the rocky moments together and look where we ended up. You helped make this book what it is—your advice and multiple chats about how I could really bring their story to life helped me in more ways than you know.

Tessa. The ultimate hype girl who no matter what will encourage me to keep writing. They way you look at my words give me hope and courage. You get all the messy things. You get all the revisions. You listen to me through everything and I am so grateful than we finally discovered we are both awkward book nerds and found each other.

Meghan and Sydney. Cash's fan girls. I love that a love for a certain fantasy novel (I take the full blame) brought us together and I love that our love for Cash keeps us together. Thank you for creating merch, giving my books sprayed edges and being there when I needed help even when the book was 'done'. You two are simply amazing.

My Betas—MJ, Kate, Heather, Cait, Meghan, Jessee (oh wait—you're the alpha! *tongue sticking out emoji*), Grayson and India. Thank you all for helping me polish this story. Without you Cash's background would still be really vague, and chapter nineteen and twenty wouldn't be here. If readers cry—I'll blame you!

My amazing writing group. Grayson, MJ, India, Cindy and Jessee. How many times did I say I couldn't do this?! How many times did you tell me I could. Thank you for the weekly meetings, for talking to me, all the laughs and being the best support group.

Michelle, Ashley and Alyssa for giving me the best writing getting away weekend. Locking ourselves in an AirBnb for four days was a fantastic idea and I hope we can do it again in the future...minus the emergency siren that only I seemed to hear at three in the morning. I cried a lot that weekend, but I also got some amazing feedback, new friends and a note I still have.

My Street Team! The way I love this team—they are simply the best! Without them, Abi and Cash wouldn't have gone as far! They truly helped with every content creation and shared every single one. Having this team was the best decision I could have made and I am so grateful for each and every one of these gals who love and support me!

My amazing editor and friend, Allie Samberts. Thank you for making the editing process smooth and stress free. Thank you for loving Abi and Cash and helping me make them even better. And mostly, thank you for helping my love my story. I don't know I would without you as my editor. (I promise I'll chill with the drama dots...oops.)

To the artists who brought these characters to life. Melody Jeffries giving me my DREAM cover, Erika Plum giving me the most perfect character art ever of Abi and Cash, even creating Stetson to perfection. Grayson Long for the sweet scene with the three of them, capturing the moment perfectly. I have an obsession with character art and you three never let me down!

I know I am forgetting people, I would thank the world if I could, but then this book would be a lot thicker. Just know, if you had anything to do with this book coming to life, I am so grateful for you. In every way imaginable.

Thank you for all your love and reading. I love you!

Stefanie K Steck

ALSO BY STEFANIE K STECK

Standalones

All Because of Elowin

Under the Marble Sky

Moments of Us Series

That Right Moment

That Next Moment

That First Moment

Hartwell Hills Series

Somebody Like Me

Never Left You

About the Author

Stefanie K Steck is a romance writer, full-time dental assistant, Army wife, mom of three crazy kids, and curator of a small zoo. She currently lives in Utah and has recently found joy in camping. In the little spare time she has, you can find her writing, reading, cuddling her favorite Guinea pig, Nugget, or rewatching the *Back to the Future Trilogy* or the *Marvel Cinematic Universe* (*The Infinity Saga* obviously) ...again...or obsessing over *Twisters*.

Follow her on Instagram @authorstefanieksteck
www.stefanieksteckbooks.com